W9-BEO-451

THE
LOST BOOK
OF
ENKI

THE
LOST BOOK
OF
ENKI

MEMOIRS AND PROPHECIES
OF AN EXTRATERRESTRIAL GOD

ZECHARIA SITCHIN

Bear & Company
Rochester, Vermont

Bear & Company
One Park Street
Rochester, Vermont 05767
www.InnerTraditions.com

Bear & Company is a division of Inner Traditions International

Copyright © 2002 by Zecharia Sitchin
First paperback edition 2004

All rights reserved. No part of this book may be reproduced or utilized in any form or by any means, electronic or mechanical, including photocopying, recording, or by any information storage and retrieval system, without permission in writing from the publisher.

The Library of Congress has cataloged the hardcover edition as follows:
Sitchin, Zecharia.
    The lost book of Enki / Zecharia Sitchin.
        p. cm.
    ISBN 1-879181-83-5 (hardcover)
    1. Civilization, Ancient—Extraterrestrial influences. 2. Lost books—
History. I. Title.
    CB156 .S5737 2002
    001.94—dc21

                                                          2001004531
ISBN of paperback edition: ISBN 978-1-59143-037-7

Printed and bound in the United States at Lake Book Manufacturing, Inc.

10

Text design and layout by Priscilla Baker
This book was typeset in Apolline, with Sparta as a display typeface

CONTENTS

INTRODUCTION

Some 445,000 years ago, astronauts from another planet came to Earth in search of gold.

Splashing down in one of Earth's seas, they waded ashore and established Eridu, "Home in the Faraway." In time the initial settlement expanded to a full-fledged Mission Earth—with a Mission Control Center, a spaceport, mining operations, and even a way station on Mars.

Short of manpower, the astronauts employed genetic engineering to fashion Primitive Workers—*Homo sapiens*. The Deluge that catastrophically swept over the Earth required a fresh start; the astronauts became gods, granting Mankind civilization, teaching it to worship.

Then, about four thousand years ago, all that had been achieved unraveled in a nuclear calamity, brought about by the visitors to Earth in the course of their own rivalries and wars.

What had taken place on Earth, and especially the events since human history began, has been culled by Zecharia Sitchin, in his *The Earth Chronicles Series,* from the Bible, clay tablets, ancient myths, and archaeological discoveries. But what had preceded the events on Earth—what had taken place on the astronauts' own planet Nibiru that caused the space journeys, the need for gold, the creation of Man?

What emotions, rivalries, beliefs, morals (or the lack thereof) motivated the principal players in the celestial and space sagas? What were the relationships that caused mounting tensions on Nibiru and on Earth, what tensions arose between old and young, between those who had come from Nibiru and those born on Earth? And to what extent was what had happened determined by Destiny—a destiny whose record of past events holds the key to the future?

Would it not be auspicious were one of the key players, an eyewitness and one who could distinguish between Fate and Destiny, to record for posterity the How and Where and When and Why of it all—the First Things and perhaps the Last Things?

But that is precisely what some of them did do; and foremost among them was the very leader who had commanded the first group of astronauts!

Scholars and theologians alike now recognize that the biblical tales of Creation, of Adam and Eve, the Garden of Eden, the Deluge, the Tower of Babel, were based on texts written down millennia earlier in Mesopotamia, especially by the Sumerians. And they, in turn, clearly stated that they obtained their knowledge of past events—many from a time before civilizations began, even before Mankind came to be—from the writings of the Anunnaki ("Those Who from Heaven to Earth Came")—the "gods" of antiquity.

As a result of a century and a half of archaeological discoveries in the ruins of the ancient civilizations, especially in the Near East, a great number of such early texts have been found; the finds have also revealed the extent of missing texts—so-called lost books—which are either mentioned in discovered texts or are inferred from such texts, or that are known to have existed because they were cataloged in royal or temple libraries.

Sometimes the "secrets of the gods" were partly revealed in epic tales, such as the *Epic of Gilgamesh,* that disclosed the debate among the gods that led to the decision to let Mankind perish in the Deluge, or in a text titled *Atra Hasis,* which recalled the mutiny of the Anunnaki who had toiled in the gold mines that led to the creation of Primitive Workers—Earthlings. From time to time the leaders of the astronauts themselves authored compositions: sometimes dictating the text to a chosen scribe, as the text called *The Erra Epos,* in which one of the two gods who had caused the nuclear calamity sought to shift the blame to his adversary; sometimes the god acted as his own scribe, as is the case regarding the *Book of the Secrets of Thoth* (the Egyptian god of knowledge), which the god had secreted in a subterranean chamber.

When the Lord God Yahweh, according to the Bible, granted the Commandments to His chosen people, He at first inscribed in His own hand two stone tablets that He gave to Moses on Mount Sinai. When Moses threw down and broke that first set of tablets in response to the golden calf incident, the replacement set was written by Moses on the tablets, on both their sides, when he stayed on the Mount forty days and forty nights recording the dictated words of the Lord.

Were it not for a tale recorded on papyrus from the time of the Egyptian king Khufu (Cheops) concerning the *Book of the Secrets of Thoth*, the existence of that book would have not become known. Were it not for the biblical narratives in Exodus and Deuteronomy, we would have never known about the divine tablets and their contents; all would have become part of the enigmatic body of "lost books" whose very existence would have never come to light. No less painful is the fact that in some instances we do know that certain texts had existed, but are in the dark regarding their contents. Such is the case regarding the *Book of the Wars of Yahweh* and the *Book of Jasher* ("Book of Righteousness"), which are specifically mentioned in the Bible. In at least two instances, the existence of olden books—earlier texts known to the biblical narrator—can be inferred. Chapter five of Genesis begins with the statement "This is the book of the *Toledoth* of Adam," the term *Toledoth* being usually translated as "generations" but more accurately meaning "historic or genealogical record." The other instance is in chapter six of Genesis, where the events concerning Noah and the Deluge begin with the words "These are the *Toledoth* of Noah." Indeed, partial versions of a book that became known as the *Book of Adam and Eve* have survived over the millennia in Armenian, Slavonic, Syriac, and Ethiopic languages; and the *Book of Enoch* (one of the so-called Apocryphal books that were not included in the canonized Bible) contains segments that are considered by scholars to be fragments from a much earlier *Book of Noah*.

An oft-quoted example of the extent of lost books is that of the famed Library of Alexandria in Egypt. Established by the general Ptolemy after Alexander's death in 323 B.C., it was said to have contained more than half a million "volumes"—books inscribed on a variety of materials (clay, stone, papyrus, parchment). That great library, where scholars gathered to study the accumulated knowledge, was burnt down and destroyed in wars that extended from 48 B.C. to the Arab conquest in A.D. 642. What has remained of its treasures is a translation of the first five books of the Hebrew Bible into Greek, and fragments retained in the writings of some of the library's resident scholars.

It is only thus that we know that the second king Ptolemy commissioned, circa 270 B.C., an Egyptian priest whom the Greeks called Manetho to compile the history and prehistory of Egypt. At first, Manetho wrote, only the gods reigned there, then demigods, and finally, circa 3100 B.C., Pharaonic dynasties began. The divine reigns, he wrote, began ten thousand years before the Flood and continued for thousands of years thereafter, the latter period having witnessed battles and wars among the gods.

In the Asiatic domains of Alexander, where reign fell into the hands of the general Seleucos and his successors, a similar effort to provide the Greek savants with a record of past events took place. A priest of the Babylonian god Marduk, Berossus, with access to libraries of clay tablets whose core was the temple library of Harran (now in southeastern Turkey), wrote down in three volumes a history of gods and men that began 432,000 years before the Deluge, when the gods came to Earth from the heavens. Listing by name and reign durations the first ten commanders, Berossus reported that the first leader, dressed as a fish, waded ashore from the sea. He was the one who gave Mankind civilization; and his name, rendered in Greek, was Oannes.

Dovetailing in many details, both priests thus rendered accounts of gods of heaven who had come to Earth, of a time when gods alone reigned on Earth, and of the catastrophic Deluge. In the fragmentary bits and pieces retained (in other contemporary writings) from the three volumes, Berossus specifically reported the existence of writings from before the Great Flood—stone tablets that were hidden for safekeeping in an ancient city called Sippar, one of the original cities established by the ancient gods.

Though Sippar, as were other pre-Diluvial cities of the gods, was overwhelmed and obliterated by the Deluge, a reference to the pre-Diluvial writings surfaced in the annals of the Assyrian king Ashurbanipal (668–633 B.C.). When archaeologists, in the mid-nineteenth century, found the ancient Assyrian capital Nineveh—until then known only from the Old Testament—they discovered in the ruins of Ashurbanipal's palace a library with the remains of some 25,000 inscribed clay tablets. An assiduous collector of "olden texts," Ashurbanipal boasted in his annals, "The god of scribes has bestowed on me the gift of the knowledge of his art; I have been initiated into the secrets of writing; I can even read the intricate tablets in Shumerian; I understand the enigmatic words in the stone carvings from the days before the Flood."

It is now known that the Shumerian (or Sumerian) civilization had blossomed in what is now Iraq almost a millennium before the beginning of the Pharaonic age in Egypt, both to be followed later by the civilization of the Indus Valley in the Indian subcontinent. It is now also known that the Sumerians were the first to write down the annals and tales of gods and men, from which all other peoples, including the Hebrews, obtained the tales of Creation, of Adam and Eve, Cain and Abel, the Deluge, the Tower of Babel; and of the wars and loves of the gods, as reflected in the writings and recollections of the Greeks, Hittites, Canaanites, Persians, and Indo-Europeans. As all these olden writings attest, their sources were even earlier texts—some found, many lost.

The volume of such early writings is staggering; not thousands but tens of thousands of clay tablets have been discovered in the ruins of the ancient Near East. Many deal with or record aspects of daily life, such as trade or workers' wages and nuptial contracts. Others, found mostly in palace libraries, constitute Royal Annals; still others, discovered in the ruins of temple libraries or of scribal schools, constitute a group of canonized texts, a secret literature, that were written down in the Sumerian language and then translated to Akkadian (the first Semitic language) and then other ancient languages. And even in those early writings—going back almost six thousand years—references are made to lost "books" (texts inscribed on stone tablets).

Among the incredible—to say fortunate does not fully convey the miracle—finds in the ruins of ancient cities and their libraries are clay prisms inscribed with the very information about the ten pre-Diluvial rulers and their 432,000 years' total reign to which Berossus had referred. Known as the *Sumerian King Lists* (and on display in the Ashmolean Museum, Oxford, England), their several versions leave no doubt that their Sumerian compilers had access to some earlier common or canonized textual material. Coupled with other equally early texts, discovered in various states of preservation, they strongly suggest that the original recorder of the Arrival, as well as of preceding events and certainly of following events, had to be one of those leaders, a key participant, an eyewitness.

One who had been an eyewitness to all those events, indeed a key participant in them, was the leader who had splashed down with the first group of astronauts. At that time his epithet-name was E.A., "He Whose Home Is Water." He experienced the disappointment of having command of Earth Mission given to his half brother and rival EN.LIL ("Lord of the Command"), a humiliation little mitigated by granting him the title EN.KI, "Lord of Earth." Relegated away from the cities of the gods and their spaceport in the E.DIN ("Eden") to supervise the mining of gold in the AB.ZU (southeastern Africa), it was Ea/Enki—a great scientist—who came across the hominids who inhabited those parts. And so when the Anunnaki toiling in the gold mines mutinied and said, "No more!" it was he who realized that the needed manpower could be obtained by jumping the gun on evolution through genetic engineering; and thus did the *Adam* (literally, "He of the Earth," Earthling) come into being. As a hybrid, the Adam could not procreate; the events echoed in the biblical tale of Adam and Eve in the Garden of Eden record the second genetic manipulation by Enki that added the extra chromosomal genes needed for sexual procreation. And when Mankind, proliferating, did not turn out the way it had been envisaged, it was he, Enki, who defied his brother Enlil's plan to let Mankind perish in the Deluge—the events whose hero has been called Noah in the Bible and Ziusudra in the earlier original Sumerian text.

The firstborn son of Anu, Nibiru's ruler, Ea/Enki was well versed in his planet's (Nibiru) and its inhabitants' past. An accomplished scientist, he bequeathed the most important aspects of the advanced knowledge of the Anunnaki especially to his two sons Marduk and Ningishzidda (who, as Egyptian gods, were known there as Ra and Thoth, respectively). But he also was instrumental in sharing with Mankind certain aspects of such advanced knowledge, by teaching to selected individuals the "secrets of the gods." In at least two instances, such initiates wrote down (as they were instructed to do) those divine teachings as Mankind's heritage. One, called Adapa and probably a son of Enki by a human female, is known to have written a book titled *Writings Regarding Time*—one of the earliest lost books. The other, called Enmeduranki, was in all probability the prototype of the biblical Enoch, the one who was taken up to heaven after he had entrusted to his sons the book of divine secrets, and of which a version has possibly survived in the extrabiblical *Book of Enoch.*

Though the firstborn of Anu, he was not destined to be his father's successor on the throne of Nibiru. Complex rules of succession, which reflected the convoluted history of the Nibiruans, gave that privilege to Enki's half brother Enlil. In the effort to resolve the bitter conflict, both Enki and Enlil ended up on a mission to an alien planet—Earth—whose gold was needed to create a shield for preserving Nibiru's dwindling atmosphere. It was against that background, made even more complex by the presence on Earth of their half sister Ninharsag (the Chief Medical Officer of the Anunnaki), that Enki decided to defy Enlil's plan to have Mankind perish in the Deluge.

The conflict carried on between the two half brothers' sons, even among their grandchildren; the fact that all of them, and especially those born on Earth, faced the loss of longevity that Nibiru's extended orbital period provided added personal agonies and sharpened ambitions. It all came to a climax in the last century of the third millennium B.C. when Marduk, Enki's firstborn by his official spouse, claimed that he and not Enlil's firstborn son, Ninurta, should inherit the Earth. The bitter conflict that included a series of wars led in the end to the use of nuclear weapons; the ensuing though unintended result was the demise of the Sumerian civilization.

The initiation of chosen individuals into the "secrets of the gods" had marked the beginning of Priesthood, the lineages of mediators between the gods and the people, the transmitters of the Divine Words to the mortal Earthlings. Oracles—interpretations of divine utterances—were commingled with the observation of the heavens for omens. And as Mankind was increasingly drawn to take sides in the godly conflicts, Prophecy began to play a role. Indeed, the term to denote such spokesmen of the gods who proclaimed what was to come, *Nabih,* was the epithet for Marduk's firstborn son, Nabu, who had tried, on behalf of his exiled father, to convince Mankind that the heavenly signs bespoke the coming supremacy of Marduk.

These developments sharpened the realization that one must distinguish between Fate and Destiny. The proclamations of Enlil, sometimes even of Anu, that used to be unquestioned were now subjected to the scrutiny of the difference between NAM—a Destiny, like the planetary orbits, whose course had been determined and was unchangeable—and NAM.TAR, literally, a destiny that could be bent, broken, changed—which was Fate. Reviewing and recalling the sequence of events, and the apparent parallelism between what had happened on Nibiru and what took place on Earth, Enki and Enlil began to ponder philosophically what indeed was destined and could not have been avoided, and what was just fated as a consequence of right or wrong decisions and free choice. The latter could not be predicted; the former could be foreseen—especially if all, as the planetary orbits, was cyclical; if what was shall again be, if the First Things shall also be the Last Things.

The climactic event of the nuclear desolation sharpened soul-searching among the leaders of the Anunnaki and raised the need to explain to the devastated human masses why it came to pass this way. Was it destined, or was it just the result of an Anunnaki-made fate? Was anyone responsible, is there someone accountable?

In the councils of the Anunnaki on the eve of the calamity, it was Enki who stood alone in opposition to the use of the forbidden weapons. It was thus important for Enki to explain to the suffering remnants how that turning point in the saga of extraterrestrials who had meant well but ended as destroyers had come to pass. And who but Ea/Enki, who was the first to come and an eyewitness to it all, was most qualified to tell the Past so that the Future could be divined? And the best way to tell it all was as a first-person report by Enki himself.

That he had recorded his autobiography is certain, for a long text (stretching over at least twelve tablets) discovered in the library of Nippur quotes Enki as saying

> When I approached Earth,
>   there was much flooding.
> When I neared its green meadows,
>   heaps and mounds were piled up
>   at my command.
> In a pure place I built my house,
>   an appropriate name I gave it.

The long text continues to describe how Ea/Enki then assigned tasks to his lieutenants, putting their Mission to Earth in motion.

Numerous other texts that relate varied aspects of Enki's role in the ensuing developments serve to complete Enki's tale; they include a cosmogony, an Epic of Creation, at whose core lay Enki's own text, which scholars call *The Eridu Genesis*. They include detailed descriptions of the fashioning of the Adam. They describe how other Anunnaki, male and female, came to Enki in his city Eridu to obtain from him the ME—a kind of data-disc that encoded all aspects of civilization; and they include texts of Enki's private life and personal problems, such as the tale of his attempts to attain a son by his half sister Ninharsag, his promiscuous affairs with both goddesses and the Daughters of Man, and the unforeseen consequences thereof. The *Atra Hasis* text throws light on Anu's efforts to prevent a flare-up of the Enki-Enlil rivalries by dividing Earth's domains between them; and texts recording the events preceding the Deluge render almost verbatim the debates in the Council of the Gods about the fate of Mankind and Enki's subterfuge known as the tale of Noah and the ark—a tale known only from the Bible until one of its original Mesopotamian versions was found in the tablets of the *Epic of Gilgamesh*.

Sumerian and Akkadian clay tablets; Babylonian and Assyrian temple libraries; Egyptian, Hittite, and Canaanite "myths"; and the biblical narratives are the main body of written-down memories of the affairs of gods and men. For the first time ever, this dispersed and fragmented material has been assembled and used by Zecharia Sitchin to re-create the eyewitness account of Enki—the autobiographical memoirs and insightful prophecies of an extraterrestrial god.

Presented as a text dictated by Enki to a chosen scribe, a Book of Witnessing to be unsealed at an appropriate time, it brings to mind Yahweh's instructions to the Prophet Isaiah (seventh century B.C.):

> Now come,
> Write it on a sealed tablet,
>   as a book engrave it;
> Let it be a witnessing until the last day,
>   a testimony for all time.
>
> *Isaiah 30:8*

In dealing with the past, Enki himself perceived the future. The notion that the Anunnaki, exercising free will, were masters of their own fates (as well as the fate of Mankind) gave way, in the end, to a realization that it was Destiny that, when all was said and done, determined the course of events; and therefore—as the Hebrew Prophets had recognized—the First Things shall be the Last Things.

The record of events dictated by Enki thus becomes a foundation for Prophecy, and the Past becomes the Future.

ATTESTATION

The words of Endubsar, master scribe, son of Eridu city,
servant of the lord Enki, great god.

In the seventh year after the Great Calamity, in the second month, on the seventeenth day, I was summoned by my master the Lord Enki, great god, benevolent fashioner of Mankind, omnipotent and merciful.

I was among the remnants of Eridu who had escaped to the arid steppe just as the Evil Wind was nearing the city. And I wandered off into the wilderness to seek withered twigs for firewood. And I looked up and lo and behold, a Whirlwind came out of the south. There was a reddish brilliance about it and it made no sound. And as it reached the ground, four straight feet spread out from its belly and the brilliance disappeared. And I threw myself to the ground and prostrated myself, for I knew that it was a divine vision.

And when I lifted my eyes, there were two divine emissaries standing near me. And they had the faces of men, and their garments were sparkling like burnished brass. And they called me by name and spoke to me, saying: You are summoned by the great god the lord Enki. Fear not, for you are blessed. And we are here to take you aloft, and carry you unto his retreat in the Land of Magan, on the island amidst the River of Magan, where the sluices are.

And as they spoke, the Whirlwind lifted itself as a fiery chariot and was gone. And they took me by my hands, each one grasping me by one hand. And they lifted me and carried me swiftly between the Earth and the heavens, as the eagle soars. And I could see the land and the waters, and the plains and the mountains. And they let me down on the island at the gateway of the great god's abode. And the moment they let go of my hands, a brilliance as I had never seen before engulfed and overwhelmed me, and I collapsed on the ground as though voided of the spirit of life.

My life senses returned to me, as if awakened from the deepest sleep, by the sound of the calling of my name. I was in some kind of an enclosure. It was dark but there was also an aura. Then my name was called again, by the deepest of voices. And although I could hear it, I could not tell whence the voice came, nor could I see whoever it was that spoke. And I said, Here I am.

Then the voice said to me: Endubsar, offspring of Adapa, I have chosen you to be my scribe, that you write down my words on the tablets.

And all at once there appeared a glowing in one part of the enclosure. And I saw a place arranged like a scribal workplace: a scribe's table and a scribe's stool, and there were finely shaped stones upon the table. But I saw no clay tablets nor containers of wet clay. And there lay upon the table only one stylus, and it glistened in the glowing as no reed stylus ever did.

And the voice spoke up again, saying: Endubsar, son of Eridu city, my faithful servant. I am your lord Enki. I have summoned you to write down my words, for I am much distraught by what has befallen Mankind by the Great Calamity. It is my wish to record the true course of the events, to let gods and men alike know that my hands are clean. Not since the Great Deluge had such a calamity befallen the Earth and the gods and the Earthlings. But the Great Deluge was destined to happen, not so the great calamity. This one, seven years ago, need not have happened. It could have been prevented, and I, Enki, did all I could to prevent it; alas, I failed. And was it fate or was it destiny? In the future shall it be judged, for at the end of days a Day of Judgment there shall be. On that day the Earth shall quake and the rivers shall change course, and there shall be darkness at noon and a fire in the heavens in the night, the day of the returning celestial god will it be. And who shall survive and who would perish, who shall be rewarded and who will be punished, gods and men alike, on that day shall it be discovered; for what shall come to pass by what had passed shall be determined; and what was destined shall in a cycle be repeated, and what was fated and only by the heart's will occurring for good or ill shall for judgment come.

The voice fell silent; then the great lord spoke up again, saying: It is for this reason that I will tell the true account of the Beginnings and of the Prior Times and of the Olden Times, for in the past the future lies hidden. For forty days and forty nights shall I speak and you will write; forty shall be the count of the days and the nights of your task here, for forty is my sacred number among the gods. For forty days and forty nights you shall neither eat nor drink; only this once of bread and water you shall partake, and it shall sustain you for the duration of your task.

And the voice paused, and all at once there appeared a glowing in another part of the enclosure. And I saw a table and upon it a plate and a cup. And I rose up thereto, and there was bread on the plate and water in the cup.

And the voice of the great lord Enki spoke up again, saying: Endubsar, eat the bread and drink the water, and be sustained for forty days and forty nights. And I did as directed. And thereafter the voice directed me to sit myself at the scribal table, and the glowing there intensified. I could see neither door nor aperture where I was, yet the glowing was as strong as the midday sun.

And the voice said: Endubsar the scribe, what do you see?

And I looked and saw the glowing rayed upon the table and the stones and the stylus, and I said: I see stone tablets, and their hue is blue as pure as the sky. And I see a stylus as I have never seen before, its stem unlike any reed and its tip shaped like an eagle's talon.

And the voice said: These are the tablets upon which you shall inscribe my words. By my wish they have been cut of the finest lapis lazuli, each with two smooth faces provided. And the stylus you see is a god's handiwork, its handle made of electrum and its tip of divine crystal. It shall firmly fit in your hand and what you shall engrave with it shall be as easy as marking upon wet clay. In two columns you shall inscribe the front face, in two columns you shall inscribe the back of each stone tablet. Do not deviate from my words and utterances!

And there was a pausing, and I touched one of the stones, and the surface thereof felt like a smooth skin, soft to the touch. And I picked up the holy stylus, and it felt like a feather in my hand.

And then the great god Enki began to speak, and I began to write down his words, exactly as he had spoken them. At times his voice was strong, at times almost a whisper. At times there was joy or pride in his voice, at times pain or agony. And as one tablet was inscribed on all its faces, I took another to continue.

And when the final words were spoken, the great god paused and I could hear a great sigh. And he said: Endubsar my servant, for forty days and forty nights you have faithfully recorded my words. Your task here is completed. Now take hold of another tablet, and on it you shall write your own attestation, and at the end thereof as a witness mark it with your seal, and take the tablet and put it together with the other tablets in the divine chest; for at a designated time chosen ones shall come hither and they shall find the chest and the tablets, and they shall learn all that I have dictated to you; and that true account of the Beginnings and the Prior Times and the Olden Times and the Great Calamity shall henceforth be known as The Words of the Lord Enki. And it shall be a Book of Witnessing of the past, and a Book of Foretelling the future, for the future in the past lies and the first things shall also be the last things.

And there was a pause, and I took the tablets, and put them one by one in their correct order in the chest. And the chest was made of acacia wood and it was inlaid with gold on the outside.

And the voice of my lord said: Now close the chest's cover and fasten its lock. And I did as directed.

And there was another pause, and my lord Enki said: And as for you, Endubsar, with a great god you have spoken, and though you have not seen me, in my presence you have been. Therefore you are blessed, and my spokesman to the people you shall be. You shall admonish them to be righteous, for in that lies a good and long life. And you shall comfort them, for in seventy years the cities will be rebuilt and the crops shall sprout again. There will be peace but there will also be wars. New nations will become mighty, kingdoms shall rise and fall. The olden gods shall step aside and new gods shall decree the fates. But at the end of days destiny shall prevail, and of that future it is foretold in my words about the past. Of all that, Endubsar, to the people you shall tell.

And there was a pause and a silence. And I, Endubsar, bowed to the ground and said: But how will I know what to say?

And the voice of the lord Enki said: The signs will be in the heavens, and the words to utter shall come to you in dreams and in visions. And after you there will be other chosen prophets. And in the end there will be a New Earth and a New Heaven, and for prophets there will be no more need.

And then there was silence, and the auras were extinguished, and the spirit left me. And when I regained my senses, I was in the fields outside Eridu.

Seal of Endubsar, master scribe

THE
WORDS
OF
LORD ENKI

Synopsis of the First Tablet

Lamentation over the desolation of Sumer

How the gods fled their cities as the nuclear cloud spread

The debates in the council of the gods

The fateful decision to unleash the Weapons of Terror

The origin of the gods and the awesome weapons on Nibiru

Nibiru's north-south wars, unification, and dynastic rules

Nibiru's place in the solar system

A dwindling atmosphere causes climate changes

Efforts to obtain gold to shield the atmosphere fail

Alalu, a usurper, uses nuclear weapons to stir volcanic gases

Anu, a dynastic heir, deposes Alalu

Alalu steals a spacecraft and escapes from Nibiru

Depictions of Nibiru as a radiant planet

THE FIRST TABLET

The words of the lord Enki, firstborn son of Anu, who reigns on Nibiru.

With heavy spirit I utter laments; laments that are bitter fill my heart.

How smitten is the land, its people delivered to the Evil Wind, its stables abandoned, its sheepfolds emptied.

How smitten are the cities, their people piled up as dead corpses, afflicted by the Evil Wind.

How smitten are the fields, their vegetation withered, touched by the Evil Wind.

How smitten are the rivers, nothing swims anymore, pure sparkling waters turned into poison.

Of its black-headed people, Shumer is emptied, gone is all life;

Of its cattle and sheep Shumer is emptied, silent is the hum of churning milk.

In its glorious cities, only the wind howls; death is the only smell.

The temples whose heads to heaven arose by their gods have been abandoned.

Of lordship and kingship command there is none; scepter and tiara are gone.

On the banks of the two great rivers, once lush and life-giving, only weeds grow.

No one treads the highways, no one seeks out the roads; flourishing Shumer is like an abandoned desert.

How smitten is the land, home of gods and men!

On that land a calamity fell, one unknown to man.

A calamity that Mankind had never before seen, one that could not be withstood.

On all the lands, from west to east, a disruptive hand of terror was placed. The gods, in their cities, were helpless as men!

An Evil Wind, a storm born in a distant plain, a Great Calamity wrought in its path.

A death-dealing wind born in the west its way to the east has made, its course set by fate.

A storm devouring as the deluge, by wind and not by water a destroyer; by poisoned air, not tidal waves, overwhelming.

By fate, not destiny, was it engendered; the great gods, in their council, the Great Calamity had caused.

By Enlil and Ninharsag it was permitted; I alone for a halt was beseeching.

Day and night to accept what the heavens decree I argued, to no avail!

Ninurta, Enlil's warrior son, and Nergal, my very own son, poisoned weapons in the great plain then unleashed.

That an Evil Wind shall follow the brilliance we knew not! they now cry in agony.

That the death-dealing storm, born in the west, its course to the east shall make, who could foretell! the gods now bemoan.

In their holy cities, the gods stood disbelieving as the Evil Wind toward Shumer made its way.

One after another the gods fled their cities, their temples abandoned to the wind.

In my city, Eridu, as the poisoned cloud approached, I could do nothing to stop it.

Escape to the open steppe! to the people I gave instructions; with Ninki, my spouse, the city I abandoned.

In his city Nippur, place of the Bond Heaven–Earth, Enlil could do nothing to stop it.

The Evil Wind against Nippur was onrushing. In his celestial boat, Enlil and his spouse hurriedly took off.

In Ur, Shumer's city of kingship, Nannar to his father Enlil for help cried;

In the place of the temple that to heaven in seven steps rises, Nannar the hand of fate refused to heed.

My father who begot me, great god who to Ur had granted kingship, turn the Evil Wind away! Nannar pleaded.

Great god who decrees the fates, let Ur and its people be spared, your praises to continue! Nannar appealed.

Enlil answered his son Nannar: Noble son, your wondrous city kingship was granted; eternal reign it was not granted.

Take hold of your spouse Ningal, flee the city! Even I who decree fates, its destiny I cannot bend!

Thus did Enlil my brother speak; alas, alas, not a destiny it was!

A calamity none greater since the deluge gods and Earthlings has befallen; alas, not a destiny it was!

The Great Deluge was destined to happen; the Great Calamity of the death-dealing storm was not.

By the breach of a vow, by a council decision it was caused; by Weapons of Terror was it created.

By a decision, not destiny, were the poisoned weapons unleashed; by deliberation was the lot cast.

Against Marduk, my firstborn, did the two sons destruction direct; vengeance was in their hearts.

Ascendancy is not Marduk's to grasp! Enlil's firstborn shouted. With weapons I shall oppose him, Ninurta said.

Of people he raised an army, Babili as Earth's navel to declare! Nergal, Marduk's brother, so shouted.

In the council of the great gods, words of venom were spread.

Day and night I raised my opposing voice; peace I counseled, deploring haste.

For the second time the people have raised his heavenly image; why does opposing continue? I asked in pleading.

Have all the instruments been checked? Did not the era of Marduk in the heavens arrive? I once more inquired.

Ningishzidda, my very son, other signs of heaven cited. His heart, I knew, Marduk's injustice to him could not forgive.

Nannar, to Enlil on Earth born, was unrelenting too. Marduk my temple in the north city his own abode made! So he said.

Ishkur, Enlil's youngest, punishment demanded; in my lands to whore after him the people he made! he said.

Utu, son of Nannar, at Marduk's son Nabu his wrath directed: The Place of the Celestial Chariots he tried to seize!

Inanna, twin of Utu, was furious of all; the punishment of Marduk for the killing of her beloved Dumuzi she still demanded.

Ninharsag, mother of gods and men, her gaze diverted. Why is not Marduk here? she only said.

Gibil, my own son, with gloom replied: Marduk has all entreaties put aside; by the signs of heaven his supremacy he claims!

Only with weapons will Marduk be stopped! Ninurta, Enlil's firstborn, shouted.

Utu about protecting the Place of the Celestial Chariots was concerned; in Marduk's hands it must not fall! So he said.

Nergal, lord of the Lower Domain, ferociously was demanding: Let the olden Weapons of Terror for obliteration be used!

At my own son I gazed in disbelief: For brother against brother the terror weapons have been foresworn!

Instead of consent, there was silence.

In the silence Enlil opened his mouth: Punishment there must be; like birds without wings the evildoers shall be,

Marduk and Nabu us of heritage are depriving; let them of the Place of the Celestial Chariots be deprived!

Let the place be scorched to oblivion! Ninurta shouted; the One Who Scorches let me be!

Excited, Nergal stood up and shouted: Let the evildoers' cities also be upheavaled,

The sinning cities let me obliterate, let the Annihilator my name thereafter be!

The Earthlings, by us created, must not be harmed; the righteous with the sinners must not be perished, I forcefully said.

Ninharsag, my creating helpmate, was consenting: The matter is between the gods alone to settle, the people must not be harmed.

Anu, from the celestial abode, to the discussions was giving much heed.

Anu, who determines fates, from his celestial abode his voice made heard:

Let the Weapons of Terror be this once used, let the place of the rocketships be obliterated, let the people be spared.

Let Ninurta the Scorcher be, let Nergal be the Annihilator! So did Enlil the decision announce.

To them, a secret of the gods I shall reveal; the hiding place of the terror weapons to them I shall disclose.

The two sons, one mine, one his, to his inner chamber Enlil summoned. Nergal, as he went by me, his gaze averted.

Alas! I cried out without words; brother has turned against brother! Are the Prior Times fated to repeat?

A secret from the Olden Times to them Enlil was revealing, the Weapons of Terror to their hands entrusting!

Clad with terror, with a brilliance they are unleashed; all they touch to a dust heap they turn.

For brother against brother on Earth they were foresworn, neither region to affect.

Now the oath was undone, like a broken jar in useless pieces.

The two sons, full of glee, with quickened step from Enlil's chamber emerged, for the weapons departing.

The other gods turned back to their cities; none of his own calamity had a foreboding!

Now this is the account of the Prior Times, and of the Weapons of Terror.

Before the Prior Times was the Beginning; after the Prior Times were the Olden Times.

In the Olden Times the gods came to Earth and created the Earthlings.

In the Prior Times, none of the gods was on the Earth, nor were the Earthlings yet fashioned.

In the Prior Times, the abode of the gods was on their own planet; Nibiru is its name.

A great planet, reddish in radiance; around the Sun an elongated circuit Nibiru makes.

For a time in the cold is Nibiru engulfed; for part of its circuit by the Sun strongly is it heated.

A thick atmosphere Nibiru envelops, by volcanic eruptions constantly fed.

All manner of life this atmosphere sustains; without it there will be only perishing!

In the cold period the inner heat of Nibiru it keeps about the planet, like a warm coat that is constantly renewed.

In the hot period it shields Nibiru from the Sun's scorching rays.

In its midst rains it holds and releases, to lakes and streams giving rise.

Lush vegetation our atmosphere feeds and protects; all manner of life in the waters and on the land to sprout it caused.

After aeons of time our own species sprouted, by our own essence
an eternal seed to procreate.

As our numbers grew, to many regions of Nibiru our ancestors
spread.

Some tilled the land, some four-legged creatures shepherded.

Some lived on the mountains, some in the valleys their home
made.

Rivalries occurred, encroachments happened; clashes occurred,
sticks became weapons.

Clans gathered into tribes, then two great nations each other faced.

The nation of the north against the nation of the south took up arms.

What was held by hand to thrusting missiles was turned; weapons
of thunder and brilliance increased the terror.

A war, long and fierce, engulfed the planet; brother amassed
against brother.

There was death and destruction both north and south.

For many circuits desolation reigned the land; all life was
diminished.

Then a truce was declared; then peacemaking was conducted.

Let the nations be united, the emissaries said to one another:

Let there be one throne on Nibiru, one king to reign over all.

Let a leader from north or from south by lot be chosen, one king
supreme to be.

If he be from north, let south choose a female to be his spouse as
equal queen to reign alongside.

If by lot a south male be chosen, let the north's female be his spouse.

Husband and wife let them be, as one flesh to become.

Let their firstborn son be the successor; let a unified dynasty thus
be formed, unity on Nibiru forever to establish!

In the midst of the ruins, peace was started. North and south by
marriage were united.

The royal throne into one flesh combined, an unbroken line of
  kingship established!

The first king after peace was made, a warrior of the north he was,
  a mighty commander.

By lots, true and fair, was he chosen; his decrees in unity were
  accepted.

For his abode he built a splendid city; Agade, Unity meaning, was
  its name.

For his reign a royal title he was granted; An it was, the Celestial
  One was its meaning.

With strong arm order in the lands he reestablished; laws and
  regulations he decreed.

Governors for each land he appointed; restoration and reclamation
  was their foremost task.

Of him in the royal annals, thus it was recorded: An the lands
  unified, peace on Nibiru he restored.

He built a new city, the canals he repaired, food to the people he
  provided; there was abundance in the lands.

For his spouse the south a maiden had chosen; for both love and
  warring she was noted.

An.Tu was her royal title; the Leader Who Is An's Spouse, the
  given name cleverly did mean.

She bore An three sons and no daughters. The firstborn son was by
  her named An.Ki; By An a Solid Foundation was its meaning.

Alone on the throne he was seated; a spouse to choose was twice
  postponed.

In his reign, concubines were brought into the palace; a son to him
  was not born.

The dynasty thus begun was by the death of Anki disrupted; on the
  foundation no offspring followed.

The middle son, though not the firstborn, the Legal Heir was
  pronounced.

From his youth, one of three brothers, Ib by his mother was
lovingly called. The One in the Middle his name did mean.

By the royal annals An.Ib he is named: In kingship celestial; by
generations, the One Who Is An's Son the name signified.

He followed his father An on Nibiru's throne; by count, he was the
third to reign.

The daughter of his younger brother he chose to be his spouse.
Nin.Ib she was called, the Lady of Ib.

A son to Anib by Ninib was born; the successor on the throne he
was, the fourth by the count of kings.

By the royal name An.Shar.Gal he wished himself to be known;
An's Prince Who Is Greatest of Princes was the meaning.

His spouse, a half sister, Ki.Shar.Gal was equally named.

Knowledge and understanding were his chief ambition; the ways of
the heavens he assiduously studied.

The great circuit of Nibiru he studied, its length a Shar to be he fixed.

As one year of Nibiru was the measure, by it the royal reigns to be
numbered and recorded.

The Shar to ten portions he divided, two festivals thereby he
pronounced.

When nearest to the Sun's quarters, a festival of the warmth was
celebrated.

When to its far abode Nibiru was distanced, the festival of coolness
was decreed.

Replacing all olden festivals of tribes and nations, to unify the
people the two were established.

Laws of husband and wife, of sons and daughters, by decree he
established;

Customs from the first tribes he proclaimed for the whole land.

From the wars females greatly outnumbered males.

Decrees he made, one male to have more than one female for
knowing.

By law, one wife as official spouse to be chosen, First Wife to be
called.

By law, the firstborn son was his father's successor.

By these laws, confusion soon came about; if the Firstborn son not
by the First Wife was born,

And thereafter by the First Wife a son was born, by law the Legal
Heir becoming,

Who shall be the successor: the one by the count of Shars firstborn?
The one by the First Wife born?

The Firstborn son? The Legal Heir? Who shall inherit? Who shall
succeed?

In the reign of Anshargal, Kishargal as First Wife was pronounced.
A half sister of the king she was.

In Anshargal's reign, concubines were again brought into the
palace.

By the concubines, sons and daughters to the king were born.

A son by one was the first to be born; the son of a concubine was
the Firstborn.

Thereafter Kishargal bore a son. The Legal Heir by law he was; the
Firstborn he was not.

In the palace Kishargal raised her voice, in anger shouting:

If by rules my son, by a First Wife born, from succession shall be
barred,

Let the double seed not be neglected!

Though of different mothers, of one father the king and I are
offspring.

I am the king's half sister; of me the king is half brother.

By that my son the double seed of our father Anib possesses!

Let henceforth the Law of the Seed, the Law of Espousal overpower!

Let henceforth a son by a half sister, whenever born, above all
other sons rise to succession!

Anshargal, contemplating, the Law of the Seed embraced with favor:

Confusion of spouse and concubines, of marriage and divorce, by it would be avoided.

In their council, the royal counselors the Law of the Seed for succession adopted.

By the king's order, the scribes the decree recorded.

Thus, the next king by the Law of the Seed for succession was proclaimed.

To him the royal name An.Shar was granted. Fifth on the throne he was.

———•·•———

Now this is the account of the reign of Anshar and the kings who followed.

When the law was changed, the other princes were contending. Words there were, rebellion there was not.

As his spouse Anshar a half sister chose. He made her First Wife; by the name Ki.Shar she was called.

Thus was by this law the dynasty continued.

In the reign of Anshar, the fields diminished their yields, fruits and grains lost abundance.

From circuit to circuit, nearing the Sun heat grew stronger; in the faraway abode, coolness was more biting.

In Agade, the throne city, the king those of great understanding assembled.

Learned savants, those of great knowledge, to inquire were commanded.

The land and the soil they examined, the lakes and streams they put to the test.

It has happened before, some gave an answer: Nibiru in the past colder or warmer has grown;

A destiny it is, in the circuit of Nibiru embedded!

Others of knowledge, the circuit observing, Nibiru's destiny to blame did not consider.

In the atmosphere a breaching has occurred; that was their finding.

Volcanoes, the atmosphere's forebears, less belching were spitting up!

Nibiru's air has thinner been made, the protective shield has been diminished!

In the reign of Anshar and Kishar, pestilences of field made appearance; toil could them not overcome.

Their son En.Shar then the throne ascended; of the dynasty the sixth he was.

Lordly Master of the Shar the name did signify.

With great understanding he was born, with much learning he mastered much knowledge.

To remedy the afflictions ways he sought; of Nibiru's heavenly circuit he made much study.

In its loop, of the Sun's family five members it embraced, planets of dazzling beauty.

For cures to the afflictions, their atmospheres he caused to be examined.

To each he gave a name, ancestral forefathers he honored; as heavenly couples he them considered.

An and Antu, the twinlike planets, he called the first two to be encountered.

Beyond in Nibiru's circuit were Anshar and Kishar, in their size the largest.

As a messenger Gaga among the others coursed, sometimes first Nibiru to meet.

Five in all were Nibiru's heavenly greeters as the Sun it circled.

Beyond, like a boundary, the Hammered Bracelet the Sun encircled;

As a guardian of the heaven's forbidden region with havoc it
    protected.

Other children of the Sun, four in number, from intrusion the
    bracelet shielded.

The atmospheres of the five greeters Enshar set out to study.

In its repeating circuit, the five in Nibiru's loop carefully were
    examined.

What atmospheres they possessed by observation and with celestial
    chariots intensely were examined.

The findings were astounding, the discoveries confusing.

From circuit to circuit Nibiru's atmosphere more breaching
    suffered.

In the councils of the learned, cures were avidly debated; ways to
    bandage the wound were urgently considered.

A new shield to embrace the planet was attempted; all that was
    thrust up back to the ground came down.

In the councils of the learned, the belching volcanoes were studied.

The atmosphere by belching volcanoes having been created, its
    wound by their diminished belching had come to be.

Let with invention new belching be encouraged, let volcanoes spew
    again! one savants group was saying.

How the feat to achieve, with what tools more belching to attain,
    none the king could inform.

In the reign of Enshar the breach in the skies grew bigger.

Rains were withheld, winds blew harder; springs from the depths
    did not arise.

In the lands there was an accursation; the breasts of mothers were
    dry.

In the palace there was distress; an accursation therein took hold.

As his First Wife, Enshar a half sister did espouse, by the Law of
    the Seed abiding.

Nin.Shar she was called, of the Shars the Lady. A son she did not bear.

By a concubine to Enshar a son was born; the Firstborn son he was.

By Ninshar, First Wife and half sister, a son was not brought forth.

By the Law of Succession, the concubine's son the throne ascended; the seventh to reign he was.

Du.Uru was his royal name; In the Dwelling Place Fashioned was its meaning;

In the House of Concubines, not in the palace, was he indeed conceived.

As his spouse a maiden from his youth beloved Duuru chose; by love, not by seed, a First Wife he selected.

Da.Uru was her royal name; She Who Is by My Side was the meaning.

In the royal court confusion was rampant. Sons were not heirs, wives were not half sisters.

In the land suffering was increasing. The fields forgot their abundance, among the people fertility was diminished.

In the palace fertility was absent; neither son nor daughter was brought forth.

Of An's seed, seven were the rulers; then of his seed the throne was dry.

Dauru a child at the palace gateway found; as a son she embraced him.

Duuru in the end as a son him adopted, Legal Heir him decreed; Lahma, meaning Dryness, was his given name.

In the palace the princes were grumbling; in the Council of Counselors there were complaints.

In the end Lahma the throne ascended. Though not of An's seed, he was the eighth to reign.

In the councils of the learned, to heal the breach there were two suggestions:

One was to use a metal, gold was its name. On Nibiru it was greatly rare; within the Hammered Bracelet it was abundant.

It was the only substance that to the finest powder could be ground; lofted high to heaven, suspended it could remain.

Thus, with replenishments, the breach it would heal, protection make better.

Let celestial boats be built, let a celestial fleet the gold to Nibiru bring over!

Let Weapons of Terror be created! was the other suggestion; weapons that the ground shake loose, the mountains split asunder;

With missiles the volcanoes to attack, their dormancy to bestir, their belching to increase,

The atmosphere to replenish, the breach to make disappear!

For a decision Lahma was too feeble; what choice to make he knew not.

One circuit Nibiru completed, two Shars Nibiru to count continued.

In the fields, affliction was not diminished. By volcanic belching the atmosphere was not repaired.

A third Shar passed, a fourth was counted. Gold was not obtained.

In the land strife was abundant; food and water were not abundant.

In the land unity was gone; accusations were abundant.

In the royal court, savants were coming and going; counselors were rushing in and rushing out.

The king to their words paid no attention. Counsel from his spouse he only sought; Lahama was her name.

If destiny it be, let us beseech the Great Creator of All, to the king she said. Beseeching, not actings, provide the only hope!

In the royal court the princes were astir; at the king accusations were directed:

Foolishly, unreasoning, greater calamities instead of cure he brought forth!

From the olden storehouses, weapons were retrieved; of rebellion there was much speaking.

A prince in the royal palace was the first to take up arms.

By words of promise, the other princes he agitated; Alalu was his name.

Let Lahma be the king no more! he shouted. Let decision supplant hesitation!

Come, let us unnerve the king in his dwelling; let him the throne abandon!

The princes to his words gave heed; the gate of the palace they rushed;

To the throne room, its entrance restricted, like onrushing waters they went.

To the tower of the palace the king escaped; Alalu was him pursuing.

In the tower there was a struggle; Lahma fell down to his death.

Lahma is no more! Alalu shouted. The king is no more, with glee he announced.

To the throne room Alalu rushed, on the throne he himself seated.

Without right or council, a king he himself pronounced.

In the land unity was lost; some by the death of Lahma rejoiced, others by Alalu's deed were saddened.

---·•·---

Now this is the account of the kingship of Alalu and of the going to Earth.

In the land unity was lost; about the kingship many were aggrieved.

In the palace princes were agitated; in the council, counselors were distraught.

From father to son, succession from An on the throne continued;

Even Lahma, the eighth, by adoption a son was proclaimed.

Who was Alalu? Was he a Legal Heir, was he Firstborn?

By what right did he usurp; was he not a king's slayer?

Before the Seven Who Judge Alalu was summoned, his fate to consider.

Before the Seven Who Judge, Alalu spread his pleas:

Though neither Legal Heir nor a son Firstborn, of royal seed indeed he was!

Of Anshargal am I descended, before the judges he claimed.

By a concubine, my ancestor was to him born; Alam was his name.

By the count of Shars, Alam was the Firstborn; the throne to him belonged;

By conniving, the queen his rights put aside!

A Law of the Seed from naught she created, for her son the kingship obtained.

Alam of kingship she deprived; to her son instead it was granted.

By descent, of Alam's generations am I continued; the seed of Anshargal is within me!

The Seven Who Judge to Alalu's words gave heed.

To the Council of Counselors they passed the matter, truth or falsehood to ascertain.

The royal annals from the House of Records were brought forth; with much care they were read.

An and Antu the first royal couple were; three sons and no daughters to them were born.

The Firstborn was Anki; he died on the throne; he had no offspring.

The middle son in his stead the throne ascended; Anib was his name.

Anshargal was his Firstborn; the throne he ascended.

After him on the throne kingship by the Firstborn did not continue;

The Law of Succession by the Law of the Seed was supplanted.

A concubine's son was the Firstborn; by the Law of the Seed of kingship he was deprived.

The kingship instead to Kishargal's son was granted; her being a half sister of the king was the reason.

Of the concubine's son, the Firstborn, the annals made no record.

Of him I am descended! Alalu to the counselors cried out.

By the Law of Succession, to him kingship belonged; by the Law of Succession, to kingship am I now entitled!

With hesitation, the counselors of Alalu an oath of truth demanded.

Alalu swore the oath of life or death; as king the council him considered.

They summoned the elders, they summoned the princes; before them the decision was pronounced.

From among the princes a young prince stepped forward; about the kingship words he wished to say.

Succession must be reconsidered, to the assembly he said.

Though neither Firstborn nor by the queen a son, of pure seed am I descended:

The essence of An in me is preserved, by no concubine diluted!

The counselors heard the words with amazement; the young prince to step closer they summoned.

They asked for his name. It is Anu; after my forefather An am I named!

They inquired about his generations; of An's three sons he them reminded:

Anki was the Firstborn, without son or daughter he died;

Anib was the middle son, instead of Anki the throne he ascended;

Anib the daughter of his younger brother took to be wife; from them onward the succession is in the annals recorded.

Who was that younger brother, a son of An and Antu, one of purest seed?

The counselors with wonderment looked at each other.

Enuru was his name! Anu to them announced; he was my great ancestor!

His spouse Ninuru was a half sister; her son was firstborn; Enama was his name.

His wife was a half sister, by laws of seed and succession a son she bore him.

Of pure descent the generations continued, by law and by seed perfect!

Anu, after our forefather An, did my parents name me;

From the throneship we were removed; from An's pure seed we were not removed!

Let Anu be king! many counselors shouted. Let Alalu be removed!

Others caution did counsel: Let strife be prevented, let unity prevail!

They called in Alalu, the discovered findings to be told.

To the prince Anu, Alalu his arm in embrace offered; to Anu he thus said:

Though by different offsprings, of one ancestor we are both descended;

Let us live in peace, together Nibiru to abundance return!

Let me keep the throne, let you keep the succession!

To the council words he directed: Let Anu Crown Prince be, let him be my successor!

Let his son my daughter espouse, let succession be united!

Anu bowed before the council, to the assembly he thus declared:

Alalu's cupbearer I shall be, his successor-in-waiting; a son of mine a daughter of his as bride shall choose.

That was the council's decision; in the royal annals it was inscribed.

In this manner Alalu on the throne remained seated.

He summoned the sages, savants and commanders he consulted; for deciding he gained much knowledge.

Let celestial boats be constructed, he decided, to seek the gold in the Hammered Bracelet, he decided.

By the Hammered Bracelets the boats were crushed; none of them returned.

Let with Weapons of Terror the bowels of Nibiru be cut open, let volcanoes again erupt! he then commanded.

With Weapons of Terror skyborne chariots were armed, with terror missiles from the skies were volcanoes struck.

The mountains swayed, the valleys shuddered as great brilliances with thunder exploded.

In the land there was much rejoicing; of abundance there were expectations.

In the palace, Anu was for Alalu the cupbearer.

He would bow at Alalu's feet, set the drinking cup in Alalu's hand.

Alalu was the king; Anu as a servant by him was treated.

In the land rejoicing receded; rains were withheld, winds blew harder.

The belching by volcanoes did not increase, the breach in the atmosphere did not heal.

In the heavens Nibiru its circuits kept coursing; from circuit to circuit heat and cold grew harder to suffer.

The people of Nibiru ceased to revere their king; instead of relief, misery he caused!

Alalu on the throne remained seated.

The strong and wise Anu, foremost among the princes, was standing before him.

He would bow to Alalu's feet, set the drinking cup in Alalu's hand.

For nine counted periods Alalu was king on Nibiru.

In the ninth Shar, Anu gave battle to Alalu.

To hand-to-hand combat, with bodies naked, Alalu he challenged. Let the winner be king, Anu said.

They grappled with each other in the public square; doorposts trembled and walls shook.

Alalu bent his knee; to the ground he fell on his chest.

Alalu in combat was defeated; by acclaim Anu was hailed as king.

Anu to the palace was escorted; Alalu to the palace did not return.

From the crowds he stealthily escaped; of dying like Lahma he was
fearful.

Unbeknownst to others, to the place of the celestial chariots he
hurriedly went.

Into a missile-throwing chariot Alalu climbed; its hatch behind him
he closed.

The forepart chamber he entered; the commander's seat he occupied.

That-Which-Shows-the-Way he lit up, with bluish aura the chamber
filling.

The Fire Stones he stirred up; their hum like music was
enthralling.

The chariot's Great Cracker he enlivened; a reddish brilliance it
was casting.

Unbeknownst to others, in the celestial boat Alalu from Nibiru
escaped.

To snow-hued Earth Alalu set his course; by a secret from the
Beginning he chose his destination.

Synopsis of the Second Tablet

Alalu's flight in a nuclear-armed spacecraft

He sets his course to Ki, the seventh planet (Earth)

Why he expects to find gold on Earth

The solar-system's cosmogony; Tiamat's water and gold

The appearance of Nibiru from outer space

The Celestial Battle and Tiamat's breakup

Earth, half of Tiamat, inherits her waters and gold

Kingu, Tiamat's main satellite, becomes the Moon of Earth

Nibiru is destined to forever orbit the Sun

Alalu's arrival and landing on Earth

Alalu, discovering gold, holds Nibiru's fate in his hands

A Babylonian depiction of the Celestial Battle

THE SECOND TABLET

To snow-hued Earth Alalu set his course; by a secret from the Beginning he chose his destination.

To regions forbidden Alalu made his way; no one has gone there before,

No one at the Hammered Bracelet a crossing had attempted.

A secret from the Beginning Alalu's course has determined,

The fate of Nibiru in his hands it placed, by a scheme his kingship to make universal!

On Nibiru exile was certain, there death itself he was chancing.

In his scheme, risk was in the journey; eternal glory of success was the reward!

Riding like an eagle, Alalu the heavens scanned; below, Nibiru was a ball in a voidness hanging.

Alluring was its figure, its radiance emblazoned the surrounding heavens.

Its measure was enormous, its belchings fire blazed forth.

Its life-sustaining envelope, its hue a redness, was like a sea churning;

In its midst the breach was distinct, like a darkened wound.

He looked down again; the wide breach turned into a small tub.

He looked again, Nibiru's great ball turned into a small fruit;

The next time he looked, in the wide dark sea Nibiru disappeared.

Remorse the heart of Alalu grasped, fear held him in its hands; decision to hesitation turned.

To halt in his tracks Alalu considered; then from audacity to decision he returned.

A hundred leagues, a thousand leagues the chariot was coursing;
   ten thousand leagues the chariot was journeying.

In the wide heavens darkness was the darkest; in the faraway, distant stars their eyes were blinking.

More leagues Alalu traveled, then a sight of great joy met his gaze:

In the expanse of the heavens, the celestials' emissary was him greeting!

Little Gaga, the One Who Shows the Way, by its circuit Alalu was greeting, to him a welcome extending.

With a leaning gait, before and after the celestial Antu it was destined to travel,

To face forward, to face backward, with two facings was it endowed.

Its appearance as first to greet Alalu as a good omen he at once considered;

By the celestial gods he is welcomed! So was his understanding.

In his chariot Alalu followed Gaga's path; to the second god of the heavens it was directing.

Soon celestial Antu, its name by King Enshar was given, in the deep's darkness was looming;

Blue as pure waters was her hue; of the Upper Waters she was the commencement.

Alalu by the sight's beauty was enchanted; to course at a distance he continued.

In the far beyond Antu's spouse began to shimmer, by size Antu's the equal;

As his spouse's double, by a greenish blueness was An distinguished.

A dazzling host encircled it on its side; with firm grounds they were provided.

To the two celestials Alalu bade a fond farewell, the path of Gaga still discerning.

The way it was showing to its olden master, of whom it was once the counselor:

To Anshar, the Foremost Prince of the heavens, the course was a-turning.

By the speeding chariot, Alalu the ensnaring pull of Anshar could tell;

With bright rings of dazzling colors the chariot it was enchanting!

His gaze Alalu to one side quickly turned, That Which Shows the Way with might he diverted.

A sight most awesome then to him appeared: In the faraway heavens the family's bright star he discerned!

A sight most frightening the revelation followed:

A giant monster, in its destiny moving, upon the Sun a darkening cast; Kishar its creator swallowed!

Frightening was the occurrence; an evil omen, Alalu indeed thought.

The giant Kishar, foremost of the Firm Planets, its size was overwhelming.

Swirling storms obscured its face, colored spots they moved about;

A host beyond counting, some quickly, some slowly, the celestial god encircled.

Troublesome were their ways, back and forth they were surging.

Kishar itself a spell was casting, divine lightnings it was thrusting.

As Alalu looked on, his course became upset,

His direction was distracted, his doings became confused.

Then the deepness darkening began to depart: Kishar on his destiny continued to circuit.

Slowly moving, its veil from the shining Sun it lifted; the One from the Beginning came fully into view.

Joy in Alalu's heart was not long-lasting;

Beyond the fifth planet the utmost danger was lurking, so indeed he knew.

The Hammered Bracelet ahead was reigning, to demolish it was awaiting!

Of rocks and boulders was it together hammered, like orphans
with no mother they banded together.

Surging back and forth, a bygone destiny they followed;

Their doings were loathsome; troubling were their ways.

Nibiru's probing chariots like preying lions they devoured;

The precious gold, needed for surviving, they refused to dislodge.

The chariot of Alalu toward the Hammered Bracelet was headlong
moving,

The ferocious boulders in close combat to boldly face.

Alalu the Fire Stones in his chariot more strongly stirred up,

That Which Shows the Way with steady hands he directed.

The ominous boulders against the chariot charged forward, like an
enemy in battle attacking.

Toward them Alalu a death-dealing missile from the chariot let
loose;

Then another and another against the enemy the terror weapons
he thrust.

As frightened warriors the boulders turned back, a path for Alalu
granting.

Like by a spell the Hammered Bracelet a doorway to the king it
opened.

In the dark deepness Alalu the heavens could clearly see;

By the Bracelet's ferocity he was not defeated, his mission was not
ended!

In the distance, the Sun's fiery ball its brilliance was sending forth;

Welcoming rays toward Alalu it was emitting.

Before it, a red-brown planet on its circuit was coursing; the sixth
in the count of celestial gods it was.

Alalu could but glimpse it: On its destined course from Alalu's
path it was quickly moving.

Then snow-hued Earth appeared, the seventh in the celestial count.

Toward the planet Alalu set his course, to a destination most inviting.

Smaller than Nibiru was its alluring ball, weaker than Nibiru's was its attracting net.

Its atmosphere thinner than Nibiru's was, clouds were within it swirling.

Below, the Earth to three regions was divided:

Snow white at the top and on the bottom, blue and brown in between.

Deftly Alalu spread the chariot's arresting wings around the Earth's ball to circle.

In the middle region dry lands and watery oceans he could discern.

The Beam That Penetrates downward he directed, Earth's innards to detect.

I have attained it! ecstatically he shouted:

Gold, much gold, the beam has indicated; it was beneath the dark-hued region, in the waters it was too!

With pounding heart Alalu a decision was contemplating:

Shall he on the dry land his chariot bring down, perchance to crash and die?

Shall he to the waters his course direct, to perchance into oblivion sink?

Which way shall he survive, will he the treasured gold discover?

In the Eagle's seat Alalu was not stirring; to fate's hands the chariot he entrusted.

Fully caught in Earth's attracting net, the chariot was moving faster.

Its spread wings became aglow; Earth's atmosphere like an oven was.

Then the chariot shook, emitting a mortifying thunder.

With abruptness the chariot crashed, with a suddenness altogether stopping.

Senseless from the shaking, stunned by the crash, Alalu was without moving.

Then he opened his eyes and knew he was among the living;

At the planet of gold he victoriously arrived.

——•——

Now this is the account of the Earth and its gold;

It is an account of the Beginning and how the celestial gods created
were.

In the Beginning,

When in the Above the gods in the heavens had not been called
into being,

And in the Below Ki, the Firm Ground, had not yet been named,

Alone in the void there existed Apsu, their Primordial Begetter.

In the heights of the Above, the celestial gods had not yet been
created;

In the waters of the Below, the celestial gods had not yet appeared.

Above and Below, the gods had not yet been formed, destinies
were not yet decreed.

No reed had yet been formed, no marshland had appeared;

Alone did Apsu reign in the void.

Then by his winds the primordial waters were mingled,

A divine and artful spell Apsu upon the waters cast.

On the void's deep he poured a sound sleep;

Tiamat, the Mother of All, as a spouse for himself he fashioned.

A celestial mother, a watery beauty she was indeed!

Beside him Apsu little Mummu then brought forth,

As his messenger he him appointed, a gift for Tiamat to present.

A gift resplendent to his spouse Apsu granted:

A shining metal, the everlasting gold, for her alone to possess!

Then it was that the two their waters mingled, divine children
between them to bring forth.

Male and female were the celestials created; Lahmu and Lahamu by names they were called.

In the Below did Apsu and Tiamat make them an abode.

Before they had grown in age and in stature,

In the waters of the Above Anshar and Kishar were formed;

Surpassing their brothers in size they were.

As a celestial couple the two were fashioned;

A son, An, in the distant heavens was their heir.

Then Antu, to be his spouse, as An's equal was brought forth;

As a boundary of the Upper Waters their abode was made.

Thus were three heavenly couples, Below and Above, in the depths created;

By names they were called, the family of Apsu with Mummu and Tiamat they formed.

At that time, Nibiru had not yet been seen,

The Earth was not yet called into being.

Mingled were the heavenly waters; by a Hammered Bracelet they were not yet separated.

At that time, circuits were not yet fully fashioned;

The destinies of the gods were not yet firmly decreed;

The celestial kinfolk banded together; erratic were their ways.

Their ways to Apsu were verily loathsome;

Tiamat, getting no rest, was aggrieved and raged.

A throng to march by her side she formed,

A growling, raging host against the sons of Apsu she brought forth.

Withal eleven of this kind she brought forth;

She made the firstborn, Kingu, chief among them.

When the celestial gods of this did hear, for council they rallied.

Kingu she has elevated, to rank as An command to him she gave! to each other they said.

A Tablet of Destiny to his chest she has attached, his own circuit to
    acquire,

To battle against the gods her offspring Kingu she instructed.

Who shall stand up to Tiamat? the gods asked each other.

None in their circuits stepped forward, none a weapon for battle
    would bear.

At that time, in the heart of the Deep a god was engendered,

In a Chamber of Fates, a place of destinies, was he born.

By an artful Creator was he fashioned, the son of his own Sun
    he was.

From the Deep where he was engendered, the god from his family
    in a rushing departed;

A gift of his Creator, the Seed of Life, with him away he carried.

To the void he set his course; a new destiny he was seeking.

The first to glimpse the wandering celestial was the ever-watchful
    Antu.

Alluring was his figure, a radiance he was beaming,

Lordly was his gait, exceedingly great was his course.

Of all the gods he was the loftiest, surpassing theirs his circuit was.

The first to glimpse him was Antu, her breast by child never
    sucked.

Come, be my son! she called to him. Let me your mother become!

She cast her net and made him welcome, made his course for the
    purpose suited.

Her words filled the newcomer's heart with pride; the one who
    would nurse him made him haughty.

His head to doubled size grew larger, four members at his sides he
    sprouted.

He moved his lips in acceptance, a godly fire from them blazed
    forth.

Toward Antu his course he turned, his face to An soon to show.

When An saw him, My son! My son! with exaltation he shouted.

To leadership you shall be consigned, a host by your side will be your servants!

Let Nibiru be your name, as Crossing forever known!

He bowed to Nibiru, turning his face at Nibiru's passage;

He spread his net, for Nibiru four servants he brought forth,

His host by his side to be: the South Wind, the North Wind, the East Wind, the West Wind.

With joyful heart An to Anshar his forebear the arrival of Nibiru announced.

Anshar upon this hearing, Gaga, who was by his side, as an emissary sent forth—

Words of wisdom to An deliver, a task to Nibiru to assign.

He charged Gaga to give voice to what was in his heart, to An thus say:

Tiamat, she who bore us, now detests us;

She has set up a warring host, she is furious with rage.

Against the gods, her children, eleven warriors march by her side;

Kingu among them she elevated, a destiny to his chest she attached without right.

No god among us against her venom can stand up, her host in us all has fear established.

Let Nibiru become our Avenger!

Let him vanquish Tiamat, let him save our lives!

For him decree a fate, let him go forth and face our mighty foe!

To An Gaga departed; he bowed before him, the words of Anshar he repeated.

An to Nibiru his forebear's words repeated, Gaga's message to him he revealed.

To the words Nibiru with wonder listened; of the mother who would her children devour with fascination he heard.

His heart, without saying, to set out against Tiamat him already prompted.

He opened his mouth, to An and Gaga he thus said:

If indeed I am to vanquish Tiamat your lives to save,

Convene the gods to assembly, my destiny proclaim supreme!

Let all the gods agree in council to make me the leader, bow to my command!

When Lahmu and Lahamu heard this, they cried out with anguish:

Strange was the demand, its meaning cannot be fathomed! Thus they said.

The gods who decree the fates with each other consulted;

To make Nibiru their Avenger they all agreed, to him an exalted fate decreed.

From this day on, unchallengeable shall be your commandments! to him they said.

No one among us gods shall transgress your bounds!

Go, Nibiru, be our Avenger!

They fashioned for him a princely circuit toward Tiamat to proceed;

They gave Nibiru blessings, they gave Nibiru awesome weapons.

Anshar three more winds of Nibiru brought forth: the Evil Wind, the Whirlwind, the Matchless Wind.

Kishar with a blazing flame filled his body, a net to enfold Tiamat therewith.

Thus ready for battle, Nibiru toward Tiamat directly set his course.

———•·•———

Now this is the account of the Celestial Battle,

And how the Earth had come to be, and of Nibiru's destiny.

The lord went forth, his fated course he followed,

Toward the raging Tiamat he set his face, a spell with his lips he
   uttered.

As a cloak for protection he the Pulser and the Emitter put on;

With a fearsome radiance his head was crowned.

On his right he posted the Smiter, on his left the Repeller he placed.

The seven winds, his host of helpers, like a storm he sent forth;

Toward the raging Tiamat he was rushing, clamoring for battle.

The gods thronged about him, then from his path they departed,

To scan Tiamat and her helpers alone he was advancing,

The scheme of Kingu, her host's commander, to conceive.

When he saw valiant Kingu, blurred became his vision;

As he gazed upon the monsters his direction was distracted,

His course became upset, his doings were confused.

Tiamat's band tightly her encircled, with terror they trembled.

Tiamat to her roots gave a shudder, a mighty roar she emitted;

On Nibiru she cast a spell, engulfed him with her charms.

The issue between them was joined, the battle was unavoided!

Face to face they came, Tiamat and Nibiru; against each other they
   were advancing.

They for battle approached, they pressed on for single combat.

The Lord spread his net, to encompass her he cast it;

With fury Tiamat cried out, like one possessed she lost her senses.

The Evil Wind, which had been behind him, Nibiru drove forward,
   in her face he let it loose;

She opened her mouth the Evil Wind to swallow, but could not
   close her lips.

The Evil Wind charged her belly, into her innards it made its way.

Her innards were howling, her body was distended, her mouth
   was open wide.

Through the opening Nibiru shot a brilliant arrow, a lightning
   most divine.

It pierced her innards, her belly it tore apart;

It tore into her womb, it split apart her heart.

Having thus subdued her, her life-breath he extinguished.

The lifeless body Nibiru surveyed, like a slaughtered carcass Tiamat now was.

Beside their lifeless mistress, her eleven helpers trembled with terror;

In Nibiru's net they were captured, unable they were to flee.

Kingu, who by Tiamat was made the host's chief, was among them.

The Lord put him in fetters, to his lifeless mistress he bound him.

He wrested from Kingu the Tablets of Destinies, unrightly to him given,

Stamped it with his own seal, fastened the Destiny to his own chest.

The others of Tiamat's band as captives he bound, in his circuit he them ensnared.

He trampled them underfoot, cut them up to pieces.

He bound them all to his circuit; to turn around he made them, backward to course.

From the Place of the Battle Nibiru then departed,

To the gods who had him appointed the victory to announce.

He made a circuit about Apsu, to Kishar and Anshar he journeyed.

Gaga came out to greet him, as a herald to the others he then journeyed.

Beyond An and Antu, Nibiru to the Abode in the Deep proceeded.

The fate of lifeless Tiamat and of Kingu he then considered,

To Tiamat, whom he had subdued, the Lord Nibiru then returned.

He made his way to her, paused to view her lifeless body;

To artfully divide the monster in his heart he was planning.

Then, as a mussel, into two parts he split her, her chest from her lower parts he separated.

Her inner channels he cut apart, her golden veins he beheld with wonder.

Trodding upon her hinder part, the Lord her upper part completely severed.

The North Wind, his helper, from his side he summoned,

To thrust away the severed head the Wind he commanded, in the void to place it.

Nibiru's Wind upon Tiamat then hovered, sweeping upon her gushing waters.

Nibiru shot a lightning, to North Wind he gave a signal;

In a brilliance was Tiamat's upper part to a region unknown carried.

With her the bound Kingu was also exiled, of the severed part a companion to be.

The hinder part's fate Nibiru then considered:

As an everlasting trophy of the battle he wished it to be,

A constant reminder in the heavens, the Place of the Battle to enshrine.

With his mace the hinder part he smashed to bits and pieces,

Then strung them together as a band to form a Hammered Bracelet.

Locking them together, as watchmen he stationed them,

A Firmament to divide the waters from the waters.

The Upper Waters above the Firmament from the Waters Below it he separated;

Artful works Nibiru thus fashioned.

The Lord then crossed the heavens to survey the regions;

From Apsu's quarter to the abode of Gaga he measured the dimensions.

The edge of the Deep Nibiru then examined, toward his birthplace he cast his gaze.

He paused and hesitated; then to the Firmament, the Place of the Battle, slowly he returned.

Passing again in Apsu's region, of the Sun's missing spouse he thought with remorse.

He gazed upon Tiamat's wounded half, to her Upper Part he gave attention;

The waters of life, her bounty, from the wounds were still pouring,

Her golden veins Apsu's rays were reflecting.

The Seed of Life, his Creator's legacy, Nibiru then remembered.

When he trod on Tiamat, when he split her asunder, to her the seed he surely imparted!

He addressed words to Apsu, to him thus saying:

With your warming rays, to the wounds give healing!

Let the broken part new life be given, in your family as a daughter to be,

Let the waters to one place be gathered, let firm land appear!

By Firm Land let her be called, Ki henceforth her name to be!

Apsu to the words of Nibiru gave heed: Let the Earth join my family,

Ki, Firm Land of the Below, let Earth her name henceforth be!

By her turning let there day and night be; in the days my healing rays to her I shall provide.

Let Kingu be a creature of the night, to shine at night I shall appoint him

Earth's companion, the Moon forever to be!

Nibiru the words of Apsu with satisfaction heard.

He crossed the heavens and surveyed the regions,

To the gods who had him elevated he granted permanent stations,

Their circuits he destined that none shall transgress nor fall short of each other.

He strengthened the heavenly locks, gates on both sides he established.

An outermost abode he chose for himself, beyond Gaga were its dimensions.

The great circuit to be his destiny he beseeched Apsu for him to decree.

All the gods spoke up from their stations: Let Nibiru's sovereignty be surpassing!

Most radiant of the gods he is, let him truly the Son of the Sun be!

From his quarter Apsu gave his blessing:

Nibiru shall hold the crossing of Heaven and Earth; Crossing shall be his name!

The gods shall cross over neither above nor below;

He shall hold the central position, the shepherd of the gods he shall be.

A Shar shall be his circuit; that his Destiny will forever be!

———•———

Now this is the account of how the Olden Times began,

And of the era that in the Annals the Golden Era by name was known,

And how from Nibiru to Earth the missions went the gold to obtain.

The escape of Alalu from Nibiru was its beginning.

With great understanding was Alalu endowed, much knowledge he by learning acquired.

By his forefather Anshargal of the heavens and the circuits much knowledge was amassed,

By Enshar was knowledge greatly augmented;

Of that Alalu made much learning; with the sages he discoursed, savants and commanders he consulted.

Thus was knowledge of the Beginning ascertained, thus did Alalu this knowledge possess.

The gold in the Hammered Bracelet was the confirmation,

The gold in the Hammered Bracelet of gold in Tiamat's Upper Half was the indication.

At the planet of gold Alalu victoriously arrived, his chariot with a
thunder crashing.

With a beam he scanned the place, his whereabouts to discover;

His chariot on dry land descended, at the edge of extended marshes
it landed.

He put on an Eagle's helmet, he put on a Fish's suit.

The chariot's hatch he opened; at the open hatch he stopped to
wonder.

Dark hued was the ground, blue-white were the skies;

No sound there was, there was no one to bid him welcome.

Alone on an alien planet he stood, perchance from Nibiru forever
exiled!

To the ground himself he lowered, on the dark-hued soil he stepped;

There were hills in the distance; nearby much vegetation there was.

Ahead of him there were marshes, into the marsh he stepped; by
the waters' coolness he shuddered.

Back to the dry ground he stepped; alone on an alien planet he
stood!

With thoughts he was possessed, of spouse and offspring with
longing he remembered;

Was he forever from Nibiru exiled? Of that again and again he
wondered.

To the chariot he soon returned, with food and drink to be sustained.

Then deep sleep him overcame, a powerful slumber.

How long he slept he could not remember; what awakened him he
could not tell.

A brightness there was outside, a brilliance on Nibiru unseen.

A pole from the chariot he extended; with a Tester it was equipped.

It breathed the planet's air; compatibility it indicated!

The chariot's hatch he opened, at the open hatch he took a breath.

Another breath he took, then another and another; the air of Ki indeed compatible was!

Alalu clapped his hands, a song of joy he was singing.

Without an Eagle's helmet, without a Fish's suit, to the ground himself he lowered.

The brightness outside was blinding; the rays of the Sun were overpowering!

Into the chariot he returned, a mask for the eyes he donned.

He picked up the carried weapon, he picked up the handy Sampler.

To the ground himself he lowered, on the dark-hued soil he stepped.

He made his way toward the marshes; dark greenish were the waters.

By the marsh's edge there were pebbles; Alalu picked a pebble, into the marsh he thrust it.

In the marsh a moving his eyes glimpsed: The waters with fishes were filled!

Into the marsh the Sampler he lowered, the murky waters to consider;

For drinking the water was not fit, Alalu greatly disappointing.

He turned away from the marshes, in the direction of the hills he went.

He made his way through vegetation; bushes to trees gave way.

The place was like an orchard, the trees with fruits were laden.

By their sweet smell enticed, Alalu picked a fruit; in his mouth he put it.

Sweet was the smell, sweeter the taste was! Alalu greatly it delighted.

Away from the Sun's rays Alalu was walking, toward the hills he set his direction.

Among the trees a wetness under his feet he sensed, a sign of closeby waters.

In the direction of the wetness he set his course;

In the midst of the forest there was a pond, a pool of silent waters.

Into the pond the Sampler he lowered; for drinking the water was good!

Alalu laughed; an unstopping laughter seized him.

The air was good, the water for drinking was fit; there was fruit, there were fishes!

With eagerness Alalu bent down, together his hands he cupped, water to his mouth he brought.

A coolness did the water have, a taste from Nibiru's water different.

Once more he drank, then with fright he asunder jumped:

A hissing sound he could hear; a slithering body by the poolside was moving!

His carried weapon he seized, a blast of its ray toward the hissing he directed.

The moving stopped, the hissing was ended.

To examine the danger Alalu stepped forward.

The slithered body lay still; dead was the creature, a sight most strange:

Like a rope its long body was, without hands or feet was the body;

Fierce eyes were in its small head, out of its mouth a long tongue was sticking.

A sight on Nibiru never beheld it was, a creature of another world!

Was it the orchard's guardian? Alalu by himself pondered. Was it the water's master? himself he asked.

In his carried flask he some water collected; with alertness to the chariot he made his way.

The sweet fruits he also picked; to the chariot he set his course.

The brightness of the Sun's rays was greatly diminished; darkness it was as the chariot he reached.

The shortness of the day Alalu pondered, its shortness him amazed.

From the direction of the marshes a cool lightness on the horizon was rising.

A white-hued ball in the heavens was quickly rising:

Kingu, the Earth's companion, he now beheld.

What in the accounts of the Beginning, his eyes the truth could now see:

The planets and their circuits, the Hammered Bracelet,

Ki the Earth, Kingu its moon, all created were, all by names were called!

In his heart Alalu knew one more truth a beholding needed:

The gold, the means of salvation, to be found was needed.

If truth be in the Beginning tales, if by the waters the golden veins of Tiamat were washed,

In the waters of Ki, its cut-off half, gold must be found!

With hands unsteady Alalu the Tester from the chariot's pole dismantled.

With trembling hands the Fish's suit he donned, the fast arriving daylight eagerly awaiting.

At daybreak the chariot he exited, to the marshes he quickly stepped.

Into deeper waters he waded, the Tester into the waters he inserted.

Its illuminated face he eagerly watched, in his chest his heart was pounding.

The water's contents was the Tester indicating, by symbols and numbers its findings disclosing.

Then Alalu's heartbeat stopped: There is gold in the waters, the Tester was telling!

Unsteady on his legs Alalu stepped forward, deeper into the marshes he made his way.

Again he the Tester into the waters inserted; again the Tester gold announced!

A cry, a cry of triumph, from Alalu's throat emanated: Nibiru's fate in his hands now was!

Back to the chariot he made his way, the Fish's suit off he took, the commander's seat he occupied.

The Tablets of Destinies that knows all circuits he enlivened, to Nibiru's circuit to find the direction.

The Speaker-of-Words he stirred up, toward Nibiru the words to carry.

Then to Nibiru words he uttered, thus he was saying:

The words of the great Alalu to Anu on Nibiru are directed.

On another world I am, the gold of salvation I have found;

The fate of Nibiru is in my hands; to my conditions you must give heed!

Synopsis of the Third Tablet

Alalu beams the news to Nibiru, reclaims the kingship

Anu, astounded, puts the issue before the royal council

Enlil, Anu's Foremost Son, suggests on-site verification

Ea, Anu's Firstborn and a son-in-law of Alalu, is chosen instead

Ea ingeniously equips the celestial boat for the journey

The spaceship, piloted by Anzu, carries fifty heroes

Overcoming perils, the Nibiruans thrill by Earth's sight

Guided by Alalu, they splash down and wade ashore

Eridu, Home Away from Home, is established in seven days

Extraction of gold from the waters begins

Though the quantity is minuscule, Nibiru demands delivery

Abgal, a pilot, chooses Alalu's spaceship for the trip

Forbidden nuclear weapons are discovered in the spaceship

Ea and Abgal remove the Weapons of Terror and hide them

Earth–Mars connection (2500 B.C. depiction)

THE THIRD TABLET

The fate of Nibiru is in my hands; to my conditions you must give heed!

Those were the words of Alalu, from dark-hued Earth to Nibiru they
were by the Speaker beamed.

When the words of Alalu to Anu, the king, were conveyed,

Anu astounded was; astounded were the counselors, amazed were the
sages.

Alalu is not dead? they each other asked. Could indeed he on another
world be living? they with disbelief were saying.

Was he not on Nibiru hiding, in the chariot to a place of concealment
gone?

The commanders of chariots were summoned, savants the beamed
words considered.

The words from Nibiru did not come; from beyond the Hammered
Bracelet were they spoken,

This was their finding, this to Anu the king they reported.

Stunned was Anu; the happening he pondered.

Let words of acknowledgment to Alalu be sent, to the assembled he was
saying.

 At the Place of the Celestial Chariots the command was given, to
  Alalu words were spoken:

   Anu, the king, to you his greetings sends; of your
    well-being to learn he is pleased;

    For your departing from Nibiru
     there was no reason,
     enmity is not in
     Anu's heart;

If gold for salvation you have indeed discovered, let Nibiru be saved!

The words of Anu Alalu's chariot did reach; Alalu them quickly answered:

If your savior I am to be, your lives to save,

Convene the princes to assembly, my ancestry declare supreme!

Let the commanders make me their leader, bow to my command!

Let the council pronounce me king, on the throne Anu to replace!

When the words of Alalu on Nibiru were heard, great was the consternation.

How could Anu be deposed? the counselors asked each other. What if Alalu mischief, not truth, is telling?

Where is his asylum? Did gold indeed he find?

They summoned the sages, of the wise and learned counseling they asked.

The oldest of them spoke: I was Alalu's master! he was saying.

He had hearkened to teachings of the Beginning, of the Celestial Battle he was learning;

Of the watery monster Tiamat and her golden veins he knowledge acquired;

If indeed beyond the Hammered Bracelet he had journeyed,

On Earth, the seventh planet, is his asylum!

In the assembly a prince spoke up; a son of Anu he was, of the womb of Antu, Anu's spouse, he was the issue.

Enlil was his name, Lord of the Command it meant. Words of caution he was saying:

Of conditions Alalu cannot speak. Calamities were his handiwork, by single combat in wrestling he the throne forfeited.

If Tiamat's gold he indeed had found, proof of that is needed;

Is it for protecting our atmosphere sufficient?

How through the Hammered Bracelet to Nibiru can it be brought?

Thus did Enlil, the son of Anu, speak; others many questions also
asked.

Much proof was greatly needed, many answers are required, all
agreed.

The words of the assembly to Alalu were conveyed, a response
demanded.

Alalu the words' merit pondered, to transmit his secrets he agreed;

Of his journey and its perils in truth he an account gave.

Of the Tester its crystal innards he removed, from the Sampler its
crystal heart he took out;

Into the Speaker he the crystals inserted, all the findings to transmit.

Now that proof has been delivered, declare me king, bow to my
command! he sternly demanded.

The sages were aghast; with Weapons of Terror Alalu on Nibiru
more havoc caused,

With Weapons of Terror a path through the Bracelet he blasted!

Once in its circuit Nibiru that region passes, calamities Alalu is
amassing!

In the council there was much consternation; the kingship to alter
was indeed a grave matter.

Anu not by ancestry alone was king: By fair wrestling the throne he
attained!

In the assembly of the princes, a son of Anu stood up to speak.

He was wise in all matters, among the sages renowned he was.

Of the secrets of waters he was a master; E.A, He Whose Home Is
Water, he was called.

Of Anu he was the Firstborn; to Damkina, Alalu's daughter, he was
espoused.

My father by birth is Anu the king, Ea was saying; Alalu by marriage
my father is.

To bring the two clans into unison was my espousal's intention;

Let me be the one in this conflict unity to bring!

Let me Anu's emissary to Alalu be, let me be the one Alalu's discoveries to uphold!

Let me in a chariot to Earth journey, a path through the Bracelet with water, not fire, I shall fashion.

On Earth, from the waters let me the precious gold obtain; to Nibiru back it will be sent.

Let Alalu be king on Earth, a verdict of the sages awaiting:

If Nibiru it will save, let there be a second wrestling; who shall Nibiru rule let it determine!

The princes, the counselors, the sages, the commanders heard Ea's words with wonder;

Full of wisdom they were, for conflict they solution found.

Let it so be! Anu announced. Let Ea journey, let the gold be tested.

Alalu a second time I shall then wrestle, let the winner be on Nibiru king!

The words of decision to Alalu were conveyed;

He pondered them and agreed: Let Ea, my son by marriage, to Earth come!

Let gold from the waters be obtained, let it for salvation on Nibiru be tested;

Let a second wrestling kingship by me or Anu settle!

So be it! Anu in the assembly decreed.

Enlil rose in objection; the king's word unalterable was.

Ea to the place of the chariots went, commanders and sages he consulted.

The mission's dangers he contemplated, how to extract and bring the gold he considered.

Alalu's transmission he carefully studied, Alalu for more testings the results he requested.

A Tablet of Destinies for the mission he was fashioning.

If water be the Force, where could it be replenished?

Where on the chariot will it be stored, how to Force will it be converted?

A full circuit of Nibiru did pass in contemplations, a Shar of Nibiru in preparations passed.

The largest celestial chariot for the mission has been fitted,

Its circuit's destiny has been calculated, a Tablet of Destiny has been firmly fixed;

Fifty heroes will for the mission be required to journey to Earth the gold to obtain!

To the journey Anu his approval gave;

The stargazers for the journey the right time to begin then selected.

At the Place of the Chariots multitudes gathered, to bid farewell to the heroes and their leader did they come.

Bearing Eagle's helmets, carrying each a Fish's suit, the heroes the chariot one by one entered.

The last to embark was Ea; to the gathering he bade farewell.

Before his father Anu he knelt down, the king's blessing to receive.

My son, the Firstborn: A far journey you have undertaken, for us all to be endangered;

Let your success calamity from Nibiru banish; go and in safety come back!

So did Anu to his son speak a blessing, bidding him farewell.

The mother of Ea, the one called Ninul, to her heart embraced him.

Why, after by Anu as a son to me you were given, did he with a restless heart you endow?

Go and come back, the hazardous road traverse safely! to him she said.

With tenderness Ea kissed his spouse, Damkina he without words embraced.

Enlil with his half brother locked arms. Be blessed, be successful! to him he said.

With heavy heart Ea the chariot entered, to soar up the command
he gave.

———•———

Now this is the account of the journey to the seventh planet,

And how the legend of the Fishgod who came from the waters was
begun.

With heavy heart Ea the chariot entered, to soar up the command
he gave.

The commander's seat by Anzu, not by Ea, was occupied; Anzu,
not Ea, was the chariot's commander;

He Who Knows the Heavens his name's meaning was; for the task
he was especially selected.

A prince among the princes he was, of royal seed his ancestry he
counted.

The celestial chariot he deftly guided; from Nibiru it powerfully
soared, toward the distant Sun he it directed.

Ten leagues, a hundred leagues the chariot was coursing, a thousand
leagues the chariot was journeying.

Little Gaga came out to greet them, a welcome to the heroes it was
extending.

To blue-hued Antu, the beautiful enchantress, it showed the way.

By her sight Anzu was attracted. Let us examine her waters! Anzu
was saying.

Ea to continue without stopping gave the word; it is a planet of no
return, he forcefully said.

Toward the heavenly An, the third in planetary counts, the chariot
continued.

On his side was An lying, his host of moons about him were
whirling.

The Tester's beams the presence of water was revealing; a stop if
needed to Ea it was indicating.

To continue the journey was Ea saying, toward Anshar, the heaven's foremost prince, he was directing.

Soon the ensnaring pull of Anshar they could tell, his colored rings with fear they admired.

Deftly did Anzu the chariot guide, the crushing dangers he cleverly avoided.

The giant Kishar, foremost of firm planets, was next to be encountered.

Her net's pull was overpowering; with great skill did Anzu the chariot's course divert.

With fury Kishar at the chariot divine lightnings was thrusting, her host at the uninvited she directed.

Slowly Kishar moved away, for the chariot the next enemy to encounter:

Beyond the fifth planet the Hammered Bracelet was lurking!

Ea his handiwork to set a-whirring commanded, the Water Thruster to prepare.

Toward the host of turning boulders the chariot was rushing,

Each one like a slingshot's stone ferociously at the chariot aimed.

The word by Ea was given, with the force of a thousand heroes the stream of water was thrust.

One by one the boulders turned face; a path for the chariot they were making!

But as one boulder fled, another in its stead was attacking;

A multitude beyond count was their number, a host for the splitting of Tiamat revenge seeking!

Again and again Ea the commands gave, the Water Thruster to keep a-whirring;

Again and again toward the host of boulders streams of water were directed;

Again and again the boulders their faces turned, a path for the chariot making.

And then at last the path was clear; unharmed the chariot could
continue!

A cry of joy the heroes sounded; double was the joy as the sight of
the Sun was now unveiled.

Amidst the elation Anzu the alarm sounded: For the path to have
fashioned, excessive waters were consumed,

Waters to feed the chariot's Fiery Stones for the remaining journey
were not sufficient!

In the dark deepness the sixth planet they could see, the Sun's rays
it was reflecting.

There is water on Lahmu, Ea was saying. Can you bring the chariot
down upon it? Anzu he was asking.

Deftly Anzu the chariot toward Lahmu directed; reaching the
celestial god, around it he the chariot made circle.

The planet's net is not great, its pull is to handle easy, Anzu was
saying.

A sight to behold was Lahmu, many hued it was; snow white was
its cap, snow white were its sandals.

Reddish hued was its middle, in its midst lakes and rivers were
aglitter!

Deftly Anzu the chariot made travel slower, by a lakeside it gently
came down.

Ea and Anzu their Eagle's helmets donned, to the firm ground they
stepped down.

On command the heroes That Which Water Sucks extended, the
chariot's bowels with the lake's waters to fill.

While the chariot was getting its fill of waters, Ea and Anzu the
whereabouts examined.

With Tester and Sampler all that matters they ascertained: The
waters were good for drinking, the air was insufficient.

All was in the chariot's annals recorded, the need for the detour
described.

With its vigor replenished the chariot soared up, to benevolent Lahmu farewell bidding.

Beyond the seventh planet was making its circuit; Earth and its companion the chariot were inviting!

In the commander's seat Anzu was without words; Ea too was silent.

Ahead was their destination, its gold Nibiru's fate for salvation or doom containing.

The chariot must be slowed or in Earth's thick atmosphere it shall perish! Anzu to Ea declared.

Around Earth's companion, the Moon, make slowing circles! Ea to him suggested.

They circled the Moon; by the vanquishing Nibiru in the Celestial Battle it prostrate and scarred was lying.

Having the chariot thus slowed down, toward the seventh planet Anzu the chariot directed.

Once, twice the Earth's globe he made the chariot circle, ever closer to the Firm Land he lowered it.

Snow hued was two thirds of the planet, dark hued was its middle.

They could see the oceans, they could see the Firm Lands; for the signal beacon from Alalu they were searching.

Where an ocean touched dry land, where four rivers were swallowed by marshes, Alalu's signal was beaconed.

Too heavy and large the chariot is for the marshes! Anzu was declaring.

The Earth's pulling net, too powerful for on dry land to descend it is! Anzu to Ea announced.

Splash down! Splash down in the ocean's waters! Ea to Anzu shouted.

Around the planet Anzu made one more circuit, the chariot with much care toward the ocean's edge he lowered.

The chariot's lungs he filled with air; into the waters down it splashed, into the depths it was not sinking.

From the Speaker a voice was heard: To Earth be welcomed! Alalu
was saying.

By his beamed words the direction of his whereabouts was
determined.

Toward the place Anzu the chariot directed, floating as a boat it
was upon the waters moving.

Soon the wide-ranging ocean narrowed, dry land on both sides as
guardian appeared.

On the left side brown-hued hills were rising, on the right
mountains to heaven their heads raised.

Toward the place of Alalu was the chariot moving, floating like a
boat upon the waters it was.

Ahead the dry land was covered with flooding, marshes the ocean
were replacing.

Anzu to heroes commands uttered, their Fishes' suits to put on he
ordered.

A hatch of the chariot was then opened, into the marshes the
heroes descended.

Strong ropes to the chariot they attached, with the ropes the chariot
they were pulling.

Alalu's beamed words more powerful were becoming. Hurry!
Hurry! he was saying.

At the edge of the marshes, a sight there was to behold:

Gleaming in the sunrays was a chariot from Nibiru; Alalu's celestial
boat it was!

The heroes their paces quickened, toward Alalu's chariot they
hurried.

Impatient, Ea donned his Fish's suit; within his chest his heart was
like a drum beating.

Into the marsh he jumped, toward its edge hurried steps he directed.

High were the marshes flooding, deeper was the bottom than he
expected.

He changed his gait to swimming, with bold strokes forward he advanced.

As dry land he was approaching, green meadows he could see.

Then his feet touched firm ground; he stood up and by walking he continued.

Ahead he could see Alalu standing, with his hands with vigor waving.

Coming out of the waters, ashore Ea stepped: On dark-hued Earth he was standing!

Alalu toward him came running; his son by marriage he powerfully embraced.

Welcome to a different planet! Alalu to Ea said.

———·•·———

Now this is the account of how Eridu on Earth was established, how the count of seven days was begun.

In silence did Alalu Ea embrace, with tears of joy his eyes were filled.

Before him Ea bowed his head, respect for his father by marriage he was showing.

In the marshes the heroes were advancing; more donned Fishes' suits, more toward the dry land were rushing.

Keep the chariot afloat! Anzu was commanding. In the waters anchor it, the mud ahead avoiding!

Ashore stepped the heroes, before Alalu they were bowing.

Ashore came Anzu, the last the chariot to depart.

Before Alalu he bowed; with him Alalu in welcome locked arms.

To all who had arrived Alalu words of welcome spoke.

To all who were assembled, Ea words of command spoke. Here on Earth I am the commander! he was saying.

On a life or death mission we have come; in our hands is Nibiru's fate!

He looked about, for a place for encampment he was searching.

Heap up soil, mounds fashion there! Ea gave command, an encampment to set up.

To a place not afar he was pointing, a reed-hut abode by Alalu erected.

To Anzu then words he directed: To Nibiru words by beaming deliver,

To the king my father, Anu, successful arrival announce!

Soon the hue of the skies was changing, from brightness to reddish it was turning.

A sight never seen before their eyes was unfolding: The Sun, as a red ball, on the horizon was disappearing!

Fear seized the heroes, of a Great Calamity afraid they were!

Alalu with laughter words of comfort was saying: A setting of the Sun it is,

The ending of one day on Earth it is marking.

For a quick rest lie down; a night on Earth is beyond imagining short.

Before you expect the Sun will an appearance make; on Earth it will be morning!

Before expecting, darkness came, the heavens from the Earth it separated.

Lightnings the darkness pierced, rains the thunders followed.

By winds were the waters blown, storms of an alien god they were.

In the chariot the heroes hunkered down, in the chariot the heroes huddled.

Resting to them did not come; they were greatly agitated.

With quickened hearts the Sun's return they awaited.

Smiling when its rays appeared they were, joyful and backslapping.

And it was evening and it was morning, their first day on Earth it was.

By daybreak Ea the ongoings considered; to separate waters from waters heed he was giving.

Engur he made of the sweet waters the master, drinking waters to provide.

To the snake pond with Alalu he went, its sweet waters to consider;

Evil serpents in the pond were swarming! so did Engur to Ea say.

The marshlands Ea then contemplated, the abundance of rainwaters he weighed.

Enbilulu he placed in charge of the marshlands, to mark out the thicket of reeds him he directed.

Enkimdu in charge of ditch and dike he placed, a boundary for the marshes to fashion,

For the waters that from heaven rain a gathering place to make.

Thus were the waters below from the waters above separated, marshwaters from sweet waters asunder were set.

And it was evening and it was morning, the second day on Earth it was.

When the Sun morning announced, the heroes their assigned tasks were performing.

With Alalu Ea to the place of grass and trees his steps directed,

All that in the orchard grows, herbs and fruits after their kind to examine.

To Isimud, his vizier, Ea questions was addressing:

What is this plant? What is that plant? him he was asking.

Isimud, one of much learning, food that grows well he could distinguish;

He tore a fruit for Ea, a honey plant it is! to Ea he was saying:

One fruit he himself ate, one fruit Ea was eating!

Of food that grows, by its good distinguished, Ea the hero Guru put in charge.

Thus were the heroes water and food provided; satiated they were not.

And it was evening and it was morning, the third day on Earth it was.

On the fourth day the winds ceased blowing, the chariot by waves was not disturbed.

Let tools from the chariot be brought, let abodes in the encampment be built! Ea thus commanded.

Kulla in charge of mold and brick Ea appointed, from the clay bricks to fashion;

Mushdammu to lay foundations he directed, dwelling abodes to erect.

All day the Sun was shining, the great light by day it was.

By evetime Kingu, Earth's moon, in fullness a pale light on Earth it cast,

A lesser light to rule the night, among the celestial gods accounted to be.

And it was evening and it was morning, the fourth day on Earth it was.

On the fifth day Ea Ningirsig a boat of reeds to fashion commanded,

The measure of the marshes to take, the stretch of the swamplands to consider.

Ulmash, he who what in the waters swarms knows, who of fowl that fly has understanding,

Ulmash as a companion Ea took, between good and bad to distinguish.

Kinds that in the waters swarm, kinds that in the skies give wing, to Ulmash many were unknown;

Bewildering was their number. Good were the carp, among the bad they were swimming.

Enbilulu, the marshlands master, Ea summoned; Enkimdu, in charge of ditch and dike, Ea summoned;

To them he gave words, in the marshlands to make a barrier;

With canebrakes and green reeds an enclosure to fashion, fish from fish there separate,

A trap for carp that from a net could not escape,

A place whose snare no bird that is good for food could escape.

Thus were fish and fowl, by their good kinds separated, for the heroes provided.

And it was evening and it was morning, the fifth day on Earth it was.

On the sixth day Ea of the orchard's creatures took account.

Enursag to the task he assigned, that which creeps and that which on feet walks to distinguish;

Their kinds Enursag astounded, of the ferocity of their wildness to Ea an account he gave.

Ea Kulla summoned, to Mushdammu urgent commands he gave:

By evetime the abodes to be completed, by a fence for protection to be surrounded!

The heroes to the task put their shoulders, bricks on the foundations were quickly laid.

With reeds were the roofings made, of cut-down trees was the fencing put up.

Anzu a Beam-That-Kills from the chariot brought over, a Speaker-That-Words-Beams at Ea's abode he set up;

By evetime, complete was the encampment! For the night therein the heroes gathered.

Ea and Alalu and Anzu the doings considered; all that was done indeed was good!

And it was evening and it was morning, the sixth day.

On the seventh day the heroes in the encampment were assembled,

To them Ea spoke these words:

A hazardous journey we have undertaken, from Nibiru to the seventh planet a dangerous way we traversed.

At Earth we with success arrived, much good we attained, an encampment we established.

Let this day be a day of rest; the seventh day hereafter a day of resting always to be!

Let this place henceforth by the name Eridu be called, Home in the Faraway the meaning thereof will be!

Let a promise be kept, let Alalu of Eridu the commander be declared!

The heroes thus assembled, in unison agreements shouted.

Words of consent Alalu uttered, then homage to Ea he greatly paid:

Let Ea a second name be given, Nudimmud, the Artful Fashioner, let him be called!

In unison the heroes agreement announced.

And it was evening and it was morning, the seventh day.

———··———

Now this is the account of how the searching for gold was begun,

And how the plans on Nibiru made to Nibiru salvation did not provide.

After the encampment of Eridu was established and the heroes with food were satiated,

Ea the task of gold from the waters obtaining started.

In the chariot the Fire Stones were stirred up, its Great Cracker was enlivened;

That Which Water Sucks from the chariot was extended, into the marsh waters it was inserted.

Into a vessel of crystals the waters were directed,

From the waters the crystals all that is metal in the vessel extracted.

Then from the vessel That Which Spits Out the waters to the fishpond spat out;

Thus were the metals that were in the waters in the vessel collected.

Ingenious was Ea's handiwork, an Artful Fashioner indeed he was!

For six Earth days marsh waters were sucked in, marsh waters were spat out;

In the vessel metals indeed were collected!

The metals on the seventh day by Ea and Alalu were examined; of many kinds were the metals in the vessel.

Iron there was, much copper there was; of gold there was no abundance.

In the chariot another vessel, the artful handiwork of Nudimmud,

The metals after their kinds were separated, ashore kind by kind they were carried.

For six days thus did the heroes toil; on the seventh day they rested.

For six days were the crystal vessels filled and emptied,

On the seventh day were the metals accounted.

There was iron and there was copper, and other metals too;

Of the gold, the smallest pile was accumulated.

In the nighttimes the Moon waxed and waned; by the name Month did Ea its circuit call.

At Month's very start, its luminous horns six days signified,

By its half crown the seventh day it announced; a day to rest it was.

At midway by a fullness was the Moon distinguished; then it paused to become diminished.

With the Sun's course was the Moon's circuit appearing, with Earth's circuit it was its face revealing.

Fascinated by the Moon's motions was Ea, its attachment as Kingu to Ki he contemplated:

What purpose did the attachment serve, what heavenly sign was it giving?

A Month did Ea the Moon's circuit call, Month to its circuit he gave the name.

For one Month, for two Months, in the chariot were the waters separated;

The Sun, every six Months, to Earth another season gave; Winter and Summer did Ea by names them call.

There was Winter and there was Summer; by Year of Earth did Ea the full circuit call.

By Year's end of the accumulated gold account was taken;

Much to dispatch to Nibiru there was not.

The swamplands' waters are deficient, let the chariot to the deeper ocean be moved! So was Ea saying.

From its moorings was the chariot untied, back whence it came it was shifted.

With great care were the crystal vessels stirred up, the saltwaters through them passing.

Metals by their kinds were separated; gold among them was sparkling!

From the chariot of the happenings Ea to Nibiru word did beam; Anu to hear it was pleased indeed.

In its destined circuit Nibiru to the Sun's abode was returning,

A closeness to Earth on its Shar circuit was Nibiru attaining.

With eagerness did Anu about the gold inquire. Is there enough for sending to Nibiru? he was asking.

Alas, not enough was of the gold from the waters collected;

Let another Shar pass, let the quantity be doubled! Ea to Anu counseled.

From the ocean's waters the obtaining of gold continued;

In his heart Ea with apprehension was filling.

From the chariot parts were hauled out, a sky chamber from them was assembled.

Abgal, he who knows piloting, of the sky chamber to take charge he appointed;

Daily in the sky chamber with Abgal did Ea upward soar, the Earth and its secrets to learn.

For the sky chamber an enclosure was constructed, by Alalu's chariot was it placed:

Daily the crystals in Alalu's chariot did Ea study, what by their beams was discovered to understand;

Whence does the gold come? he asked Alalu. Where on Earth are Tiamat's golden veins?

In the sky chamber with Abgal did Ea upward soar, the Earth and its secrets to learn.

Over great mountains they roamed, in the valleys great rivers they saw;

Steppes and forests below were stretched, thousands of leagues was their reach.

Vast lands separated by oceans they recorded, with the Beam That Scans the soils they penetrated.

On Nibiru impatience was growing. Can gold protection provide? was the outcry increasing.

Assemble the gold, on Nibiru's nearing gold you must deliver! So did Anu Ea command.

Repair Alalu's chariot, for returning to Nibiru make it fit, for the Shar's completion make it ready! So was Anu saying.

Ea his father's, the king, words was heeding; the repairing of Alalu's chariot he was contemplating.

As the sky chamber one eve by the side of the chariot they landed,

With Abgal the chariot they entered, a secret deed in the darkness to perform.

The Weapons of Terror, the seven of them, from the chariot they removed;

To the sky chamber they took them, inside the sky chamber them to give hiding.

By sunrise Ea with Abgal in the sky chamber soared, to another land was their direction.

There, in a secret place, did Ea the weapons hide; in a cave, a place unknown, he stored them.

Then to Anzu Ea words of command gave, to repair Alalu's chariot he him directed,

For returning to Nibiru to make it fit, by the Shar's completion to make it ready.

Anzu, in the ways of chariots greatly skilled, to the task his labors set;

He made its thrusters hum again, its tablets he carefully considered;

The absence of the Weapons of Terror he soon discovered!

With anger Anzu cried out; Ea of their hiding away gave the explanation:

Foresworn is the weapons' use! Ea was saying.

Neither in the heavens nor on Firm Lands shall they ever be harnessed!

Without them no passage through the Hammered Bracelet is safe! Anzu was saying.

Without them, without Water Thrusters, the danger is endurance surpassing!

Alalu, of Eridu the commander, the words of Ea considered, to the words of Anzu heed he gave:

The words of Ea by the Council of Nibiru are attested! Alalu was saying;

But without the chariot's return, Nibiru shall be doomed!

Abgal, he who knows piloting, boldly toward the leaders stepped forward.

I shall be the pilot, the dangers I shall valiantly face! he was saying.

Thus was the decision made: Abgal shall be the pilot, Anzu on Earth shall be staying!

On Nibiru, the stargazers the destinies of the celestial gods contemplated, an opportune day they were selecting.

Into Alalu's chariot basketfuls of gold were carried;

The forepart of the chariot Abgal entered, the commander's seat he occupied.

From the chariot of Ea, to him Ea a Tablet of Destiny gave;

It shall be That-Which-Shows-the-Way for you, by it the opened pathway you shall find!

The chariot's Fire Stones Abgal stirred up; their hum like music was enthralling.

The chariot's Great Cracker he enlivened, a reddish brilliance it was casting.

Ea and Alalu the multitude of heroes were standing around, farewell to him they were bidding.

Then the chariot with a roar heavenward rose, to the heavens it ascended!

To Nibiru words of the ascent were beamed; on Nibiru there was much expecting.

Synopsis of the Fourth Tablet

The Nibiruans hail even the small gold delivery

Tests of gold's use as an atmospheric shield succeed

Additional heroes and new equipment are sent to Earth

Gold extraction from the waters continues to disappoint

Ea discovers gold sources that need deep mining in the Abzu

Enlil, then Anu, come to Earth for crucial decisions

As the half brothers quarrel, lots decide the tasks

Ea, renamed Enki (Earth's Master), goes to the Abzu

Enlil stays to develop permanent facilities in the Edin

As Anu prepares to leave, he is attacked by Alalu

The Seven Who Judge sentence Alalu to exile on Lahmu

Anu's daughter Ninmah, a medical officer, is sent to Earth

Stopping off at Lahmu (Mars) she finds Alalu dead

A rock, carved to resemble Alalu's face, serves as his tomb

Anzu is given command of a Way Station on Lahmu

Enki depicted as god of waters and mining

THE FOURTH TABLET

To Nibiru words of the ascent were beamed; on Nibiru there was much
expecting.

With confidence was Abgal the chariot guiding;

Around Kingu, the Moon, he made a circuit, by its netpowers speed to
gain.

A thousand leagues, ten thousand leagues toward Lahmu he journeyed,

By its netpower a direction toward Nibiru to obtain.

Beyond Lahmu the Hammered Bracelet was awhirling;

Deftly did Abgal Ea's crystals make aglow, the opened paths to locate.

The eye of fate upon him with favor looked!

Beyond the Bracelet, the chariot beamed signals from Nibiru was receiving;

Homeward, homeward was the direction.

Ahead, in the darkness, in reddish hue glowed Nibiru; a sight to behold
it was!

By the beamed signals the chariot was now directed.

Thrice around Nibiru it made circuits, by its netforce to be slowed.

Nearing the planet, the breach in its atmosphere Abgal could see;

A squeezing in his heart he felt, of the gold he was bringing was he
thinking.

Passing through the atmosphere's thickness, aglow
was the chariot, its heat overbearing;

Deftly did Abgal spread the chariot's
wings, its descent thereby
arresting.

Beyond lay the place of the chariots, a sight most inviting;

Gently did Abgal the chariot bring down to a place by the beams selected.

He opened the hatch; a multitude of populace was there assembled!

Anu toward him stepped forward, locked arms, warm greetings uttered.

Heroes into the chariot rushed, the gold-bearing baskets they brought out.

High above their heads they the baskets held,

To the assembled, words of victory Anu shouted: Salvation is here! to them he was saying.

To the palace was Abgal accompanied, to rest and tell all he was escorted.

The gold, a sight most dazzling, by the savants was quickly taken;

To make of it the finest dust, to skyward launch it was hauled away.

A Shar did the fashioning last, a Shar did the testing continue.

With rockets was the dust heavenward carried, by crystals' beams was it dispersed.

Where there was a breach, now there was a healing!

Joy the palace filled, abundance in the land was expected.

To Earth Anu good words was beaming: Gold gives salvation! The obtaining of gold do continue!

When Nibiru near the Sun came, the golden dust was by its rays disturbed;

The healing in the atmosphere was dwindled, the breach to bigness returned.

Anu the return of Abgal to Earth then commanded; in the chariot more heroes traveled,

In its bowels more That Which the Waters Sucks In and Thrusts Out were provided;

With them Nungal to travel was commanded, a pilot-helper to Abgal to become.

Great joy there was when Abgal to Eridu returned;

Many greetings and the locking of arms there was!

The new water-workings Ea with care contemplated;

There was smiling on his face, in his heart there was a squeezing.

By Shar time, Nungal in the chariot was to depart ready;

In its bowels the chariot only a few baskets of gold carried.

The disappointment on Nibiru Ea's heart to him was predicting!

Ea with Alalu words exchanged, that which was known they
    reconsidered:

If Earth the head of Tiamat was in the Celestial Battle cut off,

Where was the neck, where were the golden veins cut asunder?

Where were the golden veins from Earth's innards protruding?

In the sky chamber Ea over mountains and valleys traveled,

The lands by oceans separated he with the Scanner examined.

Again and again there was the same indication:

Where dry land from dry land apart was torn, Earth's innards were
    revealed;

Where the landmass the shape of a heart was given, in the lower
    part thereof,

Golden veins from Earth's innards were abundant!

Abzu, of Gold the Birthplace, Ea to the region the name gave.

Ea then to Anu words of wisdom beamed:

With gold Earth indeed is filled; from the veins, not from the
    waters, the gold must be gotten.

From Earth's bowels, not from its waters, must the gold be obtained,

From a region beyond the ocean, Abzu it shall be called, can an
    abundance of gold be gotten!

In the palace there was great astonishment, savants and counselors
    to Ea's words gave consideration;

That gold must be obtained, on that unanimity there was;

How to obtain it from the bowels of the Earth, of that there was
much discussion.

In the assembly a prince spoke up; Enlil he was, the half brother
of Ea.

First Alalu, then his son by marriage, Ea, upon waters placed all
hope;

Of salvation by water's gold they were reassuring,

Shar after Shar all of us salvation were expecting,

Now different words we are hearing, a task beyond imagining to
undertake,

Proof of the golden veins is needed, a plan for success must be
ensured!

So was Enlil to the assembly saying; to his words many in agreement
listened.

Let Enlil go to Earth! Anu was saying. Let him proof obtain, a plan
put forward;

His words shall be heeded, his words a command shall be!

In unanimity the assembly its consent gave, Enlil's mission it
approved.

With Alalgar, his chief lieutenant, Enlil for Earth departed; Alalgar
his pilot was.

With each a sky chamber were the two of them provided.

To Earth the words of Anu, the king, words of decisions were beamed:

Enlil of the mission in command shall be, his word shall be the
command!

When Enlil on Earth arrived, Ea with his half brother warmly
locked arms,

As brother meets brother Ea Enlil did welcome.

To Alalu Enlil made a bowing, Alalu with weak words him bade
welcome.

The heroes to Enlil words of warm welcome were shouting; of the
commander much they were expecting.

Deftly Enlil the sky chambers to be assembled did command,

In a sky chamber he went asoaring; Alalgar, his chief lieutenant, was as the pilot with him.

Ea in a sky chamber, by Abgal piloted, to them to the Abzu showed the way.

They surveyed the dry lands, of the oceans they took careful notice.

From the Upper Sea to the Lower Sea the lands they scanned,

Of all that was above and that was below they took account.

In the Abzu the soil they tested. Gold there was indeed; with much soil and rocks it was commixed,

Refined as in the waters it was not, in an admixture it was hiding.

They went back to Eridu; what they had found they contemplated.

Eridu new tasks must be given, alone on Earth it cannot continue!

Thus was Enlil saying; a great plan he described, a wide mission he was proposing:

More heroes to bring over, more settlements to establish,

The gold from Earth's innards to obtain, the gold from the admixture to separate,

By skyships and chariots to be carried, from landing places tasks to perform.

Who of the settlements in charge will be, who of the Abzu shall take command?

Thus was Ea of Enlil asking.

Who of enlarged Eridu shall take command, who the settlements shall oversee?

Thus was Alalu saying.

Who of the skyships and the landing place shall take command? So did Anzu inquire.

Let Anu come to Earth, let him decisions provide! Thus did Enlil say in answer.

———•‑•———

Now this is the account of how Anu to Earth came,

How lots with Ea and Enlil were drawn, how Ea the title-name
Enki was given,

How Alalu for the second time with Anu wrestled.

To Earth in a celestial chariot did Anu journey; the route by the
planets it followed.

Around Lahmu Nungal, the pilot, a circuit made; by Anu was it
closely observed.

The Moon, the one who Kingu once had been, they circled and
admired.

Perchance gold thereon can also be found? in his heart Anu
wondered.

In the waters beside the marshlands his chariot splashed down;

Ea for the arrival reed boats prepared, for Anu to arrive by sailing.

Above the sky chambers were hovering, a royal welcome they were
offering.

In the lead boat Ea himself was afloat, the king his father the first
to be greeting.

Before Anu he bowed, then Anu embraced him. My son, my
Firstborn! Anu to him shouted.

In the square of Eridu in rows stood the heroes, their king to Earth
royally to welcome.

In front of them stood Enlil, their commander.

Before Anu the king he bowed, Anu him to his chest embraced.

Alalu too was there standing, of what to do he was uncertain;

Anu to him a greeting extended. Let us lock arms as comrades! to
Alalu he said.

With hesitation Alalu stepped forward, with Anu he locked arms!

A meal for Anu was prepared; by evetime to a reed hut, for him by
Ea built, Anu retired.

The next day the seventh by the count begun by Ea was, a day of
resting.

A day of backslapping and celebrating it was, as befits a king's coming.

On the day that followed, Ea and Enlil before Anu the findings presented,

What was done and what doing needed with him they discussed.

Let me see the lands by myself! Anu to them was saying.

Aloft they all in the sky chambers went, lands from sea to sea they observed.

To the Abzu they flew, on its gold-hiding soil they landed.

Difficult will the gold's extraction be! Anu was saying. To obtain the gold it is necessary;

No matter how deep the gold is below the surface, it must be gotten!

Let Ea and Enlil tools for the purpose devise, let them heroes for the task assign,

Let them find how gold from soil and rocks separates, how to Nibiru pure gold to deliver!

Let a landing place be built, let more heroes to the tasks on Earth be assigned!

So was Anu to the two sons saying; in his heart, of way stations in the heavens he was thinking.

Those were the command words of Anu; Ea and Enlil in agreement their heads were bowing.

There were evenings and there were mornings; to Eridu they all returned.

In Eridu they held a council, tasks and duties to assign.

Ea, who Eridu established, was the first to speak up:

Eridu have I established; let other settlements in this region be set up,

Let it the Edin be, Abode of the Upright Ones, by this name be known.

The commander of the Edin let me be, let Enlil the gold extraction perform!

By these words Enlil was angered; the plan is wrongful! to Anu he said.

Of commanding and tasks to perform I am the better, of skyships I have the knowledge.

Of the Earth and its secrets my half brother Ea is the knower;

The Abzu he discovered, let him of the Abzu be the master!

Anu to the angry words with a careful ear listened; the brothers were again half brothers,

The Firstborn with the Legal Heir with words as weapons were contending!

Ea was the Firstborn son, by a concubine to Anu he was born;

Enlil, thereafter born, by Antu, Anu's spouse, was conceived.

A half sister of Anu she was, thereby Enlil the Legal Heir making,

Thereby the next-born son for the succession the Firstborn overcoming.

A conflict that the obtainment of gold would endanger Anu was fearing;

One of the brothers to Nibiru must return, the succession from considering must now be removed,

So was Anu to himself thinking. Aloud to the two a startling suggestion he made:

Who to Nibiru for the throne seat shall return, who the Edin shall command, who in the Abzu shall be the master,

Let us three, I with you, by lots determine!

Silent were the brothers, the audacious words by surprise them overtook.

Let us draw lots! Anu said. By the hand of fate let there be a decision!

The three, father and two sons, clasped their hands together.

They cast lots, by the lots the tasks they divided:

Anu to Nibiru to return, its ruler on the throne to remain;

The Edin to Enlil was allotted, to be Lord of the Command as his name indicated,

More settlements to establish, of the skyships and their heroes charge to take,

Of all the lands until they the bar of the seas encounter, the leader to be.

To Ea the seas and the oceans as his domain were granted,

Lands beyond the bar of the waters by him to be governed,

In the Abzu to be the master, with ingenuity the gold to procure.

Enlil with the lots was agreeable, the hand of fate he with a bow accepted.

Ea's eyes filled with tears, of Eridu and the Edin he wished not to be parted.

Let Ea forever Eridu as his home retain! Anu to Enlil was saying,

Let his being the first to splash down forever be remembered,

Let Ea as Earth's master be known; Enki, Earth's Master, let his title be!

His father's words Enlil with a bow accepted; to his brother he thus said:

Enki, Earth's Master, your title name shall henceforth be; I Lord of the Command shall be known.

To the heroes in assembly Anu, Enki, and Enlil the decisions announced.

The tasks are assigned, success is in the offing! Anu to them was saying.

Now farewell I can bid you, to Nibiru with quiet heart I can return!

Forward toward Anu Alalu stepped. A grave matter has been forgotten! he shouted.

The mastery of Earth to me was allotted; that was the promise when the gold finds to Nibiru I announced!

Nor have I the claim to Nibiru's throne forsaken,

By Anu to share all with his sons, it is a grave abomination!

Thus did Alalu Anu and the decisions challenge.

Without words was Anu in the beginning, then with anger he
spoke up:

By a second wrestling let our dispute be decided, let us the
wrestling do here, let us do it now!

With disdain Alalu took off his clothing; likewise did Anu unrobe.

In nakedness did the two royals begin to grapple, a mighty struggle
it was.

Alalu bent his knee, to the ground Alalu fell;

Anu on the chest of Alalu with his foot pressed down, victory in
the wrestling thereby declaring.

By wrestling the decision was made; I am the king, to Nibiru Alalu
shall not return!

So was Anu saying as he removed his foot from the fallen Alalu.

Up as a lightning Alalu from the ground arose. By the legs Anu he
pulled down.

His mouth was wide open, swiftly he the malehood of Anu bit off,

The malehood of Anu did Alalu swallow!

In pained agony did Anu a cry to the heavens shout; to the ground
wounded he fell.

Enki to the fallen Anu rushed, Enlil the laughing Alalu captive held.

Heroes Anu to his hut carried, words of accursation against Alalu
he uttered.

Let justice be done! Enlil to his lieutenant shouted. With your
beam-weapon let Alalu be killed!

No! No! Enki fiercely shouted. Justice is within him, in his innards
poison has entered!

They took Alalu to a reed hut, his hands and feet as a prisoner they
bound.

Now this is the account of the judging of Alalu,

And of the happenings thereafter on Earth and on Lahmu.

In his reed hut Anu was hurting, in the reed hut to him Enki applied the healing.

In his reed hut Alalu was sitting, spittle he spat from his mouth;

In his innards the malehood of Anu was like a burden,

With Anu's semen were his innards impregnated; like a female in travail his belly grew swollen.

On the third day Anu's pains subsided; his pride was greatly hurting.

To Nibiru I wish to return! to his two sons did Anu say.

Beforehand upon Alalu there must be a judgment; a sentence the crime befitting must be imposed!

By the laws of Nibiru seven judges were required, the highest of rank on them to preside.

In the square of Eridu the heroes were assembled the trial of Alalu to observe.

For the Seven Who Judge, seven seats were provided; for Anu, presiding, the tallest seat was prepared.

To his right Enki was seated; Enlil was seated on Anu's left.

On Enki's right Anzu and Nungal were seated; Abgal and Alalgar to the left of Enlil sat.

Before these Seven Who Judge Alalu was brought; his hands and feet were untied.

Enlil was first to speak: In fairness a wrestling match was held, Alalu the kingship to Anu forfeited!

What say you, Alalu? Enki him this question asked.

In fairness the wrestling match was held, the kingship I forfeited! Alalu said.

Having been vanquished, Alalu an abominable crime performed, the malehood of Anu he bit and swallowed!

Thus did Enlil the accusation of the crime make. Death is the punishment! Enlil was saying.

What say you, Alalu? Enki his father-by-marriage asked.

There was silence; Alalu the question did not answer.

We all the crime did witness! Alalgar was saying. Judgment must be in accordance!

If words you wish to utter, speak before the judging! Enki to Alalu said.

In the silence Alalu slowly began to speak:

On Nibiru I was king, by right of succession I was reigning;

Anu was my cupbearer. The princes he aroused, to a wrestling he me challenged;

For nine counted circuits I was king on Nibiru, to my seed kingship was belonging.

On my throne seat Anu himself sat, to escape death to distant Earth I made a dangerous journey.

Salvation for Nibiru I, Alalu, on the alien planet discovered!

Return to Nibiru I was promised, in fairness the throne to regain!

Then to Earth came Ea; the one by compromise the next to reign Nibiru he was designated.

Then came Enlil, the succession from Anu to himself claiming.

Then Anu came, by lots he tricked Ea; Enki, the Lord of Earth, he was proclaimed,

Of Earth, not of Nibiru, to be the master.

Then to Enlil command was granted, Enki to the distant Abzu was delegated.

My heart of all that was aching, my chest from shame and anger was bursting;

Then Anu his foot upon my chest placed, upon my aching heart he was treading!

In the silence Anu spoke up: By royal seed and law, by fair wrestling did I gain the throne.

My malehood you bit off and swallowed, my offspring line to
discontinue!

Enlil spoke up: To the crime the accused admitted, let the judgment
come,

Let death the punishment be!

Death! said Alalgar. Death! said Abgal. Death! said Nungal.

Death to Alalu by itself will be coming, what he had swallowed in
his innards death will bring! Enki was saying.

Let Alalu for the rest of his days on Earth be in prison! Anzu was
saying.

Their words Anu was contemplating; anger and pity both him
engulfed.

To die in exile, let this be the judgment! Anu was saying.

In amazement the judges at each other glanced. What Anu was
saying they wondered.

Neither on Earth nor on Nibiru shall the exiling be! Anu was saying.

On the way there is the Lahmu planet, with waters and an
atmosphere it is endowed.

Enki, as Ea, thereon made a pause; of it as a way station have I
been thinking.

Its netforce is less than that of Earth forceful, an advantage in
wisdom to be considered;

In the celestial chariot Alalu shall be taken,

On my departing from Earth he with me shall make the journey.

Around the planet Lahmu we shall make circuits, to Alalu a sky
chamber we shall provide,

To the planet Lahmu in it he will be descended.

Alone on a strange planet an exile he shall be,

His days to his last day by himself to count!

Thus did Anu words of judgment utter, in solemnity were the
words intended.

By unanimity was this judgment upon Alalu imposed, in the
   presence of the heroes it was announced.

Let Nungal be my pilot to Nibiru, therefrom chariots bearing
   heroes again to Earth to pilot.

Let Anzu join for the journey, of the descent to Lahmu take charge!

So did Anu commandments utter.

On the morrow departing was readied; all who depart by boats to
   the chariot were ferried.

A place for landings on firm soil you must prepare! Anu to Enlil
   was saying.

How Lahmu as a way station to utilize, plans you should be making!

Farewells there were, both joy and sorrow.

Limping did Anu on the chariot embark, with his hands tied did
   Alalu the chariot enter.

Then to the heavens the chariot soared up, and the royal visit had
   ended.

They around the Moon made a circuit; Anu by the sight was
   enchanted.

Toward red-hued Lahmu they journeyed, twice about it they circled.

Lower toward the strange planet they came, mountains sky-high
   and tears in the surface they noticed.

Where Ea's chariot had once landed they observed; by a lakeside it
   was located.

Slowed by Lahmu netpower, in the chariot the sky chamber they
   readied.

Anzu, its pilot, then unexpected words to Anu was saying:

With Alalu to the firm soil of Lahmu I shall descend,

With the sky chamber to the chariot to return I wish not!

With Alalu on the strange planet I shall stay; until he dies I shall
   protect him.

When he dies of his innards' poison, as befits a king him I shall
   bury!

As for me, I shall have made my name;

Anzu, they will say, against all odds to a king in exile a companion was,

He saw things by others unseen, on a strange planet he faced unknown things!

Anzu, they will to the end of times shall say, like a hero has fallen!

There were tears in the eyes of Alalu, there was amazement in the heart of Anu.

Your wish shall be honored, to Anzu Anu said. Hereby let a promise by me to you be made,

By my raised hand to you I this swear:

On the next journey a chariot by Lahmu shall circuit, its skyship to you shall descend.

If alive it shall find you, the master of Lahmu you shall be proclaimed;

When a way station on Lahmu shall be established, its commander you shall be!

Anzu bowed his head. So be it! to Anu he said.

Into the sky chamber Alalu and Anzu were ushered,

With Eagles' helmets and Fishes' suits they were provided, with food and tools they were supplied.

From the circling chariot the skyship departed, from the chariot its descent was observed.

Then from view it disappeared, and the chariot to Nibiru continued.

For nine Shars was Alalu king on Nibiru, for eight Shars Eridu he commanded.

In the ninth Shar, to die in exile on Lahmu was his fate.

Now this is the account of the return of Anu to Nibiru,

And how Alalu on Lahmu was buried, how Enlil on Earth the Landing Place built.

On Nibiru there was for Anu a joyous welcome.

Of what had happened to the council and the princes Anu gave account;

Neither pity nor vengeance from them all he sought.

To discuss the tasks ahead he them all instructed.

To the assembled a vision great in scope he outlined:

Way stations from Nibiru to Earth to establish, all the Sun's family in one kingdom to encompass!

The first on Lahmu to be fashioned, the Moon for the plans also to be considered;

On the other planets or their circling hosts stations to set up,

A chain a constant caravan of chariots to supply and safeguard,

The gold from Earth without interruptions to Nibiru bring, perchance gold elsewhere to also find!

The counselors, the princes, the savants Anu's plans considered,

The salvation of Nibiru in the plans they all a promise saw.

Savants and commanders knowledge of the celestial gods perfected,

To chariots and skyships a new kind, rocketships, were added.

Heroes for the tasks were selected, for the tasks there was much learning.

The plans to Enki and Enlil were beamed over, preparations on Earth to hurry they were told.

On Earth of what had happened and what to be done is required there was much discussion.

Enki Alalgar to be of Eridu the Overseer appointed, his own steps to the Abzu he directed;

Where to obtain gold from Earth's bowels he then determined.

What heroes to the task are needed he calculated, what tools were required he contemplated:

An Earth Splitter with cleverness Enki designed, on Nibiru that it be fashioned he requested,

Therewith in the Earth to make a gash, its innards reach by way of tunnels;

That-Which-Crunches and That-Which-Crushes he also designed, on Nibiru for the Abzu to be fashioned.

Of other matters Nibiru's savants he to contemplate asked.

Of matters of health and well-being of heroes the needs he listed.

To the heroes Earth's quick circuits were upsetting,

Earth's quick day and night cycles dizziness were causing.

The atmosphere, though good, was in some things lacking, in others too abundant;

Of the sameness of the food the heroes were complaining.

Enlil, the commander, by the heat of the Sun on Earth was afflicted, for coolness and shade he was longing.

While in the Abzu Enki preparations was making,

Enlil in his skyship the extent of the Edin was surveying.

Of mountains and rivers he took account, of valleys and plains the measures he took.

Where a Landing Place to establish, a place for the rocketships, he was seeking.

Enlil, by the heat of the Sun afflicted, for a place of coolness and shade was searching.

To snow-covered mountains on the Edin's north side he took a liking,

The tallest trees he ever saw grew there in a cedar forest.

There above a mountain valley with power beams the surface he flattened.

Great stones from the hillside the heroes quarried and to size cut.

To uphold the platform with skyships they carried and emplaced them.

With satisfaction did Enlil the handiwork consider,

A work beyond belief indeed it was, a structure of everlasting!

An abode for himself, on the crest of the mountain, was his desire.

Of the tall trees in the cedar forest long beams were prepared,

Of them the construction of an abode for himself he decreed:

The Abode of the North Crest he named it.

On Nibiru, a new celestial chariot for soaring off was prepared,

New kinds of rocketships, skyships, and that which Enki had designed it was transporting.

A fresh group of fifty from Nibiru it was taking; chosen females among them were.

By Ninmah, Exalted Lady, were they commanded; in succor and healing were they trained.

Ninmah, Exalted Lady, a daughter of Anu she was; a half sister, not a full sister, of Enki and Enlil she was.

In succor and healing she was greatly learned, in the treating of ailments she excelled.

To the complaints from Earth she gave much attention, a healing was she preparing!

The course of prior chariots, on Tablets of Destinies recorded, Nungal its pilot did follow.

Unharmed it reached the celestial god Lahmu; it circled the planet, slowly to its surface it descended.

A faint beaming a group of heroes followed; Ninmah was going with them.

Beside a lakeshore Anzu they found; from his helmet the signals were beaming.

Anzu himself was without motion, prostrate, he lay dead.

Ninmah touched his face, to his heart she gave attention.

From her pouch she took out the Pulser; upon Anzu's heart pulsing she directed.

From her pouch she took out the Emitter, its crystals' life-giving emissions on his body she directed.

Sixty times did Ninmah direct the Pulser, sixty times the Emitter she directed;

On the sixtieth time Anzu his eyes opened, with his lips he motioned.

Gently upon his face Ninmah Water of Life poured, his lips with it wetting.

Gently into his mouth the Food of Life she placed;

Then the miracle did happen: Anzu from the dead arose!

About Alalu they him then inquired; of Alalu's death Anzu them told.

He led them to a great rock, from the plain heavenward protruding.

There to them what had happened he was telling:

Alalu soon after the landing from unremitting pain to scream began.

From his mouth his innards he was spitting; in agony he peered over the wall!

Thus was Anzu to them saying.

He led them to a great rock, like a mountain from the plain heavenward rising.

In the great rock a cave I found, Alalu's corpse therein I hid,

Its entrance with stones I covered. So was Anzu to them saying.

They followed him to the rock, the stones they removed, the cave they entered.

Inside what of Alalu remained they found;

He who once on Nibiru a king was a pile of bones was in a cave now lying!

For the first time in our annals, a king not on Nibiru has died, not on Nibiru was he buried!

So did Ninmah say. Let him in peace for eternity rest! she was saying.

They the cave's entrance again with stones covered;

The image of Alalu upon the great rock mountain with beams they carved.

They showed him wearing an Eagle's helmet; his face they made uncovered.

Let the image of Alalu forever gaze toward Nibiru that he ruled,

Toward the Earth whose gold he discovered!

So Ninmah, Exalted Lady, in the name of her father Anu did declare.

As for you, Anzu, to you Anu the king his promise shall be keeping!

Twenty heroes with you here shall remain, the way station's building to begin;

Rocketships from Earth the golden ores shall here deliver,

Celestial chariots from here the gold to Nibiru shall then transport.

Hundreds of heroes their abode on Lahmu shall make,

You, Anzu, shall be their commander!

Thus did the Great Lady, in the name of her father Anu, to Anzu say.

My life I owe to you, Great Lady! So was Anzu saying. My gratitude to Anu shall limits not have!

From the planet Lahmu the chariot departed; toward Earth the journey it continued.

Synopsis of the Fifth Tablet

Ninmah arrives on Earth with a group of female nurses

She delivers seeds to grow elixir-providing plants

She brings Enlil news of their out-of-wedlock son Ninurta

In the Abzu Enki establishes an abode and mining sites

In the Edin Enlil builds space and other facilities

Nibiruans on Earth ("Anunnaki") number six hundred

Three hundred "Igigi" operate the facilities on Lahmu (Mars)

Exiled for date-raping Sud, Enlil learns of the hidden weapons

Sud becomes Enlil's spouse Ninlil, bears a son (Nannar)

Ninmah joins Enki in the Abzu, bears him daughters

Ninki, Enki's spouse, arrives with their son Marduk

Clans form on Earth as Enki and Enlil beget more sons

Beset by hardships, the Igigi launch a coup against Enlil

Ninurta defeats their leader Anzu in aerial battles

The Anunnaki, driven to produce gold faster, mutiny

Enlil and Ninurta denounce the mutineers

Enki suggests to artificially fashion Primitive Workers

Enlil, Ninmah, Enki, and Isimud
(Sumerian depiction)

THE FIFTH TABLET

From the planet Lahmu the chariot departed, toward Earth the journey it continued.

Around the Moon they made circuits, a way station thereon to explore.

Around the Earth they made circuits, toward a splashdown slowing.

In the waters beside Eridu did Nungal the chariot bring down.

To a quay, by Enlil constructed, they stepped off; boats were no longer needed.

Enlil and Enki their sister with embraces greeted, with Nungal the pilot they locked arms.

The heroes, male and female, by the present heroes were with shouts greeted.

All that the chariot had brought was quickly unloaded:

Rocketships and skyships, and the tools by Enki designed, and provisions of all kinds.

Of all that on Nibiru transpired, of the death and burying of Alalu, Ninmah her brothers told;

Of the way station on Lahmu and the commanding by Anzu she to them related.

Enki of that uttered approval, Enlil words of bewilderment uttered.

That is Anu's decision, his word is unalterable! Ninmah to Enlil was saying.

For the maladies relief I have brought, Ninmah to her brothers said.

From her pouch a bag of seeds she brought out, seeds in the soil to be sown;

A host of bushes from the seeds shall sprout, a juicy fruit they will produce.

The juice an elixir shall form, for drinking by the heroes it shall be good.

Their ailments it will chase away; happier their mood it shall make!

In a cool place the seeds need to be sown, by warmth and water need they nourishing!

So did Ninmah to her brothers say.

The place that for this is perfect I will to you show! Enlil to her said.

It is where the Landing Place was fashioned, where an abode of cedarwood I have made!

In Enlil's skyship the two of them, Enlil and Ninmah, skyward soared;

To the Landing Place in the snow-covered mountains, by the cedar forest, brother and sister went.

On the great stone platform the skyship landed, to Enlil's abode they went.

Once inside, Enlil embraced her, with fervor he kissed Ninmah.

Oh my sister, my beloved! Enlil to her whispered. By her loins he grabbed her,

Into her womb his semen he did not pour.

Of our son Ninurta word I bring you! Ninmah to him softly said.

A young prince he is, for adventure he is ready, to join you on Earth he is prepared!

If here you stay, let us Ninurta our son bring over! Enlil to her said.

To the Landing Place heroes were arriving, rocketships by skyships to the platform they carried.

From the pouch of Ninmah the seeds were obtained, in the valley's soil they were sown,

A fruit from Nibiru on Earth to be grown!

In the skyship Enlil and Ninmah to Eridu returned.

On the way Enlil to her the landscape showed, the Edin's extent to her he showed,

From the skies Enlil to her his plans explained.

An everlasting plan have I designed! to her he was saying.

That which for all time construction shall determine I have laid out;

Away from Eridu, where dry land begins, my quarters shall be,

Laarsa will be its name, a place for directing it shall become.

On the banks of the Burannu, the River of Deep Waters, will it be located,

A twin thereof a city shall in future arise, Lagash I shall name it.

Between the two on the plans a line have I drawn,

Sixty leagues thereafter a healing city shall come into being,

A city of your own it shall be, Shurubak, the Haven City, I shall name it.

On the center line it shall be located, to the fourth city it shall be leading;

Nibru-ki, Earth's Crossing Place, I will name it, a Bond Heaven–Earth in it I shall establish.

The Tablets of Destinies it shall house, all missions it will control!

With Eridu five cities there shall be counted, to eternity they shall exist!

On a crystal tablet Enlil to Ninmah the master plan was showing;

On the tablet she saw more markings, of them of Enlil she inquired.

Beyond the five cities, a Chariot Place I shall henceforth build,

From Nibiru to Earth directly to arrive! Enlil to her was responding.

Why by Anu's plans for Lahmu Enlil was bewildered Ninmah then understood.

My brother, magnificent is your plan for the five cities! to him
    Ninmah was saying.

The creation of Shurubak, a city for healing, as my abode, for my
    own to be,

Is a matter for which grateful I am;

Beyond that plan, do not transgress your father, your brother too
    do not offend!

You are wise as well as beautiful! Enlil to her said.

In the Abzu Enki plans was also conceiving, where to build his house,

Where for heroes dwellings to prepare, where the bowels of the
    Earth to enter.

In his skyship the extent of the Abzu he measured, its districts he
    did carefully survey.

A distant land the Abzu was, beyond the waters from the Edin it
    was away;

A rich land it was, bursting with riches, perfect in fullness.

Mighty rivers rushed across the region, great waters there rapidly
    flowed;

An abode by the flowing waters Enki for himself established,

To the midst of the Abzu, to a place of pure waters Enki betook
    himself.

In that land the Place of Deepness Enki determined, for the heroes
    into Earth's bowels to descend.

The Earth Splitter Enki there established, therewith in the Earth a
    gash to make,

By way of tunnels Earth's innards to reach, the golden veins to
    uncover.

Nearby That-Which-Crunches and That-Which-Crushes he emplaced,

The gold-bearing ores to crunch and crush, by skyships to be carried,

To the Landing Place in the cedar mountains to be brought,

Therefrom by rocketships to the way station on Lahmu to be
    transported.

On Earth more heroes were arriving, some to the Edin were assigned, some in the Abzu tasks were given.

Laarsa and Lagash by Enlil were constructed, Shurubak for Ninmah he did establish.

With her therein a host of female healers were dwelling, young ones who give succor.

In Nibru-ki Enlil a Bond Heaven–Earth was assembling, from there all missions to command.

Between Eridu and the Abzu Enki was journeying, back and forth for supervising he went.

On Lahmu construction was progressing; heroes for the Way Station were also arriving.

A Shar, two Shars were the preparations lasting; then Anu gave the word.

On Earth the seventh day it was, a day of resting by Enki at the beginning decreed.

At every place the heroes were assembled, a message from Anu from Nibiru beamed they overheard;

In the Edin they were assembled, Enlil was there in command.

With him was Ninmah; her host of young ones by her side were assembled.

Alalgar who of Eridu was the master was there, Abgal who the Landing Place commanded also stood.

In the Abzu were the heroes assembled, under the gaze of Enki they stood;

With Enki was his vizier Isimud; Nungal the pilot was there too.

On Lahmu the heroes were assembled; with their proud commander Anzu they stood.

Six hundred were on Earth, three hundred on Lahmu were gathered.

In all there were nine hundred, the words of Anu the king they all heard:

Heroes, of Nibiru you are the saviors! The fate of all is in your hands!

Your success shall for eternity be recorded, by glorious names you shall be called.

Those who on Earth are shall as Anunnaki be known, Those Who from Heaven to Earth Came!

Those who on Lahmu are, Igigi shall be named, Those Who Observe and See they shall be!

All that is required is ready: Let the gold start coming, let Nibiru be saved!

———·•·———

Now this is the account of Enki and Enlil and Ninmah,

Their loves and espousals, and by their sons the rivalries.

Offspring of Anu the three leaders were, by different mothers were they born.

Enki was the Firstborn son; a concubine of Anu was his mother.

Enlil by Antu, the spouse of Anu, was born; the Legal Heir he thus became.

Ninmah by another concubine was mothered, a half sister of the two half brothers she was.

The Firstborn daughter of Anu she was, by her name-title Ninmah this was indicated.

Greatly beautiful she was, full of wisdom, one quick to learn.

Ea, as Enki then was named, by Anu to espouse Ninmah was chosen,

Thereby their offspring son the legal successor thereafter to become.

Ninmah of Enlil, a dashing commander, was enamored;

By him she was seduced, into her womb his seed he poured,

A son from Enlil's seed she bore, Ninurta the two have named him.

By the deed was Anu angered; as punishment he Ninmah ever to be a spouse forbade!

Ea his bride-to-be by Anu's decree abandoned, a princess named Damkina he instead espoused;

A son, an heir, to them was born; Marduk they named him, One in a Pure Place Born it meant.

As for Enlil, a son not by espousal he had, a spouse by his side to be he did not have.

It was on Earth, not on Nibiru, that Enlil became espoused;

The account of that is one of rape, and exile, and love that brought forgiveness,

And of more sons that were only half brothers.

On Earth it was summer; to his abode in the cedar forest Enlil retreated.

In the cedar forest was Enlil walking in the cool of the day;

In a cool mountain stream some of Ninmah's young ones, to the Landing Place assigned, were bathing.

By the beauty and grace of one, Sud was her name, Enlil was enchanted.

To his cedarwood abode Enlil her invited:

Come, partake with me in the elixir of Nibiru's fruit that grew here! So to her he said.

Sud into Enlil's abode entered, the elixir in a cup to her Enlil presented.

Sud drank, Enlil drank too; to her Enlil of intercourse was speaking.

Unwilling was the lass. My vagina is too little, it knows not copulation! to Enlil she was saying.

To her Enlil of kissing was speaking; unwilling was the lass:

My lips are too small, they know not kissing! to Enlil she was saying.

Enlil laughed and embraced her, he laughed and he kissed her;

His semen into her womb he poured!

To Ninmah, Sud's commander, the immoral deed was reported.

Enlil, immoral one! For your deed judgment you shall face! So did Ninmah to Enlil in anger say.

In the presence of fifty Anunnaki Seven Who Judge were assembled,

Seven Who Judge on Enlil a punishment decreed:

Let Enlil from all cities be banished, to a Land of No Return let him exiled be!

In a sky chamber they made Enlil leave the Landing Place; Abgal was its pilot.

To a Land of No Return Enlil was taken, never to return!

In the sky chamber the two of them journeyed, to another land was their direction.

There, amidst forbidding mountains, at a place of desolation, Abgal the sky chamber landed.

This your place of exile shall be! Abgal to Enlil was saying.

Not perchance have I it chosen! to Enlil he was saying. A secret of Enki in it is hidden,

In the nearby cave Enki seven Weapons of Terror has hidden,

From Alalu's celestial chariot he had them removed.

Take the weapons into your possession, with the weapons your freedom attain!

So was Abgal to his commander saying; a secret of Enki to Enlil he did reveal!

Then from the secret place Abgal departed; Enlil alone was there left.

In the Edin Sud to Ninmah, her commander, words was speaking:

By Enlil's seed am I pregnant, a child of Enlil in my womb has been conceived!

Ninmah Sud's words to Enki conveyed; the Lord of Earth he was, on Earth he was supreme!

They summoned Sud before Seven Who Judge: Will you take Enlil as your spouse? they her asked.

Words of consent she uttered; the words by Abgal to Enlil in his exile were conveyed.

To espouse Sud Enlil from his exile was returned; by that did Enki and Ninmah to him a pardon give.

Enlil's official spouse Sud was declared; on her the name-title
  Ninlil, Lady of the Command, was bestowed.

Thereafter to Ninlil and Enlil a son was born; Nannar, the Bright
  One, Ninlil him named.

He was the first of the Anunnaki on Earth to be conceived,

One of Nibiru's royal seed on an alien planet to be born!

It was after that that Enki to Ninmah was speaking: Come be with
  me in the Abzu!

In the midst of the Abzu, in a place of pure waters, an abode have I
  established.

With a bright metal, silver is its name, it is embellished,

With a deep blue stone, lapis lazuli, it is adorned;

Come Ninmah, be with me, your adoration of Enlil abandon!

To the Abzu, to the abode of Enki, Ninmah then journeyed;

Enki there to her words of loving spoke,

Of how for each other intended, sweet words to her he whispered.

You are still my beloved! to her he said, caressing.

He embraced her, he kissed her; she caused his phallus to water.

Enki his semen into the womb of Ninmah poured. Give me a son!
  Give me a son! he cried out.

She took the semen into her womb, the semen of Enki her
  impregnated.

One day of Nibiru was a month of Earth for her,

Two days, three days, four days of Nibiru like months of Earth
  they were,

Five and six and seven and eight days of months were completed;

The ninth count of motherhood was completed; Ninmah was in
  travail.

To a child she gave birth; the newborn was a female;

On the banks of the river in the Abzu a daughter to Enki and
  Ninmah was born!

Enki by a daughter was disappointed. Kiss the young one! to him Ninmah said.

Kiss the young one! Enki to his vizier Isimud said: A son I desired,

A son by my half sister I must have!

Again he kissed Ninmah, by her loins he grabbed her, his semen into her womb he poured.

Again she was with child, again a daughter to Enki she bore.

A son, a son by you I must have! Enki to her cried out; Ninmah he kissed again.

Thereupon Ninmah against Enki a cursing uttered,

Whatever food he ate was poison in his innards; his jaw hurt, his tooth hurt, his ribs were hurting.

Isimud the Anunnaki summoned, to Ninmah for relief they were pleading.

To distance himself from Ninmah's vulva Enki by raised arm swore;

One by one she his ailments removed, from her curse Enki was freed.

To the Edin Ninmah returned, never to be espoused; Anu's command was fulfilled!

To Earth Enki his spouse Damkina with their son Marduk summoned;

Ninki, Lady of Earth, the title she was granted.

By her and by concubines Enki five more sons had, these were their names:

Nergal and Gibil, Ninagal and Ningishzidda, and Dumuzi the youngest.

To Earth Enlil and Ninmah their son Ninurta summoned,

By his spouse Ninlil did Enlil one more son have, to Nannar a full brother; Ishkur was his name.

Three sons in all did Enlil have, none by concubines were they born.

Two clans were thus on Earth established; their rivalries to wars did lead.

———•———

Now this is the account of the mutiny of the Igigi,

And how Anzu to death was put, for stealing the Tablets of Destinies punished.

From the Abzu gold from Earth's veins to the Landing Place was carried,

Thence Igigi in rocketships to the way station on Lahmu transported.

From the planet Lahmu in celestial chariots was the precious metal to Nibiru brought;

On Nibiru was the gold to the finest dust fashioned, to protect the atmosphere it was employed.

Slowly was the breach in the heavens healing, slowly was Nibiru saved!

In the Edin the five cities were perfected.

Enki in Eridu a sparkling abode made, upon soil skyward raised he built it,

Like a mountain he raised it above the ground, in a good place he built it.

Damkina his spouse therein dwelt; to his son Marduk Enki was there wisdom teaching.

In Nibru-ki Enlil the Bond Heaven–Earth established, a sight to see it was.

At its center a heavenward tall pillar the sky itself was reaching,

On a platform that cannot be overturned it was placed;

Therewith the words of Enlil all settlements encompassed, on Lahmu and in Nibiru they were heard.

From there beams were raised, the heart of all the lands they could search;

Its eyes could scan all the lands, its net unwanted approach impossible made.

In its lofty house a crownlike chamber was the center, to distant heavens it peered;

Toward the horizon was its gaze, the heavenly zenith it perfected.

In its dark hallowed chamber, by twelve emblems was the family of the Sun marked,

On ME's were the secret formulas of Sun and Moon, Nibiru and Earth, and eight celestial gods recorded.

The Tablets of Destinies in the chamber their hues emitted,

With them Enlil all comings and goings oversaw.

On Earth the Anunnaki toiled, of work and sustenance they were complaining.

By Earth's quick cycles they were disturbed, of the elixir they only small rations were given.

In the Edin the Anunnaki toiled, in the Abzu the work was more backbreaking.

By teams were Anunnaki sent back to Nibiru, by teams new ones were arriving.

The Igigi, on Lahmu dwelling, were the loudest in complaining:

When from Lahmu to Earth they descend, a rest place on Earth they were demanding.

With Anu did Enlil and Enki words exchange, the king they consulted:

Let the leader come to Earth, with Anzu have discussions! So did Anu to them say.

Anzu to Earth from the heavens descended, the words of complaints to Enlil and Enki he delivered.

Let Anzu of the workings gain understanding! Enki to Enlil was saying.

I will the Abzu to him show, you the Bond Heaven–Earth to him reveal!

To the words of Enki, Enlil consented.

Enki to Anzu the Abzu did show, the toil in the mines to him he presented;

Enlil Anzu to Nibru-ki invited, to the hallowed dark chamber he let him enter;

In the innermost sanctuary the Tablets of Destinies to Anzu he explained.

What the Anunnaki in the five cities were doing to Anzu was shown;

To the Igigi who at the Landing Place were arriving relief he promised.

To discuss the complaints of the Igigi he to Nibru-ki then returned.

A prince among the princes was Anzu, of royal seed his ancestry he counted;

Evil thoughts filled his heart when to the Bond Heaven–Earth he returned.

To take away the Tablets of Destinies was he scheming,

Of the decrees of heaven and Earth to take control in his heart he was planning.

The removal of the Enlilship in his heart he conceived, to rule Igigi and Anunnaki was his aim!

Unsuspecting Enlil at the entrance to the sanctuary Anzu let be stationed;

Unsuspecting Enlil left the sanctuary, for a cooling swim he went away.

With evil purpose Anzu the Tablets of Destinies seized;

In a sky chamber he flew away, to the mountain of the sky chambers he swiftly went;

There, in the Landing Place, rebellious Igigi for him were waiting,

To declare Anzu king of Earth and Lahmu they were preparing!

In the sanctuary of Nibru-ki the brilliance petered out, the humming quieted down,

Silence in the place prevailed, suspended were the sacred formulas.

In Nibru-ki Enlil was speechless; by the treachery he was overwhelmed.

To Enki angry words he spoke, of the ancestry of Anzu he him questioned.

In Nibru-ki the leaders gathered, the Anunnaki who decree fates with Anu were consulting.

Anzu must be seized, the Tablets to the sanctuary must be returned! Thus did Anu decree.

Who shall the rebel face? Who shall the Tablets retrieve? the leaders asked each other.

With the Tablets of Destinies in his possession, invincible is Anzu! to each other they were saying.

Ninurta, by his mother encouraged, from the assembled stepped forward:

Enlil's warrior I shall be, Anzu I shall vanquish! Thus was Ninurta saying.

To the mountainside Ninurta set his course, to vanquish the fugitive Anzu he undertook.

Anzu from his hideout Ninurta was mocking: The Tablets are my protection, invincible I am!

Lightning darts Ninurta at Anzu directed; the arrows could not approach Anzu, backward they turned.

The battle was stilled, Ninurta's weapons Anzu did not vanquish!

Enki then to Ninurta counsel gave: With your Whirlwind stir up a storm,

Let the dust cover Anzu's face, let it the wings of his skybird ruffle!

For his son Enlil a mighty weapon fashioned, a Tillu missile it was;

To your Stormer-weapon attach it, when wing to wing near, at Anzu shoot it!

Thus did Enlil his son Ninurta instruct.

When wing to wing near each other, let the missile fly as a lightning!

Again Ninurta in his Whirlwind soared; Anzu against him in his skybird rose to challenge.

Wing to wing! Anzu in anger shouted. This battle will be your destruction!

Ninurta the advice of Enki followed; with his Whirlwind a dust storm he created.

The dust Anzu's face covered, the pinions of his skybird were exposed;

Into their midst Ninurta the missile let loose, a fiery brilliance Anzu's pinions engulfed.

Like butterflies his wings began to flutter; to the ground Anzu came falling.

The Earth shook, the skies became darkened;

The fallen Anzu Ninurta made captive, from him the Tablets he retrieved.

From the mountaintop the Igigi were watching;

When to the Landing Place Ninurta came, they trembled and kissed his feet.

Ninurta the captive Abgal and Anunnaki set free, to Anu and Enlil his victory he announced.

To Nibru-ki he then returned, in its innermost chamber the Tablets were reinstalled.

Once again the brilliance therein returned, the hum of ME's in the Tablets was restored.

Before the Seven Who Judge Anzu for a judgment was taken;

Enlil and Ninlil his spouse, Enki and his spouse Ninki, the one beforehand as Damkina known,

And the sons Nannar and Marduk were there; Ninmah also was in judging.

Ninurta of the evil deeds spoke: There was no justification, let death be the penalty! he said.

The Igigi by right were complaining, a rest place on Earth they do need! Marduk in counter argued.

By his evil deed all the Anunnaki and Igigi Anzu did endanger! Enlil said.

Enki and Ninmah with Enlil agreed; the evil must be extinguished! they said.

To death by execution the seven judged Anzu;

With a killing ray Anzu's life breath was extinguished. Let his body to the vultures be left! Ninurta said.

Let him on Lahmu be buried, in a cave next to Alalu be laid to rest! Enki was saying.

From the same ancestral seed the two of them were!

Let Marduk the body to Lahmu carry, let Marduk there as commander stay!

So was Enki to the judges suggesting. Let it so be! Enlil said.

———•·•———

Now this is the account of how Bad-Tibira, the Metal City, was established,

And how in the fortieth Shar the Anunnaki in the Abzu mutinied.

In the twenty-fifth Shar was Anzu judged and executed,

The unrest of the Igigi it subdued but left it simmering.

To Lahmu Marduk was sent, the spirits of the Igigi to raise, to their well-being pay attention.

On Earth changes were by Enlil and Enki discussed, to avoid unrest on Earth they were considering.

The stays on Earth are too prolonged, to each other they were saying.

Ninmah for counsel they asked; by her changing visage they were alarmed.

Gold to Nibiru must more quickly flow, salvation must be faster provided! they all agreed.

Ninurta in the innards of planets learned was; to his elders words of wisdom he was saying:

Let a Metal City be established, therein the gold ores to be smelted and refined,

Therefrom less weighty cargoes from Earth shall be lofted.

Each rocketship more gold could carry, room for Anunnaki to Nibiru return there shall be,

Let the tired to Nibiru return, let fresh ones them on Earth replace!

Enlil and Enki and Ninmah of Ninurta's suggestion were in favor,

Anu was consulted and his approval gave.

In the Edin was the Metal City planned, on that location Enlil did insist!

With materials from Nibiru was it constructed, with tools from Nibiru was it equipped.

Three Shars the construction lasted, Bad-Tibira was it the name given.

Ninurta, who made the suggestion, was its first commander.

The flow of gold to Nibiru was thereby eased and quickened,

Those who to Earth and Lahmu at the beginning of the Prior Times had come

To Nibiru were returning; Alalgar and Abgal and Nungal among them were.

The newcomers who them replaced were younger and eager;

To the cycles of Earth and Lahmu and the other rigors they were not accustomed.

On Nibiru, whence they had come, the breach in the atmosphere was healing;

The great calamities on the planet and in its heavens the younger ones did not know.

Of their golden mission excitement and adventure they especially cherished!

As by Ninurta conceived, the ores from the Abzu were delivered,

In Bad-Tibira they were smelted and refined, by rocketships to Lahmu they were sent;

In celestial chariots from Lahmu to Nibiru was the pure gold delivered.

As by Ninurta conceived, from the Abzu to Nibiru the gold flowed;

What was not conceived was unrest by the newcoming Anunnaki who in the Abzu toiled!

Truth be said, Enki to what was brewing heed was not giving,

To other matters in the Abzu his attention was directing.

With that which in the Abzu grows and lives fascination he acquired;

Of the differences between what on Earth and what on Nibiru
appeared he wished to learn,

How maladies by Earth's cycles and atmosphere were caused he
wished to uncover.

In the Abzu, by the gushing waters, a wondrous study place he
erected,

With all manner of tools and equipment he furnished it.

House of Life he called the place, to it his son Ningishzidda he
invited.

Sacred Formulas, tiny ME's, the secrets of life and death possessing
they shaped,

The mysteries of living and dying of Earth's creatures they to
unravel sought.

With some living creatures Enki was especially enamored;

They lived among the tall trees, their front legs as hands they were
using.

In the tall grasses of the steppes odd creatures were seen; erect
they seemed to be walking.

Absorbed was Enki in those studies; what was among the
Anunnaki brewing he noticed not.

First to notice trouble was Ninurta: A lessening of gold ores at
Bad-Tibira he observed.

By Enlil was Ninurta to the Abzu dispatched, what was ongoing to
discover.

By Ennugi, the Chief Officer, to the excavations he was accompanied,

Complaints of the Anunnaki he with his own ears heard;

They were backbiting and lamenting, in the excavations they were
grumbling;

Unbearable is the toil! to Ninurta they were saying.

Ninurta this to his uncle Enki reported. Let us Enlil summon! Enki said.

Enlil in the Abzu arrived, in a house near the excavations he was stationed.

Let us unnerve Enlil in his dwelling! mine-working heroes shouted.

Of the heavy work let him relieve us!

Let us proclaim war, with hostilities let us gain relief! others shouted.

The Anunnaki in the excavations the words of incitement heeded,

To their tools they set fire, fire to their axes they put.

They troubled Ennugi, Chief Officer of the Mining, in the tunnels they him seized;

They held him as they went, to the doorway of Enlil's dwelling they made their way.

It was night, halfway through the watch it was;

Enlil's dwelling they surrounded, their tools as torches they high held.

Kalkal, the gateway's guardian, bolted the door and Nusku aroused;

Nusku, Enlil's vizier, roused his lord, got him out of bed, thus saying:

My lord, your house is surrounded, battling Anunnaki to your gate came up!

Enlil summoned Enki, Enlil Ninurta summoned to his presence:

What do my own eyes see! Is it against me that this thing is done?

Thus was Enlil to them saying: Who is of the hostilities the instigator?

The Anunnaki stood together: Every single one of us hostilities has declared!

Excessive is the toil, our work is heavy, great is the distress! So they were to Enlil saying.

Words of the happenings Enlil to Anu beamed. Of what is Enlil accused? Anu inquired.

The work, not Enlil, is the trouble causing! Enki to Anu was saying.

The lamentation is heavy, every day the complaints we could hear!

The gold must be obtained! Anu was saying. The work must continue!

Release Ennugi for consultations! Enlil to the hostile Anunnaki said.

Ennugi was released; to the leaders he was thus saying:

Ever since Earth's heat has been rising, the toil is excruciating, unbearable it is!

Let the rebels to Nibiru return, let new ones come in their stead! Ninurta said.

Perchance new tools you can fashion? Enlil to Enki said. For the Anunnaki heroes the tunnels to avoid?

Let us summon my son Ningishzidda, counsel with him I wish to take! Enki thus responded.

They summoned Ningishzidda, from the House of Life he came;

With him Enki huddled, words amongst them they exchanged.

A solution is possible! Enki was saying:

Let us create a Lulu, a Primitive Worker, the hardship work to take over,

Let the Being the toil of the Anunnaki carry on his back!

Astounded were the besieged leaders, speechless indeed they were.

Whoever heard of a Being afresh created, a worker who the Anunnaki's work can do?

They summoned Ninmah, one who of healing and succor was much knowing.

Enki's words to her they repeated: Whoever of such a thing heard? they her asked.

The task is unheard of! she to Enki said. All beings from a seed have descended,

One being from another over aeons did develop, none from nothing ever came!

How right you are my sister! Enki said, smiling.

A secret of the Abzu let me to you all reveal:

The Being that we need, it already exists!

All that we have to do is put on it the mark of our essence,

Thereby a Lulu, a Primitive Worker, shall be created! So did Enki
to them say.

Let us hereby a decision make, a blessing to my plan give:

To create a Primitive Worker, by the mark of our essence to
fashion him!

Synopsis of the Sixth Tablet

To the incredulous leadership, Enki reveals a secret:
In the Abzu there roams a wild Being akin to the Anunnaki;
By augmenting its life essence with that of the Anunnaki,
It can be upgraded to be an intelligent Primitive Worker.
Creation belongs to the Father of All Beginning, Enlil shouted
We will give our image only to an existing being, Ninmah argued
Badly needing gold to survive, the leaders vote Yes
Enki, Ninmah, and Ningishzidda Enki's son begin experiments
After many failures the perfect-model Adamu is attained
Ninmah shouts triumphantly: My hands have made it!
She is renamed Ninti ("Lady of Life") for her achievement
Ninki, Enki's spouse, helps fashion Ti-Amat, a female Earthling
The Earthlings, being hybrids, mate but do not procreate
Ningishzidda adds two essence branches to their Life Tree
Discovering the unapproved ongoings, Enlil expels the Earthlings

The double-helix DNA emblem of Ningishzidda

THE SIXTH TABLET

To create a Primitive Worker, by the mark of our essence to fashion him!

So was Enki to the leaders saying.

The Being that we need, it already exists!

Thus did Enki to them a secret of the Abzu reveal.

With astonishment did the other leaders Enki's words hear; by the words they were fascinated.

Creatures in the Abzu there are, Enki was saying, that walk erect on two legs,

Their forelegs they use as arms, with hands they are provided.

Among the animals of the steppe they live. They know not dressing in garments,

They eat plants with their mouths, they drink water from lake and ditch.

Shaggy with hair is their whole body, their head hair is like a lion's;

With gazelles they jostle, with teeming creatures in the waters they delight!

The leaders to Enki's words with amazement listened.

No creature like that has ever in the Edin been seen! Enlil, disbelieving, said.

Aeons ago, on Nibiru, our predecessors like that might have been! Ninmah was saying.

It is a Being, not a creature!
Ninmah was saying. To behold it must be a thrill!

To the House of Life Enki led them; in strong cages there were some of the beings.

At the sight of Enki and the others they jumped up, with fists on the cage bars they were beating.

They were grunting and snorting; no words were they speaking.

Male and female they are! Enki was saying; malehoods and femalehoods they have,

Like us, from Nibiru coming, they are procreating.

Ningishzidda, my son, their Fashioning Essence has tested;

Akin to ours it is, like two serpents it is entwined;

When their with our life essence shall be combined, our mark upon them shall be,

A Primitive Worker shall be created! Our commands will he understand,

Our tools he will handle, the toil in the excavations he shall perform;

To the Anunnaki in the Abzu relief shall come!

So was Enki with enthusiasm saying, with excitement his words came forth.

Enlil at the words was hesitating: The matter is one of great importance!

On our planet, slavery has long ago been abolished, tools are the slaves, not other beings!

A new creature, beforehand nonexisting, you wish to bring into being;

Creation in the hands of the Father of All Beginning alone is held!

So was Enlil in opposing saying; stern were his words.

Enki to his brother responded: Not slaves, but helpers is my plan!

The Being already exists! Ninmah was saying. To give more ability is the plan!

Not a new creature, but one existing more in our image made! Enki with persuasion said,

With little change it can be achieved, only a drop of our essence is needed!

A grave matter it is, it is not to my liking! Enlil was saying.

Against the rules of from planet to planet journeying it is,

By the rules of to Earth coming it was forbidden.

To obtain gold was our purpose, to replace the Father of All Beginning it was not!

After Enlil thus had spoken, Ninmah was the one to respond:

My brother! Ninmah to Enlil was saying,

With wisdom and understanding has the Father of All Beginning us endowed,

To what purpose have we so been perfected, else of it utmost use to make?

With wisdom and understanding has the Creator of All our life essence filled,

To whatever using of it we capable are, is it not that for which we have been destined?

So was Ninmah words to her brother Enlil directing.

With that which in our essence was granted, tools and chariots we have perfected,

Mountains with terror weapons we shattered, skies with gold we are healing!

So was Ninurta to his birth-giving mother saying.

Let us with wisdom new tools fashion, not new beings create,

Let by new equipments, not by slave beings, the toil be relieved!

Whereto our understanding does us lead, to that we have been destined!

So was Ningishzidda saying, with Enki and Ninmah he in agreement was.

What knowledge we possess, its use cannot be prevented! Ningishzidda was saying.

Destiny indeed cannot be altered, from the Beginning to the End it
has been determined!

To them Enlil was thus saying. Destiny it is, or Fate it is,

That to this planet us has brought, to gold from the waters foil,

To put Anunnaki heroes to excavating toil, to a Primitive Worker
create to be planning?

That, my kinfolk, is the question! Thus, with graveness, Enlil was
saying.

Is it Destiny, is it Fate? That is what deciding requires,

Is it from the Beginning ordained, or by us for choosing?

To put the matter before Anu they decided; Anu before the council
the matter presented.

The elders, the savants, the commanders were consulted.

Long and bitter the discussions were, of Life and Death, Fate and
Destiny words were spoken.

Can there be another way the gold to obtain? Survival is in danger!

If gold must be obtained, let the Being be fashioned! the council
decided.

Let Anu forsake the rules of planetary journeys, let Nibiru be saved!

From Anu's palace the decision to Earth was beamed; it Enki
delighted.

Let Ninmah my helper be, of such matters understanding she has!

Thus was Enki saying. At Ninmah with a longing he was gazing.

Let it so be! Ninmah was saying. Let it so be! Enlil did say.

By Ennugi was the decision to the Anunnaki in the Abzu announced:

Until the Being is achieved, to the toil willingly you must return!
he said.

There was disappointment; rebellion there was not; to the toil the
Anunnaki returned.

In the House of Life, in the Abzu, how to fashion the Being Enki to
Ninmah was explaining.

To a place among the trees Ninmah he directed, a place of cages it was.

In the cages there were odd creatures, their likes in the wild no one had seen:

Foreparts of one kind they had, hindparts of another creature they possessed;

Creatures of two kinds by their essences combined to Ninmah Enki was showing!

To the House of Life they returned, to a clean place with brightness shining they led her.

In the clean place Ningishzidda to Ninmah the life-essence secrets was explaining,

How the essence from two kinds combined can be, he to her was showing.

The creatures in the tree cages are too odd, monstrous they are! Ninmah was saying.

Indeed so! Enki responded. To attain perfection, for that you are needed!

How the essences to combine, how much of this, how much of that to put together,

In which womb conception to begin, in which womb should the birth be given?

For that your succor and healing understanding are needed;

The understanding of one who gave birth, who a mother is, is required!

A smile on the face of Ninmah was; the two daughters that by Enki she mothered she well remembered.

With Ningishzidda she surveyed the sacred formulas that on ME's were secreted,

How this and that were done of him she inquired.

The creatures in the tree cages she examined, the two-legged creatures she contemplated.

By a male inseminating a female are the essences transmitted,

The two entwined strands separate and combine an offspring to fashion.

Let a male Anunnaki a two-legged female impregnate, let a combination offspring be born! Thus did Ninmah say.

That we have tried, with failures it resulted! to her Enki responded.

There was no conceiving, there was no birth!

------·•·------

Now this is the account of how the Primitive Worker was created,

How Enki and Ninmah, with Ningishzidda assisting, the Being fashioned.

Another way the admixture of essences to attain must be tried, Ninmah was saying.

How the two strands of essences to combine another way must be found,

That which from the Earth is the portion must not be harmed.

To receive our essence in graduations it must be shaped,

From the ME formulas of Nibiru's essence only bit by bit could be attempted!

In a crystal vessel Ninmah an admixture was preparing, the oval of a female two-legged she gently placed,

With ME Anunnaki seed containing, she the oval impregnated;

That oval back into the womb of the two-legged female she inserted.

This time there was conceiving, a birth was indeed forthcoming!

The allotted time for birth-giving the leaders awaited, with anxious hearts they results were seeking.

The allotted time arrived, there was no birth-giving!

In desperation Ninmah a cutting made, that which was conceived with tongs she drew out.

A living being it was!

With glee Enki shouted. We attained! Ningishzidda with joy cried out.

In her hands Ninmah the newborn held, with joy she was not filled:

Shaggy with hair all over was the newborn, his foreparts like of the Earth creatures were,

His hindparts to those of the Anunnaki more akin they were.

They let the two-legged female the newborn nurse, with her milk him to suckle.

Fast was the newborn growing, what on Nibiru a day was, a month in the Abzu was.

Taller the Earth child grew, in the image of the Anunnaki he was not;

His hands for tools were not suited, his speech only grunting sounds was!

We must try once more! Ninmah was saying. The admixture needs adjusting;

Let me the ME's assay, with this or that ME make the endeavor!

With Enki and Ningishzidda assisting, they repeated the procedures,

The essences in the ME's Ninmah carefully considered,

One bit she took from one, one bit she took out from another,

Then in the crystal bowl the oval of an Earth female she inseminated.

There was conception, at the appropriate time there was birth-giving!

This one more in the likeness of the Anunnaki was;

They let his birth mother him suckle, they let the newborn to a child grow.

Appealing he was by his looks, his hands to hold tools were shapen;

His senses they tested, they found them deficient:

The Earth child could not hear, his eyesight was faltered.

Again and again Ninmah rearranged the admixtures, of the ME formulas she took bits and pieces;

One Being had paralyzed feet, another his semen was dripping,

One had trembling hands, a malfunctioning liver had another;

One had hands too short to reach the mouth, one had lungs for breathing unsuited.

Enki by the results was disappointed. A Primitive Worker is not attained! to Ninmah he was saying.

What is good or is bad in this Being by trials I am discovering!

Ninmah to Enki responded. To continue for success my heart prompts me!

Once more an admixture she made, once more the newborn was deficient.

Perchance the shortfall is not in the admixture! Enki to her was saying.

Perchance neither in the female's oval nor in the essences is the hindrance?

Of what the Earth itself is fashioned, perchance that is what is missing?

Not of Nibiru's crystals use the vessel, of the clay of Earth make it!

So was Enki, with great wisdom possessed, to Ninmah saying.

Perchance what is Earth's own admixture, of gold and copper, is required!

Thus was Enki, he who knows things, prompting her to use clay of the Abzu.

In the House of Life Ninmah made a vessel, of the Abzu's clay she made it.

As a purifying bath she shaped the vessel, within it to make the admixture.

Gently into the clay vessel the oval of an Earth female, the two-legged, she put,

The life essence from an Anunnaki's blood extracted she in the vessel placed,

By the ME formulas was the essence directed, bit by correct bit was it in the vessel added,

Then the oval thus fertilized into the womb of the Earth female she inserted.

There is conception! Ninmah with joy announced. The allotted birth-giving time they awaited.

At the allotted time the Earth female began to travail,

A child, a newborn, was forthcoming!

With her hands Ninmah the newborn extracted; a male it was!

In her hands she held the child, his image she examined; it was the image of perfection.

In her hands she held up the newborn; Enki and Ningishzidda were present.

With joyful laughter the three leaders were seized,

Enki and Ningishzidda were backslapping, Ninmah Enki embraced and kissed.

Your hands have made it! Enki, with a gleaming eye, to her was saying.

They let the birth-giving mother the newborn suckle; quicker than a child on Nibiru grows he was growing.

From month to month the newborn progressed, from a baby to a child he was becoming.

His limbs for the tasks were suited, speech he knew not,

Of speaking he had no understanding, grunts and snorts were his utterings!

Enki the matter was pondering, what was done each step and admixture he considered.

Of all that we had tried and changed, one thing was never altered! to Ninmah he was saying:

Into the womb of the Earth female the fertilized oval was always inserted;

Perchance this is the remaining obstruction! Thus was Enki saying.

Ninmah at Enki gazed, with bewilderment she him beheld.

What, in truth, are you saying? Of him she an answer required.

Of the birth-giving womb am I speaking! to her Enki was responding.

Of who the fertilized oval nurtures, to birth-giving carries;

In our image and after our likeness to be, perchance an Anunnaki womb is required!

In the House of Life there was silence; words never before heard Enki was uttering!

They gazed at each other, about what in each other's mind they were thinking.

Wise are your words, my brother! Ninmah at long last was saying.

Perchance the right admixture in the wrong womb was inserted;

Now where is the female among the Anunnaki her womb to offer,

Perchance the perfect Primitive Worker to create, perchance a monster in her belly to carry?

So was Ninmah with a trembling voice saying.

Let me of Ninki, my spouse, of that inquire! Enki was saying.

Let us her to the House of Life summon, the matter before her lay out.

He was turning to depart when Ninmah put her hand on his shoulder:

No! No! to Enki she was saying.

The admixtures by me were made, reward and endangerment should be mine!

I shall be the one the Anunnaki womb to provide, for good or evil fate to face!

Enki bowed his head, gently he embraced her. So be it! to her he said.

In the clay vessel the admixture they made,

The oval of an Earth female with Anunnaki male essence they put together;

The fertilized egg into the womb of Ninmah by Enki was inserted; there was conception!

The pregnancy, by an admixture conceived, how long will it last?
    to each other they wondered.

Will it be nine months of Nibiru, will it be nine months of Earth?

Longer than on Earth, quicker than on Nibiru, travail came; to a
    male child Ninmah birth was giving!

Enki the boy child held in his hands; the image of perfection he was.

He slapped the newborn on his hindparts; the newborn uttered
    proper sounds!

He handed the newborn to Ninmah; she held him up in her hands.

My hands have made it! victoriously she shouted.

———•·•———

Now this is the account of how Adamu by name was called,

And how Ti-Amat as a counterpart female for him was fashioned.

The newborn's visage and limbs the leaders carefully examined:

Of good shape were his ears, his eyes were not clogged,

His limbs were proper, hindparts like legs, foreparts like hands
    were shaped.

Shaggy like the wild ones he was not, dark black his head hair was,

Smooth was his skin, smooth as the Anunnaki skin it was,

Like dark red blood was its color, like the clay of the Abzu was its
    hue.

They looked at his malehood: Odd was its shape, by a skin was its
    forepart surrounded,

Unlike that of Anunnaki malehood it was, a skin from its forepart
    was hanging!

Let the Earthling from us Anunnaki by this foreskin be
    distinguished! So was Enki saying.

The newborn to cry was beginning; to her chest Ninmah closely
    drew him;

Her breast to him she gave; the breast he began to suckle.

Perfection we did attain! Ningishzidda with elation was saying.

Enki at his sister was gazing; a mother and son, not Ninmah and a Being, he was seeing.

A name will you give him? Enki inquired. A Being he is, not a creature!

Ninmah cast her hand upon the newborn's body, with her fingers his dark red skin she caressed.

Adamu I shall call him! Ninmah was saying. One Who Like Earth's Clay Is, that will be his name!

For the newborn Adamu a crib they fashioned, in a corner of the House of Life they placed him.

A model for Primitive Workers we have indeed attained! Enki was saying.

Now a host of Workers like him are needed! Ningishzidda his elders reminded.

A model indeed he shall be; as for himself, like a Firstling he shall be treated,

From toil he himself shall be protected, his essence alone as a mold shall be!

So was Enki saying; by his decree Ninmah was greatly pleased.

Whose wombs henceforth the fertilized ovals shall carry? Nigishzidda was asking.

The leaders the matter pondered; Ninmah a solution offered.

From her city Shurubak Ninmah female healers summoned, the task required to them she explained,

To the crib of Adamu she led them, the newborn Earthling to perceive.

To perform the task is not a commandment! Ninmah to them was saying; your own wish is the decision!

Of the female Anunnaki assembled, seven stepped forward, seven the task accepted.

Let their names for all time be remembered! Ninmah to Enki was saying.

Their task is heroic, by them a race of Primitive Workers shall come into being!

The seven stepped forward, each one her name was announcing; the names Ningishzidda recorded:

Ninimma, Shuzianna, Ninmada, Ninbara, Ninmug, Musardu, and Ningunna,

These were the names of the seven who by their own wish birth mothers were to be,

Earthlings in their wombs to conceive and bear, Primitive Workers to create.

In seven vessels of the clay of the Abzu made, Ninmah ovals of the two-legged females placed,

The life essence of Adamu she extracted, bit by bit in the vessels she it inserted.

Then in the malepart of Adamu an incision she made, a drop of blood to let out;

Let this a Sign of Life be; that Flesh and Soul have combined let it forever proclaim!

She squeezed the malepart for blood, one drop of blood in each vessel to the admixture she added.

In this clay's admixture, Earthling with the Anunnaki shall be bound!

Thus was Ninmah saying, an incantation she was pronouncing:

To a unity shall the two essences, one of Heaven, one of Earth, together be brought,

That which is of Earth and that which is from Nibiru by a blood kinship shall be bonded!

So was Ninmah pronouncing; her words Ningishzidda also recorded.

In the wombs of the birth-giving heroines the fertilized ovals were inserted.

There was conception; with anticipation was the allotted time counted.

At the allotted time, birth-givings were occurring!

At the allotted time, seven male Earthlings were born,

Their features were proper, good sounds they were uttering; by the heroines they were suckled.

Seven Primitive Workers have been created! Ningishzidda was saying.

Let the procedure be repeated, seven more the toil to undertake!

My son! to him Enki was saying. Not even seven by seven sufficient shall be,

Of heroine healers too much is required, forever their task this way shall be!

Indeed, the task is too demanding, slow beyond enduring it is! Ninmah to them said.

Female ones we have to fashion! Enki was saying, for males counterparts to be.

Let them know each other, as one flesh the two to become,

Let them by themselves procreate, on their own the childbirthing make,

To Primitive Workers by themselves give birth, Anunnaki females to relieve!

The ME formulas you must change, from male to female adjustment make! So did Enki to Nigishzidda say.

For a counterpart to Adamu to be fashioned, in the womb of an Anunnaki female conception is needed!

So did Ningishzidda to his father Enki in responding say.

Enki at Ninmah his gaze directed; before she could speak, he raised his hand.

Let me this time Ninki my spouse summon! With strong voice he said,

If she is willing, let her the mold for the female Earthling create!

They to the Abzu, to the House of Life, Ninki summoned,

They showed her Adamu, all that matters to her they explained,

Of the task that is required they gave explanations, of success and
danger to her an account gave.

By the task Ninki was fascinated. Let it be done! she to them said.

By the ME formulas Ningishzidda adjusting made, by the admixture
was an oval fertilized,

Into the womb of his spouse Enki it inserted; with much care he
did it.

There was conception; in the allotted time Ninki was in travail;
a birth there was not.

Ninki the months counted, Ninmah the months counted;

The tenth month, a month of evil fates, they began to call.

Ninmah, the lady whose hand wombs has opened, with a cutter an
incision made.

Her head was covered, on her hands protections she wore;

With dexterity the opening she made, her face at once was brightened:

That which in the womb was from the womb came forth.

A female! A female birth was given! to Ninki with joy she shouted.

The newborn's visage and limbs they carefully examined,

Of good shape were her ears, her eyes were not clogged;

Her limbs were proper, hindparts like legs, foreparts like hands
were shaped;

Shaggy she was not, like beach sands was the hue of her head hair,

Her skin smooth was, as that of the Anunnaki in smoothness and
color it was.

Ninmah the girl child held in her hands. She slapped her hindparts;

Proper sounds the newborn uttered!

To Ninki, the spouse of Enki, she the newborn handed, to be
suckled, nourished, and raised.

A name will you give her? Enki of his spouse inquired. A Being she is, not a creature.

In your image she is and after your likeness,

Perfectly she is fashioned, a model for female workers you have attained!

Ninki cast her hand upon the newborn's body, with her fingers her skin she caressed.

Ti-Amat let her name be, the Mother of Life! Ninki was saying.

Like the planet of old of which the Earth and the Moon were fashioned, let her be called,

From her womb's life essences other birth-givers shall be molded,

To a multitude of Primitive Workers she thereby life will be giving!

Thus was Ninki saying; the others words of concurring uttered.

Now this is the account of Adamu and Ti-Amat in the Edin,

And how they Knowing of procreation were given and to the Abzu expelled.

After Ti-Amat in the womb of Ninki was fashioned,

In seven vessels of the clay of the Abzu made Ninmah ovals of the two-legged females placed.

The life essence of Ti-Amat she extracted, bit by bit in the vessels she it inserted.

In the vessels of the clay of the Abzu made, Ninmah the admixture formed;

Incantations as the procedure befits she was uttering.

In the wombs of the birth-giving heroines the fertilized ovals were inserted;

There was conception, at the allotted time birth-givings were occurring,

At the allotted time, seven female Earthlings were born.

Their features were proper, good sounds they were uttering.

Thus were seven female counterparts for the Primitive Workers created;

Seven male and seven female did the four leaders create them.

After the Earthlings were thus created,

Let the males the females inseminate, let the Primitive Workers by themselves offspring beget!

So was Enki to the others saying. After the allotted time, offsprings other offsprings will beget,

Plentiful will be the Primitive Workers' numbers, the toil of the Anunnaki they shall bear!

Enki and Ninki, Ninmah and Ningishzidda were joyful, the fruit's elixir they were drinking.

For the seven and seven cages they made, among the trees they placed them;

Let them together grow up, malehoods and femalehoods attain,

Let the males the females inseminate, let them by themselves offspring beget!

So were they to each other saying.

As for Adamu and Ti-Amat, from the toil of the excavations they shall be protected,

Let us them to the Edin bring over, to the Anunnaki therein our handiwork display!

So was Enki to the others saying; with that the others did concur.

To Eridu, in the Edin the city of Enki, Adamu and Ti-Amat were taken,

An abode in an enclosure for them was built, to roam therein they could.

The Anunnaki of the Edin came to see them, from the Landing Place they came.

Enlil came to see them; by the sight his displeasure was diminished.

Ninurta came to see them; Ninlil did as well.

From the way station on Lahmu Marduk the son of Enki also came down to see.

It was a sight most astounding, a wonder of wonders it was to behold!

Your hands have made it, the Anunnaki to the fashioners were saying.

The Igigi who between Earth and Lahmu shuttled were also all agog.

Primitive Workers have been fashioned, our days of toil to end! So were they all saying.

In the Abzu the newborns were growing, for their maturing the Anunnaki were anticipating.

Enki was the supervisor, Ninmah and Ningishzidda also came.

In the excavations the Anunnaki were grumbling, patience to impatience gave way.

Ennugi, their overseer, of Enki was often inquiring; for Primitive Workers the outcry he conveyed.

The circuits of Earth grew in number, maturity of the Earthlings was overdue;

No conceiving among the females was observed, there was no birth-giving!

By the cages among the trees Ningishzidda a couch of grass for himself made;

Day and night the Earthlings he was watching, their doings to ascertain.

Indeed he saw them mating, the males the females were inseminating!

Conceiving there was not, birth-giving there was not.

Enki the matter deeply pondered, the creatures once combined he contemplated;

None, not one of them, had offspring begotten!

By two kinds combined, a curse has been created! Enki to the others said.

Let us the essences of Adamu and Ti-Amat afresh examine! Ningishzidda was saying.

Their ME's bit by bit to be studied, what is wrong to ascertain!

In Shurubak, in the House of Healing, the essences of Adamu and Ti-Amat were contemplated,

With the life essence of Anunnaki males and females they were compared.

Like two entwined serpents Ningishzidda the essences separated,

Arranged like twenty-two branches on a Tree of Life were the essences,

Their bits were comparable, the images and likenesses they properly determined.

Twenty-two they were in number; the ability to procreate they did not include!

Another two bits of the essence in the Anunnaki present Nigishzidda to the others showed.

One male, one female; without them there was no procreating! So was he to them explaining.

In the molds of Adamu and Ti-Amat, in the combining they were not included!

Ninmah heard this and was distraught; with frustration was Enki seized.

The clamor in the Abzu is great, mutiny is again in the making! So was Enki to them saying.

Primitive Workers must be procured lest the gold extracting shall be ceasing!

Ningishzidda, in these matters learned, a solution was proposing;

To his elders, Enki and Ninmah, in the House of Healing he whispered.

They all the heroines who Ninmah were assisting sent away,

They locked the doors behind them, the three with the two
Earthlings alone remaining.

Upon the four others Ningishzidda a deep sleep caused to
descend, the four he made unfeeling.

From the rib of Enki the life essence he extracted,

Into the rib of Adamu the life essence of Enki he inserted;

From the rib of Ninmah the life essence he extracted,

Into the rib of Ti-Amat the life essence he inserted.

Where the incisions were made, the flesh thereon he closed up.

Then the four of them by Ningishzidda were awakened. It is done!
he proudly declared.

To their Tree of Life two branches have been added,

With procreating powers their life essences are now entwined!

Let them freely roam, as one flesh let them know each other!
Ninmah was saying.

In the Edin's orchards, to freely roam Adamu and Ti-Amat were
placed.

Of their nakedness they became aware, of malehood and
femalehood they were knowing.

Ti-Amat of leaves aprons made, from the wild beasts to be
distinguished.

In the heat of the day Enlil in the orchard was strolling, the shade
he was enjoying.

Without expectation Adamu and Ti-Amat he encountered, the
aprons on their loins he noticed.

What is the meaning of this? Enlil wondered; Enki for explaining
he summoned.

The matter of procreation Enki to Enlil explained:

The seven and seven had failed, to Enlil he admitted;

Ningishzidda the life essences examined, an additional combining
was needed!

Great was Enlil's anger, furious his words were:

The whole thing was not to my liking, for acting as Creators I had opposed.

The Being that we need, it already exists! So were you, Enki, saying,

All we need is put our mark on it, thereby Primitive Workers to fashion!

Healing heroines themselves put at risk, Ninmah and Ninki were endangered,

To no avail it was all, your handiwork was a failure!

Now the last bits of our life essence to these creatures you have given,

To be like us in procreation knowing, perchance our life cycles on them to bestow!

Thus did Enlil with angry words speak.

Enki Ninmah and Ningishzidda summoned, with words Enlil to pacify.

My lord Enlil! Ningishzidda was saying. Knowing for procreation they were given,

The branch of Long Living, to their essence tree was not!

Ninmah then spoke up, to her brother Enlil she was saying:

What was the choice, my brother? To end it all in failure, Nibiru in doom to face its fate,

Or to try and try and try, and by procreation let Earthlings the toil undertake?

Then let them be where they are needed! Enlil with anger said.

To the Abzu, away from the Edin, let them be expelled!

Synopsis of the Seventh Tablet

Returned to the Abzu, Adamu and Ti-Amat bear children

Earthlings proliferate, working in the mines and as servants

Enlil's grandchildren, the twins Utu and Inanna, are born

Anunnaki couples bear other offspring on Earth

Climate changes cause hardships on Earth and on Lahmu

Nibiru's orbital nearing is accompanied by upheavals

Enki and Marduk explore the Moon, find it inhospitable

Enki determines the constellations and Celestial Time

Bitter about his own fate, Enki promises supremacy to Marduk

Anu gives command of a new spaceport to Utu, not to Marduk

Enki encounters and mates with two Earthling females

One bears a son, Adapa, the other a daughter, Titi

Keeping his parenting a secret, Enki raises them as foundlings

Adapa, highly intelligent, becomes the first Civilized Man

Adapa and Titi mate, have two sons: Ka-in and Abael

Utu (Shamash) and Inanna (Ishtar)

THE SEVENTH TABLET

To the Abzu, away from the Edin, let them be expelled!

So did Enlil the command decree; from the Edin to the Abzu Adamu and Ti-Amat were expelled.

In an enclosure among the trees Enki them placed; to know each other he left them.

With joy did Enki see what Ningishzidda had done come to be: With child Ti-Amat was frolicking.

Ninmah came the birth-giving to watch: A son and a daughter, twins, to the Earth Beings were born!

With wonderment did Ninmah and Enki watch the newborns,

How they grew and developed was a marvel; days were as months, months to Earth years accumulated.

By the time Adamu and Ti-Amat had other sons and daughters, the first ones were by themselves procreating!

Before one Shar of Nibiru had passed, the Earthlings were proliferating.

With understanding were the Primitive Workers endowed, of commandments they were comprehending;

To be with the Anunnaki they were eager, for food rations they toiled well,

Of heat and dust they did not complain, of backbreaking they did not grumble;

Of the hardships of work the Anunnaki of the Abzu were relieved.

The vital gold to Nibiru was coming, Nibiru's atmosphere was slowly healing;

Earth-Mission to the satisfaction of all was proceeding.

Among the Anunnaki, Those Who from Heaven to Earth Came, there was also espousing and procreation.

The sons of Enlil and Enki, from sisters and half sisters, from healing heroines, took spouses.

To them on Earth sons and daughters were born;

Though by the life cycles of Nibiru were they endowed, by Earth's cycles were they quickened.

Who on Nibiru in diapers would still be, on Earth became a child;

Who on Nibiru began to crawl, when on Earth born was running around.

Special joy there was when to Nannar and Ningal twins were born,

A daughter and a son they were; Inanna and Utu by Ningal they were named.

With them, a third generation of Anunnaki on Earth was present!

For the offspring of the leaders, tasks were allocated;

Some olden chores were divided, easier among the offspring they were made;

To the olden chores, new tasks were added.

Upon the Earth the warmth was rising, vegetation flourished, wild creatures overran the land;

The rains were heavier, rivers were gushing, abodes repairing needed.

Upon the Earth the heat was increasing, the snow white parts to water were melting,

The bars of the seas the oceans were not containing.

From the depths of the Earth volcanoes were fire and brimstones belching,

The grounds were trembling, each time the Earth was shaking.

In the Lower World, the snow white–hued place, the Earth was grumbling;

At the tip of the Abzu, Enki a place for observing established,

To his son Nergal and his spouse Ereshkigal command thereof he
   entrusted.

A thing unknown, an untoward thing, thereunder is brewing!
   Nergal to his father Enki said.

In Nibru-ki, the place of the Bond Heaven–Earth, Enlil the heavenly
   circuits was watching,

By the ME's of the Tablets of Destinies celestial motions he was
   comparing;

There is turmoil in the heavens! Enlil to his brother Enki said.

From the planet Lahmu, the place of the way station, Marduk to
   Enki his father was complaining:

Strong winds are disturbing, annoying dust storms they are raising!

So Marduk to his father Enki words was beaming:

In the Hammered Bracelet, turmoils are occurring!

Upon the Earth, brimstones from the skies were falling.

Pitiless demons havoc causing, violently the Earth they approached,

Into flaming fires in the skies they were bursting.

In a clear day darkness they were causing, with storms and Evil
   Winds they raged around.

Like stony missiles the Earth they were attacking,

Kingu, Earth's Moon, and Lahmu too by these havocs were afflicted,

The faces of all three with countless scars were covered!

Enlil and Enki to Anu the king urgent words were beaming,
   Nibiru's savants they alerted:

The Earth and the Moon and Lahmu a calamity unknown are facing!

From Nibiru the savants were responding; their words the leaders'
   hearts were not calming:

In the heavens the family of the Sun were taking stations,

The celestials of whom Earth is the seventh in a row were choosing
   places.

In the heavens Nibiru was approaching, the Sun's abode it was nearing.

By the seven, in a row arraigned, was Nibiru distracted,

The path through the Hammered Bracelet it was missing,

From the Bracelet bits and pieces it has been displacing!

Bereft of the celestial bar, Lahamu with Mummu near the Sun were crouching,

In the heavens Lahamu her glorious dwelling place was abandoning,

Toward Nibiru the heavenly king she was attracted, a queen of heaven she wished to be!

To quell her, Nibiru from the celestial deep a monstrous demon made appear.

A monster once to Tiamat's host belonging, by the Celestial Battle fashioned,

From the celestial deep made its way, by Nibiru was it from slumber awakened.

From horizon to the midst of heaven like a flaming dragon it was stretched,

One league was its head, fifty leagues in length it was, awesome was its tail.

By day the skies of Earth it darkened,

By night upon the face of the Moon a spell of darkness it cast.

To her brothers, the celestials, Lahamu for help was calling:

Who will the dragon obstruct, who will stop and kill it? she was asking.

Only valiant Kingu, once Tiamat's protector, stepped forward to respond.

To intercept the dragon in its path Kingu was making haste:

Fierce was the encounter, a tempest of clouds upon Kingu was raised;

By its foundations was Kingu shaken, from the impact did the Moon quake and shake.

Then the heavenly havoc was calmed,

Nibiru to its distant abode in the Deep was returning,

Lahamu its dwelling place did not abandon,

The stony missiles upon the Earth and Lahmu ceased their raining.

Enki and Enlil with Marduk and Ninurta gathered, a surveying of the havoc they undertook.

The foundations of the Earth Enki surveyed, of what its platforms had befallen he examined.

The depths of the oceans he measured, in Earth's far corners the mountains of gold and copper he scanned.

Of the vital gold there will be no shortage. Thus was Enki saying.

In the Edin Ninurta was the surveyor, where mountains trembled and valleys shook,

In his skyship he soared and journeyed.

The Landing Platform was intact; in the valleys of the north the Earth fiery liquids was pouring!

So was Ninurta to his father Enlil telling; sulfuric mists and bitumens he was discovering.

On Lahmu the atmosphere was damaged, dust storms were with life and work interfering,

So Marduk to Enki was saying. To Earth return I wish! to his father he disclosed.

Enlil to his olden plans betook himself, what cities and their tasks he planned he reconsidered.

A Chariot Place in the Edin must be established! to the others he was saying.

The olden designs of the layout on the crystal tablet to them he showed.

The conveying from the Landing Place to the way station on Lahmu is no longer certain,

To soar toward Nibiru from Earth we must be able! So was Enlil to them saying.

For the count since the first splashdown, the count of eighty Shars it was.

———·—

Now this is the account of the journey to the Moon by Enki and Marduk,

And how Enki the three Ways of Heaven and the constellations determined.

Let the Place of the Chariots near Bad-Tibira, the Metal City, be established,

Therefrom, let the gold from Earth to Nibiru in the chariots directly be carried!

So Ninurta, of Bad-Tibira the commander, to them words was saying.

Enlil to the words of Ninurta, his son, gave heed; of his son's wisdom he was proud.

To Anu the king Enlil the plan quickly conveyed, to him words he was saying:

Let a Place of Celestial Chariots in the Edin be established,

Near the place where the gold ores are smelted and refined let it be built.

Let the pure gold in the chariots directly from Earth to Nibiru be carried,

Directly to Earth from Nibiru let heroes and supplies be coming!

Of great merit is the plan of my brother! Enki to their father Anu was saying.

A great disadvantage in its core it is holding:

The netpull of Earth is than Lahmu's much greater; to overcome it our powers shall be exhausted!

Before there is rush to deciding, let us an alternative examine:

Nearby the Earth a companion it has, the Moon it is!

Smaller is its netpull, ascent and descent thereon little effort will require.

Let us it as a way station consider, let me and Marduk thereto journey!

The two plans Anu the king before counselors and savants for considering presented.

Let the Moon be first examined! the king they did advise.

Let the Moon be first examined! Anu to Enki and Enlil the decision beamed.

Enki was greatly joyed; the Moon to him always was alluring,

Whether somewhere waters it is hiding, what atmosphere it possesses he did always wonder.

In sleepless nights its silvery cool disk with bewitchment he observed,

Its waxing and waning, a game with the Sun played, a wonder of wonders he deemed.

What secrets from the Beginning it held he wished to uncover.

In a rocketship did Enki and Marduk to the Moon journey;

Thrice they the Earth's companion encircled, the deep wound by the dragon caused they observed.

By many hollows, the handiwork of smashing demons, was the Moon's face marked.

In a place of rolling hills they set the rocketship down, in its midst they landed;

From the place the Earth they could observe, and the expanse of the heavens.

Eagles' helmets they had to don; the atmosphere was for breathing insufficient.

With ease they walked about, in this and that direction they went;

The evil dragon's handiwork was dryness and desolation.

Unlike Lahmu it is, for a way station it is unsuitable! to his father Marduk was saying.

Let us abandon this place, let us to Earth return!

Do not be hasty, my son! So was Enki to Marduk saying.

Are you not by the celestial dance of Earth and Moon and Sun enchanted?

Unobstructed from here is the viewing, the quarter of the Sun is at hand,

The Earth like a globe in the void by nothing is hanging.

With our instruments we can scan the distant heavens,

The handiwork of the Creator of All in this solitude we can admire!

Let us stay, the circuits observe, how the Moon circles the Earth,

How the Earth its circuits around the Sun is making!

So Enki, by the sights agitated, to his son Marduk was saying.

By his father's words Marduk was persuaded; in the rocketship they made their dwelling.

For one circuit of Earth, for three circuits on the Moon they remained;

Its motions about the Earth they measured, the duration of a month they calculated.

For six circuits of Earth, for twelve circuits about the Sun, Earth's year they measured.

How the two were entwined, causing the luminaries to disappear, they recorded.

Then to the Sun's quarter they attention gave, the paths of Mummu and Lahamu they studied.

With the Earth and the Moon, Lahmu the Sun's second quarter constituted,

Six were the celestials of the Lower Waters. So was Enki to Marduk explaining.

Six were the celestials of the Upper Waters, beyond the bar, the Hammered Bracelet, they were:

Anshar and Kishar, Anu and Nudimmud, Gaga and Nibiru; these were the six others,

Twelve were they in all, of twelve did the Sun and its family make the count.

Of the upheavals most recent, Marduk of his father was inquiring:

Why have seven celestials in a row places taken? So was he his father asking.

Their circuits about the Sun Enki then considered;

Their grand band around the Sun, their progenitor, Enki carefully observed,

The positions of Earth and Moon therein on a chart Enki marked out,

By the motions of Nibiru, of the Sun not a descendant, the width of the great band he outlined.

The Way of Anu, the king, to name it Enki decided.

In the expanse of the deep heavens, the stars did father and son observe;

By their proximities and groupings was Enki fascinated.

By the circuit of the heavens, from horizon to horizon, he drew images of twelve constellations.

In the Great Band, the Way of Anu, one each with the Sun's family of twelve he paired,

To each one he designated a station, by names they were to be called.

Then in the heavens below the Way of Anu, whence Nibiru the Sun is approaching,

A bandlike way he designed, the Way of Enki he it designated;

To it twelve constellations by their shapes he also allotted.

The heavens above the Way of Anu, the Upper Tier, the Way of Enlil he called,

Therein too the stars into twelve constellations he assembled.

Thirty-six were the stars' constellations, in the three Ways were they located.

Henceforth, when Nibiru nears and departs, from Earth by the stars' stations its course shall be known,

So will the Earth's position designated as around the Sun it travels!

The start of the cycle, of Celestial Time the measure, Enki to Marduk indicated:

When on Earth I had arrived, the station that was ending by me the Station of the Fishes was named,

The one that followed after my name title, He of the Waters, I called!

So Enki with satisfaction and pride to his son Marduk was saying.

Your wisdon the heavens embraces, your teachings my own understanding extend,

But on Earth and on Nibiru, knowledge and rulership are separated! So did Marduk to his father say.

My son! My son! What is that you do not know, what is it that you are missing? to him Enki was saying.

The secrets of the heavens, the secrets of the Earth with you have I shared!

Alas, my father! Marduk was saying. There was agony in his voice.

When the Anunnaki in the Abzu the toil ceased and the Primitive Worker you set to fashion,

Not my mother but Ninmah, the mother of Ninurta, to assist you was summoned,

Not I but Ningishzidda, of me the younger, to help you was invited,

With them, not with me, your knowledge of life and death did you share!

My son! Enki to Marduk responded. To you command was given of the Igigi and Lahmu to be supreme!

Alas, my father! to him Marduk was saying. Of supremacy by fate we are deprived!

You, my father, are Anu's Firstborn; yet Enlil, not you, is the Legal Heir;

You, my father, were first to splash down and Eridu establish,

Yet Eridu is in Enlil's domain, yours is in the distant Abzu.

I am your Firstborn, by your legitimate spouse on Nibiru was I born,

Yet the gold in the city of Ninurta is assembled, therefrom to send or to withhold,

The survival of Nibiru is in his hands, in my hands it is not.

Now to Earth we are returning; what will my task be,

Am I to fame and kingship fated, or again to humiliated be?

In silence did Enki embrace his son, on the desolate Moon to him a promise made:

Of that of which I have been deprived your future lot shall be!

Your celestial time will come, a station mine adjoining yours shall be!

----·----

Now this is the account of Sippar, the Place of the Chariots in the Edin,

And how the Primitive Workers to the Edin were returned.

For many circuits of the Earth, from the Earth were father and son absent;

On Earth no plans were implemented, on Lahmu the Igigi were in turmoil.

Enlil to Anu secret words conveyed, his concerns to Anu he from Nibru-ki beamed:

Enki and Marduk to the Moon have gone, for countless circuits there they are staying.

Their doings a mystery are, what they are scheming is not known;

Marduk the way station on Lahmu has abandoned, the Igigi are agog,

By dust storms has the way station been affected, what damage there is to us is not known.

The Place of the Chariots in the Edin must be established,

Therefrom the gold directly from Earth to Nibiru to be carried,

No way station on Lahmu shall henceforth be needed;

The plan of Ninurta it is, great in these matters is his understanding,

Let him the Place of the Chariots near Bad-Tibira establish,

Let Ninurta be its first commander!

Anu to the words of Enlil gave much consideration; to Enlil a
response he gave:

Enki and Marduk to Earth are returning;

What about the Moon they have found, let us first to their words
listen!

From the Moon Enki and Marduk departed, to Earth they did return;

Of conditions thereon they gave account; a way station is unfeasible
now! so they reported.

Let the Place of the Chariots be built! Anu was saying.

Let Marduk be its commander! Enki was saying to Anu.

The task is for Ninurta set aside! Enlil with anger shouted.

For the Igigi command is no more needed, of the tasks Marduk
knowledge has,

Of the Gateway to Heaven let Marduk be in charge! So did Enki to
his father say.

Anu the matter with concern contemplated: Rivalries now the sons
have affected!

With wisdom was Anu endowed, with wisdom were his decisions:

The Place of the Chariots for new ways the gold to handle is
designated,

Let us what henceforth comes in the hands of a new generation
place.

Neither Enlil nor Enki, neither Ninurta nor Marduk in command
shall be,

Let the third generation responsibility undertake, let Utu be the
commander!

Let the Place of the Celestial Chariots be built, let Sippar, Bird
City, be its name!

This was the word of Anu; unalterable was the word of the king.

In the eighty-first Shar was the construction started, the plans of
Enlil it followed.

Nibru-ki was in the center, a Navel of the Earth by Enlil it was designated,

As on circles by their place and distances the olden cities were
located,

Like an arrow from the Lower Sea toward the mountains pointing
they were arrayed.

A line on the twin peaks of Arrata, to the skies in the north
reaching, he drew,

Where the pointing arrow the Arrata line intersected,

The place for Sippar, the Earth's Place of the Chariots, he marked out;

To it the arrow directly led, it from Nibru-ki was by an equal circle
precisely located!

Ingenious was the plan, by its precision all were made to wonder.

In the eighty-second Shar was the construction of Sippar completed;

To the hero Utu, of Enlil the grandson, its command was given.

An Eagle's helmet for him was fashioned, with Eagle's wings was
he decorated.

In the first chariot from Nibiru to Sippar directly come, Anu was
traveling;

To view for himself the installations he desired, to marvel at what
was attained he wanted.

For the occasion the Igigi, by Marduk commanded, from Lahmu to
Earth came down,

From the Landing Place and from the Abzu Anunnaki were
assembled.

There was backslapping and hailing, a feast and a celebration.

For Anu Inanna, Enlil's granddaughter, singing and dancing
　　presented;
With affection Anu kissed her; Anunitu, Anu's Beloved, he fondly
　　called her.
Before departing, Anu the heroes and heroines assembled.
A new era has begun! So was he to them saying.
Supplied directly with the golden salvation, forthcoming is the end
　　of toil!
Once enough gold on Nibiru for protecting is piled in storage,
The toil on Earth can be diminished, heroes and heroines to
　　Nibiru will return!
Thus did Anu the king to the assembled promise, a great hope to
　　them he did extend:
A few more Shars of toil, and homeward they shall be bound!
With much pomp did Anu to Nibiru soar back; gold, pure gold,
　　with him was carried.
His new task Utu with cherish performed; Ninurta of Bad-Tibira
　　command retained.
Marduk to Lahmu did not return; with his father to the Abzu he
　　did not go.
Over all the lands he wished to roam, in his skyship the Earth to
　　comprehend,
Of the Igigi, some on Lahmu, some on Earth, Utu was the
　　commander made.
After Anu to Nibiru returned, on Earth the leaders great
　　expectations had:
With renewed vigor to labor, the Anunnaki they expected.
Gold quickly to amass, thereby quicker homebound to be.
That, alas, was not what came to pass!
In the Abzu, relief, not continued toil, was the Anunnaki's expectation,
Now that the Earthlings are proliferating, let them provide the labor!

So were the Anunnaki in the Abzu saying.

In the Edin, the tasks were greater; more abodes, more provisions were required.

For Primitive Workers, to the Abzu confined, did the Edin heroes clamor.

For forty Shars was relief only to the Abzu provided! The heroes in the Edin shouted,

Our toil has increased beyond endurance, let us have the Workers too!

While Enlil and Enki the matter were debating, Ninurta the decision into his hands took:

With fifty heroes an expedition to the Abzu he led, with weapons were they armed.

In the forests and the steppes of the Abzu, the Earthlings they chased,

With nets they them captured, male and female to the Edin they them brought.

To do all manner of chores, in the orchards and in the cities, they trained them.

By the doings was Enki angered, by them was Enlil enraged:

My expelliing of Adamu and Ti-Amat you have overturned! So Enlil to Ninurta said.

Let the mutiny once in the Abzu occurring not in the Edin be repeated!

So to Enlil Ninurta said. With the Earthlings in the Edin, the heroes are becalmed,

A few more Shars, and it will no longer matter! So did Ninurta to Enlil say.

Enlil was not appeased; with grumbling, Let it so be! to his son he said.

Let the gold pile up quickly, let us all to Nibiru soon return!

In the Edin, the Anunnaki the Earthlings with admiration observed:

Intelligence they possessed, of commands they had understanding.

They took over all manner of chores; unclothed they were the
    tasks performing.

Males with females among them were constantly mating, quick
    were their proliferations:

In one Shar, sometimes four, sometimes more, were their generations!

As the Earthlings grew in numbers, workers the Anunnaki had,

With food the Anunnaki were not satiated;

In the cities and in the orchard, in the valleys and in the hills,

The Earthlings for food were constantly foraging.

In those days grains had not yet been brought forth,

There was no ewe, a lamb had not yet been fashioned.

About these matters, Enlil to Enki angry words was saying:

By your doings confusion was created, by you let salvation be devised!

Now this is the account of how Civilized Man was brought about,

How by a secret of Enki Adapa and Titi in the Edin were brought
    forth.

By the proliferation of the Earthlings, Enki was pleased, Enki was
    worried;

The lot of the Anunnaki was greatly eased, their discontent was
    diminished,

By the proliferation the Anunnaki shunned toil, the workers as
    serfs were becoming.

For seven Shars the Anunnaki's lot was greatly eased, diminished
    was their discontent.

By the proliferation of the Earthlings, what by itself was growing
    for all insufficient was;

In three more Shars of fish and fowl there was a shortage, what by
    itself grows Anunnaki and Earthlings did not satiate.

In his heart, Enki a new undertaking was scheming; to create a
  Civilized Mankind in his heart he conceived.

Grains that are sown by them to be cultivated, ewes that become
  sheep let them shepherd!

In his heart Enki a new undertaking was scheming; how this to
  attain he contemplated.

The Primitive Workers in the Abzu he for this scheme observed,

The Earthlings in the Edin, in the cities and in the orchards he
  considered.

What could for the tasks make them suited? What by the life
  essence has not been combined?

The offspring of the Earthlings he observed, an alarming matter he
  noticed:

By their repeated copulations, back toward their wild forebears
  they were degraded!

Enki in the marshlands looked about, on the rivers he sailed and
  observed;

With him was only Isimud, his vizier, who secrets kept.

On the river's bank, bathing and frolicking Earthlings he noticed;

Two females among them were wild with beauty, firm were their
  breasts.

Their sight the phallus of Enki caused to water, a burning desire he
  had.

Shall I not kiss the young ones? Enki his vizier Isimud was asking.

I the boat will hither row, kiss the young ones! Isimud to Enki was
  saying.

The boat thereto Isimud directed, from the boat to dry land Enki
  stepped.

A young one to him Enki called, a tree fruit she to him offered.

Enki bent down, the young one he embraced, on her lips he kissed
  her;

Sweet were her lips, firm with ripeness were her breasts.

Into her womb he poured his semen, in a mating he knew her.

Into her womb she took the holy semen, by the semen of the lord Enki she was impregnated.

The second young one to him Enki called, berries from the field she him offered.

Enki bent down, the young one he embraced, on her lips he kissed her;

Sweet were her lips, firm with ripeness were her breasts.

Into her womb he poured his semen, in a mating he knew her.

Into her womb she took the holy semen, by the semen of the lord Enki she was impregnated.

With the young ones stay, whether pregnancies come about ascertain!

So was Enki to his vizier Isimud saying.

Isimud by the young ones sat down; by the fourth count their bulges appeared.

By the tenth count, the ninth having been completed,

The first young one squatted and birth gave, by her a male child was born;

The second young one squatted and birth gave, by her a female child was born.

At dawn and dusk, which a day delimit, on the same day the two were born,

The Gracious Ones, Dawn and Dusk, thereafter in legends they were known.

In the ninety-third Shar the two, by Enki fathered, in the Edin were born.

Word of the births Isimud to Enki quickly brought.

By the births Enki was ecstatic: Whoever such a thing has ever known!

Between Anunnaki and Earthling, conception was attained,

Civilized Man I have brought into being!

To his vizier Isimud Enki instructions gave: A secret must my deed remain!

Let the newborns by their mothers be suckled; thereafter into my household them bring,

Among the bulrushes in reed baskets have I them found! Thus to all you will say!

By their mothers were the newborns suckled and nurtured;

To Enki's household in Eridu thereafter Isimud them brought.

Among the bulrushes, in reed baskets, have I them found! So did Isimud to all say.

Ninki to the foundlings a liking took, as her own children she raised them.

Adapa, the Foundling, the boy she called; Titi, One with Life, the girl she named.

Unlike all other Earthling children the twosome were:

Slower to grow up than Earthlings they were, much quicker in understanding they were;

With intelligence they were endowed, of speaking with words capable they were.

Beautiful and pleasant was the girl, with her hands she was greatly dexterous;

Ninki, the spouse of Enki, to Titi took a liking; all manner of crafts she was her teaching.

To Adapa Enki himself teachings gave, how to keep records he was him instructing.

The achievements with pride Enki to Isimud was showing,

A Civilized Man have I brought forth! to Isimud he was saying.

A new kind of Earthling from my seed has been created, in my image and after my likeness!

From seed they food will grow, from ewes sheep they will shepherd,

Anunnaki and Earthlings henceforth shall be satiated!

To his brother Enlil Enki word sent; from Nibru-ki to Eridu Enlil came.

In the wilderness a new kind of Earthling has come forth! to Enlil was Enki saying.

Quick of learning they are, knowledge and craftwork to them can be taught.

Let us from Nibiru seeds that are sown bring down,

Let us from Nibiru ewes that sheep become to Earth deliver,

Let us the new breed of Earthlings farming and shepherding teach,

Let Anunnaki and Earthlings together satiated be! So was Enki to Enlil saying.

Akin to us Anunnaki in many ways, indeed they are! Enlil to his brother said.

A wonder of wonders it is, in the wilderness by themselves to have come about!

Isimud was summoned. Among the bulrushes in reed baskets I them found! he said.

Enlil the matter with graveness pondered, with amazement his head he shook.

Indeed a wonder of wonders it is, a new breed of Earthling on Earth has emerged,

A Civilized Man has the Earth itself brought forth,

Farming and shepherding, crafts and toolmaking he can be taught!

So was Enlil to Enki saying. Let us of the new breed to Anu word send!

Of the new breed word to Anu on Nibiru was beamed.

Let seeds that can be sown, let ewes that sheep become, to Earth be sent!

So did Enki and Enlil to Anu the suggestion make.

By Civilized Man let Anunnaki and Earthlings become satiated!

Anu the words heard, by the words he was amazed:

That by life essences one kind to another leads is not unheard of! to them words back he sent.

That on Earth a Civilized Man from the Adamu so quickly appeared, that is unheard of!

For sowing and husbanding, great numbers are needed; perchance the beings to proliferate are unable?

While the savants on Nibiru the matter contemplated,

In Eridu occurrences of import took place:

Adapa in a mating Titi knew, into her womb he poured his semen.

There was conception, there was birth-giving:

To twins, two brothers, Titi gave birth!

Word of the birth to Anu on Nibiru was beamed:

The twosome for conception are compatible, proliferation by them can occur!

Let seeds that are sown, ewes that sheep become, to Earth be delivered,

Let on Earth farming and shepherding begin, let us all be satiated!

So did Enki and Enlil to Anu on Nibiru say.

Let Titi in Eridu remain, the newborns to suckle and nurture,

Let Adapa the Earthling to Nibiru be brought! So did Anu his decision declare.

Synopsis of the Eighth Tablet

Adapa's wide understanding amazes Nibiru's savants
On Anu's orders Adapa is brought to Nibiru
An Earthling's first-ever space journey
Enki reveals Adapa's parenting truth to Anu
Enki justifies his deed by the need for more food
Adapa is sent back to start farming and shepherding
Enlil and Enki create crop seeds and sheep lines
Ninurta teaches Ka-in crop cultivation
Marduk teaches Abael shepherding and woolmaking
Fighting over water, Ka-in strikes and kills Abael
Ka-in is tried for murder, sentenced to exile
Adapa and Titi have other offspring who intermarry
On his deathbed Adapa blesses his son Sati as his heir
A descendant, Enkime, is taken by Marduk to Lahmu

Ninurta and his Divine Eagle symbol

THE EIGHTH TABLET

Let Adapa the Earthling to Nibiru be brought! So did Anu his decision declare.

By the decision Enlil was not pleased: Whoever of this would have thought,

That by a Primitive Worker fashioning, like us the being would become,

With knowledge, endowed, between Heaven and Earth will travel!

On Nibiru the waters of long life he will drink, the food of long life eat,

Like one of us Anunnaki shall the one of Earth become!

So was Enlil to Enki and the other leaders saying.

By the decision of Anu Enki too was not pleased; sullen was his face after Anu had spoken.

After Enlil had spoken, with Enlil his brother Enki agreed:

Indeed, who of this would have thought! So to the others did Enki say.

The brothers sat and contemplated; Ninmah with them was also deliberating.

The command of Anu cannot be avoided! to them she said.

Let Adapa by our young ones to Nibiru be accompanied, his fright to diminish, to Anu things explain!

So did Enki to the others say. Let Ningishzidda and Dumuzi his companions be,

By the way, Nibiru for the first time with their eyes also see!

By Ninmah was the suggestion favored: Our young ones, on Earth born,

Of Nibiru are forgetting, its life cycles by those of Earth are
　　overwhelmed;

Let the two sons of Enki, as yet unmarried, to Nibiru also travel,

Perchance brides there for themselves they shall find!

When the next celestial chamber from Nibiru did arrive in Sippar,

Ilabrat, a vizier of Anu, from the chamber stepped off.

I have come to fetch the Earthling Adapa! So to the leaders he said.

The leaders to Ilabrat Adapa presented; Titi and her sons to him
　　they also showed.

Indeed, in our image and after our likeness they are! So did Ilabrat
　　say.

To Ilabrat Ningishzidda and Dumuzi, sons of Enki, were presented.

To accompany Adapa on his journey they have been selected! to
　　him Enki said.

Anu his grandchildren to see will be pleased! So did Ilabrat say.

To hear instructions, Enki Adapa to him summoned. To Adapa
　　thus he said:

Adapa, to Nibiru, the planet whence we had come, you will be
　　going,

Before Anu our king you will come, to his majesty you will be
　　presented;

Before him you shall bow. Speak only when asked, to questions
　　short answers give!

New clothing you will be given; the new garments put on.

A bread on Earth not found they to you will give; the bread is
　　death, do not eat!

In a chalice an elixir to drink they to you will give; the elixir is
　　death, do not drink!

With you Ningishzidda and Dumuzi my sons will journey, to their
　　words hearken, and you shall live!

So did Enki Adapa instruct. This I shall remember! Adapa said.

Enki Ningishzidda and Dumuzi summoned, to them a blessing and advice he gave.

Before Anu the king, my father, you are coming, to him you shall bow and homage pay;

By princes and nobles do not be cowered, of them you are the equals.

To bring Adapa back to Earth is your mission, by Nibiru's delights be not charmed!

This we shall remember! Ningishzidda and Dumuzi said.

His young one, Dumuzi, Enki embraced, on the forehead he kissed him;

The wise one Ningishzidda Enki embraced, on the forehead he kissed him.

A sealed tablet in the hand of Ningishzidda unseen he placed,

To my father Anu this tablet in secret you shall give! So did Enki to Ningishzidda say.

Then the two with Adapa to Sippar departed, to the Place of the Celestial Chariots they went,

To Ilabrat, Anu's vizier, the three of them themselves presented.

To Ningishzidda and Dumuzi the garb of Igigi was given, like celestial eagles they were dressed.

As for Adapa, his unkept hair was shaven, a helmet as that of an Eagle he was given,

Instead of his loincloth a tight-fitting vestment he was made to wear,

Between Ningishzidda and Dumuzi, inside That Which Ascends he was placed.

When the signal was given, the Celestial Chariot roared and shuddered;

In fright did Adapa cower and cry out: The Eagle without wings is soaring!

Upon his sides Ningishzidda and Dumuzi their arms placed, with soothing words they him calmed.

When one league aloft they were borne, upon the Earth they
glanced out;
Its lands they saw, by seas and oceans into parts separated.
When two leagues aloft they were, the ocean to a tub grew smaller,
the land was the size of a basket.
When three leagues aloft they were, again they cast a glance
whence they had departed;
The Earth was now as a small ball, by a sea of darkness in the
vastness swallowed.
Once again Adapa agitated was; he cowered and cried out: Take me
back! he shouted.
Ningishzidda his hand on the neck of Adapa put; in an instant was
Adapa quiet.
When they on Nibiru landed, there was much curiosity,
The children of Enki, on Earth born, to see, even more so an
Earthling to encounter:
A being from another world on Nibiru has arrived! So were the
crowds shouting.
With Ilabrat to the palace they were taken to be washed and with
perfumed oils anointed.
Fresh and befitting garments they were given;
Heeding Enki's words, Adapa the new clothing did put on.
In the palace nobles and heroes milled about, in the throne room
princes and counselors gathered.
To the throne room by Ilabrat they were led, Adapa behind him,
then the two sons of Enki.
In the throne room before Anu the king they bowed; from his
throne Anu stepped forward.
My grandsons! My grandsons! he cried out. He hugged Dumuzi, he
hugged Ningishzidda,
With tears in his eyes he embraced them, he kissed them.

To his right Dumuzi he bade to be seated, on his left Ningishzidda sat.

Then Ilabrat to Anu the Earthling Adapa presented.

Does he our speech understand? Anu the king of Ilabrat inquired.

Indeed he does, by the lord Enki was he taught! Ilabrat so answered.

Come hither! Anu to Adapa said. What is your name and your occupation?

Forward Adapa stepped, again he bowed: Adapa is my name, of the lord Enki a servant!

So did Adapa in words speak; his speaking great amazement was causing.

A wonder of wonders on Earth has been attained! Anu declared.

A wonder of wonders on Earth has been attained! all the assembled shouted.

Let there a celebration be, let us our guests thus welcome! Anu was saying.

To the banquet room Anu all who were assembled led, to the laden tables he happily gestured.

At the laden tables bread of Nibiru Adapa was offered; he did not eat it.

At the laden tables elixir of Nibiru Adapa was offered; he did not drink it.

By this Anu the king was puzzled, was offended:

Why has Enki to Nibiru this ill-mannered Earthling sent, to him the celestial ways reveal?

Come now, Adapa! to Adapa Anu said. Why did you neither eat nor drink, our hospitality rejected?

My master the lord Enki commanded me: The bread do not eat, the elixir do not drink!

So did Adapa the king Anu answer.

How odd is this thing! Anu was saying. For what has Enki from an Earthling our food and elixir prevented?

He asked Ilabrat, he asked Dumuzi; Ilabrat the answer knew not,
Dumuzi could not explain.

He asked Ningishzidda. Perchance in this lies the answer!
Ningishzidda to Anu said.

The secret tablet that he carried hidden to Anu the king he then gave.

Puzzled was Anu, Anu was concerned; to his private chamber he
went the tablet to decipher.

Now this is the account of Adapa, of Civilized Mankind the
progenitor,

And how by his sons Ka-in and Abael satiation on Earth was started.

In his private chamber Anu the tablet's seal broke open,

Into the scanner the tablet he inserted, its message from Enki to
decipher.

Adapa by my seed to an Earthling woman was born! So did the
message from Enki say.

Likewise was Titi by another Earthling woman of my seed
conceived.

With wisdom and speech they are endowed; with Nibiru's long
lifetime they are not.

The bread of long-living he should not eat, the elixir of long life he
should not drink.

To live and die on Earth Adapa must return, mortality his lot
must be,

By the sowing and shepherding by his offspring on Earth satiation
shall be!

So did Enki the secret of Adapa to his father Anu reveal.

By the secret message from Enki Anu was astounded; whether to
angry be or laugh he knew not.

Ilabrat his vizier to his private chamber he summoned, to him he
thus said:

That son of mine Ea, even as Enki his free ways with females has not mended!

To Ilabrat his vizier the message on the tablet he showed.

What are the rules, what is the king to do? of his vizier Anu inquired.

Concubines by our rules are permitted; of interplanetary cohabitation no rules exist!

So did Ilabrat to the king respond. If damage there be, let it be restricted,

Let Adapa forthwith to Earth be returned, let Ningishzidda and Dumuzi longer stay!

Anu then Ningishzidda to his private chamber summoned;

Know you what your father's message said? of Ningishzidda he inquired.

Ningishzidda his head lowered, with whispering voice he said:

I know not, but guess I can. The life essence of Adapa I have tested, of Enki's seed he is!

That indeed is the message! to him Anu said. Adapa to Earth forthwith shall return,

To be of Civilized Man a progenitor his destiny shall be!

As for you, Ningishzidda, to Earth with Adapa you shall return

Of Civilized Mankind at your father's side to become the teacher!

So did Anu the king the decision make, the destiny of Adapa and Ningishzidda he determined.

To the assembled savants and nobles, princes and counselors Anu and the other two returned,

To the assembled words of decision Anu announced:

The welcome to the Earthling must not be overextended, on our planet he cannot eat or drink;

Of his astounding abilities we have all seen, let him to Earth return,

Let his offspring there on Earth fields till and in meadows shepherd!

To ensure his safety and avoid his agitation, Ningishzidda with him back will travel,

With him the seeds of Nibiru of grains which multiply to Earth will be sent;

Dumuzi, the youngest, for a Shar with us shall stay,

Then to Earth with ewes and the essence of sheep he shall return!

This was the decision of Anu, to the king's words all in agreement their heads bowed.

At the appointed time Ningishzidda and Adapa to the Place of the Celestial Chariots were taken,

Anu and Dumuzi, Ilabrat and counselors, nobles and heroes to them farewell bade.

There was roaring and shuddering, and the chariot was lofted;

The planet Nibiru grow smaller they saw, then from horizon to zenith the heavens they saw.

On their journey Ningishzidda to Adapa the planet gods explained.

Of Sun and Earth and the Moon to him lessons he gave,

Of how the months chase one another and how Earth's year is counted him he taught.

When to Earth they returned, to his father Enki Ningishzidda all that had happened related.

Enki laughed and struck his loins: It all went as I expected! with glee he said;

Except the detention of Dumuzi, that is to me a puzzle! So did Enki say.

By the prompt return of Ningishzidda and Adapa Enlil was greatly puzzled,

What is the matter, what on Nibiru transpired? of Enki and Ningishzidda he inquired.

Let Ninmah too be summoned, let her too of what transpired hear! Enki to him said.

After Ninmah arrived, to Enlil and to her Ningishzidda all did tell.

Enki his cohabitation with the Earthling females also related;

No rules have I broken, our satiation I have ensured! So Enki to them said.

No rules did you break, the fates of Anunnaki and Earthlings by a rash deed you determined!

So did Enlil in anger say. Now the lot is cast, destiny by fate is overtaken!

With fury was Enlil seized, with anger he turned and left them standing.

To Eridu Marduk came, by his mother Damkina was he summoned.

The odd ongoings to verify of his father and brother he demanded.

To keep the secret from Marduk hidden father and brother decided;

Anu by the Civilized Man was enthralled, to at once all on Earth satiate he commanded!

So they to Marduk only part of the truth revealed.

By Adapa and Titi Marduk was impressed, to the boys he took a liking.

While Ningishzidda Adapa is instructing, let me the boys' teacher be!

So did Marduk to his father Enki and to Enlil say.

Let Marduk teach one, let Ninurta teach the other! to them Enlil responded.

In Eridu Ningishzidda with Adapa and Titi stayed, numbers and writing Adapa he taught.

The twin who was first in birth Ninurta to Bad-Tibira, his city, took,

Ka-in, He Who in the Field Food Grows, he called him.

To dig canals for watering he taught him, sowing and reaping he was teaching.

A plow from the wood of trees Ninurta for Ka-in made, with it a tiller of the land to be.

The other brother, son of Adapa, by Marduk to the meadows was taken,

Abael, He of the Watered Meadows, his name was thereafter called.

How to build stalls Marduk him taught; for shepherding to start, the return of Dumuzi they awaited.

When the Shar was completed, Dumuzi to Earth returned,

The essence seed of sheep, ewes for the growing with him he brought,

Four-legged animals of Nibiru to another planet, the Earth, he conveyed!

His return with essence seed and ewes was cause for much celebration,

Into the care of his father Enki Dumuzi with his precious cargo returned.

The leaders then got together, how to proceed with the new breed they considered:

Never before was there a ewe on Earth, a lamb has never to Earth from the heavens been dropped,

A she-goat has never before to her kid given birth,

Weaving of sheep's wool has never before been established!

The Anunnaki leaders, Enki and Enlil, Ninmah and Ningishzidda, who the creators were,

A Creation Chamber, a House of Fashioning, to establish decided.

Upon the pure mound of the Landing Place, in the Cedar Mountains, it was established,

Near where the elixir seeds by Ninmah brought were planted there was the Creation Chamber established,

There was the multiplying of the grains and of the ewes on Earth begun.

Of Ka-in for sowing and reaping Ninurta was the mentor,

Of Abael the arts of ewe and lamb rearing and shepherding
    Marduk was the mentor.

When the first crops were reaped, when the first sheep matured,

Let there be a Celebration of Firsts! Enlil a decree proclaimed.

Before the assembled Anunnaki the first grains, the first lambs
    were presented,

At the feet of Enlil and Enki Ka-in, by Ninurta guided, his offering
    placed;

At the feet of Enlil and Enki Abael, by Marduk guided, his offering
    placed.

Enlil to the brothers gave a joyful blessing, their labors he extolled.

Enki his son Marduk embraced, the lamb for all to see he raised,

Meat for eating, wool for wearing to Earth have come! Enki said.

———•◦•———

Now this is the account of the generations of Adapa,

And the killing of Abael by Ka-in, and what thereafter transpired.

After the Celebration of Firsts was over, sullen was Ka-in's face;

By the lack of Enki's blessing greatly he was aggrieved.

As to their tasks the brothers returned, Abael before his brother
    was boasting:

I am the one who abundance brings, who the Anunnaki satiates,

Who gives strength to the heroes, who wool for their clothing
    provides!

Ka-in by his brother's words was offended, to his boasting strongly
    he objected:

It is I who the plains luxuriates, who furrows with grains makes
    heavy,

In whose fields birds multiply, in whose canals fish become abundant,

Sustaining bread by me is produced, with fish and fowl the
    Anunnaki's diet I variate!

On and on the twin brothers each other disputed, through the wintertime they argued.

When summer began it was not raining, the meadows were dry, the pastures dwindled.

Into the fields of his brother Abael his flocks drove, from the furrows and the canals to drink water.

By this Ka-in was angered; to move the flocks away his brother he commanded.

Farmer and shepherd, brother and brother, words of accusation uttered.

They spat on each other, with their fists they fought.

Greatly enraged, Ka-in a stone picked up, with it he Abael in the head struck.

Again and again he hit him until Abael fell, his blood from him gushing.

When Ka-in his brother's blood saw, Abael, Abael, my brother! he shouted.

Motionless on the ground did Abael remain, from him his soul had departed.

By the brother whom he had killed Ka-in remained, for a long time he sat crying.

Titi it was who of the killing was the first to know by a premonition:

In a dream-vision as she was sleeping Abael's blood she saw, in the hand of Ka-in it was.

Adapa from his sleep she awakened, her dream-vision to him she told.

A heavy sorrow fills my heart, did something terrifying happen?

So did Titi to Adapa say; greatly agitated she was.

In the morning the two from Eridu departed, to the whereabouts of Ka-in and Abael they went.

In the field they found Ka-in, by the dead Abael he was still seated.

A great cry of agony Titi shouted, Adapa spread mud on his head.

What have you done? What have you done? to Ka-in they shouted.

Silence was Ka-in's answer; to the ground he threw himself and wept.

To Eridu city Adapa returned, what had happened to the lord Enki he told.

With fury Enki Ka-in confronted. Accursed you shall be! to him he said.

From the Edin you must depart, among Anunnaki and Civilized Earthlings you shall not stay!

As to Abael, in the fields his body cannot for the wild birds remain;

As the Anunnaki custom is, he in a grave, below a stone pile, shall be buried.

How Abael to bury Enki to Adapa and Titi showed, for the custom to them was not known.

For thirty days and thirty nights was Abael by his parents mourned.

To Eridu for judgment Ka-in was brought, the exile sentence to pronounce Enki wished.

For his deed, Ka-in himself must be slain! So did Marduk with anger say.

Let the Seven Who Judge be assembled! So did Ninurta, of Ka-in the mentor, say.

Whoever of such an assembling ever heard! Marduk shouted,

That for one not from Nibiru Anunnaki leaders shall to judge be called?

Is it not enough that one by Ninurta mentored the one by me favored has killed?

Is it not that as Ninurta Anzu did vanquish, so did Ka-in against his brother rise?

Like the fate of Anzu Ka-in's fate should be, his life-breath to be extinguished!

So did Marduk in anger to Enki, Enlil, and Ninurta say.

Ninurta by the words of Marduk was saddened; silence, not words, his answer was.

Let me with Marduk my son words in private have! to them Enki said.

When in Enki's private chambers he and Marduk were,

My son! My son! to Marduk Enki softly spoke. Your agony is great. Let us not agony with agony compound!

A secret that on my heart has heavily emburdened let me to you tell!

Once upon a time, as by the river I strolled, two Earthling maidens my fancy caught,

By them from my seed were Adapa and Titi conceived,

A new kind of Earthling, a Civilized Man, by that upon the Earth was brought;

Whether they to procreate were able our king Anu in doubt was,

By the birth of Ka-in and Abael were Anu and the council on Nibiru convinced.

A new phase of Anunnaki presence on this planet was welcomed and approved;

Now that Abael has been slain, and if Ka-in too shall be extinguished,

Satiation to an end would come, mutinies will be repeated, all that was achieved shall crumble!

No wonder that to Abael a liking you took, the son of your half brother he was!

Now, on the other one have pity, let the line of Adapa survive!

So did Enki with sadness a secret to Marduk his son reveal.

By the revelation Marduk was at first astounded, then by laughter he was overcome:

Of your lovemaking prowess much to me was rumored, now of that convinced I am!

Indeed, let Ka-in's life be spared, to the ends of the Earth let him be banished!

So did Marduk, from anger to laughter changing, to his father say.

In Eridu judgment upon Ka-in by Enki was pronounced:

Eastward to a land of wandering for his evil deed Ka-in must depart,

That his life must be spared, he and his generations shall be distinguished!

By Ningishzidda was the life essence of Ka-in altered:

That his face a beard should not grow, Ka-in's life essence Ningishzidda changed.

With his sister Awan as a spouse Ka-in from the Edin departed, to the Land of Wandering he set his course.

Now the Anunnaki sat and among themselves wondered:

Without Abael, without Ka-in, who shall for us the grains grow and bread make,

Who shall be the shepherd, the ewes multiply, wool for clothing provide?

Let by Adapa and Titi more proliferation be! So did the Anunnaki say.

With the blessing of Enki, Adapa his spouse Titi knew again and again;

One daughter, another daughter, each time again and again were born.

In the ninety-fifth Shar, a son Adapa and Titi finally had;

Sati, He Who Life Binds Again, Titi him named; by him were the generations of Adapa counted.

In all, thirty sons and thirty daughters Adapa and Titi had,

Of them tillers of the land and shepherds for the Anunnaki toiled,

By them did satiation to Anunnaki and Civilized Earthlings come back.

In the ninety-seventh Shar, to Sati a son by his spouse Azura was born.

By the name Enshi in the annals he was recorded; Master of
Humanity meant his name.

By Adapa his father writing and numbers he was made to
understand,

And who the Anunnaki were and all about Nibiru by Adapa Enshi
was told.

To Nibru-ki by the sons of Enlil he was taken; secrets of the
Anunnaki him they taught.

How the perfumed oils for anointing Nannar, Enlil's on Earth the
eldest, him showed,

How the elixir from the Inbu fruits to prepare Ishkur, Enlil's
youngest, him instructed.

It was since then that by Civilized Man the Anunnaki lords were
called.

And of the rites of worship of the Anunnaki that the beginning was.

Thereafter to Enshi by his sister Noam a son was born;

Kunin, He of the Kilns, his name had the meaning.

For by Niburta in Bad-Tibira he was tutored, of furnace and kiln
there he learned,

How with bitumens fires to make, how to smelt and refine he was
taught;

In the smelting and refining of gold for Nibiru he and his offspring
toiled.

In the ninety-eighth Shar did this matter come about.

———•——

Now this is the account of the generations of Adapa after Ka-in was
exiled,

And the heavenly journeys of Enkime and the death of Adapa.

In the ninety-ninth Shar to Kunin a son was born,

By Mualit, a half sister of Kunin, he was conceived.

Malalu, He Who Plays, she named him; in music and song he excelled.

For him Ninurta a stringed harp made, a flute for him he shaped;

Hymns to Ninurta Malalu played, with his daughters before Ninurta they sang.

The spouse of Malalu the daughter of his father's brother was, Dunna was her name.

In the one hundredth Shar since the count on Earth had begun,

A son to Malalu and Dunna was born, their firstborn he was;

Irid, He of the Sweet Waters, his mother Dunna him named.

Him Dumuzi how wells to dig had taught, for flocks in distant meadows water to provide.

It was there, by the wells in the meadows, that shepherds and maidens gathered,

Where espousing and proliferation by Civilized Mankind exceedingly abounded.

In his days the Igigi to Earth were more frequently coming.

To observe and see from the heavens they increasingly abandoned,

To watch and see what on Earth was transpiring they increasingly desired;

To be with them on Lahmu Enki Marduk beseeched,

To watch and see what on Earth was transpiring Marduk more fervently wished.

At a well in the meadows did Irid his spouse meet;

Baraka was her name, the daughter of his mother's brother she was.

At the conclusion of the hundred and second Shar a son to them was born,

By the name Enki-Me, by Enki ME Understanding, in the annals he was called.

Wise and intelligent he was, numbers he quickly understood,

About the heavens and all matters celestial he was constantly curious.

To him the lord Enki took a liking, secrets once to Adapa revealed to him he told.

Of the family of the Sun and the twelve celestial gods Enki him was teaching,

And how the months by the Moon were counted and the years by the Sun,

And how by Nibiru the Shars were counted, and how the counts by Enki were combined,

How the lord Enki the circle of the heavens to twelve parts divided,

A constellation to each one how Enki assigned, twelve stations in a grand circle he arranged,

How to honor the twelve Anunnaki great leaders by names the stations were called.

To explore the heavens Enkime was eager; two celestial journeys he did make.

And this is the account of Enkime's journeys to the heavens,

And how the Igigi troubles and intermarriages by Marduk were started.

To be with Marduk in the Landing Place Enkime was sent,

From there Marduk in a rocketship to the Moon did him take.

There what Marduk from his father Enki had learned to Enkime he did teach.

When to Earth Enkime returned, to be with Utu in Sippar, the Place of the Chariots, he was sent.

There a tablet for writing what he was learning by Utu to Enkime was given,

Utu in his bright abode a Prince of Earthlings him installed.

The rites him he taught, the functions of priesthood to begin.

In Sippar with his spouse Edinni, a half sister, Enkime resided,

To them in the one hundred and fourth Shar a son was born,

Matushal his mother him named, Who by the Bright Waters
Raised the name meant.

It was after that that Enkime on his second journey to the heavens
went,

This time too Marduk was his mentor and companion.

In a celestial chariot heavenward they soared, toward the Sun and
away from it they circled.

To visit the Igigi on Lahmu by Marduk he was taken,

To him the Igigi a liking took, of Civilized Earthlings from him
they learned.

Of him it is in the Annals said that to the heavens he departed,

That in the heavens he stayed till the end of his days.

Before Enkime for the heavens departed, all that in the heavens he
was taught.

In writings Enkime a record made, for his sons to know he wrote it;

All that is in the heavens in the family of the Sun he wrote down,

And about the quarters of the Earth and its lands and its rivers too.

To the hands of Matushal, his firstborn son, the writings he
entrusted,

With his brothers Ragim and Gaidad to study and abide by.

In the one hundred and fourth Shar was Matushal born,

To the Igigi troubles and what Marduk had done he was a witness.

By his spouse Ednat a son to Matushal was born, Lu-Mach, Mighty
Man, was his name.

In his days conditions on Earth became harsher; the toilers in field
and meadow raised complaints.

As a workmaster the Anunnaki Lu-Mach appointed, the quotas to
enforce, the rations to reduce.

In his days it was that Adapa his deathtime attained;

And when Adapa knew that his days to an end were coming,

Let all my sons and sons of sons assemble themselves to me! he said,

That before I die I may bless them, and words to them speak before I die.

And when Sati and the sons of the sons had gathered,

Where is Ka-in, my firstborn? Adapa of them all asked. Let him be fetched! to them all he said.

Before the lord Enki Sati his father's wish presented, what to be done of the lord he asked.

Enki then Ninurta summoned: Let the banished one, of whom the mentor you were, to Adapa's deathbed be brought!

In his Bird of Heaven Ninurta betook himself, to the Land of Wandering he flew;

Over the lands he roamed, from the skies for Ka-in he searched.

And when he him found, like on Eagle's wings Ka-in to Adapa he brought.

When of his son's arrival Adapa was informed, Let Ka-in and Sati before me come! Adapa said.

Before their father the two came, Ka-in the firstborn on the right, Sati on the left.

And the eyesight of Adapa having failed, for recognition his sons' faces he touched;

And the face of Ka-in on the right was beardless, and the face of Sati on the left with beard was.

And Adapa put his right hand on the head of Sati, the one on the left,

And he blessed him and said: Of your seed shall the Earth be filled,

And of your seed as a tree with three branches Mankind a Great Calamity shall survive.

And he put his left hand on the head of Ka-in on his right, and to him said:

For your sin of your birthright you are deprived, but of your seed seven nations shall come,

In a realm set apart they shall thrive, distant lands they shall inhabit;

But having your brother with a stone killed, by a stone will be your end.

And when Adapa finished these words saying, his hands dropped and he sighed and said:

Now summon my spouse Titi and all the sons and all the daughters,

And after my spirit leaves me, to my birthplace by the river carry me,

And with my face toward the rising Sun there bury me.

Like a wounded beast Titi cried out, to her knees by Adapa's side she fell.

And the two sons of Adapa, Ka-in and Sati, in a cloth his body wrapped,

In a cave by the banks of the river, by Titi shown, Adapa they buried.

In the midst of the ninety-third Shar was he born, by the end of the one hundred and eighth he died.

A long life for an Earthling he had; the life cycle of Enki he did not have.

And after Adapa was buried, Ka-in to his mother and brother farewell bade.

Ninurta in his Bird of Heaven to the land of wandering him returned.

And in a distant realm Ka-in had sons and daughters,

And he for them a city built, and as he was building, by a falling stone he was killed.

In the Edin Lu-Mach as a workmaster the Anunnaki served,

In the days of Lu-Mach did Marduk and the Igigi with Earthlings intermarry.

Synopsis of the Ninth Tablet

Mankind proliferates; Adapa's line serves as royalty

Defying Enlil, Marduk espouses an Earthling female

Celestial disturbances and climate changes affect Lahmu

The Igigi descend to Earth, seize Earthling females as wives

The promiscuous Enki begets a human son, Ziusudra

Droughts and pestilences cause suffering on Earth

Enlil sees it as fated retribution, wants to return home

Ninmah, aged by Earth's cycles, also wants to return

A mystery emissary warns them not to defy their destiny

Signs increase of a coming calamitous Deluge

Most Anunnaki begin to depart back to Nibiru

Enlil enforces a plan to let Mankind perish

Enki and Ninmah start to preserve Earth's Seeds of Life

The remaining Anunnaki prepare for the Day of the Deluge

Nergal, Lord of the Lower World, is to issue the warning

Enki divulges the secret of the Deluge

THE NINTH TABLET

In the days of Lu-Mach did Marduk and the Igigi with Earthlings intermarry.

In those days on Earth the hardships were increasing,

In those days on Lahmu with dryness and dust was the planet enveloped.

The Anunnaki who decree the fates, Enlil and Enki and Ninmah, with each other consulted.

What conditions on Earth and on Lahmu were altering, they wondered.

On the Sun flarings they observed, in the netforces of Earth and Lahmu there were disruptions.

In the Abzu, at the tip the Whiteland facing, instruments for observing they installed;

In the charge of Nergal, the son of Enki, and his spouse Ereshkigal the instruments were put.

To the Land Beyond the Seas Ninurta was assigned, in the mountainland a Bond Heaven–Earth to establish.

On Lahmu the Igigi were restless; to pacify them Marduk was the task given:

Until what are the hardships causing, the way station on Lahmu must be kept! So to Marduk the leaders said.

The three who the fates decree with each other consulted;

They looked at each other. How old the others are! each one of the others thought.

Enki, who the death of Adapa was grieving, was the first one to speak.

More than one hundred Shars since my arrival have passed! to his brother and sister he said.

I was then a dashing leader; now bearded, tired, and old I am!

An enthusiastic hero I was, for command and adventure ready! Enlil then said.

Now I have children who have children, all on Earth born;

Old on Earth we became, but those on Earth born are even older sooner!

So did Enlil to his brother and sister ruefully say.

As for me, an old sheep they call me! So did Ninmah wistfully say.

While the others have been coming and going, turns on Earth to serve taking,

We the leaders have stayed and stayed! Perchance it is time to leave! So did Enlil say.

Of that did I often wonder, to them Enki was saying. Each time one of us three to revisit Nibiru wished,

Word from Nibiru always our coming thereto prevented!

Of that I too did wonder, Enlil was saying: Is it a thing on Nibiru, a thing on Earth?

Perchance the life cycles that differ it concerns, so was Ninmah saying.

To watch and see what transpires, the three leaders decided.

At that time Fate, or was it Destiny? in its hands the matters took.

For it came to pass that soon thereafter Marduk to his father Enki came,

A matter of gravity with his father Enki to discuss he wished.

Upon the Earth the three sons of Enlil spouses have chosen:

Ninurta Ba'u, of Anu a young daughter, has espoused; Nannar has chosen Ningal, Ishkur Shala has taken;

By Nergal your son Ereshkigal, of Enlil a granddaughter, as a spouse was taken,

By threats to kill her, her consent from her was extracted.

To await my espousal, being your firstborn, Nergal did not await,

The other four in deference my espousal are awaiting.

A bride I wish to choose, to have a spouse it is my desire!

So did Marduk to his father Enki say.

Your words happy make me! Enki to Marduk was saying. Your
mother too shall rejoice!

To hold his words to Ninki, Marduk with a raised hand to his
father motioned.

Is she one of the young ones who heal and succor give? Enki went
on to ask.

A descendant of Adapa she is, of Earth, not Nibiru, is she! Marduk
softly whispered.

With a puzzled look, Enki was speechless; then uncontrolled words
he shouted:

A prince of Nibiru, a Firstborn to succession entitled, an Earthling
will espouse?!

Not an Earthling but your own offspring! to him Marduk said.

A daughter of Enkime who to heaven was taken she is, Sarpanit is
her name!

Enki his spouse Ninki summoned, to her what with Marduk
transpired he related.

To Ninki, his mother, Marduk his heart's desire repeated and said:

When Enkime with me was journeying, and of heaven and Earth
him I was teaching,

What my father once had said, I with my own eyes witnessed:

Step by step on this planet a Primitive Being, one like us to be, we
have created,

In our image and in our likeness Civilized Earthling is, except for
the long life, he is we!

A daughter of Enkime my fancy caught, her to espouse I wish!

Ninki her son's words pondered. And the maiden, does she your gaze appreciate? So did she Marduk ask.

Indeed she does, Marduk to his mother said.

This is not the matter to consider! Enki with a raised voice said.

If our son this shall do, to Nibiru with his spouse he would never go,

His princely rights on Nibiru he forever will forsake!

To this Marduk with a bitter laughter responded: My rights on Nibiru are nonexistent,

Even on Earth my rights as Firstborn have been trampled.

This indeed is my decision: From prince a king on Earth become, the master of this planet!

Let it so be! Ninki said. Let it so be! Enki also said.

They summoned Matushal, the bride's brother; of Marduk's wish they him told.

Humbled but with joy overwhelmed Matushal was. Let it so be! he said.

When of the decision Enlil was told, with fury he was seized.

It was one thing for the father with Earthlings intercourse have,

It is another matter for the son an Earthling to espouse, lordship on her to bestow!

When Ninmah of the matter was told, greatly disappointed she was.

Marduk any maiden of ours could espouse, even from my own daughters by Enki he could choose,

Half sisters, as is the royal custom, he could espouse! So did Ninmah say.

With fury Enlil to Anu on Nibiru of the matter words beamed up:

Too far has this behavior gone, it cannot be allowed! to Anu the king Enlil said.

On Nibiru Anu the counselors summoned, the matter with urgency to discuss.

In the rule books of such a matter no rule they found.

Anu the savants also summoned, the matter's consequences to discuss.

On Nibiru Adapa, the maiden's progenitor, could not stay! to Anu they were saying.

Therefore to return to Nibiru with her, Marduk forever must be barred!

Indeed, having to Earth cycles become accustomed, even without her Marduk's return impossible might be!

So were the savants to Anu saying; with that the counselors too agreed.

Let the decision to Earth be beamed! Anu was saying: Marduk marry can,

But on Nibiru a prince he shall no more be!

The decision by Enki and Marduk was accepted, Enlil too to the word from Nibiru bowed.

Let there be a wedding celebration, in Eridu let it be! Ninki to them said.

In the Edin Marduk and his bride cannot stay! Enlil, the commander, announced.

Let us to Marduk and his bride a wedding gift make,

A domain of their own, away from the Edin, in another land! So did Enki to Enlil say.

Of Marduk being sent away Enlil with consent to himself was thinking:

To what land, of what domain, are you speaking? Enlil to his brother Enki said.

A domain above the Abzu, in the land that the Upper Sea reaches,

One that by waters from the Edin is separated, that by ships can be reached!

So did Enki to Enlil say. Let it so be! Enlil said.

In Eridu a wedding celebration Ninki for Marduk and Sarpanit arranged.

Her people by the sound of a copper drum the ceremony announced,

With seven tambourines her sisters the bride to her spouse presented.

A great multitude of Civilized Earthlings in Eridu assembled, like a coronation to them the wedding was.

Young Anunnaki also attended, Igigi from Lahmu in great numbers came.

To celebrate our leader's wedding, of Nibiru and Earth a union, to witness we came!

So did the Igigi their arrival in large numbers explain.

———•·•———

Now this is the account of how the Igigi the daughters of the Earthlings abducted,

And how afflictions followed and Ziusudra oddly was born.

In a great number did the Igigi from Lahmu to Earth come,

Only one third of them on Lahmu stayed, to Earth came two hundred.

To be with their leader Marduk, his wedding celebration to attend, was their explanation;

Unbeknownst to Enki and Enlil was their secret: To abduct and have conjugation was their plot.

Unbeknownst to the leaders on Earth, a multitude of the Igigi on Lahmu got together,

What to Marduk permitted is from us too should not be deprived! to each other they said.

Enough of suffering and loneliness, of not offspring ever having! was their slogan.

During their comings and goings between Lahmu and Earth,

The daughters of the Earthlings, the Adapite Females as them they called,

They saw and after them they lusted; and to each other the plotters said:

Come, let us choose wives from among the Adapite Females, and children beget!

One among them, Shamgaz his name was, their leader became.

Even if none of you agrees, I alone the deed shall do! to the others he said.

If a penalty for this sin shall be imposed, I alone for all of you shall it bear!

One by one others in the plot joined together, by an oath together to do it they swore.

By the time of Marduk's wedding, two hundred of them on the Landing Place descended,

Upon the great platform in the Cedar Mountains they came down.

From there to Eridu they journeyed, among the toiling Earthlings they passed,

Together with the Earthling throng in Eridu they arrived.

After the wedding ceremony of Marduk and Sarpanit had taken place,

By a signal prearranged Shamgaz to the others a sign gave.

An Earthling maiden each one of the Igigi seized, by force they them abducted,

To the Landing Place in the Cedar Mountains the Igigi with the females went,

Into a stronghold the place they made, to the leaders a challenge they issued:

Enough of deprivation and not having offspring! The Adapite daughters to marry we wish.

Your blessing to this you must give, else by fire all on Earth destroy we will!

Alarmed the leaders were, of Marduk, the Igigi commander, charge to take they demanded.

If in the matter I a solution must seek, with the Igigi my heart in agreement is!

So did Marduk to the others say. What I have done from them cannot be deprived!

Enki and Ninmah their heads shook, with begrudging agreement they voiced.

Only Enlil was enraged without pacification:

One evil deed by another has been followed, fornication from Enki and Marduk the Igigi have adopted,

Our pride and sacred mission to the winds have been abandoned,

By our own hands this planet with Earthling multitudes shall be overrun!

With much disgust was Enlil speaking. Let the Igigi and their females from Earth depart!

On Lahmu conditions unbearable have become, surviving is not possible!

So did Marduk to Enlil and Enki say.

In the Edin they cannot remain! Enlil with anger shouted. With much disgust the gathering he left;

In his heart things against Marduk and his Earthlings was Enlil plotting.

Upon the Landing Platform in the Cedar Mountains were the Igigi and their females secluded,

Children there to them were born, Children of the Rocketships they were called.

Marduk and Sarpanit his spouse also had children, Asar and Satu were the first two sons called.

To the domain above the Abzu, to him and Sarpanit granted, Marduk the Igigi invited,

To dwell in two cities that for his sons he had built, Marduk the Igigi summoned.

Some of the Igigi and their offspring to the domain in the dark-hued land came;

On the Landing Platform in the Cedar Mountains Shamgaz and others did remain,

To the far eastlands, lands of high mountains, some of their offspring went.

How Marduk of Earthlings his strength increases, Ninurta carefully observed.

What are Enki and Marduk scheming? to his father Enlil Ninurta said.

The Earth by the Earthlings inherited will be! Enlil to Ninurta said.

Go, the offspring of Ka-in find, with them a domain of your own prepare!

To the other side of Earth Ninurta went; the offspring of Ka-in he found.

How tools to make and music to play he them taught,

How in mining to engage and smelt and refine he showed them,

How to build rafts of balsam trees he showed them, to cross a great sea he them guided.

In a new land a domain they established, a city with twin towers there they built.

A domain beyond the seas it was, the mountainland of the new Bond Heaven–Earth it was not.

In the Edin Lu-Mach was the workmaster, quotas to enforce was his duty,

The Earthlings' rations to reduce was his task.

His spouse was Batanash, the daughter of Lu-Mach's father's brother she was.

Of a beauty outstanding she was, by her beauty was Enki charmed.

Enki to his son Marduk a word did send: To your domain Lu-Mach do summon,

How by Earthlings a city to build there him teach!

And when Lu-Mach to the domain of Marduk was summoned,

To the household of Ninmah, in Shurubak, the Haven City, his
spouse Batanash he brought,

From the angry Earthling masses protected and safe to be.

Thereafter Enki his sister Ninmah in Shurubak was quick to visit.

On the roof of a dwelling when Batanash was bathing

Enki by her loins took hold, he kissed her, his semen into her
womb he poured.

With a child Batanash was, her belly was truly swelling;

To Lu-Mach from Shurubak word was sent: To the Edin return, a
son you have!

To the Edin, to Shurubak, Lu-Mach returned, to him Batanash the
son showed.

White as the snow his skin was, the color of wool was his hair,

Like the skies were his eyes, in a brilliance were his eyes shining.

Amazed and frightened was Lu-Mach; to his father Matushal he
hurried.

A son unlike an Earthling to Batanash was born, by this birth greatly
puzzled I am!

Matushal to Batanash came, the newborn boy he saw, by his likeness
amazed he was.

Is one of the Igigi the boy's father? Of Batanash Matushal the truth
demanded;

To Lu-Mach your spouse whether this boy his son is, the truth
reveal!

None of the Igigi is the boy's father, of this upon my life I swear!
So did Batanash him answer

To his son Lu-Mach Matushal then turned, a calming arm on his
shoulders he put.

A mystery the boy is, but in his oddness an omen to you is revealed,

Unique he is, for a task unique by destiny he was chosen.

What that task is, I know not; in time appropriate, known it shall become!

So was Matushal to his son Lu-Mach saying; to what on Earth was transpiring, he was alluding:

In those days the sufferings on Earth were increasing,

The days colder grew, the skies their rains were holding back,

Fields their crops diminished, in the sheepfolds ewe lambs were few.

Let the son to you born, unusual as he is, an omen be that a respite is coming!

So did Matushal to his son Lu-Mach say. Let Respite be his name!

To Matushal and Lu-Mach Batanash her son's secret did not reveal;

Ziusudra, He of Long Bright Lifedays, she called him; in Shurubak he was raised.

Ninmah on the child her protection and affection bestowed.

Of much understanding he was endowed, with knowledge he was by her provided.

Enki the child greatly adored, to read the writings of Adapa him he taught,

The priestly rites how to observe and perform the boy as a young man learned.

In the one hundred and tenth Shar was Ziusudra born,

In Shurubak he grew up and espoused Emzara, and she bore him three sons.

In his days the sufferings on Earth intensified; plagues and starvations the Earth afflicted.

———·•·———

Now this is the account of Earth's tribulations before the Deluge,

And how the mysterious Galzu decisions of life and death in secret guided.

By the conjugations of Igigi and the Earthling daughters was Enlil greatly disturbed,

By Marduk's espousal of an Earthling female Enlil was much distraught.

In his eyes the Anunnaki mission to Earth had become perverted,

To him the howling, shouting Earthling masses an anathema became;

Oppressive the pronouncements of the Earthlings have become,

The conjugations of sleep deprive me! So did Enlil to the other leaders say.

In the days of Ziusudra plagues and pestilences the Earth afflicted,

Aches, dizziness, chills, fevers the Earthlings overwhelmed.

Let us the Earthlings curing teach, how themselves to remedy to learn! So did Ninmah say.

This by decree I forbid! Enlil to her pleas retorted.

In the lands whereto the Earthlings have spread, waters from their sources did not rise,

The earth shut its womb, vegetation did not sprout.

Let us the Earthlings pond- and canal-building teach, let them from the seas fish and sustenance obtain!

So did Enki to the other leaders say.

This by decree I forbid! Enlil to Enki said. Let the Earthlings by hunger and pestilence perish!

For one Shar the Earthlings ate the grasses of the fields,

For the second Shar, the third Shar, the vengeance of Enlil they suffered.

In Shurubak, Ziusudra's city, the suffering unbearable was becoming.

To Eridu Ziusudra, of the Earthlings a spokesman, journeyed,

To the house of the lord Enki he made his way, by the name of his lord he called,

For help and salvation to him he pleaded; Enki by Enlil's decrees was bound.

In those days the Anunnaki for their own surviving were concerned;

Their own rations were diminished, by Earth's changes they themselves afflicted became.

On Earth as on Lahmu the seasons their regularity lost.

For one Shar, for two Shars, from Nibiru the heavenly circuits were studied,

Oddities in the planetary destinies from Nibiru were observed.

On the Sun's face black spots were appearing, from its face flames shot up;

Kishar also was misbehaving, its host its footings lost, dizzying were their circuits.

The Hammered Bracelet was by unseen netforces pulled and pushed,

For reasons unfathomed, the Sun its family was upsetting;

The destinies of the celestials by unsavory fates were overtaken!

On Nibiru the savants alarms raised, in the public squares the people gathered;

The Creator of All, to primordial days the heavens is returning,

Angry is the Creator of All! voices from amongst the people shouted.

On Earth the tribulations were increasing, fear and famine their heads reared.

For three Shars, for four Shars the instruments the Whiteland facing were observed,

By Nergal and Ereshkigal odd rumblings in the Whiteland's snows were recorded:

The snow-ice that the Whiteland covers to sliding has taken! So did they from Abzu's tip report.

In the Land Beyond the Seas, Ninurta in his haven foretelling instruments established,

Quakes and jitters at the Earth's bottom with the instruments he noticed.

An odd matter is afoot! So did Enlil to Anu on Nibiru words of alarm send.

For the fifth Shar, for the sixth Shar the phenomena gained strength,

On Nibiru the savants an alarm raised, of calamities to the king they forewarnings gave:

The next time Nibiru the Sun shall be nearing, Earth to Nibiru's netforce exposed shall be,

Lahmu in its circuits on the Sun's other side shall a station take.

From the netforce of Nibiru Earth in the heavens protection shall not have,

Kishar and its host agitated shall be, Lahamu shall also shake and wobble;

In Earth's great Below, the snow-ice of the Whiteland its footing is losing;

The next time Nibiru the closest to Earth shall approach,

The snow-ice off the Whiteland's surface shall come a-sliding.

A watery calamity it shall cause: By a huge wave, a Deluge, the Earth will be overwhelmed!

On Nibiru great was the consternation, uncertain about Nibiru's own fate,

King, savants, and counselors about Earth and Lahmu also greatly worried.

The king and the counselors a decision made: for evacuating Earth and Lahmu to prepare!

In the Abzu the gold mines shut down, therefrom the Anunnaki to the Edin came;

In Bad-Tibira smelting and refining ceased, all gold to Nibiru was lofted.

Empty, for evacuating ready, a fleet of fast celestial chariots to Earth returned;

On Nibiru the heavenly signs were watched, on Earth the tremors recorded were.

It was at that time that from one of the Celestial Chariots a white-haired Anunnaki stepped off,

Galzu, Great Knower, was his name.

With steps majestic to Enlil his way he made, to him a sealed message from Anu he presented.

I am Galzu, emissary plenipotentiary of King and Council, to Enlil he said.

By his coming Enlil was surprised: No word from Anu of that did forecome.

Enlil the seal of Anu examined; unbroken and authentic it was.

In Nibru-ki the message tablet was read, its encoding was trustworthy.

For King and Council Galzu speaks, his words are my command! So did the message from Anu state.

That Enki and Ninmah be also summoned was Galzu's request.

When they came, to Ninmah Galzu pleasantly smiled. Of the same school and age we are! to her he said.

This Ninmah could not recall; the emissary was as young as a son, she was as his olden mother!

Simple is the explanation! Galzu to her said: By our winter's slumbered life cycles it is caused!

Indeed, this matter is of my mission a part; about the evacuation it is a secret.

Ever since Dumuzi on Nibiru had stayed, returning Anunnaki on Nibiru examined were;

Those who on Earth the longest stayed by the returning harshly were afflicted:

Their bodies to Nibiru's cycles were accustomed no longer,

Their sleep was disturbed, their eyesight was failing, the netforce of Nibiru weighted their walk.

Their minds were also affected, as sons were older than the parents they had left!

Death, my comrades, to the returnees quickly came; of that I am here a warning to give!

The three leaders, on Earth the longest, by the words silent became.

Ninmah was the first to speak: That much was to be expected! she was saying.

Enki, the wise one, to her words consented: That much was clear! he said.

Enlil with anger was seized: Before, the Earthlings like us were becoming,

Now we as Earthlings have become to this planet imprisoned!

This whole mission to a nightmare turned, by Enki and his Earthlings from masters, slaves we were made!

To the outburst Galzu with compassion listened. Indeed much there is to ponder, he said,

On Nibiru much thinking and soul-searching deep questions were raising:

Should Nibiru to its fate been left, whatever by the Creator of All intended, to be let to happen,

Or was the coming to Earth by the Creator of All conceived, and we only unwitting emissaries?

Of that, my comrades, the debate will continue! So was Galzu to them saying.

Now this is the secret command from Nibiru:

The three of you on Earth will remain; only to die to Nibiru you will return!

In celestial chariots, the Earth encircling, the calamity you shall outwait;

To each of the other Anunnaki, a choice to leave or the calamity outwait must be given.

The Igigi who Earthlings espoused must between departure and spouses choose:

No Earthling, Marduk's Sarpanit included, to Nibiru to journey is allowed!

For all who stay and what happens see, in celestial chariots they safety must seek!

As for all the others, to depart for Nibiru forthwith they ready must be!

So did Galzu Nibiru's commands to the leaders in secret reveal.

————•—————

Now this is the account of how the Anunnaki to abandon Earth decided,

And how an oath they took Mankind to let in the Deluge perish.

In Nibru-ki Enlil a council of Anunnaki and Igigi commanders summoned,

The leaders' sons and their children also were present.

Word of the impending calamity Enlil to them as a secret revealed.

To a bitter end Earth Mission has come! to them he solemnly said.

All who to leave wish in celestial boats that are ready to Nibiru will be evacuated,

But if Earthling spouses they have, without the spouses they must leave.

Igigi who to their spouses and offspring attached are, let them to the highest peaks on Earth escape!

As for a few of us Anunnaki who will choose to stay, in Boats of Heaven in Earth's skies will we remain,

The calamity to outwait, the fate of Earth to witness!

As the commander, I shall be the first one to stay! So was Enlil saying.

By their own choice will be the others!

With my father I choose to stay, the calamity to face! So did
Ninurta announce.

To the Lands Beyond the Oceans after the Deluge I will return!

Nannar, Enlil's on Earth firstborn, an odd wish announced:

The Deluge to outwait not in Earth's skies but on the Moon; that
was his wish.

Enki an eyebrow raised; Enlil, though puzzled, approved.

Ishkur, Enlil's youngest, to remain on Earth with his father his decision made.

Utu and Inanna, Nannar's children who on Earth were born, to
stay declared.

Enki and Ninki, to stay and Earth not abandon chose; proudly they
so announced.

The Igigi and Sarpanit I shall not desert! Marduk with anger stated.

One by one Enki's other sons their choice to stay announced:
Nergal and Gibil, Ninagal and Ningishzidda and Dumuzi too.

All eyes to Ninmah then turned; with pride her choice to stay she
declared:

My lifework is here! The Earthlings, my created, I shall not abandon!

By her words Anunnaki and Igigi to a clamor were stirred; about
the Earthlings' fate they inquired.

Let the Earthlings for the abominations perish; so did Enlil proclaim.

A wonderous Being by us was created, by us saved it must be, Enki
to Enlil shouted.

To this Enlil with his own shouted words retorted:

From the very beginning, at every turn, the decisions by you
modified were!

To Primitive Workers procreating you gave, to them Knowing you
endowed!

The powers of the Creator of All into your hands you have taken,

Thereafter even that by abominations you fouled.

With fornication Adapa you conceived, Understanding to his line you gave!

His offspring to the heavens you have taken, our Wisdom with them you shared!

Every rule you have broken, decisions and command you ignored,

Because of you by a Civilized Earthling brother a brother murdered,

Because of Marduk your son the Igigi like him with Earthlings intermarried.

Who is lordly from Nibiru, to whom the Earth alone belongs, to no one is no longer known!

Enough! Enough! to all that I say. The abominations cannot continue!

Now that a calamity by a destiny unknown has been ordained,

Let what must happen, happen! So did Enlil angrily proclaim;

That all leaders solemnly swear to let events unhindered occur, of all Enlil demanded.

First to take the oath of silence was Ninurta; others of Enlil's side followed.

Nergal of Enki's sons was first to take the oath; others of Enki's sons followed.

To your command I bow! Marduk to Enlil said. But of what worth is the swearing?

If Igigi their spouses will abandon, would not the fear among the Earthlings spread?

Ninmah was in tears; the words of the oath she faintly whispered.

Enlil at his brother Enki gazed. It is the wish of king and council! to him he said.

Why will you bind me with an oath? Enki his brother Enlil asked.

The decision by you was made, on Earth it is a commandment!

The floodwaters I cannot arrest, the Earthling multitudes I cannot save,

To what oath to bind me you therefore desire? So did Enki his brother ask.

To let it all happen as if by fate decreed, let it as Enlil's Decision be known,

On Enlil alone let the responsibility forever rest! So did Enki to all pronounce.

Then Enki from the assembly departed; Marduk with him also left.

With quick words of command Enlil the assembly to order brought.

Tasks for what was to be done he with firm decisions assigned,

Between those who will depart and those who will stay the grouping arrange,

Places for assembly to designate, equipment to collect, chariots to assign.

First to depart were those who to Nibiru were returning,

With much embracing and the locking of arms, in joy mixed with sorrow, the celestial boats they boarded;

One after the other the vehicles from Sippar roared aloft.

At first those left behind Journey safely! shouted, then muted were the cries.

After the launchings toward Nibiru completed were,

The turn of Marduk and the Igigi with Earthling spouses came;

Marduk them all on the Landing Place assembled, a choice to them he gave:

With him and Sarpanit and two sons and the daughters to Lahmu go, there the calamity outwait,

Or to distant mountainlands on Earth disperse, a haven from the Deluge to find.

Enlil then of those who remained took account, by groupings to them chariots he assigned.

Ninurta to the mountainlands beyond the oceans Enlil directed on Earth's rumblings to report;

To Nergal and Ereshkigal, the task the Whiteland to watch Enlil assigned;

To guard against an onrush of Earthlings, to Ishkur the task Enlil
gave,

To bar access, barrier and bolt to erect and bolster.

Of all preparations Sippar, the Place of the Celestial Chariots, was
the center;

To Sippar Enlil the Tablets of Destinies from Nibru-ki moved, a
temporary Bond Heaven–Earth was there established.

His brother Enki Enlil then addressed, to him he was thus saying:

However if ever the calamity might be survived, let all that had
happened be remembered.

Let us tablets of records in Sippar, in the depths of the Earth, safely
bury,

Let what from one planet on another done in days to come
uncovered be!

Enki his brother's words with approving accepted. ME's and other
tablets in golden chests they stored,

In the depths of the Earth, in Sippar, for posterity they buried.

Thus ready, for the signal to depart the leaders awaited,

The approach of Nibiru in its great circuit with apprehension they
watched.

It was at that time of anxious waiting that Enki his sister Ninmah
addressed,

To her was Enki thus saying:

In his preoccupation with the Earthlings, of all other living
creatures Enlil lost attention!

When the avalanche of waters sweeps over the lands,

Other living creatures, some by us from Nibiru originated, most
from Earth itself evolved,

In one sudden swoop to an extinction shall be doomed.

Let us, you and me, their seed of life preserve, their life essences
for safekeeping extract!

Ninmah, she who gave life, to the words of Enki favor gave:

I shall do it in Shurubak, you do so with the Abzu's living creatures! So to Enki she said.

While the others sat idly waiting, Enki and Ninmah a challenging task undertook;

Ninmah in Shurubak by some of her female assistants was helped,

Enki by Ningishzidda in the Abzu, at the olden House of Life, was assisted.

Male and female essences and life-eggs they collected,

Of each kind two by two, two by two they in Shurubak and the Abzu preserved,

For safekeeping while in Earth circuit to be taken, thereafter the living kinds to recombine.

At that time word from Ninurta came: Earth's rumblings ominous are!

At that time word from Nergal and Ereshkigal came: The Whiteland is shaken!

In Sippar all the Anunnaki gathered, the Day of the Deluge they awaited.

Synopsis of the Tenth Tablet

The mystery emissary appears to Enki in a dream-vision
Enki is told to save Mankind through his son Ziusudra
By subterfuge Enki directs Ziusudra to build a submarine
A navigator comes aboard, bringing Earth's seeds of life
Nibiru's approach causes the Whiteland's icesheet to slip
The resulting tidal wave engulfs the Earth with water
The remaining Anunnaki bewail the calamity from Earth orbit
The waters recede; Ziusudra's boat rests on Mount Salvation
Descending in a Whirlwind, Enlil discovers Enki's duplicity
Enki convinces Enlil it was destined by the Creator of All
They use the surviving Landing Platform as a temporary base
In a Creation Chamber there, crops and cattle are fashioned
Abundant gold is discovered in the Lands Beyond the Seas
New space facilities are established in the olden lands
They include two artificial mounds and a lion-shaped carving
Ninmah offers a peace plan to resolve erupting rivalries

Cattle and grains are granted to Mankind

THE TENTH TABLET

In Sippar all the Anunnaki gathered, the Day of the Deluge they awaited.

It was at that time, as the tension of awaiting was mounting,

That the lord Enki, asleep in his quarters, had a dream-vision.

In the dream-vision there appeared the image of a man, bright and shining like the heavens;

And as the man Enki approached, Enki saw that the white-haired Galzu he was!

In his right hand an engraver's stylus he was holding,

And in his left hand a tablet of lapis lazuli, shining smooth, he held.

And as he approached near enough by Enki's bed to stand, Galzu spoke up and said:

Unwarranted your accusations against Enlil were, for only the truth he spoke;

And the decision that as Enlil's Decision will be known, not he but Destiny decreed.

Now into your hands Fate take, for the Earthlings the Earth will inherit;

Summon your son Ziusudra, without breaking the oath to him the coming calamity reveal.

A boat that the watery avalanche can withstand, a submersible one, to build him tell,

The likes of which on this tablet to you I am showing;

Let him in it save himself and his kinfolk,

And the seed of all that is useful, be it plant or animal, also take;

That is the will of the Creator of All!

And Galzu, in the dream-vision, with the stylus on the tablet an image drew,

And placed the engraved tablet by the side of Enki's bed;

And after that the image faded, the dream-vision ended, and Enki with a shudder awoke.

In his bed Enki for a while lying remained, with wonder the dream-vision he pondered:

What was thereof the meaning, what omen did it hold?

Then, as off his bed he stepped, lo and behold there was the tablet;

What in a mere dream-vision he had seen now by his bedside materially was!

With trembling hands the lord Enki the tablet picked up,

A design of a curious-shaped boat upon the tablet he saw,

By the tablet's edge measuring markings there were, the boat's measures indicating!

Astir with awe and hope the lord Enki by sunrise for his emissaries quickly sent,

Find the one called Galzu, to him I must speak! So to them he said.

By sundown all came back, to Enki thus reporting: None Galzu to find was able,

Galzu, they said, to Nibiru did long ago return!

Greatly baffled Enki was, the mystery and its omen to understand he strove.

Unravel the mystery he could not, yet the message to him was clear!

That night to the reed hut where Ziusudra was sleeping Enki stealthily went;

The oath not breaking, the lord Enki not to Ziusudra but to the hut's wall spoke:

Wake up! Wake up! to the reed wall Enki was saying, from behind the reed screen he was speaking.

When Ziusudra by the words was awakened, to him Enki from behind the reed screen said:

Reed hut, reed hut! To my words pay attention, to my instructions heed pay!

On all the habitations, over the cities, a calamitous storm will sweep,

The destruction of Mankind and its offspring it will be.

This is the final ruling, the word of the assembly by Enlil convened,

This is the decision by Anu and Enlil and Ninmah spoken.

Now heed my words, observe the message that to you I am speaking:

Abandon your house, build a boat; spurn possessions, save the life!

The boat that you must build, its design and measurements on a tablet are shown,

By the reed hut's wall the tablet I shall leave.

Make sure that the boat shall be roofed throughout, the sun from the inside must not be seen.

The tackle must be very strong, the pitch strong and tight to ward off the water.

Let the boat be one that can turn and tumble, the watery avalanche to survive!

In seven days build the boat, into it your family and kinfolk gather,

In the boat food and water for drinking heap up, household animals also bring.

Then, on the appointed day, a signal to you shall be given;

A boatguide who knows the waters, by me appointed, to you that day will come;

On that day the boat you must enter, its hatch tightly close you must.

An overwhelming Deluge, coming from the south, lands and life shall devastate;

Your boat from its moorings it shall lift, the boat it shall turn and tumble.

Fear not: To a safe haven the boatguide will navigate you,

By you shall the seed of Civilized Mankind survive!

When Enki's voice fell silent, agog was Ziusudra, on his knees
prostrate he fell:

My lord! My lord! he shouted. Your voice I heard, let me see your
face!

Not to you, Ziusudra, have I spoken, to the reed wall did I speak!
So Enki said.

By Enlil's decision, by an oath upheld am I bound to that all the
Anunnaki swore;

If my face you shall see, surely like all Earthlings you will die!

Now reed hut, to my words pay heed:

The purpose of the boat, a secret of the Anunnaki with you must
remain!

When the townspeople will inquire, to them you will so say:

The lord Enlil with my lord Enki has angry been,

To Enki's abode in the Abzu I am sailing, perchance Enlil will be
appeased!

For a while a silence followed. Ziusudra from behind the reed wall
came,

A tablet of lapis lazuli, in the moonlight shining, he saw and
picked up;

The image of a boat upon it was drawn, notches its measurements
gave;

Wisest of Civilized Men was Ziusudra, what he had heard he
understood.

In the morning, to the townspeople he so announced:

The lord Enlil with the Lord Enki, my master, angry has been,

On that account to me the lord Enlil is hostile.

In this city I no longer reside can, nor in the Edin my foot
anymore set;

To the Abzu, the lord Enki's domain, I will there a-sailing go.

In a boat that must quickly be built I will away from here depart;

Thereby the lord Enlil's anger will subside, hardships will end,

Upon you the lord Enlil abundance henceforth will shower!

The morning was not yet gone when the people about Ziusudra gathered,

To speedily for him the boat build they each other encouraged.

Timbers of boat-wood the elders were hauling, the little ones bitumen from the marshes carried.

As woodworkers the planks together hammered, Ziusudra in a cauldron the bitumen melted.

With bitumen the boat he waterproofed inside and out,

As in the drawing upon the tablet the boat on the fifth day was completed.

Eager to see Ziusudra depart, the townspeople to the boat food and water brought,

From their own mouths sustenance they took; to appease Enlil they were in a hurry!

Four-legged animals into the boat were also driven, birds from the field by themselves flew in.

Into the boat Ziusudra his spouse and sons made embark, their wives and children also came.

Any who to the abode of the lord Enki wish to go, let them too aboard come!

So did Ziusudra to the gathered people announce.

Envisioning Enlil's abundance, only some of the craftsmen the call heeded.

On the sixth day Ninagal, Lord of the Great Waters, to the boat came,

A son of Enki he was, to be the boat's navigator he was selected.

A box of cedarwood in his hands he held, by his side in the boat he kept it;

The life essences and life eggs of living creatures it contains, by the lord Enki and Ninmah collected,

From the wrath of Enlil to be hidden, to life resurrect if Earth be
willing!

So did Ninagal to Ziusudra explain; thus were all beasts by their
twos in the boat hidden.

Now Ninagal and Ziusudra in the boat the arrival of the seventh
day awaited.

In the one hundred and twentieth Shar was the Deluge awaited,

In the tenth Shar in the life age of Ziusudra was the Deluge
forthcoming,

In the station of the Constellation of the Lion was the avalanche
looming.

———•◦•———

Now this is the account of the Deluge that over the Earth swept

And how the Anunnaki escaped, and how Ziusudra in the boat
survived.

For days before the Day of the Deluge the Earth was rumbling,
groan as with pain it did;

For nights before the calamity struck, in the heavens Nibiru as a
glowing star was seen;

Then there was darkness in daytime, and at night the Moon as
though by a monster was swallowed.

The Earth began to shake, by a netforce before unknown it was
agitated.

In the glow of dawn, a black cloud arose from the horizon,

The morning's light to darkness changed, as though by death's
shadow veiled.

Then the sound of a rolling thunder boomed, lightnings the skies
lit up.

Depart! Depart! Utu to the Anunnaki gave the signal.

Crouched in the boats of heaven, the Anunnaki heavenward were
lofted.

In Shurubak, eighteen leagues away, the bright eruptions by
    Ninagal were seen:
Button up! Button up the hatch! Ninagal to Ziusudra shouted.
Together the trapdoor that the hatch concealed they pulled down;
Watertight, enclosed completely, was the boat; inside not a ray of
    light penetrated.
On that day, on that unforgettable day, the Deluge with a roar
    began;
In the Whiteland, at the Earth's bottom, the Earth's foundations
    were shaking;
Then with a roar to a thousand thunders equal, off its foundations
    the icesheet slipped,
By Nibiru's unseen netforce it was pulled away, into the south sea
    crashing.
One sheet of ice into another icesheet was smashing,
The Whiteland's surface like a broken eggshell was crumbling.
All at once a tidal wave arose, the very skies was the wall of waters
    reaching.
A storm, its ferocity never before seen, at the Earth's bottom began
    to howl,
Its winds the wall of water were driving, the tidal wave northward
    was spreading;
Northward was the wall of waters onrushing, the Abzu lands it was
    reaching.
Therefrom toward the settled lands it traveled, the Edin it
    overwhelmed.
When the tidal wave, the wall of waters, Shurubak reached,
The boat of Ziusudra the tidal wave from its moorings lifted,
Tossed it about, like a watery abyss the boat it swallowed.
Though completely submerged, the boat held firm, not a drop of
    water into it did enter.

Outside the storm's wave the people overtook like a killing battle,

No one his fellow man could see, the ground vanished, there was only water.

All that once on the ground stood by the mighty waters away was swept;

Before day's end the watery wall, gathering speed, the mountains overwhelmed.

In their celestial boats the Anunnaki the Earth were circling.

Crowding the compartments, against the outer walls they crouched,

What was happening upon the Earth, down below, to see they strained.

From the celestial boat in which she was, Ninmah like a woman in travail cried out:

My created like drowned dragonflies in a pond the waters fill,

All life by the rolling sea wave away was taken! Thus did Ninmah cry and moan.

Inanna, who was with her, also cried and lamented:

Everything down below, all that lived, has turned into clay!

Thus did Ninmah and Inanna weep; they wept and eased their feelings.

In the other celestial boats the Anunnaki by the sight of unbridled fury were humbled,

A power greater than theirs they with awe those days witnessed.

For the fruits of Earth they hungered, for fermented elixir they thirsted.

The olden days, alas, to clay have turned! So to each other the Anunnaki said.

After the immense tidal wave that over the Earth swept,

The sluices of heaven opened, a downpour from the skies upon the Earth was unleashed.

For seven days the waters from above with the waters of the Great Below were mingled;

Then the wall of water, its limits reaching, its onslaught ceased,

But the rains from the skies for forty more days and nights continued.

From their perches the Anunnaki looked down: Where there were dry lands, now was a sea of water,

And where mountains once to the heavens their peaks raised,

Their tops now like islands were in the waters;

And all that on the dry lands was living in the avalanche of waters perished.

Then, as in the Beginning, the waters to their basins were gathered,

Waving back and forth, day by day the water level came lower.

Then, forty days after the Deluge over the Earth swept, the rains also stopped.

After the forty days Ziusudra the boat's hatch opened, his whereabouts to survey.

A bright day it was, a gentle breeze was blowing;

All alone, with no other sign of life, the boat upon a vast sea was lolling.

Mankind, all living things, off the Earth's face are wiped out,

No one except us few survived, but there is no dry land to set a foot upon!

So did Ziusudra to his kinfolk say as he sat down and lamented.

At that time Ninagal, by Enki appointed, the boat toward the twin peaks of Arrata directed,

A sail for her he shaped, toward the Mount of Salvation he the boat guided.

Impatient Ziusudra was; birds that were on board he released

To check for dry land, for surviving vegetation to verify he sent them.

He sent forth a swallow, he sent forth a raven; both to the boat returned.

He sent forth a dove; with a twig from a tree to the boat it returned!

Now Ziusudra knew that the dry land from under the waters had emerged.

A few more days, and the boat by rocks was arrested:

The Deluge is over, at the Mount of Salvation we are! So did Ninagal to Ziusudra say.

Opening the watertight hatch, from the boat Ziusudra emerged;

The sky was clear, the Sun was shining, a gentle wind was blowing.

Hurriedly upon his spouse and children he to come out called.

The lord Enki let us praise, to him thanks give! to them Ziusudra said.

With his sons stones he gathered, with them an altar he built,

Then a fire on the altar he lit, with aromatic incense he made a fire.

A ewe-lamb, one without blemish, for a sacrifice he selected,

And upon the altar to Enki the ewe-lamb as a sacrifice he offered.

At that time Enlil from his celestial boat to Enki words conveyed:

Let us in Whirlwinds from the celestial boats upon the peak of Arrata descend,

The situation to review, what to be done to determine!

While the others in their celestial boats the Earth to circuit continued,

Enlil and Enki in Whirlwinds upon the peak of Arrata descended.

Smiling the two brothers met, with joy their arms they locked.

Then Enlil by the whiffs of fire and roasting meat was puzzled.

What is that? to his brother he shouted. Has anyone the Deluge survived?

Let us go and see! meekly to him Enki responded.

In their Whirlwinds to the other peak of Arrata they flew over,

The boat of Ziusudra they saw, by the altar that he had built they landed.

When Enlil the survivors saw, Ninagal among them, his fury no bounds had.

Every Earthling had to perish! he with fury shouted; at Enki with anger he lunged,

To kill his brother with his bare hands he was ready.

He is no mere mortal, my son he is! Enki, to Ziusudra pointing, cried out.

For a moment Enlil was hesitating. You broke your oath! at Enki he shouted.

To a reed wall I spoke, not to Ziususdra! Enki said, then to Enlil the dream-vision related.

By then, by Ninagal alerted, Ninurta and Ninmah in their Whirlwinds also touched down;

When the account of events they heard, Ninurta and Ninmah by the account were not angered.

The survival of Mankind the will of the Creator of All must be! So did Ninurta to his father say.

Ninmah her necklace of crystals, a gift of Anu, touched and swore:

On my oath, the annihilation of Mankind shall never be repeated!

Relenting, Enlil by the hands Ziusudra and Emzara his spouse took and blessed them thus:

Be fruitful and multiply, and the Earth replenish!

Thus were the Olden Times ended.

————•◦•————

Now this is the account of how survival on Earth was restored,

And how a new source of gold and other Earthlings beyond the oceans were found.

It was after the encounter at Arrata that the waters of the Deluge to recede continued,

And the face of the Earth gradually from under the waters was showing.

The mountainlands were mostly unscathed, but the valleys under mud and silt were buried.

From the celestial boats and from the Whirlwinds the Anunnaki
the landscapes surveyed:

All that in the Olden Times in the Edin and the Abzu had existed
under the mud was buried!

Eridu, Nibru-ki, Shurubak, Sippar, all were gone, completely
vanished;

But in the Cedar Mountains the great stone platform in the sunlight glistened,

The Landing Place, in the Olden Times established, was still
standing!

One after another the Whirlwinds upon the platform landed;

The platform was intact; at the launch corner the huge stone blocks
held firm.

Clearing debris and tree branches away, the first to land to the
chariots signaled;

One after the other the celestial chariots came, upon the platform
they touched down.

Then to Marduk on Lahmu and Nannar on the Moon words were
sent,

And they too to Earth returned, upon the Landing Place they came
down.

Now the Anunnaki and Igigi who were thus gathered by Enlil to
assembly were called.

The Deluge we have survived, but the Earth is devastated! So did
Enlil to them say.

All ways to recover we must assess, be it on Earth, be it elsewhere!

Lahmu by the passage of Nibiru was devastated! So did Marduk
relate:

Its atmosphere was sucked out, its waters thereafter evaporated, a
place of dust storms it is!

The Moon by itself life cannot sustain, only with Eagle masks is
staying enabled!

So did Nannar to the others account give, and then words of enamor he added:

Once there, that it was Tiamat's host's leader one must recall,

Of Earth a companion it is, with it Earth's destiny is connected!

Lovingly Enlil on his son's shoulders his arm put. With survival now we are concerned!

So did Enlil to Nannar mildly retort; now, sustenance is our first concern!

Let us the sealed Creation Chamber examine; perchance Nibiru's seeds we shall still find!

So did Enlil to Enki say, of the grains once created him reminding.

At the side of the platform, clearing some mud, the shaft from times remote they found,

The stone that blocked it they lifted off, the sanctuary they entered.

The diorite chests with seals were fastened, the seals with a copper key they made open.

Inside the chests, in crystal vessels, the seeds of Nibiru's grain were there!

Once outside, to Ninurta Enlil the seeds gave, to him he was thus saying:

Go, the mountainside terrace, let the grains of Nibiru once again bread provide!

In the Cedar Mountains, on other mountains too, Ninurta water-falls dammed,

Terraces constructed, the eldest son of Ziusudra to raise crops he taught.

To Ishkur, his youngest, Enlil another task assigned:

Where the waters have receded, go and remaining fruit-bearing trees find!

To him as fruit cultivator Ziusudra's youngest son was assigned:

The first fruit they found, the vine that by Ninmah was brought it was;

Of its juice, as the Anunnaki's elixir renowned, Ziusudra took a sip.

By one sip, then another and another, Ziusudra was overpowered, like a drunkard he fell asleep!

Then a gift to Anunnaki and Earthlings Enki presented:

The chest that Ninagal had carried he unveiled, its surprising contents to all he announced:

The life essences and life eggs, in the wombs of the four-legged animals from Ziusudra's boat can be combined,

Sheep for wool and meat will multiply, cattle for milk and hides will all have,

Then with other living creatures the Earth we shall replenish!

To Dumuzi the shepherding tasks Enki gave, in the task was Ziusudra's middle son assisting.

Then to the dark-hued landmass, where his and his sons' domains had been, Enki his attention turned.

With Ninagal, at the confluence of mighty waters the mountains he dammed,

Fierce waterfalls to a lake he channeled to let the waters as a lake accumulate.

Then the lands between the Abzu and the Great Sea with Marduk he surveyed:

Where habitations once were, the river's valley how to drain he considered.

At midstream where the river's waters cascaded, an island from the waters he raised.

In its bowels twin caverns he carved out, above them from stones sluices he fashioned.

From there two channels in the rocks he cut, for the waters two narrows he fashioned,

Thus the flowing waters from the highlands coming he could slow or let go faster;

With dams and sluices and the two narrows the waters he regulated.

From the Cavern Island, the island of Abu, the river's serpentine valley from under the waters he raised:

In the Land of the Two Narrows for Dumuzi and the shepherds a habitation did Enki fashion.

With satisfaction did Enlil all this to Nibiru words send; with words of concern Nibiru responded:

The close passage that Earth and Lahmu affected on Nibiru too much damage caused;

The shield of gold dust was torn, the atmosphere was dwindling again,

Now new supplies of gold quickly were needed!

Fervently to the Abzu Enki went, with Gibil his son to survey and search he journeyed.

All the gold mines were gone, by the avalanche of water they were buried.

In the Edin, Bad-Tibira too no longer existed, in Sippar a place for the chariots was no more!

The hundreds of Anunnaki who in the mines and Bad-Tibira toiled, from the Earth were gone,

The multitude of Earthlings, as Primitive Workers serving, by the Deluge were to clay turned;

No gold can from Earth anymore be provided! So did Enlil and Enki to Nibiru announce.

On Earth and on Nibiru there was desperation.

At that time Ninurta, his tasks in the mountains of cedars completed,

To the mountainland beyond the oceans once again journeyed.

From that land, on the other side of Earth, astounding words he delivered:

The avalanche of waters deep cuts into the mountainsides there tore,

From the mountainsides uncounted gold, in nuggets large and small,

To the rivers below fell down, without mining can the gold be hauled!

Enlil and Enki to the distant mountainland hurried, with amazement they the discovery viewed:

Gold, pure gold, refining and smelting not requiring, all about was lying!

A miracle it is! So was Enki to Enlil saying. What by Nibiru was wrought, by Nibiru was amended!

The unseen hand of the Creator of All it is life on Nibiru to enable! So did Enlil say.

Now who could collect the nuggets, how to Nibiru they will be sent? the leaders each other asked.

Of the first question, Ninurta had the answer:

In the high mountainland on this side of Earth, some Earthlings have survived!

Descendants of Ka-in they are, with the handling of metals they are knowing;

Four brothers and four sisters are their leaders, on rafts they themselves saved,

Now their mountaintop in the midst of a great lake is an island.

As the protector of their forefathers they me recall, the Great Protector they call me!

By the report that other Earthlings had survived the leaders were heartened,

Even Enlil, who the end of all flesh planned, was no longer angered.

It is the will of the Creator of All! to each other they said.

Now let us a new Place for Celestial Chariots establish, therefrom the gold to Nibiru send!

For a new plain whose soil has dried and hardened they searched,

In the proximity of the Landing Place, in a desolate peninsula, such a plain they found.

Flat as a quiet lake it was, by white mountains it was surrounded.

Now this is the account of the new Place of the Celestial Chariots,

And the artificed twin mounts and how the image of the lion by Marduk was usurped.

In the peninsula by the Anunnaki chosen, the heavenly Ways of Anu and Enlil on Earth were reflected;

Let the new Place of the Chariots precisely on that boundary be located,

Let the heart of the plain the heavens reflect! So did Enlil to Enki suggest.

Once Enki to this agreed, Enlil from the skies of distances took measures;

On a tablet a grand design for all to see he marked out.

Let the Landing Place in the Cedar Mountains be a part of the facilities! he said.

The distance between the Landing Place and the Chariot Place he measured,

In the midst thereof a place for a new Mission Control Center he designated:

There a suitable mount he selected, the Mount of Way Showing he named it.

A platform of stones, akin but smaller than the Landing Place, to be built there he ordered;

In its midst a great rock was carved inside and out, to house a new Bond Heaven–Earth it was made.

A new Navel of the Earth, the role of Nibru-ki before the Deluge to replace.

The Landing Path on the twin peaks of Arrata in the north were anchored;

To demarcate the Landing Corridor Enlil two other sets of twin peaks required,

To delimit the Landing Corridor's boundary, ascent and descent to secure.

In the southern part of the desolate peninsula, a place of mountains,

Twin adjoining peaks Enlil selected, on them the southern delimit he anchored.

Where the second set of twin peaks was required, mountains there were none,

Only a flatland above the water-clogged valley from the ground protruded.

Artificial peaks thereon we can raise! So did Ningishzidda to the leaders say.

On a tablet the image of smooth-sided, skyward rising peaks for them he drew.

If it can be done, let it so be! Enlil with approval said. Let them also as beacons serve!

On the flatland, above the river's valley, Ningishzidda a scale model built,

The rising angles and four smooth sides with it he perfected.

Next to it a larger peak he placed, its sides to Earth's four corners he set;

By the Anunnaki, with their tools of power, were its stones cut and erected.

Beside it, in a precise location, the peak that was its twin he placed;

With galleries and chambers for pulsating crystals he designed it.

When this artful peak to the heavens rose, to place upon it the capstone the leaders were invited.

Of electrum, an admixture by Gibil fashioned, was the Apex Stone made.

The sunlight to the horizon it reflected, by night like a pillar of fire it was,

The power of all the crystals to the heavens in a beam it focused.

When the artful works, by Ningishzidda designed, were completed and ready,

The Anunnaki leaders the Great Twin Peak entered, at what they saw they marveled;

Ekur, House Which Like a Mountain Is, they named it, a beacon to the heavens it was.

That the Anunnaki the Deluge survived and prevailed forever it proclaimed.

Now the new Place of the Celestial Chariots gold from across the seas can receive,

From it the chariots to Nibiru the gold for survival shall carry;

From it to the east, where the Sun on the designated day rises, they will ascend,

To it to the southwest, where the Sun on the designated day sets, they will descend!

Then Enlil by his own hand the Nibiru crystals activated.

Inside eerie lights began to flicker, an enchanting hum the stillness broke;

Outside the capstone all at once was shining, brighter than the Sun it was.

The multitude of assembled Anunnaki a great cry of joy uttered;

Ninmah, by the occasion moved, a poem recited and sang:

House that is like a mountain, house with a pointed peak,

For Heaven–Earth it is equipped, the handiwork of the Anunnaki it is.

House bright and dark, house of heaven and Earth,

For the celestial boats it was put together, by the Anunnaki built.

House whose interior with a reddish light of heaven glows,

A pulsating beam that far and high reaches it emits;

Lofty mountain of mountains, great and lofty fashioned,

Beyond the understanding of Earthlings it is.

House of equipment, lofty house of eternity,

Its foundation stones the waters touch, its great circumference in clay is set.

House whose parts are skilfully together woven,

The great ones who in the skies circle to a resting make descent;

House that for the rocketships is a landmark, with unfathomable insides,

By Anu himself is the Ekur blessed.

Thus did Ninmah at the celebration recite and sing.

While the Anunnaki their remarkable handiwork were celebrating,

Enki to Enlil words of suggestion said: When in future days it will be asked:

When and by whom has this marvel been fashioned?

Let us beside the twin peaks a monument create, the Age of the Lion let it announce,

The image of Ningishzidda, the peaks' designer, let its face be,

Let it precisely toward the Place of the Celestial Chariots gaze,

When, by whom, and the purpose let it to future generations reveal!

So did Enki to Enlil suggest. To the words Enlil consented and to Enki said:

Of the Place of the Celestial Chariots, Utu must again the commander be;

Let the gazing lion, precisely eastward facing, with Ningishzidda's image be!

When the work to cut and shape the lion from the bedrock was proceeding,

Marduk to his father Enki words of aggrievement said:

To dominate the whole Earth to me did you promise,

Now command and glory to others are granted, without task or dominion I am left.

In my erstwhile domain are the artificed mounts situated, on the lion the image mine must be!

By these words of Marduk Ningishzidda was angered, the other sons were also annoyed,

By the clamor for domains Ninurta and his brothers were also aroused,

Lands for themselves and devoted Earthlings everyone was demanding!

Let not the celebration a contest become! Ninmah amidst the raised voices shouted.

The Earth is still in havoc, we Anunnaki are few, of the Earthlings there are only survivors!

Let Marduk Ningishzidda of the honor not deprive, let us Marduk's words also heed!

So did Ninmah, the peacemaker, to the contending leaders say.

For peace to prevail, the habitable lands between us should be apart set! Enlil to Enki said.

To make the peninsula an uncontested divider they agreed, to the peacemaker Ninmah they it allotted.

Tilmun, Land of the Missiles, they named it; to Earthlings it was beyond bounds.

The habitable lands to the east thereof to Enlil and his offspring were set apart,

For the descendants of two sons of Ziusudra, Shem and Yafet, therein to dwell.

The dark-hued landmass that the Abzu included to Enki and his clan was for domains granted,

The people of Ziusudra's middle son, Ham, to inhabit it were chosen.

To make Marduk their lord, of their lands the master, Enki to appease his son suggested.

By your wish let it so be! Enlil to Enki about it said.

In Tilmun, in its mountainous south, an abode for Ninmah his mother Ninurta built;

Near a spring with date trees, a verdant valley, it was located,

The mountain peak Ninurta terraced, a fragrant garden for Ninmah he planted.

When all was thus completed, a signal to all outposts on Earth was given:

From the mountainlands across the ocean Whirlwinds the gold nuggets brought,

From the Place of the Celestial Chariots to Nibiru the gold was lofted.

On that memorable day Enlil and Enki to each other said and agreed:

Let us Ninmah, the peacemaker, with a new epithet-name honor:

Ninharsag, Mistress of the Mountainhead, let us name her!

By acclamation was Ninmah the honor given, henceforth Ninharsag she was called.

Praise to Ninharsag, on Earth the peacemaker! in unison the Anunnaki proclaimed.

Synopsis of the Eleventh Tablet

The spaceport's land, Tilmun, is declared a neutral zone
It is granted to Ninmah, who is renamed Ninharsag
Marduk gets the Dark Lands, the Enlilites the Olden Lands
Marduk's grandsons quarrel, Satu murders Asar
Impregnating herself, Asar's wife Asta bears Horon
In aerial battles over Tilmun, Horon vanquishes Satu
The Enlilites deem it prudent to prepare another spaceport
Enki's son Dumuzi and Inanna, Enlil's granddaughter, fall in love
Fearing the consequences, Marduk causes Dumuzi's death
Seeking his body, Inanna is put to death, then resurrected
Inanna launches a war to seize and punish Marduk
The Enlilites break into his hideaway in the Great Mount
They seal the uppermost chamber to entomb Marduk alive
Marduk's wife Sarpanit and his son Nabu plead for his life
Ningishzidda, knowing the Mount's secrets, reaches Marduk
Marduk, his life spared, goes into exile
Enki and Enlil divide the Earth among their other sons

The triumph of Ninurta and the Great Pyramids

THE ELEVENTH TABLET

Praise to Ninharsag, on Earth the Peacemaker! in unison the Anunnaki proclaimed.

During the first Shar after the Deluge, Ninharsag to cool down tempers managed;

Nibiru with gold to resupply was over ambitions and rivalries paramount.

Slowly the Earth to teem with life returned; with the seeds of life by Enki preserved

What by itself survived was augmented on land and in the air and waters.

Most precious of all, the Anunnaki discovered, were Mankind's own remnants!

As in bygone days, when the Primitive Workers were created,

The Anunnaki, few and strained, for Civilized Workers now clamored.

By the time the first Shar after the Deluge was completed,

The peaceful truce by an unexpected occurrence was shattered.

Not between Marduk and Ninurta, not between the Enki and Enlil clans, was the eruption:

Between Marduk's own sons, by the Igigi abetted, was tranquillity broken.

When Marduk and Sarpanit and their sons and daughters on Lahmu the Deluge outwaited,

The two sons, Asar and Satu, to the daughters of Shamgaz, the Igigi leader, a liking took;

When to Earth they all returned, the two brothers the two sisters espoused,

Asar the one called Asta chose, Satu the one called Nebat betrothed.

Asar with his father Marduk in the dark-hued lands to abide chose,

Satu near the Landing Place, where the Igigi dwelt, with Shamgaz his dwelling made.

About the domains on Earth was Shamgaz concerned: Where shall the Igigi the masters be?

So did Shamgaz the other Igigi incite, of that Nebat to Satu daily spoke;

By staying with his father, Asar the successor alone shall be, the fertile lands he will inherit!

So did Shamgaz and his daughter Nebat to Satu day after day say.

How the succession in the hands of Satu alone to retain, father and daughter schemed.

On an auspicious day they made a banquet; Igigi and Anunnaki to it they invited.

Asar, unsuspecting, to celebrate with his brother also came.

Nebat, his spouse's sister, prepared the tables, footstools she also set,

She beautified herself, with lyre in hand a song to mighty Asar she sang.

Satu before him choice roast meat cut, with salted knife for him fatlings he served.

Shamgaz in a large goblet new wine to Asar offered, an admixture for him he made,

A large vessel, mighty to look upon, with elixired wine he gave him.

In good humor was Asar; merrily he arose and sang, with cymbals in his hand he chanted.

Then by the admixtured wine he was overcome, to the ground he fell down.

Let us for a sound sleep take him! the hosts to the others at the banquet said.

They Asar to another chamber carried, in a coffin they him laid,

The coffin with tight seals they closed, into the sea they threw it.

When word of what had happened Asta reached, to Marduk her husband's father she raised a wailing:

Asar to his death in the sea depths was brutally thrown, quickly must the coffin be found!

They searched the sea for Asar's coffin, by the shores of the dark-hued land it was found.

Inside the stiff body of Asar lay, from its nostrils the breath of life departed.

Marduk his clothes rent, on his forehead he put ashes.

My son! My son! Sarpanit cried and wept, great were her grief and mourning.

Enki was distraught and wept: The curse of Ka-in is repeated! to his son in agony he said.

Asta to high heavens a wailing raised, to Marduk for revenge and an heir an appeal she made:

Satu his death must meet. By your own seed a successor let me conceive,

Let by your name his name remembered be, the lineage surviving!

This, alas, cannot be done! Enki to Marduk and Asta said:

The brother who killed, the brother's brother must be the keeper,

For this Satu must be spared, by his seed an heir to Asar you must conceive!

By these twists of fate Asta was baffled; distraught, the rules to defy she was determined.

Before the body of Asar was wrapped and in the shroud in a shrine preserved,

From his phallus Asta the life seed of Asar extracted.

With it Asta herself made conceive, an heir and avenger to Asar to be born.

To Enki and his sons, to Marduk and his brothers, Satu word delivered:

The sole heir and Marduk's successor am I, of the Land of the Two
    Narrows I will be the master!

Before the Anunnaki's council Asta the claim refuted: With Asar's
    heir I am with child.

Among the river's bull rushes with the child she hid, the wrath of
    Satu she was avoiding;

Horon she called the boy, to be his father's avenger she raised him.

Satu by this was disconcerted; Shamgaz from ambitions did not
    retreat.

From Earth year to Earth year the Igigi and their offspring from the
    Landing Place spread,

Unto the borders of Tilmun, Ninharsag's sacred region, closer they
    moved.

To overrun the Place of the Celestial Chariots the Igigi and their
    Earthlings threatened.

In the dark-hued lands the child Horon by Earth's quick life cycles
    to a hero grew,

By his great-uncle Gibil was Horon adopted, by him was he trained
    and instructed.

For him Gibil winged sandals for soaring fashioned, to fly like a
    falcon he was able;

For him Gibil a divine harpoon made, its arrows bolts of missiles
    were.

In the highlands of the south did him Gibil the arts of metals and
    smithing teach.

The secret of a metal called iron Gibil to Horon revealed.

From it weapons Horon made, from loyal Earthlings an army he
    raised.

To challenge Satu and the Igigi northward, across land and river
    they marched.

When Horon and his Earthlings army the border of Tilmun, the
    Land of the Missiles, reached,

Satu to Horon words of challenge sent:

Between us two alone is the conflict, let us one on one in contest meet!

In the skies above Tilmun Satu in his Whirlwind for combat Horon awaited.

When Horon toward him like a falcon skyward soared,

A poisoned dart at him Satu shot, like a scorpion's sting it Horon felled.

When Asta this saw, a cry to heaven she sent forth, for Ningishzidda she cried out.

From his celestial boat Ningishzidda came down, to save the hero for his mother he came.

With magic powers Ningishzidda the poison to benevolent blood converted,

By morning was Horon healed, from the dead was he returned.

Then with a Fiery Pillar, like a heavenly fish with fins and a fiery tail,

Ningishzidda to Horon provided, its eyes from blue to red to blue their colors changed.

Toward the triumphant Satu Horon in the Fiery Pillar soared.

Far and wide each other they chased; fierce and deadly was the battle.

At first Horon's Fiery Pillar was hit, then with his harpoon Horon Satu smote.

To the ground Satu crashing down came; by Horon in tethers he was bound.

When before the council Horon with his captive uncle came,

They saw that he was blinded, his testicles squashed, like a discarded jar he stood.

Let Satu, blind and heirless, live! So did Asta to the council say.

To end his days as a mortal, among the Igigi, the council his fate determined.

Triumphant was Horon declared, the throne of his father to inherit;

On a metal tablet was the council's decision inscribed, in the Hall of Records they placed it.

In his abode Marduk with the decision was pleased; by what had happened he was sorrowed:

Though Horon a son of Asar his son was, from Shamgaz the Igigi he was descended,

A domain, one as among the Anunnaki allocated, to him was not given.

Having lost both sons, in each other Marduk and Sarpanit solace sought.

In time to them another son was born; Nabu, Prophecy Bearer, they named him.

Now this is the account of why in the faraway a new chariot's place was built,

And the love of Dumuzi and Inanna that Marduk by Dumuzi's death disrupted.

It was after the contesting of Horon and Satu, and their aerial battle over Tilmun,

That Enlil his three sons to a council summoned.

With concern to them of what was happening, he said:

In the beginning the Earthlings in our image and after our likeness we made,

Now the Anunnaki offspring in the image and likeness of the Earthlings became!

Then it was Ka-in who his brother killed, now a son of Marduk is his brother's killer!

For the first time ever, an Anunnaki offspring from Earthlings an army raised,

Weapons from a metal, of the Anunnaki a secret, in their hands he placed!

From the days when by Alalu and Anzu our legitimacy was challenged,

Disruption and rule-breaking by the Igigi continued.

Now the beacon peaks in the domain of Marduk are located, the Landing Place by the Igigi is held,

Now toward the Place of the Chariots the Igigi are advancing,

In the name of Satu to all the Heaven–Earth facilities they claim will lay!

So did Enlil to his three sons say, to take countersteps to them he proposed:

An alternative Heaven–Earth facility in secret establish we must!

Let it in Ninurta's land beyond the oceans, in the midst of trusted Earthlings, come to be!

Thus was the secret mission in the hands of Ninurta entrusted;

In the mountainlands beyond the oceans, beside the great lake,

A new Bond Heaven–Earth he was setting up, within an enclosure he placed it;

At the foot of the mountains where the gold nuggets were scattered

A plain with firm ground he chose; on it for ascent and descent markings he made.

Primitive are the facilities, but the purpose they will serve!

So did Ninurta to his father Enlil in good time declare:

From there gold shipments to Nibiru can continue, from there in need we too can ascend!

At that time what as a blessed event began as a horrible occurrence ended.

At that time Dumuzi, Enki's youngest son, to Inanna, Nannar's daughter, a liking took;

Inanna, Enlil's granddaughter, by the lord of herding was captivated.

A love that knows no bounds engulfed them, a passion their hearts inflamed.

Many of the love songs that for a long time thereafter were sung,

Inanna and Dumuzi were the first to sing them, by song their love they recounted.

To Dumuzi, his youngest son, Enki a large domain above the Abzu allotted;

Meluhha, the Black Land, was its name, highland trees there grew, its waters abundant were.

Large bulls among its river reeds roamed, greatly numbered were its cattle,

Silver from its mountains came, its copper bright as gold was aglitter.

Greatly beloved was Dumuzi; by Enki after the death of Asar he was favored.

Of his youngest brother Marduk was jealous.

Inanna by her parents Nannar and Ningal was beloved, Enlil by her cradle sat.

Beautiful beyond describing she was, in martial arts with Anunnanki heroes she competed.

Of journeys in the heavens and of celestial boats from her brother Utu she learned;

A skyship of her own, to roam in Earth's skies, to her the Anunnaki presented.

After the Deluge, on the Landing Platform, Dumuzi and Inanna their eyes on each other set;

At the dedication of the artificed mounts was between them a warm encounter.

Hesitant at first they were, he of Enki's clan, she of Enlil an offspring.

When Ninharsag for peace the disputing clans together brought,

Inanna and Dumuzi away from the others to be together managed, love to each other they professed.

As they went strolling together, sweet words of alluring love to each other they said.

Side by side they lay down, one heart with the other heart chatted;

Around her waist Dumuzi put his arm, like a wild bull to take her he wished,

Let me teach you! Let me teach you! to Inanna Dumuzi said.

Gently she kissed him, then to him of her mother she spoke:

What fib could I tell my mother? What words will you tell Ningal?

Let us of our love my mother tell, of joy cedar perfume she will on us sprinkle!

To the dwelling place of Ningal, Inanna's mother, the lovers went,

To them Ningal her blessing gave, of Dumuzi the mother of Inanna approved.

Lord Dumuzi, as a son-in-law of Nannar you are worthy! to him she said.

Dumuzi as bridegroom by Nannar himself was welcomed, Inanna's brother Utu, Let it so be! said.

Perchance the espousing peace between the clans truly will bring! Enlil to them all said.

When of the love and bethrothal Dumuzi to his father and brothers spoke,

Enki of peace through espousal also was thinking, his blessing to Dumuzi he gave.

Dumuzi's brothers, all except Marduk, about the espousal were joyful.

A bethrothal bed of gold by Gibil was fashioned, Nergal blue-hued lapis stones sent.

Sweet dates, a fruit by Inanna favored, beside the bed they in a pile placed,

Under the fruits the beads of lapis they hid for Inanna to discover.

As the custom was, to perfume and clothe Inanna a sister of Dumuzi was sent,

Geshtinanna, a sister-in-law-to-be, was her name.

To her Inanna what was in her heart revealed, of her future with Dumuzi to her she said:

A vision of a great nation I have, as a Great Anunnaki Dumuzi there will rise.

His name over others shall be exalted, his queen-spouse I shall be.

Princely status we will share, rebellious countries we shall together subdue,

To Dumuzi I will status give, the country I will rightly direct!

Inanna's visions of rulership and glory by Geshtinanna to her brother Marduk were reported.

By Inanna's ambitions Marduk was greatly disturbed; to Geshtinanna a secret plan he told.

To her brother Dumuzi, to the herder's dwelling, Geshtinanna went.

Lovely to behold and perfumed, to her brother Dumuzi thus she said:

Before with your young wife in your embrace with you will sleep,

A legitimate heir, by a sister born, you must have!

Inanna's son to succession shall not be entitled, on your mother's knees he will not be raised!

She put his hand in her hand, she pressed her body against his body.

My brother, with you I will lie down! Bridegroom, with you a peer of Enki we shall have!

So did Geshtinanna to Dumuzi whisper, a noble issue from her womb to have.

Into her womb Dumuzi poured the semen, by her caressing he fell asleep.

During the night Dumuzi had a dream, a premonition of death he envisioned:

In the dream seven evil bandits he saw coming into his dwelling.

The Master has sent us for you, son of Duttur! to him they said.

They chased away his ewes, his lambs and kids they drove away,

The headdress of lordship they took off his head, the royal robe off his body they tore,

The staff of shepherding they took and broke, his cup from its peg they threw down.

Naked and barefooted they seized him, in fetters they his hands bound,

In the name of the Princely Bird and the Falcon they left him dying.

Disturbed and startled Dumuzi in the middle of the night awoke, to Geshtinanna the dream he told.

The dream is not favorable! Geshtinanna to the distraught Dumuzi said.

Marduk of raping me will accuse you, evil emissaries to arrest you he will send.

To try you and disgrace you he will order, the liaison with an Enlilite to disunite!

As a wounded beast Dumuzi a cry roared out: Betrayal! Betrayal! he shouted.

To Utu, Inanna's brother, Help me! word he sent; the name of his father Enki as a talisman he uttered.

Through the desert of Emush, the Snakes Desert, Dumuzi rushed to escape,

To the place of mighty waterfalls from the evildoers he ran to hide.

Where the gushing waters the rocks to slippery smoothness made, Dumuzi slipped and fell;

The onrushing waters his lifeless body in a white froth swept away.

———————

Now this is the account of Inanna's descent to the Lower Abzu,

And the Great Anunnaki War, and how Marduk in the Ekur alive was imprisoned.

When the lifeless body of Dumuzi from the great lake's waters by
Ninagal was retrieved,

To the abode of Nergal and Ereshkigal in the Lower Abzu the body
was brought.

On a stone slab was the dead body of Dumuzi, a son of Enki, placed.

When of what had happened word to Enki was sent, Enki rent his
clothes, on his forehead he put ashes.

My son! My son! for Dumuzi he lamented. What have I sinned to
be so punished? out loud he asked.

When I to Earth from Nibiru came, EA, He Whose Home Is
Waters, was my name,

With waters did the Celestial Chariots obtain their thrustpower, in
waters I splashed down;

Then by an avalanche of waters the Earth was swept over,

In waters did Asar my grandchild drown, by waters my beloved
Dumuzi is now dead!

Everything I had done, for righteous purpose did I do it.

Why am I punished, why has Fate against me turned?

So did Enki bewail and lament.

When from Geshtinanna the veracity of occurrences was discovered,

Greater was Enki's agony: Now Marduk, my firstborn, for his deed
will also suffer!

By the disappearance and death of Dumuzi was Inanna worried,
then grieved;

Then to the Lower Abzu she hurried, Dumuzi's body for burial to
retrieve.

When Ereshkigal, her sister, of the arrival of Inanna at the
precinct's gates was told,

Ereshkigal a devious scheme on the part of Inanna suspected.

At each of the seven gates, one of Inanna's accoutrements and
weapons was from her removed,

Then, unclothed and powerless before Ereshkigal's throne,

Of scheming an heir by Nergal, Dumuzi's brother, she was accused!

Trembling with fury, Ereshkigal to her sister's explanations would not listen.

Let loose against her the sixty diseases! Ereshkigal her vizier, Namtar, in anger ordered.

By the disappearance of Inanna in the Lower Abzu were her parents much worried,

Nannar to Enlil in the matter went, Enlil to Enki a message sent.

From Nergal his son, Ereshkigal's spouse, Enki what had happened learned,

From clay of the Abzu Enki two emissaries fashioned, beings without blood, by death rays unharmed,

To the Lower Abzu he sent them, Inanna to bring back, whether alive or dead.

When before Ereshkigal they came, Ereshkigal by their appearance was puzzled:

Are you Anunnaki? Are you Earthlings? with bewilderment she asked them.

Namtar the magical weapons of power against them directed, but unharmed the two were.

To the lifeless body of Inanna he took them, hanging from a stake she was.

Upon the corpse the clay emissaries a Pulser and an Emitter directed,

Then the Water of Life on her they sprinkled, in her mouth the Plant of Life they placed.

Then Inanna stirred, her eyes she opened; from the dead Inanna arose.

When the two emissaries Inanna to the Upper World were ready to return,

Inanna the lifeless body of Dumuzi to take along them ordered.

At the seven gates of the Lower Abzu, to Inanna her accoutrements and attributes were returned.

To the abode of Dumuzi in the Black Land the lover of her youth to take the emissaries she ordered,

There to wash him with pure water, with sweet oil him anoint,

Then to clothe him in a red shroud, upon a slab of lapis lay him;

Then in the rocks for him a rest place carve out, the Day of Arising there to await.

As for herself, to the abode of Enki Inanna set her steps,

Retribution for her beloved's death she wanted, the death of Marduk the culprit she demanded.

There has been death enough! Enki to her said. Marduk an instigator was, but murder he committed not!

When Inanna learned that Marduk would not by Enki be punished, Inanna to her parents and brother went.

To high heaven she a wailing raised: Justice! Revenge! Death to Marduk! she cried for.

At Enlil's abode his sons Inanna and Utu joined, for a council of war they gathered.

Ninurta, whom the rebel Anzu defeated, for strong measures argued;

Of secret words between Marduk and the Igigi exchanged, Utu to them reported.

Of Marduk, an evil serpent, Earth must be rid! Enlil with them agreed.

When the demand for Marduk's surrender to Enki his father was sent,

Enki to his abode Marduk and all the other sons summoned.

Though for my beloved Dumuzi I am still grieving, Marduk's rights I must defend!

Though evil did Marduk instigate, by ill fate, not by Marduk's hand, did Dumuzi die;

Marduk is my firstborn, Ninki is his mother, for succession he is destined,

From death by Ninurta's gang by us all he must be protected! So did Enki say.

Only Gibil and Ninagal their father's call heeded; Ningishzidda was opposed,

Nergal was hesitant: Only if in mortal danger he will be will I help! he said.

It was after that that a war, of ferocity unknown, between the two clans erupted.

Unlike the contending of Horon and Satu, of Earthlings descended, it was:

A battle between Anunnaki, Nibiruan-born among them, on another planet was loosed.

By Inanna was the warfare begun, in her skyship to the domains of Enki's sons she crossed over;

Marduk to battle she challenged, to the domains of Ninagal and Gibil she him pursued.

To assist her Ninurta from his Storm Bird withering beams at the enemy's strongholds shot,

Ishkur from the skies with scorching lightnings and smashing thunders attacked.

In the Abzu from the rivers fish he washed away, cattle in the fields he dispersed.

To the north, the place of the artificed mounts, Marduk then retreated;

Pursuing him, Ninurta on the habitations poison-bearing missiles rained.

His Weapon That Tears Apart the people in those lands robbed of their senses,

The canals that the river's waters bore, red from blood became;

Ishkur's brilliances the nights' darkness into flaming days converted.

As the devastating battles northward advanced, Marduk in the
Ekur himself ensconced,

Gibil for it an unseen shield devised, Nergal to heaven its
all-seeing eye raised.

With a Weapon of Brilliance, by a horn directed, Inanna the hiding
place attacked;

Horon to defend his grandfather came; by her Brilliance was his
right eye damaged.

While Utu the Igigi and their horde of Earthlings beyond Tilmun
held off,

At the foot of the artificed mounts Anunnaki, this and that clan
supporting, in battle clashed.

Let Marduk surrender, let the bloodshed end! So did Enlil to Enki
words convey;

Let brother talk to brother! to Enki Ninharsag a message sent.

In his hideout, within the Ekur, Marduk his pursuers to defy
continued,

Within the House Which Like a Mountain Is his final stand he made.

Inanna the massive stone structure could not surmount, its smooth
sides her weapons deflected.

Then Ninurta of the secret entrance learned, the swivel stone on
the north side he found!

Through a dark corridor Ninurta passed, the grand gallery he
reached,

Its vault by the many-hued emissions of the crystals like a rainbow
was aglitter.

Inside, by the intrusion alerted, Marduk with ready weapons
Ninurta awaited;

With weapons responding, smashing the wonder crystals, Ninurta
up the gallery kept going.

Into the upper chamber, the place of the Great Pulsating Stone,
Marduk retreated,

At its entrance Marduk the sliding stone locks lowered; from one and all admission they barred.

Into the Ekur Inanna and Ishkur Ninurta followed; what next to do they contemplated.

Let the encased hiding chamber be Marduk's stone coffin! to them Ishkur said.

To three blocking stones, ready for down gliding, Ishkur their attention drew.

Let slow death, by alive being buried, be Marduk's sentence! Inanna her consent gave.

At the end of the gallery, the three the blocking stones let loose,

Each one of them one stone for plugging slid down, Marduk as in a tomb to seal.

———•———

Now this is the account of how Marduk was saved and to exile departed,

And how the Ekur was dismantled and lordship over the lands rearranged.

Away from the Sun and light, without food or water, Marduk within the Ekur alive was entombed;

By his imprisonment and punishment without trial Sarpanit, his spouse, a wailing raised.

To Enki her father-in-law she hurried, with the young son Nabu to him she came.

To be among the living Marduk must be returned! to Enki Sarpanit said.

He sent her to Utu and Nannar, who with Inanna can intercede.

Wearing a garment of atonement, To the lord Marduk give life! she pleaded.

Let him humbly life continue, rulership he will lay aside!

Appeased was not Inanna. For the death of my beloved, the Instigator must die! Inanna retorted.

Ninharsag, the peacemaker, the brothers Enki and Enlil summoned,

Punishment to Marduk must come, death is not warranted! to them she said.

Let Marduk in exile live, the succession on Earth to Ninurta submit!

Enlil by her words was pleased and smiled: Ninurta was his son, of Ninurta she was the mother!

If between succession and life the choice is, what can I, a father, say?

So did Enki with heavy heart answer. In my lands widespread is the desolation,

Warfare must end, for Dumuzi I am still in mourning; let Marduk live in exile!

If peace is to be returned and Marduk shall live, binding arrangements must be made! Enlil to Enki said.

All facilities that heaven and Earth bond, to my hands alone must be entrusted,

The mastery over the Land of the Two Narrows to another son of yours you must give.

The Igigi who Marduk follow, the Landing Place must give up and abandon,

To a Land of No Return, by no descendant of Ziusudra inhabited, must Marduk in exile go!

So did Enlil forcefully declare, to be foremost among the brothers he meant.

The hand of fate Enki in his heart acknowledged: Let it so be! with bowed head he said.

Ningishzidda alone the Ekur innards knows; let him over its land the master be!

After the decisions by the Great Anunnaki were announced, Ningishzidda for the rescue they summoned.

How Marduk from the blocked and sealed innards to extricate was
   his challenge;
To let free the one who alive is buried, a task beyond conceiving to
   him they gave.
Ningishzidda the Ekur's secret designs contemplated, how to
   circumvent the blockings he planned:
Through a chiseled upper opening Marduk will be rescued! to the
   leaders he said.
At a place which I will show them, a doorway in the stones they
   will cut,
From it upward a twisting passageway they shall bore, a rescue
   shaft creating.
Through hidden hollowings to the Ekur's midst they will continue,
At the vortex of the hollowings through the stones they will break
   through.
A doorway to the insides they will blow open, thereby the blockings
   circumventing;
Up the grand gallery they will continue, the three stone bars they
   will raise,
The uppermost chamber, Marduk's death prison, they will reach!
Anunnaki, by Ningishzidda guided, his outlined plan then followed,
With tools that crack the stones the opening they made, the rescue
   shaft they fashioned,
The insides of the artificed mount they reached, an exit they blew
   open.
Circumventing the three blocking stones, the uppermost chamber
   they reached,
On a small platform the portcullises they raised; Marduk, fainted,
   they rescued.
Carefully through the twisting shaft they the lord lowered, to fresh
   air they him brought;

Outside Sarpanit and Nabu spouse and father were awaiting;
   a joyful reunion it was.

When to Marduk his father Enki the terms of release conveyed,

Marduk was enraged: I would rather die than my birthright forfeit!
   he shouted.

Sarpanit into his arms Nabu thrust. We are part of your future! she
   softly said.

Marduk was angered, Marduk was humbled. To Fate I yield! he
   inaudibly said.

With Sarpanit and Nabu to a Land of No Return he departed,

To a place where horned beasts are hunted with wife and son he
   went.

After Marduk had departed, Ninurta the Ekur through the shaft
   reentered,

Through a horizontal corridor to the Ekur's vulva he went.

In its east wall, in a niche artfully fashioned, the Destiny Stone a
   red radiance was emitting.

Its power to kill me grabs, with a killing tracking it me seizes!
   Ninurta inside the chamber cried.

Take it away! To obliteration destroy it! to his lieutenants Ninurta
   shouted.

Retracing his steps, through the grand gallery to the topmost
   chamber Ninurta went,

In a hollowed-out chest the heart of the Ekur pulsated, its netforce
   by five compartments was enhanced.

With his baton Ninurta the stone chest struck; with a resonating
   sound it responded.

Its Gug Stone, that directions determined, Ninurta ordered to be
   taken out, to a place of his choice carried.

Coming down the grand gallery, Ninurta the twenty-seven pairs of
   Nibiru crystals examined.

Many in his fight with Marduk were damaged; some the struggle intact survived.

To remove the whole ones from their grooves Ninurta ordered, the others with his beam he pulverized.

Outside the House Which Like a Mountain Is Ninurta in his Black Bird soared,

To the Apex Stone his attention he turned; his enemy's epitome it represented.

With his weapons he shook it loose, to the ground in pieces it toppled.

By this the fear of Marduk is forever ended! Ninurta, victorious, declared.

On the battleground the assembled Anunnaki the praise of Ninurta announced:

Like Anu you are made! to their hero and leader they shouted.

To replace the incapacitated beacon a mount near the Place of the Celestial Chariots was chosen,

Within its innards the salvaged crystals were rearranged.

Upon its peak the Gug Stone, the Stone of Directing, was installed;

Mount Mashu, Mount of the Supreme Celestial Barque, the mount was called.

At that time Enlil his three sons summoned; Ninlil and Ninharsag also attended.

Commands over olden lands to confirm, lordships over new lands to assign they met.

To Ninurta, who Anzu and Marduk had vanquished, the Enlilship powers were granted,

In all the lands his father's surrogate to be.

Of the Landing Place in the Cedar Mountains, lordship to Ishkur was granted,

To his domain northward thereof was the Landing Place joined.

The lands south and east thereof, where the Igigi and their offspring had spread,

To Nannar as an everlasting endowment were given, by his descendants and followers to keep and to hold.

The peninsula wherein the Place of the Chariots was, in Nannar's lands was included,

Utu as commander of the Place and of the Navel of the Earth was confirmed.

In the Land of the Two Narrows, as agreed, Enki to Ningishzidda the lordship did assign.

To that none of Enki's other sons objected; to that Inanna was opposed!

To the heritage of Dumuzi, her deceased bridegroom, did Inanna claim lay,

A dominion of her own she of Enki and Enlil demanded.

How Inanna's demands to satisfy the leaders contemplated,

About the lands and the peoples the Great Anunnaki who the fates decree counsel took,

Regarding the Earth and its resettling words with Anu they exchanged.

From the time of the Deluge, the Great Calamity, almost two Shars have passed,

The Earthlings have proliferated, from mountainlands to dried lowlands they went.

Of Civilized Mankind by Ziusudra there were descendants, with Anunnaki seed they were intermixed.

Offspring of Igigi who intermarried roamed about, in the distant lands Ka-in's kinfolk survived.

Few and lofty were the Anunnaki who from Nibiru had come, few were their perfect descendants.

How settlements for themselves and for Earthlings to establish the Great Anunnaki considered,

How over Mankind lofty to remain, how to make the many the few obey and serve.

About all that, about the future the leaders with Anu words exchanged.

To come to Earth one more time Anu decided; with Antu his spouse he wished to come.

Synopsis of the Twelfth Tablet

The soil dries, plains and river valleys are resettled

Plentiful gold comes from the Lands Beyond the Seas

Anu and his spouse Antu arrive for a memorable visit

Reminiscing, the leaders realize they are Destiny's pawns

They allocate three regions of civilization to Mankind

Pardoned by the departing Anu, Marduk remains rebellious

The First Region and space facilities are Enlilite lands

Man's first civilization begins in the First Region (Sumer)

Marduk usurps a site to build an illicit launch tower

Frustrated by the Enlilites, Marduk seizes the Second Region

He deposes and exiles Ningishzidda (Thoth) to distant lands

He declares himself Ra, supreme god, in a new religion

He introduces Pharaonic reigns to mark a new civilization

Enlil assigns his son Ishkur to protect the metal sources

Inanna is granted dominion in the Third Region (Indus Valley)

The gods grant kingship, wars begin

THE TWELFTH TABLET

To come to Earth one more time Anu decided, with Antu his spouse he wished to come.

While his arrival they awaited, the Anunnaki abodes in the Edin to reestablish began.

From the mountainlands where descendants of Shem dwelt, to the olden land the black-headed people migrated.

Upon the newly dried soil the Anunnaki let them settle, food for all to provide.

Where Eridu, Enki's first city, before the Deluge had stood,

On top of the myriads of mud and silt a new Eridu was marked out.

In its center, upon a raised platform, an abode for Enki and Ninki was built,

House of the Lord Whose Return Is Triumphant it was called;

With gold and silver and precious metals by Enki's sons provided it was adorned.

Above, in a circle skyward pointing, the twelve constellations by their signs were marked out.

Below, as in the Abzu, waters with swimming fishes flowed.

In a sanctuary, a place that no uninvited can enter, Enki the ME formulas kept.

For Enlil and Ninlil, a new Nibru-ki atop the mud and silt was established;

Amid its people's dwellings and cattlefolds and stalls a sacred precinct was walled off.

An abode for Enlil and Ninlil therein was built, in seven stages it
     arose;

A stairway, rising as to heaven, to the topmost platform led.

His Tablets of Destinies did Enlil there keep, with his weapons it
     was protected:

The Lifted Eye that scans the lands, the Lifted Beam that penetrates
     all.

In the courtyard, in its own enclosure, Enlil's fast-stepping Skybird
     was kept.

As the time for the arrival of Anu and Antu neared,

For their stay in the Edin a new place was selected, neither Enlil's
     nor Enki's to be.

Unug-ki, the Delightful Place, it was named. Shade trees in it were
     planted,

A pure white structure, the House of Anu, in its midst was built.

Its exterior in seven stages rose; its interior like a king's quarters was.

When the celestial chariot of Anu at Earth arrived, Anunnaki
     skyships toward it soared;

For a safe landing at the Place of the Chariots, in Tilmun, it was
     guided.

Utu, the Place's commander, his great-grandparents to Planet Earth
     welcomed.

The three children of Anu, Enlil and Enki and Ninharsag, stood
     there to greet them.

They embraced and kissed, they laughed and cried. So long, so
     long has the separation been!

They to each other kept saying. At each other they looked, aging to
     examine:

Though greater in Shars were the parents, younger than the children
     they looked!

The two sons looked old and bearded; Ninharsag, once a beauty,
     was bent and wrinkled.

All five of them with tears were filled; tears of joy with sorrowed tears were mingled.

In skyships were the guests and their hosts to the Edin taken,

In a prepared place beside Unug-ki the skyships landed.

All the Anunnaki that on Earth had stayed as an honor guard were standing.

Hail and welcome! Hail and welcome! in unison to Anu and Antu they were shouting.

Then in a procession, singing and music playing, the Anunnaki to the House of Anu the guests accompanied.

In the House of Anu, Anu washed and rested, then he was perfumed and clothed;

Antu by female Anunnaki to the House of the Golden Bed was escorted;

There she too washed and rested, then she was perfumed and clothed.

In the open courtyard, as an evening breeze the tree leaves rustled,

Anu and Antu on thrones were seated. Flanking them were Enlil and Enki and Ninharsag.

Attendants, Earthlings who were completely naked, wine and good oil served;

Others, in a corner of the courtyard, a bull and a ram, gifts of Enlil and Enki, on a fire were roasting.

A great banquet was for Anu and Antu prepared, for the sign in the heavens its start was awaiting.

On Enlil's instructions Zumul, who in matters of stars and planets was learned,

The steps of the House of Anu ascended, the rising of the planets at evetime to announce.

On the first step Kishar in the eastern skies appeared, Lahamu on the second step was seen,

Mummu on the third step was announced, Anshar by the fourth step rose,

Lahmu on the fifth step was seen, the Moon from the sixth step was announced.

Then, on a signal from Zumul, the hymn The Planet of Anu in the Skies Rises began to be sung,

For from the topmost step, the seventh, the red-haloed Nibiru into view came.

To music the Anunnaki clapped and danced, to music they danced and sang;

To the one who grows bright, the heavenly planet of the lord Anu, they sang.

On the signal a bonfire was lit, seen from place to place were the bonfires started:

Before the night was over, the whole land of Edin was with bonfires lit!

After a meal of bull meat and ram meat, of fish and fowl, with wine and beer accompanied,

Anu and Antu to their overnight quarters were accompanied; by Anu and Antu were all the Anunnaki thanked.

For several Earth days and nights Anu and Antu slept; on the sixth day his two sons and daughter Anu summoned.

Of what had on Earth transpired their accounts he heard, of the peace and the warfare he learned.

Of how the Earthlings, by the oath of Enlil to be wiped off, had again proliferated Anu heard;

Of the gold discovery in the land beyond the oceans and the chariot's place there, Enlil to him revealed.

It was then that of the dream and the tablet from Galzu Enki to his father told.

By that was Anu greatly puzzled: A secret emissary by that name

To Earth by me was never sent! So did Anu to the three leaders say.

Puzzled were Enki and Enlil, baffled they at each other looked.

On account of Galzu Ziusudra and the seed of life were saved! Enki said.

On account of Galzu on Earth we remained! Enlil to his father said.

The day to Nibiru you return you shall die, so did Galzu to us say.

Incredulous of that was Anu; the change of cycles indeed havoc did cause, but with elixirs cured it was!

Whose emissary, if not yours, was Galzu? Enki and Enlil in unison said.

Who the Earthlings to save wanted, who on Earth made us stay?

Ninharsag her head slowly nodded: For the Creator of All did Galzu appear!

Was the creation of the Earthlings also destined, of that I must wonder!

For a while the four of them were silent; each one past events in his heart recounted.

While fates we decreed, the hand of destiny every step directed! So did Anu say.

The will of the Creator of All is clear to see: On Earth and for Earthlings, only emissaries we are.

The Earth to the Earthlings belongs, to preserve and advance them we were intended!

If that is our mission here, let us accordingly act! So did Enki say.

The great Anunnaki who the fates decree counsels exchanged regarding the lands:

To create civilized regions the Great Anunnaki decided, therein knowledge to Mankind provide;

Cities of Man to establish, therein in sacred precincts abodes for the Anunnaki create;

Kingship as on Nibiru on Earth establish, crown and scepter to a chosen man give;

By him the word of the Anunnaki to the people convey, work and dexterity to enforce;

In the sacred precincts a priesthood to establish, the Anunnaki as lofty lords to serve and worship.

Secret knowledge to be taught, civilization to Mankind convey.

To create four regions, three for Mankind, one restricted, the Anunnaki resolved:

The first region in the olden Edin-land to establish, for Enlil and his sons to dominate;

The second region in the Land of the Two Narrows thereafter to follow, for Enki and his sons to lord;

The third region, with the other two not mingling, in a distant land to Inanna grant;

The fourth region, for the Anunnaki alone consecrated, the peninsula of the Place of the Chariots will be.

Now this is the account of Anu's journey to the lands beyond the oceans,

And how in the First Region for the Anunnaki cities were reestablished.

Having the decision about the four regions and Mankind's civilizations made,

Anu about his grandson Marduk inquired. I must see him again! to the leaders Anu said.

Whether by Dumuzi and Ningishzidda to Nibiru inviting, Marduk's ire I myself have caused!

So did Anu wonder; to reconsider the punishment of Marduk he wished.

When to the lands beyond the oceans you journey, Marduk to meet you will be told!

The land where he roams, in those parts of the Earth it is! So did Enlil to Anu say.

Before for the distant lands the royal couple went, the Edin and its lands Anu and Antu surveyed;

Eridu and Nibru-ki they visited, where the cities of the first region were planned they saw.

In Eridu Enlil about Enki complained: The ME formulas to himself Enki is keeping!

Anu, on the seat of honor seated, words of praise to Enki said:

My son for himself a magnificent house built, beautifully on a platform it is raised.

To the people that the House surround and serve, great knowledge will Enki give;

Now, the knowledge that in the ME's is secreted, with other Anunnaki must be shared!

Embarrassed was Enki; to share with all the divine formulas to Anu he promised.

In the ensuing days, in skyships traveling, Anu and Antu the other regions surveyed.

Then, on the seventeenth day, to Unug-ki the royal couple returned for one more night of rest.

In the morrow, when the younger Anunnaki before Anu and Antu for a blessing came,

Anu to his great-granddaughter Inanna took a liking; he drew her closely, he hugged and kissed her.

Let all my words heed! to the congregated he announced:

This place, after we leave, to Inanna as a dowry is given,

Let the skyship in which we the Earth shall survey to Inanna my present be!

Joyed, Inanna to dance and sing began, her praises of Anu as hymns in times to come were chanted.

Thereafter, bidding farewells to the Anunnaki, for the lands
beyond the oceans Anu and Antu departed;

Enlil and Enki, Ninurta and Ishkur with them to the golden land
went.

To impress Anu the king with the great golden richess, Ninurta an
abode for Anu and Antu built;

Its stone blocks, to perfection cut, with pure gold inside were
covered.

A golden enclosure, with flowers of carnelian stones carved, the
royal couple awaited!

By the shore of the great mountain lake was the abode erected.

How the gold nuggets are collected the visitors were shown;

There is gold here enough for many Shars to come! Anu, satisfied,
said.

To a place nearby Ninurta to Anu and Antu an artificed mound
showed,

How to a place for melting and refining metals it was made
Ninurta explained.

How a new metal from stones was extracted he showed them:
Anak, Anunnaki-made, he called it,

How by combining it with the abundant copper a strong metal he
invented, he showed them.

On the great lake, from whose shores the metals came, Anu and
Antu sailed;

The Lake of Anak Anu called it, henceforth this was its name.

Then from lands from the north, lands where great horned beasts
are hunted,

Marduk before his father Enki and his grandfather Anu came;
Nabu his son with him was.

When Enki about Sarpanit inquired, Marduk with sorrow of her
death them told.

Now Nabu alone with me has remained! to his father and grandfather Marduk said.

Anu Marduk to his chest pressed: Enough you have been punished! to him he said;

With his right hand on Marduk's head, Anu Marduk to be forgiven blessed.

From the golden place, high in the mountains, all who had gathered to the plain below went.

There, stretching to the horizon, Ninurta a new place for the chariots has prepared.

Anu and Antu's celestial chariot stood there ready, with gold to the brim it was loaded.

As the time for departing came, Anu to his children words of good-bye and guidance said:

Whatever Destiny for the Earth and the Earthlings intended, let it so be!

If Man, not Anunnaki, to inherit the Earth is destined, let us destiny help.

Give Mankind knowledge, up to a measure secrets of heaven and Earth them teach,

Laws of justice and righteousness teach them, then depart and leave!

So did Anu to his children fatherly instructions give.

Once more they hugged, embraced and kissed, and from the new chariots' place Anu and Antu for Nibiru left.

The first to break the sorrowed silence was Marduk; with anger were his words:

What is this new Place of Celestial Chariots? of the others an explanation he demanded.

What after my exile without my knowledge has transpired?

When Enki of the decisions about the four regions to Marduk told,

Marduk's fury knew no bounds: Why will Inanna, a cause of Dumuzi's death, her own region get?

The decisions have been made, they cannot be altered! So did Enlil
to Marduk say.

In separate skyships to the Edin and its adjoining lands they
returned;

Sensing trouble, Enlil Ishkur to stay behind instructed, over the
gold watch to keep.

To commemorate Anu's visit, a new count of time passage was
introduced:

By Earth years, not by Nibiru Shars, was what on Earth transpired
to be counted.

In the Age of the Bull, to Enlil dedicated, was the count of Earth
years begun.

When to the Edin the leaders returned, the place of the first
civilized region,

How to make bricks from mud the Anunnaki the Earthlings
taught, therewith cities to build.

But where once cities of the Anunnaki alone had stood, cities for
both them and Earthlings now arose;

Therein and in new cities for the great Anunnaki sacred precincts
were consecrated,

Therein the Anunnaki with lofty abodes were provided, Temples
by Mankind they were called;

Therein the Anunnaki as Lofty Lords were served and worshiped,

By number-ranks were they honored, the heirship to Mankind
made known:

Anu, the heavenly, the rank of sixty held, to Enlil the fifty rank was
given,

On Ninurta his foremost son did Enlil the same rank bestow.

Next in succession was the lord Enki, the rank of forty he held;

To Nannar, the son of Enlil and Ninlil, the rank of thirty was
assigned.

To his son and successor, Utu, the rank of twenty was allotted;

Ten as a number-rank to the other Anunnaki leaders' sons was granted.

Ranks by the fives between the female Anunnaki and spouses were shared.

When after Eridu and Nibru-ki and their temple-abodes were completed,

In Lagash the Girsu precinct for Ninurta was built, his Black Skybird there was kept.

Eninnu, House of Fifty, was the temple-abode for Ninurta and Bau his spouse called;

The Supreme Hunter and the Supreme Smiter, weapons a gift of Anu, the Eninnu protected.

Where Sippar before the Deluge had been, on top of the mud-soil Utu a new Sippar established.

In the Ebabbar, the Shining House, an abode for Utu and his spouse Aya was raised;

From there Utu for Mankind laws of justice promulgated.

Where because of silt-mud the olden plans could not be followed, new sites were chosen.

Adab, a site from Shurubak not distant, for Ninharsag as a new center was made.

The House of Succor and Healing Knowledge was her temple-abode therein named;

The ME's of how the Earthlings were fashioned Ninharsag in its holy shrine kept.

For Nannar a city with straight streets, canals, and wharves was provided; Urim was its name,

House of the Throne's Seed was its temple-abode called, the Moon's beams to the lands it reflected.

Ishkur to the mountainlands of the north returned, the House of Seven Storms his abode was called;

Inanna in Unug-ki resided, in the abode by Anu bequeathed to her she dwelt.

Marduk and Nabu in Eridu dwelt, in the Edin their own abodes they did not have.

———•••———

Now this is the account of the first City of Men and of kingship on Earth,

And how Marduk to build a tower schemed and wherefor Inanna the ME's stole.

In the First Region, in the lands of Edin and in the cities with precincts,

By their Anunnaki lords the Earthlings handiworks and crafts were taught.

Before long were the fields irrigated, on canal and river boats soon sailed;

The sheepfolds and granaries were overflowing, prosperity the land filled.

Ki-Engi, Land of the Lofty Watchers, the First Region was called.

Then to let the black-headed people a city of their own possess it was decided;

Kishi, Scepter City, it was called, in Kishi did the kingship of Man begin.

Therein, in consecrated soil, Anu and Enlil the Heavenly Bright Object implanted.

In it Ninurta the first king appointed, Mighty Man was his royal title.

To make it a center for Civilized Mankind, Ninurta to Eridu journeyed,

The ME tablets that for kingship divine formulas hold from Enki to obtain.

Properly attired, with respect Ninurta Eridu entered, for the ME of kingship he asked:

Enki, the lord who all the ME's safeguards, fifty ME to Ninurta granted.

In Kishi were the black-headed people with numbers to calculate taught,

Heavenly Nisaba writing them taught, heavenly Ninkashi beermaking them showed.

In Kishi, by Ninurta guided, kilnwork and smithing proliferated,

Wheeled wagons, to male asses harnessed, craftily in Kishi first were fashioned.

Laws of justice and righteous behavior in Kishi were promulgated.

It was in Kishi that the people hymns of praise to Ninurta composed:

Of his heroic deeds and victories they sang, of his awe-inspiring Black Bird they chanted,

How in faraway lands the bisons he subdued, how the white metal to mix with copper he found.

Ninurta's glorious time it was, with the Constellation of the Archer he was honored.

All the while Inanna in Unug-ki her lordship in the Third Region awaited,

All the while the domain of her own of the leaders she demanded.

The Third Region after the second one will come! her leaders thus assured her.

Having seen how Ninurta to Eridu journeyed, how the ME of kingship he obtained,

Inanna in her heart a plan devised, to obtain ME from Enki she schemed.

Her chambermaid Ninshubur to Eridu she dispatched, a visit by Inanna to announce.

On this hearing Enki to Isimud, his housemaster, quickly instructions gave:

The maiden, all alone, to my city Eridu her step is directing,

When all alone she will arrive, my inner chambers let her enter.

Pour for her cold water to freshen her heart, barley cakes with butter give her,

Sweet wine prepare, the beer vessels to the rim fill up!

When Inanna alone the abode of Enki entered, Isimud Enki's commands followed;

Then when Enki Inanna greeted, by Inanna's beauty he was overwhelmed:

With jewelry was Inanna bedecked, by her thin dress her body she revealed;

When she bent down, her vulva by Enki was thoroughly admired.

From the wine cups sweet wine they drank, for beer drinking a competition they had.

Show me the ME's, Inanna to Enki playfully said; let me ME in my hand hold!

Seven times in the course of the competition Enki to Inanna ME's to hold gave,

The divine formulas for lordship and kingship, for priesthood and scribeship,

For lovedressing and for warring ME's to Inanna Enki to hold gave;

For music and singing, woodworking and metals and precious stones,

Ninety-four ME's that for civilized kingdoms are needed Enki to Inanna gave.

Holding her prizes tightly, Inanna from the slumbering Enki slipped away;

To her Boat of Heaven she rushed out, to soar away her pilot she instructed.

When Enki from his slumber by Isimud was awakened, Get hold of Inanna! to Isimud he said.

When from Isimud that Inanna had already in her Boat of Heaven departed Enki heard,

To chase Inanna in Enki's skyship Isimud he instructed. All the ME's you must retrieve! to him he said.

At the approach to Unug-ki Isimud Inanna's Boat of Heaven intercepted,

To return to Eridu and the wrath of Enki face he made her.

But when Inanna back to Eridu was brought, the ME's with her no more were:

To her chambermaid, Ninshubur, she gave them, to the House of Anu in Unug-ki Ninshubur took them.

In the name of my power, in the name of my father Anu, I command you the ME's to return!

So did Enki angrily to Inanna say, in his abode captive he held her.

When of this Enlil heard, to Eridu to face his brother he came.

By right the ME's have I obtained, Enki himself in my hand placed them!

So did Inanna to Enlil say; the truth of that Enki meekly admitted.

When the time term of Kishi shall be completed, to Unug-ki kingship shall pass! So did Enlil declare.

When Marduk all this did hear, greatly he was enraged, his anger no bounds knew.

Enough has my humiliation been! to his father Enki Marduk shouted.

A sacred city of his own in the Edin from Enlil he forthwith demanded.

When Enlil to Marduk's appeal no heed paid, Marduk fate in his own hands grasped.

To a place that for Anu's arrival, before Unug-ki was selected, was considered,

Nabu the Igigi and their offspring from their dispersal lands summoned,

For Marduk therein a sacred city, a place for skyships, to establish!

When his followers at the place assembled, stones to build with
 they found not.

Marduk how to make bricks and burn them by fire, to serve as
 stone, to them he showed,

Therewith a tower whose head the heavens can reach they were
 building.

To thwart the plan Enlil to the place hurried, to placate Marduk
 with soothing words he tried;

To stop Marduk and Nabu in their endeavor Enlil did not succeed.

In Nibru-ki Enlil his sons and grandchildren assembled; what to do
 they all considered.

Marduk an unpermitted Gateway to Heaven is building, to
 Earthlings it he is entrusting!

So did Enlil to his sons and grandchildren say.

If this we allow to happen, no other matter of Mankind shall be
 unreached!

This evil plan must be stopped! Ninurta said; all with that agreed.

It was nighttime when from Nibru-ki the Enlilite Anunnaki came,

From their skyships havoc upon the rising tower, fire and
 brimstones they rained;

To the tower and the whole encampment a complete end they made.

To scatter abroad the leader and his followers Enlil thereupon
 decided,

Henceforth their counsels to confuse, their unity to shatter, Enlil
 decreed:

Until now all the Earthlings one language had, in a single tongue
 they speak.

Henceforth their language I shall confound, that they each other's
 speech will not understand!

In the three hundred and tenth year since the count of Earth years
 began did all this happen:

In each region and every land the people a different tongue he made to speak,

A different form of writing thereafter to each was given, that one the other will not comprehend.

Twenty-three kings did in Kishi reign, for four hundred and eight years was it the Scepter City;

It was also in Kishi that a beloved king, Etana, for a heavenly journey was taken.

At the allotted time, let kingship to Unug-ki be transferred! So did Enlil decree.

To its soil the Heavenly Bright Object from Kishi was transferred.

When the decision to the people was announced, to Inanna an exaltation hymn they sang:

Lady of the ME's, Queen, brightly resplendent,

Righteous, in radiance clothed, of heaven and Earth beloved;

By the love of Anu consecrated, great adorations wearing,

Seven times the ME's she obtained, in her hand she them is holding.

For the tiara of kingship they are appropriate, for high priesthood suitable,

Lady of the great ME's, of them she is the guardian!

In the four hundred and ninth year after the count of Earth years began,

Kingship of the First Region to Unug-ki was transferred;

Its first king was the high priest of the Eanna temple-abode, a son of Utu he was!

As for Marduk, to the Land of the Two Narrows he went,

To be the master of the Second Region, once established, he expected.

———

Now this is the account of how the Second and Third Regions were established,

And how Ningishzidda was exiled and Unug-ki Aratta threatened.

When Marduk, after a long absence, to the Land of the Two Narrows returned,

Ningishzidda as its master he there found, its Lofty Lord Ningishzidda was.

With the aid of offspring of Anunnaki who Earthlings espoused did Ningishzidda the lands oversee,

What Marduk had once planned and instructed, by Ningishzidda was overturned.

What is it that happened? Marduk of Ningishzidda to know demanded.

Of the destruction of hidden things Marduk Ningishzidda accused,

Of making Horon to a desert place depart, a place that has no water,

A boundless place where sexual pleasures are not enjoyed!

The two brothers an uproar made, upon quarreling bitterly they embarked.

Pay heed, I am here in my proper place! Marduk to Ningishzidda said.

You have been my place-taker; from now on only a deputy of mine you can be.

But if to rebellion you are inclined, to another land go away you must!

For three hundred and fifty Earth years did the brothers in the Land of the Two Narrows quarrel,

For three hundred and fifty years was the land in chaos, between the brothers it was split;

Then Enki, their father, to Ningishzidda said: For the sake of peace, to other lands depart!

To go to a land beyond the oceans Ningishzidda chose, with a band of followers thereto he went.

Six hundred and fifty Earth years was at that time the count,

But in the new domain, where Ningishzidda the Winged Serpent was called, a new count of its own began.

In the Land of the Two Narrows the Second Region under Marduk's lordship was established;

In the annals of the First Region, Magan, Land of the Cascading River, it was called.

But by the Second Region's people, when languages were confounded,

Hem-Ta, the Dark Brown Land, it was henceforth called.

Neteru, Guardian Watchers, the Anunnaki were there in the new language called.

Marduk as Ra, the Bright One, was worshiped; Enki as Ptah, the Developer, was venerated.

Ningishzidda as Tehuti, the Divine Measurer, was recalled;

To erase his memory Ra on the Stone Lion his image with that of his son Asar replaced.

To count by tens, not by sixty, Ra the people made; the year he also by tens divided,

The watching of the Moon by the watching of the Sun he replaced.

Whereas under the lordship of Tehuti the olden City of the North and City of the South were reestablished,

Marduk/Ra the two lands, of the North and of the South, into one Crown City united.

A king, an offspring of Neteru and Earthling, he there appointed; Mena was his name.

Where the two lands meet and the great river divides, a Scepter City Ra established.

Splendor to surpass Kishi in the First Region he gave it, Mena-Nefer, Mena's Beauty, it was called.

To honor his elders Ra a holy city built, to honor Nibiru's king Annu he named it;

Therein on a platform a temple-abode for his father Enki-Ptah he erected,

Its head, within a high tower, like a sharp rocket skyward rose.

In its shrine Ra the upper part of his Celestial Barge deposited, the Ben-Ben it was called;

It was the one in which from the Planet of Countless Years he had traveled.

On the day of the New Year, the king as High Priest the ceremonies performed,

On that day only alone the innermost Star Room he entered, before the Ben-Ben offerings he put.

To benefit the Second Region, Ptah to Ra all manner of ME's gave.

What do I know that you do not know? the father his son asked.

Then all manner of knowledge, except that of the dead reviving, to Ra he gave.

As a Great One of the Twelve Celestials, Ptah to Ra the constellation sign of the Ram allotted.

The waterflow of Hapi, the land's great river, Ptah for Ra and his people regulated,

Abundance in the fertile soils quickly came, man and cattle proliferated.

By the success of the Second Region the leaders were encouraged; the Third Region to establish they proceeded.

To make it a domain of Inanna, as she was promised, they decreed.

As befits the mistress of a region, a celestial constellation to her was assigned:

Beforehand with her brother Utu the Station of the Twins she shared,

Henceforth, as a gift from Ninharsag, her Constellation of the Maiden to Inanna was allotted;

In the eight hundred and sixtieth year, according to the Earth year count, was Inanna so honored.

Far away in the eastern lands, beyond seven mountain ranges, was the Third Region;

Zamush, Land of Sixty Precious Stones, was its highland realm called.

Aratta, the Wooded Realm, was in the valley of a meandering great river located;

In the great plain did the people cultivate crops of grains and horned cattle herd.

There too two cities with mud bricks they built, with granaries they were filled.

As by Enlil's decree required, the Lord Enki, Lord of Wisdom,

For the Third Region a changed tongue devised, a new kind of writing signs he for it fashioned,

A tongue of man heretofore unknown, for Aratta Enki in his wisdom created;

But the ME's of civilized kingdoms for the Third Region Enki did not give:

Let Inanna what for Unug-ki had obtained with the new region share! So did Enki declare.

In Aratta Inanna a shepherd-chief appointed, akin to her beloved Dumuzi he was.

In her skyship from Unug-ki to Aratta Inanna journeyed, over mountains and valleys she flew.

The precious stones of Zamush she cherished, pure lapis lazuli with her to Unug-ki she carried.

At that time the king in Unug-ki was Enmerkar, the second one to reign therein he was;

It was he who the boundaries of Unug-ki expanded, by its glories was Inanna exalted.

It was he who the wealth of Aratta coveted, to be over Aratta supreme he schemed.

To Aratta Enmerkar an emissary dispatched as a tribute Aratta's riches to demand.

Over seven mountain ranges, through parched lands and then soaked by rains, the emissary to Aratta went,

To the king of Aratta the demand words of Enmerkar word for word he repeated.

His language the king of Aratta to understand was unable; like the bray of a donkey its sound was.

A wooden scepter, inscribed with a message, the king of Aratta to the emissary gave.

To share Unug-ki's ME's with Aratta the king's message requested,

As a royal gift to Unug-ki grains on donkeys were loaded, with the emissary to Unug-ki they went.

When Enmerkar the inscribed scepter received, its message in Unug-ki no one understood.

He brought it forth from light to shade, he brought it forth from shade to light;

What kind of wood is this? he asked. Then to plant it in the garden he ordered.

After five years, after ten years had passed, from the scepter a tree grew, a tree of shade it was.

What shall I do? Enmerkar in frustration his grandfather Utu asked.

With heavenly Nisaba, the mistress of scribes and writing, Utu interceded.

On a clay tablet his message to inscribe Nisaba Enmerkar taught, in the tongue of Aratta it was;

By the hand of his son Banda was the message delivered: Submission or war! it said.

By Inanna Aratta was not abandoned, to Unug-ki Aratta will not submit! the king of Aratta said.

If warfare Unug-ki desires, let one warrior one warrior in combat
  meet!

Better yet, let us peacefully treasures exchange; let Unug-ki its
  ME's for Aratta's riches give!

On the way back, carrying the peace message, Banda fell sick; his
  spirit left him.

His comrades raised his neck, without the breath of life it was;

On Mount Hurum, on the way from Aratta, to his death was
  Banda abandoned,

The riches of Aratta Unug-ki did not receive, the ME's of Unug-ki
  Aratta did not obtain;

In the Third Region, Civilized Mankind did not fully blossom.

Synopsis of the Thirteenth Tablet

Royal cities sprout with sacred precincts for the gods

Demigods serve as kings and priests in palaces and temples

Marduk promises his royal followers an eternal Afterlife

In Sumer, Inanna encourages belief in Resurrection

Celestial omens and foretelling oracles gain followings

Marduk proclaims the coming Age of the Ram as his sign

Ningishzidda builds stone observatories to show otherwise

Insurrections, wars, and invasions destabilize Enlilite lands

The mystery emissary appears to Enlil, foretells a calamity

Instructs Enlil to select a Worthy Man to lead survival

Enlil chooses Ibruum, scion of priestly royal family

Armies raised by Nabu attempt to seize the spaceport

Overruling Enki, the gods resort to Weapons of Terror

Ninurta and Nergal obliterate the spaceport and sinning cities

The drifting nuclear cloud brings death to all in Sumer

God of the Mounts and the Chosen Man

THE THIRTEENTH TABLET

In the Third Region, Civilized Mankind did not fully blossom;

What to Inanna was entrusted she neglected, other domains, not to her granted, in her heart she coveted.

When from Unug-ki, at the count of a thousand years, kingship away was taken,

Who the calamity by the end of the next millennium could foresee, who the disaster would have prevented?

That in less than a third of one Shar a calamity unknown would befall, who could foretell?

By Inanna was the bitter end started, Marduk as Ra with Destiny tangled;

Ninurta and Nergal the unspeakable end with their own hands delivered!

Why was Inanna with her granted domain not satisfied, why to Marduk did unforgiving she remain?

Journeying between Unug-ki and Aratta, Inanna restless and ungratified was;

For her beloved Dumuzi she still mourned, her love's desire unquenched remained.

> When she flew about, in the sunrays Dumuzi's image she saw shimmering and beckoning,

>> In the nighttime in dream-visions he appeared; I will return! he was saying.

>>> The glories of his domain in the Land of the Two Narrows to her he was promising.

In the sacred precinct of Unug-ki, a House for Nighttime Pleasure she established.

To this Gigunu young heroes, on the night of their weddings, with sweet words she lured:

Long life, a blissful future to them she promised; that her lover Dumuzi was she imagined.

Each one in the morning in her bed was found dead.

It was at that time that the hero Banda, left for dead, alive to Unug-ki returned!

By the grace of Utu, of whose seed he was, did Banda from the dead return.

A miracle! A miracle! excited Inanna shouted. My beloved Dumuzi to me came back!

In her abode Banda was bathed, with a sash a fringed cloak on him was fastened.

Dumuzi, my beloved! she called him. To her bed, with flowers bedecked, she lured him.

When in the morning Banda was alive, with joy Inanna shouted:

The power of not dying in my hands was placed, immortality by me is granted!

Then to call herself a goddess Inanna decided, the Power of Immortality it implied.

Nannar and Ningal, Inanna's parents, by her proclamation were not pleased;

Enlil and Ninurta by Inanna's words were disconcerted; Utu, her brother, was bemused;

The dead to revive is not possible! Enki and Ninharsag to each other said.

In the lands of Ki-Engi, the people their good fortune praised:

The gods are among us, death they can abolish! So to each other the people said.

On the throne of Unug-ki Banda his father Enmerkar succeeded;
  Lugal, Great Man, his title was.

The goddess Ninsun, of Enlil's seed, took him to be her spouse,

The hero Gilgamesh, their son, on the throne of Unug-ki
  Lugal-Banda followed.

As the years passed and Gilgamesh older grew, of life and death to
  his mother Ninsun he spoke,

About the death of his forebears, though of Anunnaki descended,
  he wondered. Do gods die? his mother he asked.

Shall I too, though two thirds divine, as a mortal over the wall
  climb? So to her he said.

As long as on Earth you abide, the death of an Earthling will you
  overwhelm! Ninsun to her son said.

But if to Nibiru you will be taken, long life thereon you will attain!

To take Gilgamesh aloft, to Nibiru journey, Ninsun to Utu the
  commander appealed,

Endlessly Ninsun to Utu appealed, day after day with him she
  pleaded:

Let Gilgamesh to the Landing Place go! Utu in the end agreed.

To guide and protect him, Ninharsag a double of Gilgamesh
  fashioned.

Enkidu, As by Enki Created, was he called, of a womb he was not
  born, blood in his veins was not.

With the comrade Enkidu Gilgamesh to the Landing Place
  journeyed, Utu with oracles his progress oversaw;

At the entrance to the cedar forest, its fire-belching monster their
  way blocked.

With trickery they the monster confused, to pieces it they broke.

When the secret entrance to the tunnels of the Anunnaki they found,

By the Bull of Heaven, a creature of Enlil, with deathly snorts they
  were challenged.

To the gates of Unug-ki the monster them chased; at the city's ramparts by Enkidu it was smitten.

When Enlil this heard, with agony he cried, in the heavens of Anu was his wailing heard;

For in his heart Enlil well knew: Bad indeed was the omen!

For having the Bull of Heaven slain, to perish in waters Enkidu was punished;

Gilgamesh, having by Ninsun and Utu been instructed, of the slaying was absolved.

Still the long life of Nibiru seeking, Gilgamesh to proceed to the Place of the Chariots by Utu was permitted.

After many adventures the Land of Tilmun, the Fourth Region, he reached;

Through its subterranean tunnels he proceeded, in a garden of precious stones Ziusudra he met!

The events of the Deluge Ziusudra to Gilgamesh related, the secret of long living to Gilgamesh he revealed:

A plant in the garden's well was growing, Ziusudra and his spouse from getting old it prevented!

Unique of all the plants on Earth it was; by it a man full vigor can regain.

Man at Old Age Is Young Again! This is the plant's name, Ziusudra to Gilgamesh said.

A gift of Enki, with Enlil's blessing, on the Mount of Salvation to us was granted!

When Ziusudra and his spouse were asleep, Gilgamesh to his feet stones tied.

Into the well he dived, the plant of Being Young Again he grasped and uprooted.

With the plant in his satchel through the tunnels he hurried, to Unug-ki he made his way.

When he tired and was asleep, a snake by the plant's fragrance was attracted.

The plant did the snake snatch from the sleeping Gilgamesh; with the plant it vanished.

In the morning, his loss discovering, Gilgamesh sat and wept.

To Unug-ki empty-handed he returned, as a mortal therein he died.

Seven more kings in Unug-ki after Gilgamesh reigned, then its kingship to an end came;

Precisely when the count of a thousand Earth years was completed it was!

To Urim, the city of Nannar and Ningal, was kingship of the First Region transferred.

To all these matters that in the other Regions were occurring, Marduk much heed gave.

By Inanna's dreams and visions, to Dumuzi's domain alluding, Ra was disturbed.

To counteract Inanna's schemes of expansions he was determined;

In the matters of resurrection and immortality he found much to ponder.

The thought of divine godship to him greatly appealed, to be a great god himself he announced!

By what to Gilgamesh, in good measure an Earthling, was permitted, Ra was angered,

But a clever way wherewith the loyalty of kings and people to retain he deemed it:

If demigods the gateway to immortality are shown, let this to the kings of my region apply!

So did Marduk, in the Second Region by the name Ra known, to himself words say:

Let the kings of my Region of Neteru offspring be, to Nibiru in an Afterlife journey!

So did Ra in his realm decree. The kings how to build tombs facing eastward he taught,

To the priest-scribes a long book he dictated, the Afterlife journey in detail in it was described.

How to reach the Duat, the Place of the Celestial Boats, in the book was told,

How to there, by a Stairway to Heaven, to the Imperishable Planet journey,

Of the Plant of Life partake, the Waters of Youth to satiation drink.

Of the coming of the gods to Earth by Ra were the priests taught,

Gold is the splendor of Life, to them he said. The flesh of the gods it is! to the kings Ra said.

To make expeditions to the Abzu and the Lower Domain, gold to obtain, the kings he instructed.

When by the force of weapons the kings of Ra lands not theirs conquer,

His brothers' realms he invaded, their ire he caused to arise and grow:

What is Marduk up to, the brothers each other asked, that over us he tramples?

To their father Enki they appealed; to Ptah his father Ra did not listen.

To capture all adjoining lands the kings of Magan and Meluhha Ra directed,

To be the master of the Four Regions was his heart's plan.

The Earth is mine to rule! So adamantly to his father he said.

———·—·———

Now this is the account of how Marduk supreme himself declared and Babili built,

And how Inanna, warrior kings commanding, blood made flow and sacrileges allowed.

After kingship to Urim from Unug-ki was transferred, Nannar and Ningal on the people smiled.

As his Rank of Thirty befitting, as the god of the Moon Nannar was worshiped;

As the count of the Moon months in a year, twelve festivals each year he decreed,

To each of the twelve great Anunnaki a month and its festival were dedicated.

Throughout the First Region to the Anunnaki gods, great and lesser ones,

Shrines and sanctuaries were built, the people to their gods could directly pray.

In the First Region, civilization from Ki-Engi to other neighboring lands spread,

In Cities of Man local rulers as Righteous Shepherds were designated;

Artisans and farmers, shepherds and weavers their products far and wide exchanged,

Laws of justice were decreed, contracts of trade, of espousal and divorce were honored.

In schools the young ones studied, scribes hymns and proverbs and wisdom recorded.

Abundance and happiness were in the lands; quarrels and encroachments there also were.

All the while Inanna in her skyship from land to land roamed; near the Upper Sea with Utu she frolicked.

To the domain of her uncle Ishkur she went, Dudu, Beloved, she called him.

To the people who in the upper plain of the two rivers dwelt Inanna took a liking;

The sound of their tongue she found pleasant, to speak their language she learned.

By the name of the planet Lahamu in their tongue Ishtar they
     called her,
Uruk her city Unug-ki they called, Dudu as Adad in their language
     they pronounced.
Sin, Lord of Oracles, her father Nannar they named; Urim-city by
     them Ur was called.
Shamash, Bright Sun, in their tongue Utu they called, him too
     they worshiped.
Enlil by them Father Elil was called, Nippur by them was Nibru-ki;
Ki-Engi, Land of the Lofty Watchers, Shumer in their language was
     named.
In Shumer, the First Region, kingship between the cities was rotated;
In the Second Region, diversity by Ra was not permitted, alone to
     reign he wished.
The eldest of Heaven, firstborn who is on Earth! Thus by the
     priests to be known he wanted.
The foremost from the earliest times! So he decreed in the hymns
     to be called;
Lord of eternity, he who everlastingness has made, over all the
     gods presiding,
The one who is without equal, the great solitary and sole one!
So did Marduk, as Ra, above all other gods himself emplace,
Their powers and attributes to himself he by himself assigned:
As Enlil I am for lordship and decrees, as Ninurta for the hoe and
     combat;
As Adad for lightning and thunder, as Nannar for illuminating the
     night;
As Utu I am Shamash, as Nergal over the Lower World I reign;
As Gibil the golden depths I know, whence copper and silver come
     I have found;
As Ningishzidda numbers and their count I command, the heavens
     my glory bespeak!

By these proclamations the Anunnaki leaders were greatly alarmed,

To their father Enki the brothers of Marduk spoke, Nergal to Ninurta their concerns conveyed.

What has you overpowered? Enki to his son Marduk said. Unheard of are your pretensions!

The heavens, the heavens my supremacy bespeak! Marduk his father Enki answered.

The Bull of Heaven, Enlil's constellation sign, by his own offspring was slain,

In the heavens the Age of the Ram, my age, is coming, unmistakable the omens are!

In his abode, in Eridu, the circle of the twelve constellations Enki examined,

On the first day of spring, the beginning of a year, sunrise was carefully observed;

In the constellation stars of the Bull was the sun that day rising.

In Nibru-ki and Urim Enlil and Nannar the observations made,

In the Lower World, where the Instruments Station had been, Nergal the results attested:

Still remote was the time of the Ram, the Age of the Bull of Enlil it still was!

In his domains, Marduk in his assertions did not relent. By Nabu he was assisted,

To domains not his emissaries he sent, to the people that his time has come to announce.

To Ningishzidda the Anunnaki leaders appealed, how to the people the skies to observe to teach.

In his wisdom stone structures Ningishzidda devised, Ninurta and Ishkur to erect them helped.

In the settled lands, near and far, the people how the skies to observe they taught,

That the sun in the Constellation of the Bull was still rising to the
people they showed.

With sorrow did Enki these ongoings watch, how Fate the rightful
order twisted he pondered:

After the Anunnaki as gods themselves declared, on Mankind's
support they instead are dependent!

In the First Region to unify the lands under one leader the
Anunnaki decided, a warrior king they desired.

To Inanna, of Marduk the adversary, the task of the right man to
find they entrusted.

A strong man whom on her journeys she had met and loved,
Inanna to Enlil indicated,

Arbakad, of four garrisons the commander, was his father, a high
priestess his mother was.

Scepter and crown Enlil him gave, Sharru-kin, Righteous Regent,
Enlil him appointed.

As on Nibiru once was done, a new crown city, the lands to unify,
was established,

Agade, the Unified City, they named it, not far from Kishi it was
located.

By Enlil was Sharru-kin empowered; Inanna with her weapons of
brilliance his warriors accompanied.

All the lands from the Lower Sea to the Upper Sea to his throne
obedience gave,

At the borders of the Fourth Region, to protect it, his troops were
stationed.

With a cautious eye Ra on Inanna and Sharru-kin constantly gazed,
then as a falcon on his prey he pounced:

From the place where Marduk the tower to heaven reaching to
build had attempted,

Sacred soil from there to Agade did Sharru-kin move, therein the
Heavenly Bright Object to implant.

Enraged did Marduk to the First Region rush, with Nabu and followers to the tower's place they came.

Of the sacred soil, I alone the possessor am, by me shall a gateway of the gods be established!

So did Marduk vehemently announce, instructions the river to divert to his followers he gave.

Dikes and walls in the Place of the Tower they raised, the Esagil, House for the Utmost God, for Marduk they built;

Babili, the Gateway of the Gods, Nabu in his father's honor named it,

In the heart of the Edin, in the midst of the First Region, Marduk himself established!

Inanna's fury no boundary knew; with her weapons on Marduk's followers death she inflicted.

The blood of people, as never before on Earth, like rivers flowed.

To his brother Marduk Nergal to Babili came, for the sake of the people Babili to leave him he persuaded:

Let us peacefully wait for the true signs of heaven! Nergal to his brother said.

To depart Marduk agreed, from land to land the skies to watch he traveled,

Amun, the Unseen One, in the Second Region was Ra henceforth called.

For a while was Inanna appeased, two sons of Sharru-kin his peaceful successors were.

Then on the throne of Agade Sharru-kin's grandson ascended; Naram-Sin, by Sin Loved, he was called.

In the First Region Enlil and Ninurta absent were, to the lands beyond the oceans they went;

In the Second Region Ra was away, as Marduk in other lands he traveled;

Her chance in her hands to seize all powers Inanna envisioned, Naram-Sin to seize all lands she commanded.

To march against Magan and Meluhha, Marduk domains, Naram-Sin she instructed.

The sacrilege of an Earthlings' army through the Fourth Region passing Naram-Sin committed,

Magan he invaded, the sealed Ekur, House Which Like a Mountain Is, to enter he attempted.

By the sacrileges and transgressions Enlil was infuriated; upon Naram-Sin and Agade a curse he put:

By a bite of a scorpion did Naram-Sin die, by the command of Enlil was Agade wiped out.

At the count of a thousand and five hundred Earth years did this happen.

———·——

Now this is the account of the prophecy by Galzu to Enlil in a vision given;

About Marduk's supremacy it was, how a calamity to survive a man to choose.

After Marduk Amun became, kingship in the Second Region disintegrated, disorder and confusion reigned;

After Agade was wiped out, in the First Region there was disorder, confusion reigned.

In the First Region kingship was in disarray, from Cities of Gods to Cities of Man it moved about,

Unug-ki, Lagash, Urim and Kish, Isin and to faraway places kingship was shifting.

Then Enlil, with Anu consulting, kingship in the hands of Nannar deposited;

To Urim, in whose soil the divine Heavenly Bright Object remained implanted, kingship for the third time was granted.

In Urim a Righteous Shepherd of men Nannar as king appointed, Ur-Nammu was his name.

Equity in the lands Ur-Nammu established, to violence and strife an end he made, in all the lands prosperity was abundant.

It was at that time that in the nighttime Enlil a dream-vision had:

The image of a man to him appeared, bright and shining like the heavens he was;

As he approached and by Enlil's bed stood, Enlil the white-haired Galzu recognized!

In his left hand a tablet of lapis lazuli he was holding, the starry heavens on it were designed;

By the twelve constellation signs were the heavens divided, to them with his left hand Galzu pointed.

From the Bull to the Ram Galzu his pointing shifted; three times the pointing he repeated.

Then in the dream-vision Galzu spoke up and to Enlil thus said:

The righteous time of benevolence and peace by evildoing and bloodshed will be followed.

In three celestial portions the Ram of Marduk the Bull of Enlil will replace,

One who himself as Supreme God has declared supremacy on Earth will seize.

A calamity as has never before occurred, by Fate decreed, will happen!

As at the time of the Deluge, a righteous and worthy man must be chosen,

By him and his seed will Civilized Mankind, as by the Creator of All intended, be preserved!

So did Galzu, the divine emissary, to Enlil in the dream-vision say.

When Enlil from the nighttime dream-vision awakened, there was no tablet beside his bed.

Was it an oracle from heaven or did I it all in my heart imagine? Enlil to himself wondered.

To none of his sons, Nannar among them, nor to Ninlil did he of the dream-vision tell.

Among the priests in the Nibru-ki temple Enlil of celestial savants inquired,

Tirhu, an oracle priest, to him the high priest indicated.

Of Ibru, of Arbakad the grandson, he was descended, sixth generation of Nibru-ki priests he was,

With the royal daughters of Urim's kings they were intermarried.

Get yourself to Nannar's temple in Urim, the heavens for celestial time observe:

Seventy-two Earth years is the count of a Celestial Portion, the passage of three thereof carefully record!

So did Enlil to Tirhu the priest say, the prophesied time he made him count.

While Enlil the dream-vision and its portents pondered, Marduk from land to land went.

Of his supremacy the people he was telling, to followers gain was his purpose.

In the lands of the Upper Sea and the lands on Ki-Engi bordering,

Nabu, Marduk's son, was the people inciting; to seize the Fourth Region was his plan.

Between the dwellers of the west and the dwellers of the east clashes were occurring,

Kings hosts of warriors formed, caravans ceased going, the walls of cities were raised.

What Galzu had foretold indeed is happening! Enlil to himself said.

Upon Tirhu and his sons, of worthy lineage descended, Enlil set his gaze:

This is the man to choose, by Galzu indicated! Enlil to himself said.

To Nannar, without the dream-vision revealing, Enlil to his son thus said:

In the land between the rivers whence Arbakad had come, a city like Urim establish,

A home-abode away from Urim let it for you and Ningal be.

In its midst a temple-shrine establish, the Priest-Prince Tirhu in charge thereof appoint!

By his father's word abiding, Nannar in the land of Arbakad the city of Harran established.

To be high priest in its temple-shrine Tirhu he sent, his family with him;

When two Celestial Portions out of the prophesied three were completed did Tirhu to Harran go.

At that time Ur-Nammu, the Joy of Urim, in the western lands from his chariot fell and died.

On the throne of Urim his son Shulgi him succeeded; full of vile and eager for battles Shulgi was.

In Nibru-ki himself high priest he anointed, in Unug-ki the joys of Inanna's vulva he sought;

Warriors from the mountainlands, to Nannar not beholden, in his army he enlisted,

With their help the western lands he overran, the sanctity of Mission Control Center he ignored.

In the sacred Fourth Region his foot he set, King of the Four Regions himself he declared.

About the defilements Enlil was angered, about the invadings Enki to Enlil spoke:

The rulers of your region all bounds have exceeded! Enki to Enlil bitterly said.

Of all the troubles Marduk is the fountainhead! Enlil to Enki retorted.

Still the dream-vision to himself keeping, Enlil to Tirhu his attention turned.

Upon Ibru-Um, the eldest son of Tirhu, Enlil cast the choosing gaze.

A princely offspring, valiant and with priestly secrets acquainted
    Ibruum was;

To protect the sacred places, the chariots' ascents and descents
    enable, Enlil Ibruum to go commanded.

No sooner did Ibruum from Harran depart than in that city
    Marduk arrived;

The defilements he too had observed, as birth pangs of a New
    Order he them deemed.

From Harran, on the threshold of Shumer, his final thrust he
    planned,

From Harran, at the edge of Ishkur's domains situated, the raising
    of armies he directed.

When twenty-and-four Earth years of his sojourn in Harran had
    passed,

Marduk to the other gods, of whomever descended, tearfully an
    appeal made;

Confessing his transgressions but insisting on his lordship, to them
    he thus said:

Oh gods of Harran, oh great gods who judge, learn my secrets!

As I girdle my belt, my memories I remember:

I am the divine Marduk, a great god, in my domains as Ra am I
    known.

For my sins to exile I went, to the mountains have I gone, in many
    lands I wandered,

From where the sun rises to where the sun sets I went, to the land
    of Ishkur I came.

Twenty-four years in the midst of Harran I nested, an omen in its
    temple I sought;

Until when? about my lordship an omen in the temple I asked.

Your days of exile are completed! to me the oracle in the temple said.

Oh great gods who the fates determine, let me to my city set my
    course,

My temple Esagil as an everlasting abode establish, a king in Babili install;

In my temple house let all the Anunnaki gods assemble, my covenant accept!

So did Marduk, confessing and appealing, to the other gods his coming announce.

By his appeal for their submission the Anunnaki gods were disturbed and alarmed.

To a great assembly, counsel to take, Enlil them all summoned.

All the Anunnaki leaders in Nibru-ki gathered; Enki and Marduk's brothers also came.

About the happenings all of them were agitated, opposed to Marduk and Nabu they all were.

In the council of the great gods, accusations were rampant, recriminations filled the chamber.

What is coming no one can prevent; let us Marduk's supremacy accept! Enki alone counseled.

If the time of the Ram is coming, let us Marduk of the Bond Heaven–Earth deprive! Enlil in anger proposed.

To obliterate the Place of the Celestial Chariots all except Enki agreed;

To use therefore the Weapons of Terror Nergal suggested; only Enki was opposed:

Of the decision, Earth to Anu the words pronounced; Anu to Earth the words repeated.

What was destined to be, by your decision to undo will fail! So did Enki say as he departed.

The evil thing to carry out Ninurta and Nergal were selected.

Now this is the account of how Fate to Destiny did lead,

How step by step, some in long forgotten times taken, the Great Calamity made happen!

Now let it for all time be recorded and remembered:

When the decision to use the Weapons of Terror was made, to himself Enlil two secrets kept:

To no one, before the terrible decision was taken, did Enlil the secret of Galzu's dream-vision reveal;

To no one, until the fateful decision was made, did Enlil his knowledge of the terror's hiding place disclose!

When, despite all protestations, the council to use the Weapons of Terror permitted,

When Enki, angry and distraught the council chamber left,

In his heart was Enki smiling: Only he knew where the weapons were hidden! So did Enki think,

For it was he, before Enlil to Earth had come, who with Abgal in a place unknown the weapons did hide.

That Abgal, to the exiled Enlil, the place disclosed, that to Enki was unknown!

When Enki this second secret heard, in his heart a wishful thought he harbored:

That after such a long sojourn, the weapons' terror would have evaporated!

Little did Enki expect the long sojourn a calamity as never before known on Earth to cause.

Thus it was that without Enki needing, Enlil to the two heroes the hiding place disclosed:

Those seven Weapons of Terror, in a mountain they abide! to them Enlil said.

In a cavity inside the earth they dwell, with the terror to clad them is required!

Then the secret of how the weapons from their deep sleep awaken, Enlil to them did reveal.

Before the two sons, one of Enlil, one of Enki, to the hiding place departed,

Enlil to them words of forewarning said: Ere the weapons are used, by the Anunnaki must the chariots' place be vacated;

The cities must be spared, the people must not perish!

In his skyship Nergal to the hiding place soared, Ninurta by his father was delayed;

A word to his son alone Enlil wished to say, a secret to him alone reveal:

About the prophecy of Galzu and the choosing of Ibruum to Ninurta he told.

Hot-headed is Nergal, make sure that the cities are spared, that Ibruum is forewarned! to Ninurta Enlil said.

When Ninurta at the weapons' place arrived, Nergal from the cavity had already them brought out,

As their ME's from the long slumber he awakened, to each one of the seven Nergal a taskname gave:

The One Without Rival the first weapon he called, the Blazing Flame he named the second,

The One Who with Terror Crumbles he called the third, Mountain Melter the fourth he called,

Wind That the Rim of the World Seeks he named the fifth, the One Who Above and Below No One Spares was the sixth,

The seventh with monstrous venom was filled, Vaporizer of Living Things he called it.

With Anu's blessing were the seven to Nergal and Ninurta given, therewith to destruction wreak.

When Ninurta at the place of the Weapons of Terror arrived, to destroy and annihilate was Nergal ready.

I shall kill the son, I will annihilate the father! Nergal with vengeance was shouting.

The lands they covet will vanish, the sinning cities I will upheaval! So did Nergal enraged announce.

Valiant Nergal, will you the righteous with the unrighteous destroy? So did Ninurta his comrade ask.

The instructions of Enlil are clear! To the selected targets the way I will lead, you behind me will follow!

The decision of the Anunnaki to me is known! Nergal to Ninurta said.

For seven days and seven nights the signal from Enlil the two awaited.

As was his intention, when his waiting was completed, Marduk to Babili returned,

In the presence of his followers, with weapons armed, his supremacy he declared;

A thousand and seven hundred and thirty-six was the count of Earth years then.

On that day, on that fateful day, Enlil to Ninurta the signal sent;

To Mount Mashu Ninurta departed, behind him Nergal followed.

The Mount and the plain, in the heart of the Fourth Region, Ninurta from the skies surveyed.

With a squeezing in his heart, to Nergal a sign he gave: Keep off! to him he signaled.

Then the first terror weapon from the skies Ninurta let loose;

The top of Mount Mashu with a flash it sliced off, the mount's innards in an instant it melted.

Above the Place of the Celestial Chariots the second weapon he unleashed,

With a brilliance of seven suns the plain's rocks into a gushing wound were made,

The Earth shook and crumbled, the heavens after the brilliance were darkened;

With burnt and crushed stones was the plain of the chariots covered,

Of all the forests that the plain had surrounded, only tree stems were left standing.

It is done! Ninurta from the skyship, his Black Divine Bird, words shouted.

The control that Marduk and Nabu so coveted, of it they are forever deprived!

Then to emulate Ninurta Nergal desired, to be Erra the Annihilator his heart him urged;

Following the King's Highway, to the verdant valley of the five cities he flew.

In the verdant valley where Nabu the people was converting, Nergal as a caged bird to squash him planned!

Over the five cities, one after the other, Erra upon each from the skies a terror weapon sent,

The five cities of the valley he finished off, to desolation they were overturned.

With fire and brimstones were they upheavaled, all that lived there to vapor was turned.

By the awesome weapons were mountains toppled, where the sea waters were barred the bolt broke open,

Down into the valley the sea's waters poured, by the waters was the valley flooded;

When upon the cities' ashes the waters poured, steam to the heavens was rising.

It is done! Erra in his skyship shouted. In Nergal's heart there was no more vengeance.

Surveying their evil handiwork, the two heroes by what they saw were puzzled:

By a darkening of the skies were the brilliances followed, then a storm to blow began.

Swirling within a dark cloud, gloom from the skies an Evil Wind carried,

As the day wore on, the Sun on the horizon with darkness it obliterated,

At nighttime a dreaded brilliance skirted its edges, the Moon at its rising it made disappear.

When dawn the next morning came, from the west, from the Upper Sea, a stormwind began blowing,

The dark-brown cloud eastward it directed, toward the settled lands did the cloud spread;

Wherever it reached, death to all that lives mercilessly it delivered;

From the Valley of No Pity, by the brilliances spawned, toward Shumer the death was carried.

To Enlil and Enki Ninurta and Nergal the alarm sounded: Unstoppable the Evil Wind death to all delivers!

The alarm Enlil and Enki to the gods of Shumer transmitted: Escape! Escape! to them all they cried out.

Let the people disperse, let the people hide!

From their cities the gods did flee, like frightened birds from their nests escaping they were.

The people of the lands by the Evil Storm's hand were clutched; futile was the running.

Stealthy was the death, like a ghost the fields and cities it attacked;

The highest walls, the thickest walls, like floodwaters it passed,

No door could shut it out, no bolt could turn it back.

Those who behind locked doors hid inside their houses like flies were felled,

Those who to the streets fled, in the streets were their corpses piled up.

Cough and phlegm the chests filled, the mouths with spittle and foam filled up;

As the Evil Wind the people unseen engulfed, their mouths were drenched with blood.

Slowly over the lands the Evil Wind blew, from west to east over plains and mountains it traveled;

Everything that lived, behind it was dead and dying, people and cattle, all alike perished.

The waters were poisoned, in the fields all vegetation withered.

From Eridu in the south to Sippar in the north did the Evil Wind the land overwhelm;

Babili, where Marduk supremacy declared, by the Evil Wind was spared.

Synopsis of the Fourteenth Tablet

Babili, Marduk's chosen center, survives the calamity
Enki sees it as an omen of Marduk's inevitable supremacy
Enlil ponders the past, Fate, and Destiny
Accepts Marduk's supremacy, retreats to faraway lands
The brothers bid a sentimental good-bye
Enki sees the Past as a guide foretelling the Future
He decides to commit all as a record for posterity.
Colophon by the scribe Endubsar

Babylonian depiction of a resplendent Marduk

THE FOURTEENTH TABLET

Babili, where Marduk supremacy declared, by the Evil Wind was spared;

All the lands south of Babili the Evil Wind devoured, the heart of the Second Region it also touched.

When in the aftermath of the Great Calamity Enlil and Enki to survey the havoc met,

Enki to Enlil the sparing of Babili as a divine omen considered.

That Marduk to supremacy has been destined, by the sparing of Babili is confirmed! So did Enki to Enlil say.

The will of the Creator of All it must have been! Enlil to Enki said.

Then to him the dream-vision and prophecy of Galzu Enlil revealed.

If that by you was known, why did you the use of the Weapons of Terror not prevent? Enki him asked.

My brother! Enlil to Enki with a sorrowed voice said. Enough seen was the reason.

Whenever after your coming to Earth the mission by an obstacle obstructed was,

A way the obstruction to circumvent we have found;

Of that, the fashioning of the Earthlings, the greatest solution,

Also the fountain of a myriad unwanted twists and turns was.

When you have the celestial cycles fathomed and the constellations assigned,

Who in them the hands of Destiny could foresee,

Who could between our chosen fates and our unbending destiny distinguish?

Who false omens proclaimed, who true prophecies could pronounce?

Therefore to keep to myself the words of Galzu I decided—

Was he truly the Creator of All's emissary, was he my hallucination?

Let whatever has to happen, happen! so to myself I said.

To his brother's words Enki listened, his head up and down he nodded.

The First Region is desolate, the Second Region is in confusion, the Third Region is wounded,

The Place of the Celestial Chariots is no more; that is what has happened! Enki to Enlil said.

If that was the will of the Creator of All, that is what of our Mission to Earth remained!

By the ambitions of Marduk was the seed sown, what the crop resulted is for him to reap!

So did Enlil to his brother Enki say, then he the triumph of Marduk accepted.

Let the rank of fifty, by me for Ninurta intended, to Marduk instead be given,

Let Marduk over the desolation in the Regions his supremacy declare!

As for me and Ninurta, we will in his way no longer stand.

To the Lands Beyond the Oceans we will depart, what we had all had come for,

The mission to obtain for Nibiru gold we will complete!

So did Enlil to Enki say; dejection was in his words.

Would different matters have been were the Weapons of Terror unused? Enki his brother challenged.

Should we have the words of Galzu to Nibiru not return heeded? Enlil retorted.

Should Earth Mission been stopped when the Anunnaki mutinied?

I what I did did, you what you did did. The past undone cannot become!

Is not in that too a lesson? Enki asked them both.

Is not what on Earth happened, what on Nibiru had taken place mirrored?

Is not in that tale of the Past the outline of the Future written—

Will Mankind, in our image created, our attainments and failures repeat?

Enlil was silent. As he stood up to leave, Enki to him his arm extended.

Let us lock arms as brothers, as comrades who together challenges on an alien planet confronted!

So did Enki to his brother say.

And Enlil, grasping his brother's arm, hugged him as well.

Shall we meet again, on Earth or on Nibiru? Enki asked.

Was Galzu right that we die if we to Nibiru go? Enlil responded. Then he turned and departed.

Alone was Enki left; only by the thoughts of his heart was he accompanied.

How it all began and how it thus far ended, he sat and pondered.

Was it all destined, or was it fate by this and that decision fashioned?

If Heaven and Earth by cycles within cycles regulated,

What had happened will again occur? Is the Past—the Future?

Will the Earthlings the Anunnaki emulate, will Earth relive Nibiru?

Will he, the first to arrive, the last to leave be?

Beseiged by thoughts, Enki a decision made:

All the events and decisions, starting with Nibiru to this day on Earth,

To put in a record, a guide to future generations to become;

Let posterity, at a time by destiny designated,

The record read, the Past remember, the Future as prophecy
    understand,
Let the Future of the Past the judge be!
These are the words of Enki, Firstborn of Anu of Nibiru.

———·—

Fourteenth tablet: The Words of the lord Enki.
Written from the mouth of the great lord Enki,
not one word missed, not one word added,
by the master scribe Endubsar, a man of Eridu,
son of Udbar.
By the lord Enki with long life I have been blessed.

GLOSSARY

Abael: The biblical Abel, killed by his brother Ka-in

Abgal: Spacecraft pilot; first commander of the Landing Place

Abzu: Enki's gold-mining domain in southeast Africa

Adab: Ninharsag's post-Diluvial city in Sumer

Adad: Akkadian name of Ishkur, Enlil's youngest son

Adamu: The first successfully genetically engineered Primitive Worker, The Adam

Adapa: Son of Enki by an Earthling female, first Civilized Man; the biblical Adam

Agade: First postwar capital of Nibiru; unified capital of Sumer and Akkad

Akkad: The northern lands added to Sumer under Sargon I

Akkadian: The mother tongue of all Semitic languages

Alalgar: Spacecraft pilot; second commander of Eridu

Alalu: The deposed king of Nibiru who escaped to Earth and discovered gold; died on Mars; his image was carved on a rock that was his tomb

Alam: Son of Anshargal by a concubine

Amun: Egyptian name for the exiled god Ra

An: First unity king on Nibiru; name of the planet we call Uranus

Anak: The metal tin

Anib: Royal title of Ib, a successor on Nibiru's throne

Anki: Firstborn son of An on Nibiru

Annu: Sacred city in Egypt, the biblical On, Heliopolis in Greek

Anshar: The fifth ruler on Nibiru of the unified dynasty; the planet we call Saturn

Anshargal: The fourth ruler on Nibiru of the unified dynasty

Antu: Spouse of An; spouse of Anu; early name of the planet we call Neptune

Anu: Nibiru's ruler when the Anunnaki came to Earth; also, the planet called Uranus

Anunitu: Endearment name for the goddess Inanna

Anunnaki: "Those Who from Heaven to Earth Came" (from Nibiru to Earth)

Anzu: Spacecraft pilot; first commander of the way station on Mars

Apsu: Primordial progenitor of the solar system, the Sun

Aratta: A domain granted to Inanna, part of the Third Region

Arbakad: The biblical Arpakhshad (one of Shem's sons)

Arrata: The land and mountains of Ararat

Asar: The Egyptian god called Osiris

Asta: The Egyptian goddess called Isis, sister-wife of Asar

Awan: Sister-wife of Ka-in (the biblical Cain)

Aya: Spouse of Utu (the god called Shamash in Akkadian)

Azura: Spouse of Sati, mother of Enshi (the biblical Enosh)

Bab-Ili: "Gateway of the gods"; Babylon, Marduk's city in Mesopotamia

Bad-Tibira: Ninurta's city of smelting and refining gold

Banda: Heroic ruler of Uruk (biblical Erech), father of Gilgamesh

Baraka: Spouse of Irid (the biblical Jared)

Batanash: Spouse of Lu-Mach (biblical Lamech), mother of the hero of the Deluge

Bau: Spouse of Ninurta, a healer

Beacon peaks: The two Great Pyramids of Giza; afterward, Mount Mashu in the Sinai

Ben-Ben: Conical upper part of Ra's celestial boat

Black-headed people: The Sumerian people

Black land: The African domain of the god Dumuzi

Black skybird: The aerial vehicle of Ninurta

Boat of heaven: Aerial vehicle of various gods and goddesses

Bond Heaven–Earth: The complex instruments in Mission Control Center

Branch of life essence: DNA-holding chromosome

Bull of Heaven: Enlil's guardian of the Landing Place, symbol of his constellation

Burannu: The river Euphrates

Cedar forest: Location of the Landing Place (in present-day Lebanon)

Cedar Mountains: Location of Enlil's abode in the cedar forest

Celestial barque: Egyptian term for a god's spacecraft

Celestial Battle: The primordial collision between Nibiru and Tiamat

Celestial chariots: Interplanetary spacecraft

Celestial portions: The 72-year period for 1° zodiacal shift due to Precession

Celestial stations: The twelve houses of the zodiacal constellations

Celestial Time: Time measured by the precessional shifts of zodiacal constellations

Chariots' place: Spaceport

Circuit: Orbit of a planet around the Sun

Civilized Man: Homo sapiens-sapiens, of which Adapa was the first one

Count of Earth years: The count of years since Anu's visit to Earth, the Nippur calendar begun in 3760 B.C.

Creation Chamber: Genetic engineering and domestication facility on the Cedar Mountains

Creator of All: The universal, cosmic God

Damkina: Spouse of Enki, renamed Ninki; daughter of Alalu

Dark-hued land: Africa

Dauru: Spouse of the Nibiruan king Du-Uru

Dawn and Dusk: Earthling females impregnated by Enki, mothers of Adapa and Titi

Deluge: The Great Flood

Destiny: Predetermined course (of events, of orbit) that is unchangeable

Duat: Egyptian name for the restricted zone of the spaceport in the Sinai

Dudu: Endearment name for the god Adad (Ishkur), Enlil's youngest son, Inanna's uncle

Dumuzi: Enki's youngest son, in charge of shepherding in his Egyptian domain

Dunna: Spouse of Malalu, mother of Irid (the biblical Mahalalel and Jared)

Duttur: Concubine of Enki, Dumuzi's mother

Du-Uru (Duuru): Seventh ruler on Nibiru

E-A: "Whose home is water," the prototype Aquarius; firstborn son of Anu, half brother of Enlil; leader of the first group of Anunnaki to arrive on Earth; the fashioner of Mankind and its savior from the Deluge; given the epithets Nudimmud ("the Fashioner"), Ptah ("the Developer" in Egypt), Enki ("Lord Earth"); father of Marduk

Eanna: The seven-staged temple of Anu in Uruk, given by him as a present to Inanna

East Wind: A satellite (moon) of Nibiru

Edin: Location of the Anunnaki's first settlements, the biblical Eden, in southern Mesopotamia; later the area of Shumer

Edinni: Spouse of Enkime, mother of Matushal (the biblical Enoch and Methuselah)

Ednat: Spouse of Matushal, mother of Lumach (the biblical Lamech)

Ekur: The tall structure in the pre-Diluvial Mission Control Center; the Great Pyramid (of Giza) after the Deluge

Emitter: Instrument used together with Pulser to revive Inanna

Emush: Snake-infested desert where Dumuzi sought to hide

Emzara: Spouse of Ziusudra (the biblical Noah) and mother of his three sons

Enbilulu: A lieutenant of Ea with the first landing party

Endubsar: The scribe to whom Enki dictated his memoir

Engur: A lieutenant of Ea with the first landing party

Enki: Ea's epithet-title after the division of duties and powers between him and his half brother and rival Enlil; father of Marduk by his spouse Damkina; failed to have a son by his half sister Ninmah, but fathered five other sons by concubines and also children by Earthling females

Enkidu: Artificially created companion of Gilgamesh

Enkimdu: A lieutenant of Ea with the first landing party

Enkime: Taken heavenward and granted much knowledge; the biblical Enoch; father of Sarpanit, Marduk's spouse

Eninnu: The temple-abode of Ninurta in the sacred precinct of Lagash

Enlil: Son of Anu and his sister-spouse Antu and thus the Foremost Son entitled to the succession to Nibiru's throne ahead of the firstborn Ea; military commander and administrator, sent to Earth to organize wide-scale gold-obtainment operations; father of Ninurta by his half sister Ninmah, and of Nannar and Ishkur by his spouse Ninlil; opposed the fashioning of the Earthlings, sought Mankind's demise by the Deluge; authorized the use of nuclear weapons against Marduk

Enmerkar: Heroic ruler of Unug-ki (Uruk), grandfather of Gilgamesh

Ennugi: Commander of the Anunnaki assigned to the gold mines in the Abzu

Enshar: Sixth dynastic ruler on Nibiru; named the planets embraced by Nibiru's orbit

Enshi: The biblical Enosh, the first to be taught rites and worship

Enursag: A lieutenant of Ea with the first landing party

Enuru: Third son of An and Antu and father of Nibiru's ruler Anu

Ereshkigal: Granddaughter of Enlil, mistress of the Lower World (southern Africa); spouse of Nergal; sister of Inanna

Eridu: The first settlement on Earth, established by Ea; his everlasting center and abode in Shumer

Erra: Epithet of Nergal after the nuclear holocaust, meaning the Annihilator

Esagil: Temple of Marduk in Babylon

Essence of life: The genetically encoded DNA

Etana: A king of Uruk who was carried heavenward but was too afraid to continue

Evil serpent: Derogatory epithet for Marduk by his enemies

Evil Wind: The death-bearing nuclear cloud drifting eastward toward Shumer

Fate: A course of events that is subject to free choice and is alterable

Father of All Beginning: The universal Creator of All; the cosmic God

Firmament: The Asteroid Belt, the remnant of the broken-up half of Tiamat

First Region: The first region of civilization granted to Mankind, Shumer

Foremost son: The son born to a ruler by a half sister and thus the legal heir

Fourth Region: The Sinai peninsula, location of the post-Diluvial spaceport

Gaga: The moon of Anshar (Saturn) that after Nibiru's passage became the planet Pluto

Gaida: Youngest son of Enkime (Enoch in the Bible)

Galzu: A mysterious divine emissary who conveyed the messages in dreams and visions

Gateway to heaven: The purpose of the launch tower built by Marduk in Babylon

Geshtinanna: Dumuzi's sister who betrayed him

Gibil: A son of Enki, in charge of metallurgy, maker of magical artifacts

Gigunu: Inanna's House of Nighttime Pleasure

Gilgamesh: King in Uruk; being a son of a goddess, went in search of immortality

Girsu: Sacred precinct of Ninurta in Lagash

Great Below: The continent of Antarctica

Great Calamity: The devastation in the aftermath of the nuclear holocaust in 2024 B.C.

Great Deep: The Antarctic Ocean

Great Sea: The Mediterranean Sea; also called the Upper Sea

Gug Stone: Beam emitting crystal, transferred from the Great Pyramid to Mount Mashu

Guru: A lieutenant of Ea at the first landing

Ham: Second son of the hero of the Deluge, brother of Shem and Japhet

Hammered Bracelet: The Asteroid Belt; also called the Firmament

Hapi: The ancient Egyptian name for the Nile River

Harran: City in northwestern Mesopotamia (now in Turkey) that served as a twin city of Ur; sojourn place of Abraham; staging place of Marduk for usurpation of supremacy on Earth

Heavenly Bright Object: A secret divine device enshrining the site of kingship

Hem-Ta: Egyptian name for ancient Egypt

Horon: The Egyptian god now called Horus

House of Fashioning: Genetic laboratory in the cedar forest for crops and livestock

House of Healing: The medical-biological facilities of Ninmah in Shurubak

House of Life: The biogenetic facilities of Enki in the Abzu

Hurum: A mountain where the hero Banda died and came back to life

Ib: Third dynastic king on Nibiru, given the royal title An-Ib

Ibru: Grandson of Arbakad, the biblical Eber (forebear of Abraham)

Ibru-Um (Ibruum): Scion of a priestly royal family from Nippur and Ur, the biblical Abraham

Igigi: The three hundred Anunnaki assigned to shuttlecraft and the way station on Mars; abducted female Earthlings as wives; frequent rebels

Ilabrat: A vizier and emissary of Anu; fetched Adapa for the journey to Nibiru

Imperishable Star: The Egyptian name for the planet from which Ra had come to Earth

Inanna: Daughter of Nannar and Ningal, twin sister of Utu; was betrothed to Dumuzi; ferocious in war, lusty in lovemaking; mistress of Uruk and of the Third Region; known as Ishtar in Akkadian; associated with the planet we call Venus

Inbu: A fruit brought from Nibiru to Earth, source of the Anunnaki's elixir

Irid: The biblical Jared; father of Enkime (the biblical Enoch)

Ishkur: Youngest son of Enlil by his spouse Ninlil, the Akkadian god Adad

Ishtar: The Akkadian name for the goddess Inanna

Ishum: Epithet given to Ninurta after the nuclear holocaust, meaning "the Scorcher"

Isimud: Housemaster and vizier of Enki

Ka-in: The biblical Cain, who killed his brother Abael (Abel) and was banished

Kalkal: Gatekeeper of Enlil's residence in the Abzu

Ki: "Firm Ground," the planet Earth

Ki-Engi: Shumer ("Land of Lofty Watchers"), the First Region of civilization

Kingu: Tiamat's principal satellite; Earth's Moon after the Celestial Battle

Kishar: Spouse of Nibiru's fifth ruler; the planet we call Jupiter

Kishargal: Spouse of Nibiru's fourth ruler

Kishi: The first City of Men in Shumer where kingship began

Kulla: A lieutenant of Ea during the first landing

Kunin: The biblical Kenan, son of Enshi and Noam

Laarsa: One of the Anunnaki's pre-Diluvial cities; reestablished after the Deluge

Lagash: Built the same time as Laarsa, both to serve as Beacon Cities; after the Deluge, reestablished as Ninurta's principal city

Lahama: Spouse of Lahma

Lahamu: The planet we call Venus

Lahma: The eighth dynastic king on Nibiru

Lahmu: The planet we call Mars

Land Beyond the Seas: The Americas; settled by Ka-in's descendants, overseen by Ninurta

Land of the Two Narrows: The lands along the Nile River

Landing Place: The platform for skyships and rocketships in the Cedar Mountains

Law of the Seed: The rule giving succession precedence to a son by a half sister

Life seed: DNA extracted from semen

Lower Abzu: The southern tip of Africa, domain of Nergal and Ereshkigal

Lower Sea: The body of water now called the Persian Gulf

Lower World: The southern hemisphere, including southern Africa and Antarctica

Lugal: Literally, "Great Man"; epithet for a chosen king

Lulu: The genetically engineered hybrid, the Primitive Worker

Lu-Mach: Son of Matushal and Ednat, the biblical Lamech

Magan: Ancient Egypt

Malalu: Son of Kunin and Mualit, the biblical Mahalalel

Marduk: Firstborn son and legal heir of Enki and Damkina; worshiped as Ra in

Egypt; jealous of his brothers, unsatisfied with Egypt alone as his domain, claimed and after exiles and wars attained supremacy on Earth from his city Babylon

Matushal: Son of Enkime and Edinni, the biblical Methuselah

ME: Tiny objects encoded with formulas for all aspects of science and civilization

Meluhha: Ancient Nubia

Mena: The king whose reign began the First Dynasty of Egyptian Pharaohs

Mena-Nefer: Egypt's first capital, Memphis

Mission Control Center: In Nibru-ki (Nippur) before the Deluge, on Mount Moriah after the Deluge

Mount Mashu: The instrument-equipped mount at the post-Diluvial Sinai spaceport

Mount of Salvation: The peaks of Ararat, where the ark rested after the Deluge

Mount of Showing the Way: Mount Moriah, site of post-Diluvial Mission Control Center

Mualit: Spouse of Kunin, mother of Malalu

Musardu: One of seven birth mothers of the first Earthlings

Mushdammu: A lieutenant of Ea at the first landing

Nabu: Son of Marduk and Sarpanit; organized human followers of Marduk

Namtar: "Fate"; Vizier of Ereshkigal in her Lower World domain

Nannar: Son of Enlil and Ninlil, the first Anunnaki leader to be born on Earth; patron god of Urim (Ur) and Harran; associated with the Moon; known as Sin in Akkadian; father of Utu and Inanna

Naram-Sin: Grandson of Sargon and a successor of his as King of Shumer and Akkad

Navel of the Earth: Epithet for the location of Mission Control Center

Nebat: Sister-wife of the Egyptian god Satu, the one we call Nephtys

Nergal: A son of Enki, ruler of the Lower Abzu with his spouse Ereshkigal; unleashed the nuclear weapons together with Ninurta

Neteru: Egyptian word for *gods* meaning Guardian Watchers

Nibiru: Home planet of the Anunnaki; its orbital period, a Shar, equals 3,600 Earth years; became the twelfth member of the solar system after the Celestial Battle

Nibru-ki: The original Mission Control Center; Enlil's city in Shumer, called Nippur in Akkadian

Nimug: One of seven birth mothers of the first Earthlings

Nimul: Mother of Ea/Enki by Anu; not being an official spouse and half sister, her son, though firstborn, lost the succession to Enlil, whose mother was Antu

Ninagal: A son of Enki, appointed by him to navigate the boat of the hero of the Deluge

Ninbara: One of seven birth mothers of the first Earthlings

Ningal: Spouse of Nannar (Sin), mother of Inanna and Utu

Ningirsig: A lieutenant of Ea at the first landing

Ningishzidda: Son of Enki, master of genetics and other sciences; called Tehuti (Thoth) in ancient Egypt; went with followers to the Americas after he was deposed by his brother Marduk

Ninguanna: One of seven birth mothers of the first Earthlings

Ninharsag: Epithet of Ninmah after she was granted an abode in the Sinai peninsula

Ninkashi: Female Anunnaki in charge of beermaking

Ninki: Title of Damkina, Ea's spouse, when he was entitled Enki ("Lord of Earth")

Ninib: Spouse of Ib, the third dynastic king on Nibiru

Ninimma: One of seven birth mothers of the first Earthlings

Ninlil: Espoused by Enlil after she forgave his date rape; Mother of Nannar and Ishkur

Ninmada: One of seven birth mothers of the first Earthlings

Ninmah: Half sister of Enki and Enlil, mother of Ninurta by Enlil; chief medical officer of the Anunnaki; helped Enki to genetically engineer the Primitive Worker; peacemaker among the rival and warring Anunnaki clans; renamed Ninharsag

Ninmug: One of seven birth mothers of the first Earthlings

Ninshubur: Chambermaid of Inanna

Ninsun: The Anunnaki mother of Gilgamesh

Ninurta: Enlil's Foremost son, mothered by Enlil's half sister Ninmah, and his legal successor; battled with Anzu, who seized the Tablets of Destinies, and with Marduk; found the alternative sources for gold and established alternative space facilities in the Americas; patron-god of Lagash

Nippur: Akkadian name of Nibru-ki, where the calendar of Earth years was begun in 3760 B.C.; birthplace of Ibru-Um (Abraham)

Nisaba: Goddess of writing and measuring

Noam: Sister-wife of Enshi, mother of Kunin

North Crest: Abode of Enlil in the Cedar Mountains

North Wind: One of Nibiru's satellite-moons

Nudimmud: An epithet for Ea meaning He Who Fashions Things; the planet Neptune

Nungal: Pilot of spacecraft

Nusku: Enlil's vizier and emissary

Olden Times: The period that began with the first landing and ended with the Deluge

Place of Celestial Chariots: Spaceport of the Anunnaki

Plant of Being Young Again: The secret rejuvenation plant found by Gilgamesh

Plant of Life: Used by Enki's robotic emissaries to revive Inanna

Primitive Worker: The first genetically engineered Earthling

Primordial Begetter: "Apsu"—the Sun—in the creation cosmogony

Prior Times: The period of events on Nibiru before the missions to Earth

Ptah: Enki's name in Egypt; meaning "the Developer," it commemorates his deeds in raising the land from under the Flood's waters

Pulser: Instrument used, together with the Emitter, to revive the dead

Ra: The Egyptian name for Marduk, meaning the Bright One

Sarpanit: An Earthling, the spouse of Marduk, mother of Nabu

Sati: Third son of Adapa and Titi (the biblical Seth)

Satu: Son of Marduk and Sarpanit, the Egyptian god known as Seth

Scorcher: Epithet for Ninurta in his role in the use of nuclear weapons

Second Region: Egypt and Nubia when they were granted civilization

Seed of life: The genetic material encoding all life-forms, DNA

Shamash: Akkadian name for Utu

Shamgaz: A leader of the Igigi and instigator of the abduction of Earthling females

Shar: One orbital period of Nibiru around the Sun, equal to 3,600 Earth years

Sharru-kin: The first king of unified Shumer and Akkad, the one we call Sargon I

Shem: The eldest son of the hero of the Deluge

Shumer: Land of the Watchers, the First Region of post-Diluvial civilization; Sumer

Shurubak: Healing center of Ninmah from before the Deluge and reestablished thereafter

Sin: The Akkadian name for Nannar

Sippar: The spaceport city in pre-Diluvial times commanded by Utu; his cult center after the Deluge

Skybirds: Aircraft of the Anunnaki for flying in Earth's skies

Snow-hued place: Antarctica

South Wind: A satellite-moon of Nibiru

Storm Bird: Ninurta's aerial battlecraft

Sud: A nurse; also the epithet-name for Ninlil before she became Enlil's spouse

Suzianna: One of seven birth mothers of the first Earthlings

Tablets of Destinies: Devices used in Mission Control Center to track and control orbits and trajectories; later on, a record of unalterable decisions

Tehuti: Egyptian name for Ningishzidda as "Thoth," the god of science and knowledge

Third Region: Domain allotted to Inanna; the Indus Valley civilization

Tiamat: Primordial planet that broke up in the Celestial Battle, giving rise to the Asteroid Belt and to the Earth

Ti-Amat: Wife of Adamu; first Earthling female able to procreate

Tilmun: "Land of the Missiles," the Fourth Region in the Sinai peninsula

Tirhu: Oracle priest in Nippur, Ur, and Harran (the biblical Terah, father of Abraham)

Titi: Spouse of the first Civilized Man, Adapa, mother of Ka-in and Abael

Udbar: Father of the scribe Endubsar

Ulmash: A lieutenant of Ea at the first landing

Unug-ki: City built for Anu's visit, granted by him to Inanna; later called Uruk (the biblical Erech); throne-city of Gilgamesh and other demigods

Upper Plain: Area in northern Mesopotamia where the descendants of Arpakad dwelt

Upper Sea: The Mediterranean Sea

Ur: Akkadian name for Urim; the rulers of Shumer and Akkad when the nuclear calamity happened are known as kings of the Third Dynasty of Ur; the biblical "Ur of the Chaldees" from which Abraham migrated to Harran

Urim: Nannar's city in Shumer and the land's capital three times (including at the time of the Great Calamity); a thriving center of culture, industry, and international trade

Ur-Nammu: First king of the Third Dynasty of Ur

Uruk: Akkadian name for Unug-ki (the biblical Erech)

Utu: "Shamash" in Akkadian; twin brother of Inanna; commander of the Spaceport of Sippar in pre-Diluvial times and of the one in the Sinai after the Deluge; giver of laws from his cult center in Sippar after the Deluge; Godfather of Gilgamesh

Water of Life: Used to revive Inanna and bring her back from the dead

Water of Youth: Promised by Ra to his followers in an Afterlife

Way of Anu: The central band of the celestial sphere containing the zodiacal constellations; on Earth, the central band between the northern Way of Enlil and the southern Way of Enki

Way of Enki: The celestial sphere below the 30th parallel south

Way of Enlil: The celestial sphere above the 30th parallel north

Weapons of Terror: Nuclear weapons, used at first on Nibiru and then finally on Earth

West Wind: A satellite-moon of Nibiru, one of seven

Whirlwind: A satellite-moon of Nibiru, one of seven

Whirlwinds: Helicopter-like aerial vehicles of the Anunnaki

Whiteland: Antarctica

Winged Serpent: Epithet of Ningishzidda in the Americas

Zamush: Land of precious stones, part of Inanna's Third Region

Ziusudra: Hero of the Deluge, a son of Enki by an Earthling (the biblical Noah)

Zumul: Astronomer-priest in Uruk during Anu's visit